ILLUSION

HELENA BRADY

ILLUSION

Also by Helena Brady:

The Secrets of the Forest
(Available on Amazon and Kindle)

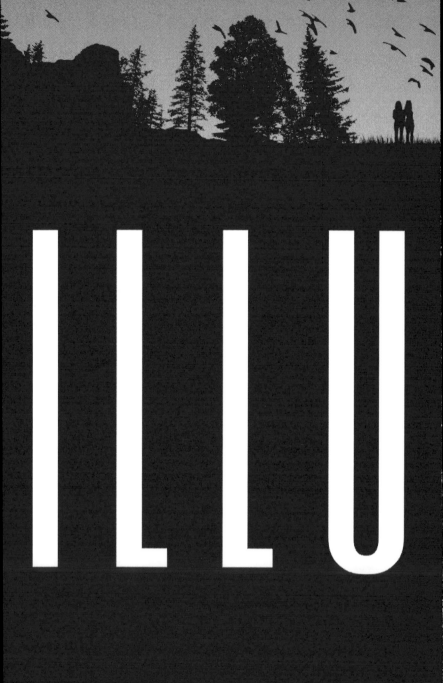

SION

Content warning:

Please be advised this book contains graphic description of violence, injury, murder and death, and contains several references to trauma (including family trauma), suicide, abuse (including physical and emotional abuse), homophobia, anxiety and panic attacks.
This book contains themes that may not be suitable for all readers, including strong language and intimate scenes.

For Carolina,
Without whom this book would never have made it this far.

CHAPTER 1

Olivia woke to the door squeaking as it slowly opened downstairs. She blinked a few times, her eyes adjusting to the darkness that enveloped her small bedroom. Gradually, dark shapes came into focus that formed the rest of her furniture. Beside her dinosaur bookcase, the bedroom door was open just a crack, and a slit of pale yellow light poked through, casting a soft glow across the floor.

The sound of the door clicking shut downstairs barely reached her ears. It couldn't be Mummy—she was asleep in the other room.

Wasn't she?

Maybe that was the sound of her leaving? Olivia's panicked breath started to become ragged, and she sat up in bed, the duvet falling away from her. No, Mummy wouldn't leave without her, would she? The panic started to spread through her, a lump of it landing in the pit of her stomach where it buried itself—an infestation of panic-lice eating away at her stomach lining. Her little heart beat hard against her chest, and the thumping radiated through her whole body until her fingers started to tremble.

She closed her eyes.

No, Mummy would never leave without me, she told herself.

Then what was that noise downstairs?

She decided she better go check Mummy's room, just in case. Just to be absolutely sure. She swung her legs over the side of the bed, letting them dangle just above the floor. Her thoughts instantly turned to the monsters that could be hiding under the bed, eyes glowing red and pointy, white teeth so bright they could be seen in the darkness. They would be ready to grab her feet as she set them on the floor, their long claws waiting to dig into her ankles and pull her screaming under the bed to eat her—

"No," she whispered to herself. "Monsters aren't real. Mummy says they aren't real." She took a deep breath as she set her feet on the soft carpet, waiting with her eyes scrunched closed for the claws to grab her and drag her away.

But no claws took hold of her, and she exhaled with a long sigh.

"Monsters aren't real," she affirmed to herself, then crept quickly towards the door, just in case the monsters were only stirring from their sleep and hadn't realized their next meal was within arm's reach.

A beam of light shone through the crack in the door, guiding her towards it. She nudged toys and teddies out of her way with her feet as she went, careful not to make too much noise. A delicate silence hung over the house, fragile, ready to be broken and alert everyone within its walls. She put her hand on the doorknob, about to open it, when the stairs started creaking.

She paused.

The steps squeaked and groaned as someone climbed them, getting closer and closer to the landing. Closer and closer to *her*. Maybe Mummy was coming home? Maybe she had to go to the shops, and now she was back? But why would she be out when it was still dark? Olivia waited at the door, peering out through the crack into the hall. She would just check if it was Mummy, then she could go back to bed and return to her world of sweet dreams. If Mummy caught her out of bed, she might get into trouble.

The person was climbing higher, and Olivia could see the top of their head through the banisters now. They had black hair…

But Mummy didn't have black hair.

The person ascended until their head and torso came into view, but there was something not right about this person, about this stranger that made her stomach sink. They *looked* like a person, but there was a smoky haze surrounding them, black as midnight yet somehow slightly transparent. It swirled and churned, reaching out into the air like hungry fingers grasping and searching, then falling back on itself and returning to the stranger on the stairs.

This person was made out of smoke and shadow.

Olivia's eyes widened, her lungs freezing, and she slowly backed away from the door.

There was a stranger in their house.

Where was Mummy?

The Shadow Person reached the top of the stairs and paused for a moment before continuing along the landing, towards Olivia's room.

She gasped into her tiny hands. She stood completely rigid,

muscles locked into place, her small heart hammering away at her chest, trying to burst through it and escape her frozen body. Sweat was clinging to her skin, covering her in a sticky film and plastering her clothes to her.

But the Shadow Person moved past her door, hardly making a sound as they walked. They blocked out the light from the hall, and she was momentarily submerged in complete darkness. Her heart stopped as the light went out, and only restarted with manic pounding as they moved past and light trickled into her room once again.

Olivia tip-toed up to her door and quietly pulled it open, just enough so she could peer after them. The Shadow Person was standing at Mummy's door, their shadow hand closing over the doorknob. Trails of shadow snapped at the air, feeling along the walls and wrapping around the banister. Olivia's heart skipped a beat, and her eyes blurred for a second as tears filled them. She brought her shaking hands up to press firmly on her chest, making sure her heart was still beating and this wasn't all a dream. It pumped hard against her palm, reassuring her that she was still alive. Mummy's door only gave a small squeak as it opened, not loud enough to wake her up.

Olivia swallowed, trying to move the lump that was blocking her throat. She blinked away tears. They were going to hurt Mummy, she knew it. They were a bad person, a person Mummy would tell her to run away from. And they were going to hurt her!

She couldn't let that happen!

She had to warn her.

She had to do something.

The Shadow Person stepped into Mummy's room and seemed to melt into the darkness there. They blended in perfectly with the black veil that covered the room.

In a surge of panic, Olivia flung her door open and ran towards Mummy's bedroom. Her feet made soft thuds on the scratched wooden floor as she ran. The Shadow Person had probably heard her, but she didn't care anymore. She had to tell Mummy, and they had to run away. Right now. Her heart was racing, a stampede of horses in her chest, booming loudly in her ears. Her throat was squeezing, shrinking smaller and smaller. Her eyes stung with tears.

She made it to Mummy's room but hesitated at the door. Light from the hall shone past her and into the bedroom, piercing through that black veil, but she couldn't see the Shadow Person. Maybe they were hiding? Were they hiding under the bed, like the monsters under hers?

Were they a monster?

She quickly pushed the thoughts away. She couldn't worry about that just yet; she had to get Mummy up, and they had to run.

Olivia reached her hand up the bedroom wall and flicked on the light. She squinted as the light blinded her, but when they finally adjusted to the room, the Shadow Person was nowhere to be seen. Mummy groaned and rolled over in bed. The light reflected on her pale blue eyes like sunlight on a still pond, glittering with diamonds. They were kind eyes, a peaceful place you could get lost in and be safe from the world.

"Olivia, what are you doing up?" she asked quietly, her voice croaky. Tears started falling down Olivia's face as she reached the bed, letting out a whimper.

"There's someone in the house," she whispered urgently, her voice breaking as more tears rolled down her cheeks.

Mummy frowned at her. "What?"

Olivia screamed as the Shadow Person rose up on the other side of the bed, looming over them. Shadows reached out of the dark corners and latched onto the Person as they rose in height, adding to their mass. Olivia noticed for the first time that this person had no eyes, no mouth, no defining features at all. There was just a blank face, shifting and moving in the light. They were like a nightmare, something that had crawled from her dreams—a real monster. Even though Mummy said monsters aren't real, Olivia knew this one was.

Mummy swore and pushed Olivia backwards. She stumbled and fell, landing with a loud thump. Her head was thrown backwards as she hit the ground, and she was barely able to save herself from smashing her skull off the floor.

Then the room changed.

A brick wall rose from the duvet and up towards the ceiling, slicing the bed in half, cutting the Shadow Person off from them. They were red bricks with crusty, white cement holding them in place and blocking off the other half of the room. She couldn't tell if it was real or not—if it was just her panicked imagination, or if this wall had really just risen from the bedroom floor. Just as she was starting to register what was going on, Olivia was jerked off her feet, and her head was thrown backwards again with the sudden force. A hand pushed her face tight against Mummy's shoulder, and Olivia's forehead knocked against Mummy's collarbone. They started to run.

The pound of Mummy's footsteps on the ground sent jolts through Olivia's body. Olivia just held on tight to Mummy's top, forgetting the wall that had just appeared in the bedroom. Her chest was starting to hurt from all the battering her heart had done to her ribs.

Then they violently jerked to a stop, and Olivia lost her grip and flew from Mummy's arms. She cried out as she landed.

Mummy shrieked, her hands flying to her throat as she was

pulled backwards with a dark trail of shadow wrapped around her neck. The artery that ran up her neck was bulging, ready to burst. Olivia screamed, struggling to stand up again. Bullets of pain shot through her with every move she made. Tears ran steadily down her face and soaked into her already-stained pyjamas.

"Run, Olivia!" Mummy choked out, wrestling with the shadow that was pulling her back into the bedroom, back to the monster that lived in shadow and fed on pain.

The brick wall was gone now, and there stood the Shadow Person, one arm outstretched with trails of smoke and shadow streaming from their dark fingers.

"No, Mummy!" Olivia finally managed to stand on weak legs, but her knees were trembling, and she almost fell again.

"Run!" Mummy screamed between gasps of air.

Now there was another shadow snaking along the floor towards Olivia, slithering across the floorboards, reaching towards her. Olivia let out a cry but turned and ran along the landing, then stumbled her way down the stairs. She almost fell twice, almost slipped and tumbled down to a possible death.

As she reached the bottom step, Mummy gave a wailing howl that echoed through the whole house, following Olivia as she ran. Olivia covered her mouth with her hands to stop herself from screaming as she ran, her stubby legs moving as quickly as they could. Her whole body was shaking, and her legs were starting to give up, ready to accept the inevitable.

Downstairs was completely dark, except for the light that shone from the landing upstairs. But Olivia knew her way well enough to hurry into the kitchen. She moved as quietly as she could, barely able to contain her sobs as her lungs begged for air. Each breath hurt and closed her throat even more. Soon, she feared, she wouldn't be able to breathe anymore.

Mummy screamed again, and this time, Olivia couldn't stop her own scream. It tore its way out of her lips, ragged and wild, digging knives into her throat as it forced its way out of her lungs.

Her small legs buckled from under her, and jarring pain shot up her wrists as she landed. She crawled her way to the cabinets and fumbled with the handles, her hands shaking so much she could hardly move her fingers. Eventually, she managed to pull one open and stuff herself inside. She pushed the boxes of cereal and packets of biscuits over so she could fit. She pulled the door closed but left a crack to peer through to see if the Shadow Person came looking for her.

She waited in silence, struggling to control her noisy, quivering breaths. She was starting to feel sick, an awful heaviness in her stomach, but willed herself not to throw up. Not now.

The stairs started creaking again.

Olivia closed her eyes and kept her hands clasped firmly over her mouth, forcing herself to take slow, deep breaths. There was a tight pressure in her head, and it pulsed with each creak of the stairs, blurring her vision.

The Shadow Person stepped onto the hall floor and paused.

Olivia held her breath.

The footsteps started again, but they went into the sitting room. Olivia turned her head slightly, trying to listen through the faint ringing in her ears. Through the crack in the door, it was too dark to make out anything except the black outlines of the furniture and the vague yellow glow from upstairs that spilled across the hall floor.

The footsteps came back towards her, and Olivia peaked

out of the crack. The Shadow Person was walking past the stairs, coming into the kitchen. Their black mass glided through the glow from the upstairs light and into the darkness of the kitchen, where they disappeared from sight.

Olivia slowly moved her head away from the cabinet door, and did her best to slow her breathing.

The footsteps got louder, tapping against the tiles. Tears filled her eyes again, but she wouldn't let herself cry or try to wipe them away. She couldn't give away her hiding place. They couldn't find her. They were going to hurt her, she knew it.

Had they hurt Mummy?

The Person stopped, and Olivia risked a peek out, but she couldn't see them.

The tapping started again as they moved back into the hall. Olivia almost sighed with relief, stopping herself just before it escaped her lips. She looked out the crack to where they were standing in plain view at the foot of the stairs. Smoke and shadows swirled around them, trailing off into the house in search of their prey. In search of her.

She shrunk herself into an even smaller ball despite the pain that flared in her neck and back. Her stomach heaved, and she nearly spewed its contents out all over herself.

She waited for what seemed like an eternity, and everywhere was starting to hurt. Her head, her feet, her arms…everywhere. But she didn't dare shift her position. If she did that, if she made any noise at all, they would hear, and the game would be up. They would drag her out of the cabinet and—

She stopped herself as her heart started to flutter and panic with the thoughts.

The Person turned, looking up the stairs. They held up a hand and shadow burst from their fingertips, darting to the second floor to search for her. It seemed like forever that they stood there, waiting for those shadowy snakes to find something. But eventually the Shadow Person lowered their hand, and the shadow returned to swirl around their body.

Then they left.

As the door clicked closed, Olivia let out a heavy sigh.

Yet she stayed still, hidden away in her hole under the counters. Just in case they came back. Just in case they were waiting for her to put her feet on the floor, just like the monsters under the bed were. But she also wanted to wait for Mummy to come down the stairs and find her. But what if Mummy was hiding too, waiting to see if they came back?

What if they'd hurt her?

The thought made a cry rise in her throat, but this one slipped past her defences. She squeezed her cheeks and mouth with trembling hands, but it didn't stop the noise. It rang through the house, and she froze. Her muscles cramped painfully. Beads of cold sweat rolled down the back of her neck and soaked into her sky blue pyjama top, leaving dark stains.

She waited.

But the Shadow Person didn't come back.

She pushed the cabinet door open and crawled back out. A packet of oats fell out after her and spilled across the floor. For a second, she had the urge to clean it up quickly before Mummy came down and saw, but then she realized Mummy wouldn't mind, not after what had happened. Not after the stranger with the shadows had been in their house and tried to hurt them. Olivia stood and dusted herself off. She looked around the dark kitchen, and her eyes started to tear up again.

"Mummy!" she cried out. She broke into a run and clambered up the stairs, tears rolling off her cheeks in fat droplets and splashing onto the steps.

She tripped and landed hard, the edge of the step digging into her ribs. She winced but pushed past the pain and kept climbing.

She reached the top of the stairs and stood upright but nearly fell backwards as the blood dropped from her head. She used the wall to steady herself. Lights exploded in front of her eyes, and she blinked furiously before wiping away the tears with her spare hand. Her vision slowly came back into focus, and the world stopped spinning.

Mummy was lying face-down on the landing.

Blood was pooling beneath her, creeping outwards over the wood. Olivia dropped to her knees and let out a wail, grabbing Mummy's hair and pulling it, trying to wake her up. But Mummy was still, and the blood kept coming. It soaked into Olivia's pyjamas and coated her hands. Olivia went cold. The trembling returned, much more violent this time.

"Mummy! Mummy!" she screamed, pulling her and shaking her. Olivia began batting her with balled-up fists, screaming until her throat was raw. A sharp pain shot through her stomach, and she curled over on top of Mummy, crying into her matted, stained hair.

"Mummy, please!" she begged, struggling to suck in air through her swollen throat.

But Mummy never moved, never spoke. She lay completely still.

Olivia stayed bent over Mummy, wailing and screaming until she couldn't bear the pain in her throat and her tears ran dry. Sunlight broke over the horizon, and the room lightened. Mummy's body was turning cold, and the pool of blood had spread so much that it had cascaded down the stairs like a waterfall. Now, though, it was starting to slow its spread, lazily creeping over the floor. Olivia slowly uncurled herself when warm sunlight fell across her back. She sat upright. Her head was spinning, and she swayed so much to one side that she had to put her hand out to stop herself from falling. Speckles of blood splashed upwards as her hand met the floor.

She sat like that for a few moments, starting to form thoughts, but then they escaped her like feathers in the wind. Her legs were numb, and pins and needles poked at her feet. Sometimes it felt like she was floating, looking down at her body from above, not connected to this earth anymore. The shrill ringing in her ears was all she could seem to focus on.

Eventually, she could form a sentence of a thought in her mind. *Help Mummy.*

She struggled to her feet. They were heavy as lead, and she couldn't move her toes.

She had to do something. Mummy wouldn't move or get up, so she needed a doctor. A doctor would help her. Yes, a doctor. She needed a doctor.

She walked carefully around Mummy, dragging her weight through the thick blood and making her way towards Mummy's bedroom. The floorboards were slick, and her feet shot out from under her. The ground rose to meet her face, so fast she didn't have time to put her hands out to stop herself. Her small nose crunched as it slammed into the wood, and she screamed. Throbbing pain flared all over her face, spreading and growing until it covered her whole head. She sobbed as she pushed herself to her knees.

Blood dripped from her face and splashed back into the sea of red she had landed in. She slowly stood, heaving for breath between her sobs. Her face was still throbbing, and blood ran over her chin and down her neck. She tried to wipe it with her sleeves, but they were soaked in it too, so the motion only served to spread it further, staining her flesh.

She gave another cry then pushed herself up and started walking again on shaky legs. She still had to call the doctor. She still had to help Mummy. Red footprints followed her across the landing and into the bedroom. They stained Mummy's carpet. Her phone was on the dressing table. She picked it up and stared at it for a moment. The grey casing was smeared with red where her stubby fingers touched.

Mummy had told her the number to call if there was ever an emergency. This was an emergency, she told herself. Mummy was cold, and she wouldn't get off the floor. She was hurt really bad. She needed a doctor, and she needed the police. The police could find the Shadow Person and put them in jail for what they did.

She pressed the three numbers Mummy had told her and held the phone to her ear with a shaking hand. Her heart was starting to beat fast again. Faster and faster, pounding her lungs and forcing air in and out of them too quick.

"Emergency services—"

"You need to help Mummy, please!" Olivia begged, her voice breaking.

"Hello, dear. Can you tell me what happened to your Mummy?" the operator asked kindly.

"She's lying on the floor, and she's cold, and she won't get up! That person hurt her, the person who came to the house! And-and she's bleeding! She needs to go to the doctor!" Her legs shook violently, and her stomach lurched. Vomit rose in her throat, and she struggled to swallow it back down. She sat herself down on the floor, her back against the leg of the dresser. The world was starting to spin again.

"Okay, dear. What's your name?"

"O-Olivia."

"Olivia, sweetheart, everything is going to be okay."

CHAPTER 2

Olivia sat on the patio steps, looking down the long garden. The short grass was covered with daisies, buttercups, and clovers poking their heads out between the green blades. Apart from these wildflowers and the single tree at the end of the garden, it was pretty bland here. There were no flowerbeds, no small vegetable patches or pots filled with herbs. There were no toys on the lawn either. Aunt Stephanie had told her to keep her toys inside, so the garden could stay looking nice and neat. Not that Olivia played with toys much anymore. Aunt Stephanie had bought her a box of LEGO shortly after she had moved in here. Olivia loved—*had* loved—LEGO, but now she couldn't even bring herself to open the packets. After that, Aunt Stephanie stopped trying.

Aunt Stephanie was behind her, humming as she hung the washing out to dry in the warm spring air. But Olivia sat in silence, the humming behind her only a ringing in her ears. Her small hands were closed around a teddy bear—the only thing they would let her take from her own house. Everything else was *evidence*, the detective had said. She didn't really know what that meant, but she didn't like it. Her bear was brown and fluffy, with a big, black nose and green eyes that almost looked like her eyes. Mummy had tied a red bow around his neck a few months ago, but now it was starting to droop and fray at the ends.

"Are you okay, Olivia?" She barely heard Aunt Stephanie speak, but she didn't answer anyway. Her eyes were fixed on the oak tree at the end of the garden, where birds chirped and hopped happily along the branches, scanning the ground below for their next meal.

There was a nest of birds on the higher branches. Aunt Stephanie had said they were ravens. The mummy bird had gone to get food, and the little baby ravens were crying out for her to come back. Their heads poked out of the nest, grey beaks wide open and wings flapping as they fought for space.

The hand on her back made her jump.

"Sorry, Olivia. I just wanted to make sure you're okay." Aunt Stephanie smiled.

Olivia nodded quickly, her heart thudding loudly in her chest. Aunt Stephanie stood up, and when her back was turned, Olivia wiped tears from her eyes. She had to consciously loosen her grip on the teddy bear, then hugged tighter him against her chest. Mummy had given him to her as a birthday present when she'd turned four, and she had slept with him beside her every night since then. He wasn't afraid of the monsters under her bed, but he had been afraid of the stranger who had come to their house. He was still afraid of the shadows that moved in the night, and no matter how hard she hugged him, he did nothing to protect her from them. They both just cowered under the blankets together, hoping that no shadow reached out and grabbed them. She rested her head on top of his and let her eyes close while her heartbeat started to slow.

She opened them again once the tears were gone and went

back to staring at the tree down the garden. The little ravens were getting hungry, screaming for their mother to come home, to bring them food. To make sure they were safe and secure, and that nothing would hurt them.

Just like Olivia had hoped Mummy would come home, that the doctors would ring and tell her that she was okay, that she was in the hospital while she got better, that one day she could come home. The thought made her heart ache.

But Mummy was dead.

And she was never coming back.

Aunt Stephanie had told her so.

Aunt Stephanie's phone started ringing, the sound of sweet wind chimes blowing in the wind, breaking Olivia from her trance. She glanced over her shoulder as Aunt Stephanie answered the call.

"Hello?" she greeted.

A silence followed that was almost too painful to bear.

"Oh, hello. How can I help you?" Aunt Stephanie finally spoke as she left the basket of washing under the washing line and went through the kitchen door, back into the house. She left the door open.

Olivia gulped.

Thoughts started to pick up speed, swirling around her head like a whirlpool, sucking everything into it before spewing it out again in a jumbled, tangled mess. She closed her eyes again and buried her face into the top of her teddy bear's head. Aunt Stephanie had washed him not too long ago, so he still faintly smelled of lemon.

"Yes, she's outside right now." Olivia's ears perked up.

Could it be Mummy?

"Yes… Yes… I've tried to get her to talk to me, Doctor, but she just…won't."

It wasn't Mummy, then. Her chest deflated, and more tears pricked the corners of her eyes. Why was Aunt Stephanie talking to a doctor? Were they going to take Olivia away? Were they coming here to look at her? What did they want?

A stabbing pain shot through her stomach, and she squeezed the teddy bear tighter. She didn't like the doctors. They asked too many questions, always prodding and poking for information, invading her private space. Her throat clenched.

"She's very quiet, yes. She's like a ghost, Doctor."

The tears came again.

She rubbed her face against the soft fur of the teddy, trying to wipe them from her cheeks.

"Yes, okay."

Her head was starting to pound now, pressure building inside it. She didn't want the doctor to come see her. She didn't want the doctor to talk to Aunt Stephanie about her. She didn't want him to take her away. Her fingertips were starting to buzz now, pins and needles travelling up her fingers and towards her palms. She didn't want to see a doctor! She *hated* the doctor! No, she didn't want any doctor to come near her ever again!

She looked up and gasped in what little air she could squeeze through her throat. Through her blurry eyes, she saw a black shape flying into the tree. Her heart stopped, her mind taking her back to that night. There was so much blood, everywhere, everywhere, everywhere. She blinked rapidly and rubbed her eyes.

But it wasn't the Shadow Person searching for her.

The mother raven had returned, three worms dangling from her beak. The baby birds went into a frenzy, trying to leap up and grab them from her mouth. Wings flapped violently in an effort to push the others away. They screeched and cawed, begging to be the first fed, begging for the sweet juices to run down the back of their throats.

"I will, Doctor. Thank you very much. Goodbye now. Bye,

bye, bye," Aunt Stephanie finished on the phone. Her heels clacked on the patio.

Olivia focused intensely on the birds at the end of the garden, willing herself not to cry anymore. Tears stabbed her eyes like millions of little needles. If she started crying, Aunt Stephanie would start talking to her, invading her private little bubble that she had built around herself. She didn't want to talk. Olivia only allowed herself to cry late into the night, when the shadows would jump out at her and try to grab her hair, and she had to pull the duvet over her head to stop them reaching her. That was when she cried, as quietly as she could, so Aunt Stephanie wouldn't hear her.

"Oh, look, Olivia. The mummy bird has come back!" Aunt Stephanie said happily from behind her. Olivia sensed her legs only centimetres from her back. She merely nodded, trying her hardest just to focus on the birds. Everything else became a blur, colours smeared across a palette in no particular order or shape.

The mother raven leaned down into the nest and fed her babies. They squawked and squirmed, trying to reach the food before the others. Sibling rivalry. A fight to the death, almost, preparing them for life outside the safety and familiarity of the nest.

There was one little raven, however, that wasn't interested in getting a worm. It sat at the back of the nest, watching the others with small, sunken eyes. They didn't squawk, or squirm, or fight to get food. They just sat there silently, observing.

The mother noticed and hopped along the side of the nest around to the little runt of the flock. She peered down at it, tilting her head from side to side, then pecked it once. The bird gave a little squeal, the noise barely reaching Olivia's ears. The baby tried to shuffle away from its mother, but she picked it up by its head and threw it over the side of the nest.

"No!" Olivia cried out, jumping to her feet.

Aunt Stephanie put her hand on Olivia's shoulder, keeping her from running down the garden.

"Aunt Stephanie, please go help it! Please, please!" Olivia begged, pointing frantically down the garden, to where the little raven was lying helplessly on the grass, flapping its wings as it tried to stand.

"Okay, dear. Will you go find a box to put him in?" Aunt Stephanie asked, a hint of a smile playing on her lips. This was the most words Olivia had ever spoken in one go since that night, and her own voice sounded strange to her.

Olivia dropped the teddy bear and ran inside to find the recycling box in the kitchen. She opened the lid and dug around inside, shoving paper and plastic aside. She pulled out a yellow shoe box. It was a little tattered and torn at the edges, but it would do. She ran back outside, holding it in front of her. She had to help the little baby raven, she had to help him! She didn't want to let him die!

She now knew what happened when things died.

Aunt Stephanie was walking back up the garden, the small raven in her cupped hand. He didn't struggle or try to flap away. He just sat there, eyes half closed and beak half open. His down feathers were so fluffy, so soft, yet they were starting to wilt along his back.

"We'll put him in the box to rest, then we can find him some food later on," she said.

Olivia nodded and opened the box. Aunt Stephanie gently placed the bird inside. Olivia stared down at him, feeling a little better now that it was safe in the shoe box. She would take care of it now. It was going to be okay. It looked up at her and gave one little squawk. She smiled at him, looking at his mismatched eyes—one ashy grey and one sky blue.

"We have to cut some air holes before we close the top. Will you get me the scissors, please?" Aunt Stephanie asked.

Olivia nodded, handed the box over, and ran back inside.

Protecting this bird was the only thing on her mind. Nothing else mattered. Now that its mother didn't want it, she had to take care of it. Protect it. Keep it safe. She climbed up onto the counter and took the scissors, then slid back to the floor. But this time, she walked with the scissors, just like Mummy had told her over and over again. She held them out in front of her and gripped the closed blade, pointed end down to the ground. Just like Mummy had told her. She carefully brought it outside, taking extra care with each step.

She gave the scissors to Aunt Stephanie and watched her as she set the box down on the patio and cut holes in the lid. When she was finished, she set the scissors down beside her and closed the lid over the silent bird. Olivia smiled to herself. She had done it. She had saved the baby bird. Her smile grew the more she thought about it.

"There, now we have to leave him here for a while so he calms down, then you can give him some food. Okay?" Aunt Stephanie said.

Olivia nodded, her face beaming. "Can I hold the box?" she asked.

There was a hesitation. "Why don't you sit beside it on the patio? It's best if we keep him as still as we can so he doesn't get scared," Aunt Stephanie said before standing up. Olivia nodded and sat herself down next to the box. She peered in through one of the air holes, but Aunt Stephanie gently pulled her away.

"Remember, we don't want to scare him," she said gently. Olivia nodded with a sigh. She stared at the box for a few moments, then curled her legs under her. She picked her teddy bear up off the ground and held him against her chest, swaying from side to side and smiling into the top of his head.

Aunt Stephanie went back to doing the washing, and Olivia just watched the box. The bird gave a single squawk, then went back to being silent.

"Poor little birdy," she whispered under her breath to her teddy bear. Abandoned by its mother. Thrown out of the nest, left all alone to die. Olivia put one hand on the top of the box quietly, so Aunt Stephanie wouldn't hear. She knew how it felt. One minute Mummy is there, and the next…

Dead.

Gone.

And you're all alone.

"I understand," she whispered. Memories tried to flood her mind, but she managed to keep them down. She didn't want to remember what had happened to Mummy. She was so cold…so still…so much blood. It made her cry, every time. And she couldn't cry in front of Aunt Stephanie. No, she refused to think about Mummy.

A single tear started to roll down her cheek, and she wiped it quickly. Aunt Stephanie couldn't see her crying.

The raven gave another little squawk. It knew. It understood her, just like she understood it. Olivia gave a sad smile, one that didn't quite reach her eyes.

"I'm going to take care of you, don't worry," she whispered, tapping the box with one finger. She could be this bird's Mummy now. She would take care of it, feed it, make sure it was warm… She didn't know if she could teach it to fly, but she could try. Yes, she would be a Mummy for this bird now. It wasn't going to be abandoned, not by her.

"I know. I'll call myself Ravyn, so I can be your Mummy," Ravyn told it, and the bird gave a small chirp in reply.

12 YEARS
LATER

CHAPTER 3

The day had been horrible. A pure shitshow, where everything that could have gone wrong, went wrong. It was almost comical, now that she was looking back on it. The moment she had taken that disgusting school uniform off and dumped it on the floor, a little ray of sunshine broke through the dark clouds that had been hanging over her all day. Her mind was still drowning in murky water, but it was better than the tornado that had been there earlier in the day, during classes.

She had left Math ten minutes into the lesson and gone to the bathroom to have a panic attack. She had felt it coming before she even sat down in her seat and silently prayed that it would pass. But it hadn't. The anxiety had built in the back of her head until it couldn't be ignored any longer, and she couldn't even sit still in her seat. She knew she had to leave to save herself from facing public humiliation as her body broke down, succumbing to the raging mess that was her thoughts.

Mr. Carey had screamed at her when she'd returned,

accusing her of ditching for a smoke or to get out of doing work. *This is the most important year of your life!* he had shouted as she stood red-faced and teary-eyed at the top of the room, with twenty-two other sets of eyes glaring at her, driving daggers into her skull. *You will fail—you will not get your points to get into college, and you'll have to resit your exams! You will never make it in any career, not with the track record you have! Nobody will take on someone who half-arses work and disappears for an hour at a time doing God knows what!*

She never mentioned this to Aunt Stephanie when asked about her day. Instead, she had fabricated a fantasy where everything had gone fantastically well. Aunt Stephanie had wanted to know all about James in Biology, who had asked her out last week. She had turned him down instantly but had told Aunt Steph that she still was thinking about it, that James was a nice boy, but he just wasn't really her type.

He was the only thing Aunt Stephanie was interested in right now, and if she picked up on any hints Ravyn had dropped, she ignored them. There was no doubt that when exams rolled around in a few weeks, James would be forgotten, and grades would be the only thing they would talk about, and Ravyn wasn't sure if that would be a blessing or a curse. The Leaving Cert, Aunt Stephanie always reminded her, is the beginning of the rest of your life, and it was so important to get enough points to get into a good college course.

Ravyn thought that was all bullshit.

Aunt Stephanie didn't know about the panic attacks or the sobbing episodes that hit her across the head every so often. She didn't know about the sleepless nights where anxiety convinced Ravyn that she was going to die. And she definitely didn't know about the shadows swirling in the corner, forming human figures that watched her, that teased her and hurt her, and gave her bruises she had to cover up. She didn't need that burden—things were hard enough for Aunt Steph. Single parent, working full time trying to pay for the mortgage, school, food, and everything else that came with having an adopted child. She had sacrificed enough for Ravyn, as she was often told, and these little secrets would shatter her heart.

Ravyn pushed a lock of honey-blonde hair back behind her ear and closed her wardrobe door with her other hand. Her head was starting to thump, a dull pain gathering at the bridge of her nose.

A sigh escaped her lips.

Rain pattered against the glass pane beside her. Outside, the world was dark, enveloped in the embrace of spring showers. Fat water droplets ran in streaks down the window, creating their own maze. New droplets joined in the race as they sped down, choosing their paths carefully, trying to reach the bottom before its brothers and sisters. The sound created a dull drumming in the room. Normally, this sound would be soothing, gentle background noise to listen to as she studied or scrolled through Instagram. Now, however, it was irritating. The rain was pellets shooting at the window, a harsh sound that pricked her eardrums.

She turned around and leaned against the wardrobe. The flimsy door creaked. She rested her head against the wood and stared up at the popcorn ceiling. Her breath shuddered as it left her lips. She briefly thought about starting her homework but decided it could wait until after she got something to eat. There was half a bar of chocolate waiting for her in the cupboard downstairs.

A cold hand closed over her wrist.

She was yanked to the floor and hit it with a loud thud. What little air was left in her lungs was expelled suddenly, and dull pain shot through her ribs and across her back. She lay on her back, her wide eyes staring at the ceiling as her brain tried to comprehend what had just happened. Her lungs sucked in a gasp of air that was cold against the back of her throat. For a moment, the world around her blurred, and piercing pain stabbed her skull. She winced, and slowly her vision came back to her. One edge of her vision was dark and hazy, covered with a veil of grey smoke. She planted her hands on either side of her, but a foot connected with her ribs, and she was knocked down again. Sharp pain shot down her side and into her lungs as she heaved for air.

She groaned and rolled over.

Standing there, looking down on her, was a Shadow Person. Black smoke swirled around them and rose towards the ceiling. Coils of shadow reached out into the room, slithering like snakes as they floated through the air.

A scream rose in her throat, but they stomped down on her ribs and knocked the breath out of her before her lungs had a chance to release it. She grunted and tried to roll away, but long trails of shadow leaked from the Person's fingers and wrapped themselves around her hair, pulling her to her knees. Her heart was in her throat, beating violently against her already-restricted airway.

"Wh—" She couldn't even get the words out before a fist of black shadow and smoke smashed into her chest.

Tears sprang to her eyes and memories flashed in her mind, making her body freeze. She was trapped watching herself try to save her mother as the Shadow Person dragged her away. Blood smeared across the wooden floor as her body was pulled away, into the darkness. Gone, out of reach, never to sing her a lullaby again. And blood, so much blood…

A punch to the head knocked Ravyn's memories out of her

brain, and she fell sideways. Lights burst in front of her eyes, and her ears rang loud like funeral bells, tolling their awful shrieks. Pain shot through her skull, ricocheting around in her brain. Tears were rolling now, falling from her face and splashing onto the floor.

She lashed out, trying to strike the Person with her fist, but they were made of black sponge, and her fist sunk deep into their torso and bounced back out, doing no damage. Her lungs were trying desperately to grasp oxygen, but it struggled to get down her pinhole throat. The edges of her vision were darkening.

And in the midst of the chaos, her mind decided to take her back to that night once again, but this time, it showed her the wall that had risen from the floor in her mother's room. It showed it to her, until she could almost see it in her own room, until it could almost protect her. Until her eyes actually saw it in her room, blocking her off from the shadows for just a moment before the Shadow Person stepped through the red brick as if it was nothing, and the hallucination disappeared.

The Person held their hand up, fingers poised elegantly, and shadow swirled from their palm. It rose and twisted to form a knife, with a sharp, pointed blade that seemed all too capable of carving into her flesh.

Ravyn's eyes widened.

Before she even had the chance to open her mouth, there was a kick in the stomach, and the words disintegrated on her lips. Ravyn lashed out again, trying to kick the Person away from her, but her foot simply bounced off their swirling, smoky body.

A realization dawned on her, and it made her heart skip a beat. She was going to die. They were going to kill her. All the moisture in her mouth evaporated with her pained breath. The darkness at the edges of her vision was starting to close in, and black spots appeared in front of her eyes. Her hands were shaking uncontrollably, and the tremors travelled up her arms.

More shadows snaked out from the Person, taking hold of her wrists and suspending her in the air so her feet were inches off the ground. Ravyn struggled, thrashing her legs and trying desperately to break free. Other shadows took hold of her ankles, holding her in place. Then they pulled, and Ravyn screamed as she was stretched. All the muscles in her body clenched tight, trying to hold her together, adding to the pain already flaring through her. Her bones and joints were being prised apart, creaking and aching as they were. She couldn't move.

The shadowy blade was rising up to meet her skin. Ravyn sobbed, twisting her ankles and wrists to try and break the shadows' grasp, but it held tight, only getting tighter as she squirmed. The blood supply to her hands was cut off, and her fingers started to go numb.

The Person brought the blade to her wrist, and for a moment, she thought maybe it wouldn't pierce her flesh, that maybe it was just to scare her. But the blade pressed against the skin and broke it. Blood welled in the cut, then dribbled freely down her arms and soaked into her black t-shirt. Ravyn cried out, squirming again.

"Olivia, are you okay? What are you doing?" Aunt Stephanie called from downstairs. Ravyn opened her mouth to scream, but then shadows wrapped themselves around her mouth, squeezing tight and crushing her jaw. The pressure travelled upwards and into her skull, collecting at the top of her head. It kept building, growing more painful as it did. The image of her teeth starting to fall out under the pressure flashed in her mind, and even more alarm bells started to ring.

She could barely hear her own muffled screams. She tried to struggle, but the shadows grip on her was immense, trying to rip her in half.

The blade travelled down her arm, right down to her elbow. Ravyn screamed against the gag on her mouth, her arm on fire, sizzling and burning. Blood flowed heavily from the gaping wound, soaking into her clothes and her hair. It pattered like heavy rain as it hit the floor.

"Olivia? What's going on?" Aunt Stephanie called again, but this time, she was much closer. The Shadow Person, sensing the game was up, released her, and she dropped to the floor, crumpling into a heap of blood and tears. Then they simply melted away, joining the long shadows on the floor cast by the gloomy clouds outside.

Ravyn sucked in a heaving breath, grabbing her arm. Dark blood trickled between her fingers, running down her hand and splashing onto the floor between her legs. Tears ran off her face and joined the blood, mixing with it and dissolving into it, and made the wound sting. She hugged her arm to her chest, and heaved another tearful breath. Pins and needles filled her hand, and was starting to move down into her wrist. Her whole arm was on fire, burning so hot her skin blistered and peeled away. She pressed her arm tighter against her chest, barely managing to keep herself from screaming in pain.

The door opened with a click, and the light from the hall spilled into her bedroom. There was a loud gasp behind her, and Ravyn squeezed her eyes shut.

"Oh my god, Olivia!" Aunt Stephanie hurried over, and crouched down beside her. Ravyn turned her face away, hard sobs rattling her chest. Aunt Stephanie took her hand, and pulled her sliced arm away from her chest. Blood spurt out, the pressure of her chest now gone and there was nothing to stop her from bleeding to death.

There was a gasp, and Ravyn's heart exploded.

"Oh, Olivia! Oh my god!"

Aunt Stephanie shot to her feet and grabbed one of Ravyn's old t-shirts which was lying half hidden under her bed. She came back and took Ravyn's arm again, pressing the t-shirt to her wound. It stung badly, like venom eating away at her nerves, and Ravyn cried out. Her whole body was starting to tremble, and her muscles seized up tightly.

"Olivia! What— Did you do this? How— What?!" Aunt Stephanie asked, her voice crackling and frayed, her words coming too quick. She pulled Ravyn to her chest.

Ravyn opened her eyes slowly, tears still flowing and sobs scratching her throat as they rose to her mouth.

Aunt Stephanie gave a small cry. "Oh, no, no, no. Oh my god!" Her voice broke, and one of her tears landed on the top of Ravyn's head.

Ravyn's head spun so fast that she forgot about the pain, about the blood which was soaking into her clothes and staining her floor. She would have to take the blame for this whole thing. Because Aunt Stephanie couldn't see the Shadow People. Even when there was one watching them in the corner of the room, she never saw. She looked straight through them, like there was nothing there. She had said it was the trauma from what happened to her mother, because that's what the doctors told her. It was all trauma; it wasn't real. There had been many times that Ravyn had questioned herself too.

But this… This proved it was all too real. This proved that it wasn't just trauma, that there was actually something there, and only she could see it.

Only she could see it and feel it. Only she could suffer the wounds that they would inflict.

But Ravyn just had to bottle it up and look the other way, hoping that the People melted into the shadows and left her alone.

She just had to hope she wouldn't share her mother's fate.

CHAPTER 4

Olivia, don't argue with me—"

"Stop calling me that!" Ravyn snapped back, staring out the car window, tears blurring her vision. Outside, the world passed by in a smear of grey—grey clouds, grey buildings, grey people.

Aunt Stephanie sighed heavily, annoyance on her breath. "I am not calling you a silly name like that, *Olivia*."

Ravyn thought about arguing, like she had the past ten thousand times they'd had this conversation, but decided to save her breath. There was no point, and it would only make things worse.

They had already argued three times this morning, over various things, but mainly the fact that Aunt Stephanie wanted her to see a doctor about "all this stuff" that had been going on.

It didn't help that during one of those arguments, there was a Shadow Person breathing down Ravyn's neck, standing right behind her the whole time. It moved with her, teased the back of her neck with cold fingers. Aunt Stephanie said nothing about it, because she couldn't see the damn thing. But Ravyn could, and the whole time her heart was beating fast, her brain whirring like an old computer as it struggled to function with this creature of death and darkness standing right behind her, waiting to finish the job and kill her.

After the attack, she had hardly slept, always in fear of being murdered in her sleep. Her heart rate never went below a hundred, and every little flicker in the corner of her eye sent her mind into a panicked frenzy. She saw Death everywhere, as if He was following her, waiting for the time when a Shadow sneaked past her defences and slit her throat.

Ever since the attack, they had been showing up more often, teasing her, playing games with her mind. And every time, without fail, she knew that she was going to die. There was never any doubt in her mind of that fact. But when it didn't come to fruition, the drop from the adrenaline high was so forceful, it nearly killed her anyway.

Ravyn stared out the window, and a single tear rolled down her cheek. It was warm against her skin, gliding all the way down her face until it gathered at the corner of her mouth and seeped onto her taste buds.

The scar on her arm burned, and she massaged it gently, comforting herself that maybe this wouldn't be as bad as she thought.

Aunt Stephanie said something, but Ravyn didn't hear. There was a constant hum in her ears, a mind-numbing noise that she tuned into in the hopes that it would numb her into non-existence.

Aunt Stephanie grabbed her arm and jerked her off the window. Ravyn startled, her heart leaping.

"Don't ignore me!" Aunt Stephanie snapped, and Ravyn's

lips pressed tighter together.

The car behind them blared their horn. The light had turned green, and they were still sitting stationary.

Aunt Stephanie let go of Ravyn's arm and started driving again.

Ravyn stared at her a moment longer before turning her head back to face the window. Another tear rolled down her face, followed instantly by another. She wiped her eyes quickly and pulled her hoodie strings tighter to cover her face. Blonde hair poked out of her hood, and she shoved it all back inside the thick, grey fabric.

"Stop behaving like a child, for God's sake! You should have known something like this was going to happen, with the way you've been carrying on," Aunt Stephanie said harshly, her words like nettles rubbing against Ravyn's skin.

Maybe the best thing would be to run away, Ravyn thought to herself. She couldn't think of any other solution. Running away would only solve one of her problems though. The shadows would undoubtedly follow.

They pulled into a parking space, and the car engine shut off. The silence that followed was almost unbearable.

"I can't believe I have to do this. I'm at my wit's end with you," Aunt Stephanie huffed before stepping out of the car. She slammed her door, and Ravyn flinched at the noise. She stared down at the door handle, waiting for her arm to move itself. But it didn't.

She didn't want to be here. At this fucking appointment that was supposed to "*help her.*" There was nothing that could help her, nothing that could make them leave her alone. How was anybody supposed to *help her* when they couldn't even see the problem?

Aunt Stephanie pulled the door open, and Ravyn nearly fell

out of the car. Only the seatbelt saved her from face planting on the concrete path.

"Get out of the car, now."

Ravyn undid her seatbelt and stepped out onto the curb. The cool air wrapped around her, and a chill ran through her bones. She closed the door and tucked her hands into the pockets of her hoodie. Aunt Stephanie's face hardened; her lips pursed as she trapped words in her mouth. She turned on her heel and led the way down the street. Her heels clacked on the concrete in their distinctive way—quick and heavy. Ravyn sighed before following, the soles of her runners dragging on the ground.

It would be so easy to run away.

But where would she go?

So she kept walking, following Aunt Stephanie the short distance to the doctor's surgery. With each step, her feet became heavier, trying to stop her. And she would have stopped if Aunt Stephanie hadn't turned around and grabbed her arm, dragging her the rest of the way.

The reception to the surgery was brightly lit by two large windows, spanning the height of the wall. Cracked leather seats were lined in front of them, and stacks of disorganized newspapers and magazines were piled onto the side tables. Aunt Stephanie only let go of Ravyn's arm once they were through the door.

The weight of the room pressed down on her as she stood there, staring at the dismal surroundings. There were only three other people here, one of them being the receptionist who was on the phone behind the desk. Aunt Stephanie stood patiently at the desk, glaring at Ravyn and beckoning her forwards with her eyes.

But the room was too heavy to move through. Even the air

was too thick to breathe. It was trying to suffocate her, holding her in heavy hands and watching as she slowly died, unable to escape its grasp. She tried to suck in a breath, but the weight on her chest prevented the air from reaching her lungs.

Aunt Stephanie started to move towards her, her mouth scrunching up.

Her movement kick-started Ravyn's body, and she took a step backwards.

Aunt Stephanie's eyes were dangerous, spitting fire across the space between them.

Ravyn's mind screamed at her to leave, to turn and just run. Her heart pounded, sending blood around her body so she could move again. The receptionist was still on the phone, tapping away at a keyboard as they did. The other patients had their heads stuck in their phone screens.

Go, now.

Leave!

Ravyn turned and walked out the door, leaving Aunt Stephanie standing stunned in the middle of the reception. It was only a second, however, before the clack of her heels followed Ravyn outside.

Out here, the sun had found a hole in the clouds and was shining down on Ravyn as she hurried back up the street, her hands fidgeting in her pockets. She threw a glance over her shoulder, and her eyes caught a glimpse of Aunt Stephanie's fuming face.

"Olivia!" she called out, the sound of her heels speeding up.

Go! Ravyn's brain screamed at her. Her legs responded, and she started to run.

She was running to nowhere in particular, just anywhere except here. Anywhere except back to Aunt Stephanie and her suffocating grasp. Anywhere except back to this fucking hell that she had been trapped in for years and years.

Her legs started to move faster.

"Olivia! Get back here!"

It was too late when she saw the sliver of shadow dart across the corner of her eye. She knew instantly what it was, but it was too late anyway. The shape grew into a figure, standing at the corner of a building that she was running towards. She looked to her left, out towards the road, but there was no break in the traffic—

A tendril of shadow snaked out while her head was turned, sliding across the pavement towards her legs. It snapped out as she approached and wrapped around her foot while it was mid-air.

She flew towards the ground, barely able to take her hands out of her pockets to break her fall.

She groaned, her palms scraping the pavement, tearing her skin open.

The Shadow Person stood there and watched her for a moment, mockingly, before melting back into the darkened corner of the street. And her opportunity was taken from her, melting into the shadows with it. It was exactly as it wanted—keeping her trapped here so they could have fun tormenting their toy.

There was no escaping the darkness.

"Olivia! Get off the ground!"

Aunt Stephanie's voice was a painful reminder of reality. She had failed. She stared at the street, at the possibilities of what could have been if that thing hadn't stopped her.

A single tear skimmed down her cheek.

Aunt Stephanie's hand closed around the collar of her hoodie and pulled her to her knees. Ravyn stared down at her bloodied hands, where bits of dirt and stones had gathered in the wounds. Tears joined them then as they dribbled from her face.

"Stop acting like a fucking child! I have had enough of this!" Aunt Stephanie snapped, giving the collar of her hoodie a yank. Her fingers grazed the back of Ravyn's neck, cold against her skin.

Aunt Stephanie let her go and shook her hand as though she had touched something filthy, something rotten.

*****

Ravyn sat alone on the stone wall, her hood pulled up over her head, earphones in her ears blaring music to which she gently swung her foot in the air. It blocked out the noise of the world around her, with only the occasional low hum of a passing car breaking through the music barricade. It was almost time for her appointment with her new therapist that the doctor had sent her to, but she was on the other side of town, wishing she could be anywhere else but here.

The world passed by in front of her, and she went unnoticed by everyone.

The sky was a light grey, with some darker patches in the clouds, promising rain later today. She hadn't dressed for rain, so she was hopeful that it would pass and that she could make it home later without getting wet. The occasional flock of birds flew overhead, and she watched them every time, as if she could magically grow a pair of wings and join them in the sky. How nice that would be, to get away from the fuckery of the world and make the sky her new home.

Her fourth appointment began in exactly five minutes. It

was the only day Aunt Stephanie hadn't been able to drive her there because she had a hair appointment at the exact same time, so, with a stern word of warning, she had let Ravyn walk there herself.

Bad idea.

She had walked Ravyn down to the bus stop and waited until the bus had moved out of sight before leaving for her own appointment. But Ravyn had simply stared out the window as the stop she was supposed to get off at passed by, and instead she'd ridden it to the end of the line, leaving her on the opposite side of town. She hadn't really planned to do that, but she was here now, and it was too late to do anything about it. Besides, while she sat on this wall, ideas flooded her head.

The thought of running away and hopping on a train to the other side of the country with only a handful of cash was becoming more appealing by the second. And she could do it right now, if she wanted to. She could walk her sorry ass to the Luas and catch a free ride into the city centre, dodging the ticket-checkers like she always did.

She could hop on a train to Galway maybe? Cork? Somewhere far from here at least. Somewhere Aunt Stephanie couldn't find her.

She pulled out her purse and counted her cash. Well, not *her* cash, but she had more use for it than Aunt Stephanie right now.

One hundred and fifteen.

She sighed.

Well, it was enough for a one-way train ticket at least. Maybe a cheap hotel for the night, but that was about it.

She closed her eyes and held back another sigh, then put her purse away. She kept her hands in her pockets and took hold of her phone. There would no doubt be a phone call any minute now—an angry phone call, and more threats. Maybe she would even be told to never come back again, if she was lucky. That would be the final straw she needed to draw to get the fuck away from this place.

Someone tapped her on the shoulder.

She jumped, pulled from her thoughts back into the real world.

A girl was sitting beside her, probably about her age, swinging her legs as she sat on the wall. Ravyn pulled one of the earphones from her ears and raised her eyebrows at this strange girl who had seemingly appeared from nowhere.

"Hi! I called you, but you couldn't hear me," the girl greeted, a little too enthusiastically. Ravyn's eyebrows raised higher as she stared at the girl she didn't recognize.

"Hi?" she said hesitantly, eyeing her up and down. She was wearing a light pink zip-up jumper, a baby pink that looked nearly white in the light of the day. The girl smiled widely at her, her slightly crooked teeth showing between her lips.

"Hello," she said again, still kicking her legs out and bouncing her heels off the stone wall. The noise was starting to annoy Ravyn.

"Can I help you?" Ravyn asked. The girl just shrugged.

"I just wanted to say hi. You seemed lonely," she replied, turning to stare out in front of them, watching as a double-decker bus trundled up the road towards the next stop. Behind them, kids shouted and screamed as they played in the mini playground that covered one corner of the park.

Ravyn didn't reply. She didn't know how to respond to that. Music still blared in one of her ears, and she tuned back into the words. She wasn't really in the mood for a conversation, not when she was trying to plot her escape from this place.

"My name is Brooklyn, by the way. Call me Brook though. I hate when people call me Brooklyn. It's too long." Brook turned back to face Ravyn. Ravyn nodded, only throwing a glance her way. She was about to put the other earphone back into her ear when Brook spoke again.

"Are you not going to tell me your name?"

Ravyn sighed and just rolled her head to her left shoulder to look at Brook.

"Ravyn," she said flatly, already wanting to leave. She pulled out her phone and checked the bus timetable. She stared at the different bus numbers, debating if she would take one home or go further towards Dublin City, further away from Aunt Stephanie.

She pulled the hood down from her head and fixed her blonde hair back into a messy ponytail.

"I have something to tell you," Brook said, her voice lowered. Ravyn stared at her, her hands behind her head as she adjusted the ponytail, before she shook her head and rolled her eyes.

"I don't care," she mumbled, staring back down at her phone.

Was she going home or running away?

Home, or the other side of the country?

Would she still be haunted by the people made of shadow if she left here? Would they follow her, torture her for the rest of her life? It was very likely they would. And Ravyn couldn't even live hiding in the shadows, because they would find her there. That was their home.

She rubbed her eyes and dragged her hands down her face.

"I can help you," Brook said, trying again to get her attention. She shifted closer to Ravyn, but Ravyn just pushed herself off the wall and stood in front of her on the pavement.

"I don't need help. Leave me alone, please. I don't want to talk to you," Ravyn said, staring directly into Brook's eyes. Brook didn't even flinch. She just shrugged, a faint smirk playing in the corner of her lips.

Ravyn turned and started walking, following the flow of traffic. She pulled her hood back over her head and fixed her earphones.

Brook walked beside her.

Ravyn picked up her pace and pulled the hood further over her head, covering the side of her face. Brook's footsteps cut through the music, refusing to leave her alone.

Ravyn finally stopped and pulled the earphones from her ears. She spun around to face Brook.

"What the fuck do you want? Just leave me alone. I don't need you following me around like some fucking psychopath," Ravyn snapped. Brook's face became amused, that little smirk still on her lips.

"I'm not leaving you, not while they're around," Brook said, motioning with her head to something on the other side of the road. Ravyn turned to look, and her eyes widened.

It was staring back at her from across the road. A person made of shadow, out in broad daylight. People passed by it, unaware of its presence. Unaware that one of these people had tried to kill her just a few weeks ago, unaware of the danger she was suddenly in. Her breath caught in her throat as she stared at it. It sucked all the oxygen from her lungs and pulled it into the dark mass of its body.

"They won't touch you while I'm here, don't worry. Oh, that sounded way cockier out loud than it did in my head." Brook gave a short laugh. Ravyn's head whipped around to her, her eyes wide. How could she laugh when there was one right here?

Wait—

"I can see it too," Brook said once she stopped laughing, and realization dawned on Ravyn. Her heart sped up, pushing leftover oxygen around her body while her lungs forgot how to work. "And I want to help you."

Ravyn only caught a glimpse of it as it melted away, becoming part of the shadows on the ground cast by the low wall on the other side of the road.

A chill ran through her whole body, right up her spine, making her jaw clench. She pulled the earphones from her ear and shoved them into her pocket. Her legs almost buckled under her as the wave of chills reached them. Brook watched her, not even a hint of worry on her face.

"You can see it? What the hell—what the hell are they?" Ravyn demanded, struggling to keep the quiver out of her voice. Her heart was beating hard against her chest, radiating the pulses through her whole body. The scar on her arm was starting to burn with memories.

Brook reached over and took Ravyn's hand, startling her. Ravyn tried to pull away, but her grip was strong.

"Let's talk somewhere more private. Can we go back to your house? I feel like that would be best." Brook was already starting to walk, pulling Ravyn along with her.

So much for running away, was the first thought that sprang to her mind, and she shook it away. Now was not the time to be thinking of that. Brook could see it! Brook could see the Shadow Person!

That meant Ravyn wasn't the only one who could see them!

This was too much for her brain to process all at once. Words swam in her mind, clogging up the space as they refused to sink in.

Behind the overwhelming fear that was pulsing through her blood with the beat of her heart, there was a hint of relief. Relief that she was not in this alone, that she wasn't the only one who could see these people.

Relief that she wasn't crazy, like everybody told her she was.

Ravyn guided Brook towards the bus stop, her steps surer now, her strides more confident. And soon, the thud of her heart wasn't the song of fear anymore. Her head was still clouded with millions of thoughts, but she silenced them for now. Just for the forty minutes it would take to get home.

And once they got there, Brook would have a lot of explaining to do.

CHAPTER 5

Ravyn locked the door behind her, testing the handle to ensure that it was locked securely.

The house was quiet. Aunt Stephanie was still at the hairdressers. Being here—just standing in the hallway—took every ounce of hope that she had built up during that long, mostly silent bus journey and beat it with a mace. The air was heavy, and suddenly she wanted to rip the door open and just run. She couldn't be here. When Aunt Stephanie got home, she couldn't be here, or God only knows what might happen.

But she took a deep breath and turned around to face Brook.

Aunt Stephanie would kill her if she knew Ravyn had let a stranger into their house. A stranger she might consider "crazy" because she could see the shadows moving too.

But this stranger was Ravyn's key to finding out what the fuck was going on.

Ravyn stared into Brook's dark hazel eyes.

"You need to tell me what's going on," Ravyn said, urgency

lacing her words. Aunt Stephanie would be home soon, and Brook needed to be gone by then. Ravyn would be in enough trouble as it is, but if Brook was here when Aunt Steph came banging down the door…

Brook smirked.

"Where are your manners? You have a guest in the house." Brook tried to sound stern, but the wide grin on her face gave it away. She spun on the spot, admiring the tiny, bare entrance to the house that Ravyn lived in.

Ravyn opened her mouth to apologize but caught herself and frowned.

"You said you were going to help me," she reminded Brook. Brook threw a glance at Ravyn over her shoulder and smiled. She started walking down the hallway, peeking through the opened doors into messy rooms. Ravyn followed, wringing her hands in front of her. Brook let herself into the small kitchen at the back of the house. The setting sunlight streamed in through the windows, and dust particles floated in the air through the beams of light.

"Let's sit." Brook pulled out a chair for herself and sat down. She rested her elbows on the stained, floral tablecloth, looking up at Ravyn with a broad smile, her white teeth peeking through her lips. Ravyn stared at her, her lips pressed tightly together.

"Do you have biscuits? Actually, no. I don't want anything, forget I asked." Brook grinned cheekily.

There was a moment of silence between them.

Ravyn glanced up at the clock hanging above the table. Nearly five o'clock.

They didn't have much time.

Ravyn sat down opposite Brook, holding back her sigh.

"Anyway, I'm here to give you a choice," Brook finally

began, and Ravyn lapped up her words. "You can stay here and I can just explain what the hell is going on, *or* you can come with us and I can *show* you what the hell is going on."

Ravyn frowned. She shook her head and rubbed her temples in a circular motion. "Wait, no. Hold on a second. Who is 'us'? And why won't you just tell me what those things are?"

"They're called Shades," Brook answered instantly. Ravyn opened her mouth, but any forthcoming words evaporated. She closed her mouth, trying to come up with something to say. The ticking clock above her didn't help.

So she just nodded.

Shades. Okay.

"You're not the only one who can see them, Ravyn. There are loads of us, all over the world."

Ravyn tried to digest the words, but her mind was working in overdrive and was starting to overheat. Nearing full capacity. There was too much going on up there to properly understand the words Brook was saying.

"There's a lot more to this than just seeing Shades every so often—"

That Ravyn knew already. One had tried to kill her.

"—but I don't know if I'll be able to explain it all to you. That's why I suggest packing a bag and coming with me so I can show you. You can always come back if you change your mind. But if I were you, I'd really consider coming. Besides, I want to get to know you better! I've heard about you for so long, it's so nice to actually meet you!"

Ravyn was struggling to dissect the information Brook kept throwing at her. Her brain was swelling, unable to contain it all.

She held up her hands again, not even sure where to start.

"But… How did you know? Who told you about me? And how the fuck did you find me?" She sighed, frustrated. They didn't have time for this.

Maybe it was better to go with Brook, no questions asked and no looking back.

"Oh, you'll come and meet all the others like us! Everyone's really nice, don't worry. And like I said, you can always come back if you change your mind—"

"I don't want to come back," Ravyn said, cutting Brook off. It was decided, her mouth moving before her brain could dwell on it any longer. Brook raised an eyebrow and nodded slowly.

"So are you going to pack a bag, or do I need to do that for you? I'm not letting you only bring hoodies and jeans though, girl. Where is your sense of fashion?"

Says the one sitting in an oversized pink jumper and ripped jeans, Ravyn couldn't help but think. She ignored the joke and started rubbing her temples again to try and relieve the pressure in her head.

"Will we be safe from them though? The Shades?" Ravyn asked. Her scar was starting to burn.

Brook only shrugged. "For the most part."

"What does that mean?"

Brook spoke again, but Ravyn didn't even hear her words because a key slid into the lock on the front door, and the hinges squeaked as it was pushed open.

Ravyn's eyes widened, and her heart skipped a beat.

Well, shit.

Brook raised an eyebrow, stopping mid-sentence.

Every inch of Ravyn's being just wanted the earth to swallow her whole, to take her away from this place. She shouldn't have asked questions, shouldn't have come back here in the first place. She should have just let Brook take her to wherever it is she wanted to take her. An active war zone would be better than staying here. Buried six feet under in a wooden box would be better than this.

Aunt Stephanie's heels clacked over the wooden hall floors, the noise pounding in Ravyn's ears as she made her way into the kitchen.

Ravyn couldn't even look up at her as she stood in the kitchen door. Her heart was pounding, pounding so hard it hurt. Her stomach was threatening to throw up everything she had eaten today.

"Olivia." Aunt Stephanie's sharpened tone sliced right through her centre. Ravyn dragged her eyes up to look at Aunt Stephanie's scowl.

"What are you doing here?" she hissed. "And who is this?"

"I'm Brook. It's nice to meet you, but we won't be staying long, unfortunately. Ravyn and I have planned this impromptu trip for a few days, hope you don't mind. We'll be back in a few days though, won't we, Ravyn? Okay, we're just gonna—"

"Get out of my house. Olivia is not going anywhere," Aunt Stephanie said. Brook's smile faltered, and she looked over to Ravyn with raised eyebrows. Ravyn bit her lip and filled her lungs to explain herself.

But Aunt Stephanie didn't even give her a chance.

"And what are you even doing here, Olivia?! I *trusted* you to go to your counselling yourself, and you just throw it back in my face? I am fucking sick of this," Aunt Stephanie snapped. She dropped her bags on the floor. They tipped over, and shopping fell out over the tiles.

"I'm sorry, I—"

"*Sorry* is not good enough, Olivia! Do you think this is

funny? Do you think I am going to keep bending over backwards for you? I have had enough!" Aunt Stephanie marched over, her heels pounding the tiles, the noise deafening.

Brook stood up and reached down towards Ravyn's hand.

"We're actually just about to leave, sorry. We've already paid for the hotel and everything, haven't we? Yeah, so we're gonna go now, but it was nice to meet you," she said, pulling Ravyn to stand.

"Olivia is not going anywhere! I don't know who you are, trying to take *my child* away from me, but I swear if you try to take her one foot out that door, I will kill you."

Aunt Stephanie pushed Brook to the side and grabbed Ravyn's arm. She squeezed it tight, her fingernails digging through Ravyn's hoodie and pressing sharply into her skin.

"What are you playing at, Olivia?! Stop this nonsense, you are *not* leaving!" Aunt Stephanie shouted. Ravyn grabbed Aunt Stephanie's hands and ripped them from her arms, her nail scraping Ravyn's skin as she did. Her heart was beating a million times a second, beating so hard her vision was pulsing.

"I'm going with Brook," she told her. Not that she had much of a choice. She could not stay here, she knew that much. Not if she wanted her head to stay on her shoulders. Not if she wanted to find out what the hell was going on, and what those Shades are—

"You're not going anywhere—"

"I thought you were sick of seeing me, and now you want me to stay?" Ravyn snapped back before she could stop the words, quoting her own words back at her.

Aunt Stephanie's hand slapped Ravyn across the face before she could react. Her head whipped to the side with the force of the blow. The noise rang in her ear, and the skin of her cheek burned hotter than the sun. Her hands flew to her face, tenderly covering her cheek, and she winced at the contact.

"Do not talk back to me," Aunt Stephanie hissed. Ravyn stared at her with widened eyes, her lower lip quivering.

"What the fuck?" Brook was there, and she grabbed Aunt Stephanie by the arm, spinning her around. Aunt Stephanie smacked her across the face with an open palm.

"I told you to leave! Go! Olivia is not going anywhere, she belongs *here*!" Aunt Stephanie screamed, pointing Brook towards the front door. Brook rubbed her cheek. Ravyn stared at her, watching as the skin on her face turned bright red. Ravyn could almost feel the heat of it from where she stood.

A surge of fire shot through Ravyn's body as she watched Aunt Stephanie scream at the only person who could help her figure out what was going on.

The only person who could keep her safe from the Shades.

The only person who might be able to tell her why her mother died.

Her mother's face came into view, beautiful and sweet, with kind eyes that Ravyn never wanted to forget. There was a gentle smile on her cherry-blossom pink lips. And all too quickly, blood started to dribble from her hairline and down her face, and her skin turned pale. A trail of shadow was wrapped around her throat, choking her, pulling her away. Ravyn closed her eyes, shutting the image off in her brain.

Tears gathered behind her eyelids.

"Ravyn is not *your child,* and we both know that. We are leaving, right now. Come on, Ravyn," Brook said. Ravyn opened her eyes and saw Brook reaching for her. She reached out and took her hand, sealing the deal. They were leaving.

Aunt Stephanie pulled open the top drawer beside her, and

the blade of a bread knife sparkled in the evening sunlight as she pulled it out.

Ravyn's eyes widened.

"Olivia is not going anywhere. Get out of my house, and stay the fuck away from my daughter," she hissed. Brook stared at the knife, all the giddiness gone and replaced with fear. Ravyn could feel it through her skin, and it started to leak into her own body, contaminating her bloodstream.

"What are you doing? Put that down!" Ravyn said, unable to stop the quiver in her voice.

"Olivia, you are staying here. That is *final*."

Ravyn dropped Brook's hand.

She didn't expect herself to reach over and grab Aunt Stephanie's hand which was closed over the handle of the knife. But her body did it anyway. Her fingers had their own mind. They wanted to know what had happened to her mother, and Aunt Stephanie was in the way of that.

Aunt Stephanie was in the way of everything.

Everything.

Aunt Stephanie stared at Ravyn, looking between her face and Ravyn's hand closed tightly over hers.

And she laughed.

She fucking *laughed*.

Ravyn's jaw clenched.

"I'm leaving. I'm going with Brook—"

"*YOU ARE NOT LEAVING!*" Aunt Stephanie screamed, pulling her hand away from Ravyn. She pushed Ravyn, sending her backwards so she tripped over the chair and was suddenly staring at the ceiling, pain gripping the back of her head. The knife clattered to the floor beside her, just about missing her skin. Ravyn slowly brought her hand up to her head. It was tender to the touch, and she winced again.

She rolled slowly onto her side, the movement making her ears ring.

"What are you doing? Leave her alone!" she heard Brook shout over the ringing.

Ravyn propped herself up on her elbows.

A drop of blood hit the tiles, right in front of her face. She reached back around to her head, her fingers carefully parting her hair to feel the cut on her scalp. Warm, red blood oozed from it and stained her hair.

"Get out of my fucking house!" Aunt Stephanie shouted back at Brook.

Ravyn's vision was pulsing with the beat of her heart. She took her hand away from her head, and her fingertips were stained dark red.

The knife glinted on the kitchen floor, the blade singing to her.

And her fingers responded to its call.

She reached over and closed her hand around the handle. It was an extension of her now, a part of her own body. And it was hungry. She didn't need to command it; it just knew what to do.

She stumbled as she tried to stand, using the overturned chair to help her. Once she was upright, she swayed, her vision darkening. She blinked it away, and her eyes readjusted to find Aunt Stephanie screaming in Brook's face.

The knife dragged her hand behind it as it reached out in hunger, only wanting a warm meal to satisfy its cravings. Ravyn watched as her arm followed the blade, watched how the light reflected off the metal. Everything moved in slow motion.

So slow she even had time to see Aunt Stephanie's face before the knife plunged into the side of her neck. Her head was only starting to turn, her eyes leading the way. And they were open wide, so wide Ravyn could see every strand of colour in her irises—the deep blue, the hints of sea green, even wisps of oak and pine bark. Her mouth hung open, mid-sentence.

As soon as the knife pierced her skin, time sped up again. There was a sickening squelch as it cut straight through her flesh, tore open her artery, and even managed to dig as deep as her windpipe.

Blood splashed out instantly, covering Ravyn's hoodie in deep red stains.

Aunt Stephanie dropped to the floor instantly. The knife went down with her, its teeth feasting on her body. It was a hunter posing with its kill, proclaiming its trophy.

Ravyn stood frozen to the spot, staring at the place where Aunt Stephanie had just been. Her hand was stretched out in front of her, still closed in a fist.

It was only when Brook pulled her out of the kitchen that her mind restarted, kicking back into action. Her knees buckled, and she pulled Brook to the ground with her. Ravyn sucked in a gasp, oxygen struggling to get through her tightening airway.

"What have I done?" she tried to say, but her own words barely reached her ears. A sob rattled her chest, and she covered her face with her hands, her own blood mixing with Aunt Stephanie's as it ran over her fingers.

"Ravyn!" Brook grabbed her by the shoulders and tried to pull her to her feet, but Ravyn's body was dead weight. Tears streamed down her face, mixing with her blood as it splashed onto the tile floor.

"We have to go, Ravyn!" Brook said urgently, trying again to get Ravyn to her feet. Ravyn's legs refused to move.

She had killed her.

She had killed Aunt Stephanie.

What the fuck had she done?

"Oh my god!" Ravyn cried. Her chest was tight, too tight to breathe. The sobs that shook her were painful, scratching her throat raw. The edges of her vision were starting to darken.

"Nat, you need to pick us up, right now," she heard Brook say but paid no attention to her words.

She had just killed someone.

She had just killed her own aunt.

She was a murderer.

Brook gripped at the hem of Ravyn's hoodie and ripped it off over her head. She balled it up and left it on the ground beside them. Some of the blood had soaked through to Ravyn's t-shirt—a light blue now spotted with crimson.

"I killed her!" Ravyn sobbed. Pain flared in her chest and started to spread, like vines reaching through her body and wrapping themselves around every organ. It was an infection, the infection of a murderer.

Her hands were covered in blood. Some of it her own, most of it not.

The tiles were covered with blood. There was so much blood everywhere. She closed her eyes, tried to block it out, but her brain wanted to show her what she had done. It kept her eyes open, staring at Aunt Stephanie's unmoving body, no matter how much she willed her eyes to shut.

Ravyn tried to wipe her hands on her shirt, only making the stains larger. Brook grabbed her wrists and stopped her. Ravyn dragged her eyes up, tears making her vision blurry. Brook stared intently at her.

"We have to go. Nat is picking us up, but we have to leave," she said slowly. Ravyn nodded, her lips trembling. Her whole body was starting to follow suit, shaking violently. Brook took Ravyn's bloody hand and helped her to stand.

Her legs threatened to buckle beneath her.

But the house didn't want them to leave. It showed Ravyn her mother's body, laying on the ground in front of them. It showed her Aunt Stephanie's body, lying right beside her mother's. Their blood mixed on the ground, their skin white as paper, drained of all life.

She had become like one of them.

Like one of the Shades.

She had killed somebody.

Brook recoiled, her hand jerking away from Ravyn's. Without the support, Ravyn collapsed again. She hit the floor with a thud, and her vision darkened. One of the bodies disappeared; the other didn't.

Brook sank to the ground beside her, her eyes wide.

"What…" Ravyn heard her mumble to herself, but over the ringing in her ears, she didn't hear if she said anything else.

Her vision was continuing to darken. The ringing in her ears was getting louder, drowning out everything. She was spinning, spiralling downwards into an abyss. There was something in her head, a presence she had never felt before. It was growing, spreading through her brain like roots, corrupting everything and shutting it all down, flicking every single switch to off.

Then her mind gave up completely.

CHAPTER 6

Sunlight crept across her face, gently waking her from her sleep. She scrunched up her eyes before opening them. There was a dull pain behind them, pulsing gently, syncing up with the rhythm of her heart. She blinked a few times, allowing her eyes to adjust to the brightness. The room startled her. This was not her bedroom, or any room she had ever been in before. No, definitely not. The walls were an off-cream colour, with a window opposite the bed. The wine-red curtains were drawn, but there was a large slit down the middle, allowing the sun to poke its head in to say good morning. Beside the window was a wardrobe, painted red. The paint was starting to wear and chip off, especially on the doors.

Where the hell was she?

She slowly sat up, rubbing her eyes. She hugged the duvet to her chest as she looked around the room, trying to remember how she got here. Her memory was hazy and cloudy, a dense fog covering her mind. She sat silently for a moment. trying to coax the memories to come out of their hiding place, but they refused to come.

She sighed, hunching her shoulders. They would come back to her later, she figured, and she climbed out of the bed. It was a much nicer bed than her old one. This one had a thick duvet, cosy and warm, and the mattress was just perfect. Her shoulders weren't aching or cramping. She swayed as the blood rushed down from her head and black spots floated across her vision. She closed her eyes and took a deep breath; it quivered as it left her mouth. The back of her head ached, and she reached her fingers around to touch it. There was something dried into her hair, and she picked at it and pulled some of it out, examining it.

It was dried blood.

She flicked the flake off her fingers, staring as it floated slowly to the ground.

Her fingers reached back again, this time feeling the scab that had formed over a wound. Had she hit her head? She didn't remember.

She didn't remember anything.

Anxiety was starting to build in her chest, spreading like a disease through her blood, latching onto her organs and infecting them, rotting them. She looked down at herself and found bloodstains on her shirt. A *lot* of stains, darkened and hardened into a crust. It was probably from when she'd hit her head. But how had she hit her head?

She didn't remember.

She only remembered… Brook? Yes, she was going to run away with Brook. Was this where she was? Had she actually managed to escape? It must be, she told herself. She looked around the room, and her eyes fell on the clothes draped over the end of the bed. There was a scrap of paper lying on top. She picked it up.

For you ;), was scrawled on it in messy handwriting.

There was a black, turtle-neck top and black leggings with a thin, white stripe down the legs. She held them out in front of her, looking for bloodstains. There was none. She undressed and pulled them on clumsily, leaving her own clothes in a pile on the floor. They fit snugly. Maybe Brook had lent them to her?

She wished she could remember what had happened. Everything past getting home with Brook was a haze, damaged film with black streaks and muffled audio that just got worse the longer it played until it was completely unintelligible.

They must have run away as they'd planned. How else could she have ended up here?

There was only one door to this room, so she inched towards it. Before she opened it, she pressed her ear against it, quieting her breath to hear beyond it. The wood was surprisingly warm. There were muffled voices in the other room.

"You're sure?" someone said, their voice louder than the others. There was a mumble in reply, the words lost to her. She listened closer, moving her ear to the crack between the door and the frame, hoping the spoken words would reach her.

"Damn. Should we tell Jay?" It was the same voice.

Ravyn gritted her teeth as she tried to coax memories to come to her. Who were these other people? She could only remember Brook… Her hands were starting to shake, the tips of her fingers being poked by pins and needles.

She swallowed a lump in her throat and slowly opened the door. The talking ceased, and three people turned their heads to look at her standing in the doorway.

The room was a kitchen, sitting room, and dining room merged into one tiny space that barely managed to contain it all. There were two windows on the far wall, and the mesh, cream curtains were pulled open. The sun lit up the room with a subtle golden glow. Two people—one of them Brook, the other a boy she had never seen before—sat at the table. There was another girl standing by the counter, making food. The scents of a cooked breakfast filled Ravyn's nostrils and made her stomach turn and she suppressed a wretch.

"Ravyn! You're up." Brook stood and made her way over to Ravyn. Her chest was getting tight, her throat wanting to close up and cut off her oxygen. Brook gave her a quick hug, adding more pressure to her already collapsing lungs.

"How are you feeling?" She asked sweetly. Ravyn shrugged. She glanced nervously at the two others in the room.

"I don't know if these are for me, or…?" She dodged the question, looking down at herself and taking hold of the hem of the top. Brook gave her a smile.

"Yeah, they're for you. Did you not see my note? Nat donated them." Brook threw a glance behind her at the girl in the kitchen, who had her back to them. "Come sit with us while we wait for breakfast. You look hungry." Brook took Ravyn's nearly numb hand and led her over to the table. The somewhat familiar, warm skin against hers did nothing to combat the wave that was washing her away, taking over every inch of her body, trying to drown her. The boy smiled at her as she approached.

"I'm Alec," he said. Ravyn held up her hand in greeting as Brook pulled out a chair for her, opposite him. She sat and took a breath to calm herself. Her heart was beating a little harder, but she tried her best to ignore it.

Brook sat beside her.

"You sure you're okay?" Brook put a hand on her shoulder, her head tilted to one side. Ravyn just nodded, not trusting her voice. There was a knot in her throat, with the ends being pulled tighter.

Alec softened his gaze. "Don't worry, we don't bite," he chuckled, and Ravyn flashed a small smile. Brook gave her shoulder a squeeze, then took her hand away.

"You hit your head pretty hard last night. How are you now?" Brook asked cautiously, leaning back to look at Ravyn's skull. As soon as the words left her mouth, Nat shot Brook a warning glance. Ravyn caught it out of the corner of her eye and swallowed hard. She brought her hand to the back of her head, and covered over the matted strands with clean hair. Butterflies were invading her stomach, and she felt sick.

"Ehm…I'm okay. I don't really…remember much," she admitted. Some of her memories were staying hidden from her, hiding in the dark depths of her mind, down in places she couldn't reach, places she didn't dare try to explore.

"That's okay. Don't worry about it for now. Are you hungry? Nat is making a good proper breakfast for us. You look like you need a decent breakfast," Brook said. Ravyn had smelled it, but her stomach was not too happy about it. She just smiled and nodded, afraid of throwing up despite her empty stomach.

"Well, I am fucking starving," Alec said, biting one of his fingernails, which was coated in chipped, white nail polish. He smiled at her again. He had warm, tanned skin and a mop of dark brown hair that fell in front of his burnt-amber eyes. Stubble was starting to grow down his cheeks and chin. He wore a green hoodie that was too big for him but looked cosy.

Nat brought five plates to the table and set them out. Ravyn kept her eyes on the table as she did so, tracing the patterns of the scratched wood while her fingers drummed against her lap.

"John has just gone to get teabags. We forgot to buy them yesterday. The most essential item on the shopping list and we forgot the fucking things." Brook scoffed and shook her head. Ravyn cracked a small smile and nodded, her eyes cast down on the plate in front of her. There was a chip in the side, but otherwise, it looked brand new.

The pulse of blood in her was becoming more noticeable.

Ravyn, calm down!

"Coffee or tea, Ravyn?" Nat said, her back to her. Ravyn looked up at her figure. Wavy, black hair cascaded down to the bottom of her shoulder blades like the sea in the night, silky and glowing in the morning light.

"Oh, um, tea. Thanks," Ravyn said, and Nat nodded without turning around.

"You'll have to wait until John gets here, then," she told her. Ravyn didn't respond. She was focused on keeping her breathing calm, so she didn't spiral out of control. She couldn't—not here, not now.

Not in front of these people she had only just met.

"Nat and John are the only ones here who drink coffee. I don't know why, it's rotten shite, ugh," Brook said, trying not to let silence settle over them, but nobody responded so silence fell anyway.

Nat carried two plates over to the table and set them down in the centre. One was full of toast, rashers, and white pudding, the other had eggs, beans, and sausages. The smell was much stronger now, and Ravyn's stomach tied itself into a knot. Bile rose in her throat, and she forced herself to swallow it back down. Alec eyed the food lovingly, rubbing his hands together.

Nat went back to get cutlery and to fill the kettle.

"Tuck in," she said as she sat back down. Alec started piling food onto his plate, and Brook followed suit. Ravyn gingerly took a slice of toast, though she wasn't sure if she could even manage to eat it. She set it on her plate and stared at it until she sensed eyes on her; looking up, she met Nat's gaze.

"Not hungry?" Nat asked. Her eyes were a piercing blue, so bright and vivid that they startled Ravyn. Like the hot summer sky, with not a single cloud to be seen.

"Oh, uh…not really," she stammered, and her cheeks flushed with colour.

"Understandable," Nat said as she took her own serving of food. Ravyn watched her. Her dark eyebrows arched softly, perfectly framing her bright eyes. She caught herself staring and looked away.

"What happened last night?" Ravyn asked, looking down at her single piece of toast. Before anyone had a chance to answer, there was a knock at the door, and Ravyn flinched.

"That's John. And just in time, too." Brook stood. The kettle was nearly finished boiling, climbing steadily towards its climax. Ravyn watched Brook walk to the door at the opposite end of the room. Ravyn's leg was starting to tremble, so she pressed her foot firmly into the floor. Brook undid the lock and pulled the door open. A man walked in, swinging a white plastic bag in circles at his side.

He was tall, with muscles rolling under his dark skin. He had an undercut, and she could see some stubble poking through on his cheeks, like Alec. He wore camo cargo trousers, and a black shirt that clung to his biceps. Brook closed the door, and they walked over together. He towered above her, the top of her head only barely reaching his shoulder.

"I come with gifts," John said, pulling the box of tea from

the bag.

Alec grinned at him. "Go make the tea, then."

John scoffed. "Tea is for weaklings." He threw the box at Alec's head. Ravyn flinched away from the missile. Alec caught it and went over to the counter. The kettle clicked off, and mugs clinked together.

"You must be Ravyn." John held out his hand. Ravyn shook it tentatively. He had a firm grip.

She nodded. "Yeah."

John sat in the chair beside Alec. He started loading breakfast onto his plate with a grin on his face. Ravyn took a bite out of her toast, much to the displeasure of her stomach. It heaved, and she brought a hand to her mouth. A cup of steaming tea was placed in front of her. The steam swirled up around her face, warming it. Brook put a carton of milk on the table, and the feast was ready. Ravyn waited patiently as the milk was passed between them and poured into cups. John and Nat had coffee.

The anxiety was still bubbling in her. Her chest was still tight, as though there was a rope tied around her, squeezing her ribs together. These were a bunch of strangers. And she was in their house, eating with them. She was wearing their clothes. She had slept in their bed. She hardly knew them.

"You'll feel better when you eat something." Brook gave her a nudge, breaking her out of her trance. Ravyn just nodded and brought her cup to her lips. The tea scalded the inside of her mouth, and she swallowed it quickly. It burned all the way down to her stomach. Her tongue turned to sandpaper, and she rubbed it against the roof of her mouth.

"I suppose I did promise to explain everything to you," Brook commented, looking around at the others. Alec paused for a moment, in the middle of shovelling a forkful of beans into his mouth. Then he shrugged and continued eating. John made no comment.

"What do you know already?" Nat asked.

Ravyn looked at her, into her piercing eyes, and her cheeks started to heat up. "I don't know," she muttered, and Nat smiled gently.

Those memories still would not come to her. They were buried deep, hidden beneath the surface, lying alongside the corpses of her mind.

"You know about the Shades," Brook said, giving her another nudge. This deepened Ravyn's blush until her whole face started burning, and she looked down into her mug. Shades…? It sounded familiar, and she knew Brook had explained it to her already, but she couldn't quite remember what that explanation was.

"I—"

"*They* are the Shades. And we are the Ethereal," Nat cut in, saving her from embarrassment. Slowly, the memory from the kitchen pieced itself back together, word by word, dragging itself to the surface. Yes, Brook had told her she could see the Shadow People too. The *Shades*, she corrected herself.

We? We are Ethereal? Me?

"Okay…" She frowned and rubbed her forehead.

"You are an Ethereal, Ravyn. Do you know what that means?" Nat asked, tilting her head to the right. Her dark hair fell to the side, hanging over her right shoulder. Everyone else was silent. John was on his phone with a slice of toast in his other hand, Alec focused on eating, and Brook was listening in to the conversation, her eyes flicking between Ravyn and Nat.

"Um…" Ravyn trailed off. Her scar burned, and she rubbed it with her thumb. "No."

"The Ethereal can see the Shades, but other people can't. But we can also...do things. I suppose you could call it...magic, if you like. Abilities. Dare I say, superpowers." Nat smirked. "For example, I can manipulate water. John and Brook can manipulate the earth—"

"But I'm more powerful!" John cut in before Brook could and got a slap across the side of his head. He pushed Brook away with a chuckle. A smile somehow managed to push its way onto Ravyn's face, but it faltered quickly. She turned her attention back to Nat and her words, which were barely sinking in.

"But that's the most common type, so you're nothing special," Nat shot back playfully, and Brook shot her a glare.

"That's just bullshit." Brook shook her head at Ravyn, and a small chuckle rose in her throat. Ravyn's smile returned for just a moment. Her leg had stopped shaking, and the sickness in her stomach was starting to fade. But her head was still crammed; there was no space for the words which were being thrown at her.

"Anyway." Nat cleared her throat, a smile still playing on her face. Tiny dimples appeared on her cheeks when she smiled. "Alec can manipulate fire. There are also some people who can manipulate the air. So, together, we have all the elements. Cheesy, right?" She flashed a grin. "But you have something rare. You are an Illusionist. Want to take a guess as to what that is?"

Ravyn ignored her question. "Wait, how do you know?"

Nat didn't know her, so how could she know? Ravyn didn't even know herself. How could anyone else? Was this even real? Were they telling the truth, or was this all a big lie, a set-up from the very beginning to make a show out of her and prove her insanity to Aunt Stephanie?

"Your mother was an Illusionist too." It was Alec's turn to speak. Ravyn turned to him, eyes wide and mouth open. Her eyebrows were pushed right up her forehead as far as the muscles would allow, but they wanted to rise higher. Words failed her, so he just continued.

"Your mother was an Illusionist. One of our best, actually. I didn't get a chance to meet her, but I heard from my parents she was…exceptional." He finished his piece by tearing hungrily into his toast. Ravyn blinked a few times, not sure what to say. She sat back in her chair and ran her hand through her hair, and flakes of dried blood gathered under her fingernails.

Her mother was one of them?

"But how do you know I'm one? Could I not be something else? What if I'm not like her?" Ravyn asked slowly, still trying to process the news.

"Unlike our abilities, Illusionism is hereditary. There is no way you couldn't have it," Nat said, taking over.

"But wouldn't my aunt have it then?" Ravyn asked, frowning. This was too confusing. Her brain was spinning, information whirling around and around; she wasn't even sure what was factual or not anymore. Her foot was starting to tremble again.

"Um…no, not exactly." Nat glanced at John and Alec, then cleared her throat. "You see, your 'aunt' is not your real aunt. She was just a close friend of your mother's, but she is not part of our world. Your mother made her your legal guardian before— Sorry, I thought you knew."

Another punch to the stomach, a full fist tearing through her flesh and ripping her organs out of her body. Ravyn fell silent, shrinking in on herself. That nausea in her stomach returned as her insides churned themselves. Brook put a hand on her arm, and she stared at it, her brain struggling to keep up with it all. Nobody spoke, and an uncomfortable silence fell over the room, heavy on their shoulders.

"Oh," she said flatly.

She took a second to allow her brain to process and sort everything into neat little sections. Time ticked by slowly. The others never interrupted her thoughts. Brook's hand never left her arm, but it wasn't comforting anymore, it was just another weight that suppressed her.

Finally, Ravyn took a deep breath and nodded. While her brain had been placing information into different piles, a memory had come back, rising out of the dark waters and making itself known. The night her mother had died. The brick wall. She could remember the whole thing in clear detail, like she was watching a movie being played out in front of her. Yes, she remembered it, the wall rising out of the ground and granting them a second to start running.

"What do Illusionists do?" Ravyn asked slowly. The name suggested one thing, but she wanted to be sure. That brick wall, was that…?

"They can project illusions into the real world and make it so realistic that everyone who sees it thinks it's real. It's very cool, actually." Nat offered her a supportive smile. Ravyn nodded slowly, replaying that scene in her head, when the brick wall had risen out of the floor that night, and they had tried to run…

Then there was blood.

And her mother's body.

She had tried to save them both that night.

But it hadn't worked.

She tried to swallow a lump in her throat, but it held tight and refused to leave. It pressed on her windpipe, threatening to close it and kill her, to choke her to death.

"Okay." Her voice quivered, and she cleared her throat.

"Illusionism is one of the rarest abilities an Ethereal can have. There are only seven in the world that we know of, one of them being you. That's why we want you to come with us, so we can show you our little Ethereal world. You're special," Alec said, his mouth half full. He gulped down his food.

"Can we talk about something else now, please? I think we're frying her brain a little," Brook protested, staring down into her mug of tea that had probably gone cold. Nat nodded in agreement, and the boys started to clear the table.

"What's our next step, then?" Alec asked, taking Ravyn's plate and her half-eaten slice of toast away.

"We start moving tonight, to the house, like Jay said," Nat told him. Alec nodded. Ravyn was about to ask who Jay was, but Brook spoke first.

"Should we not wait until tomorrow? I think Ravyn needs to rest. She's had a rough day." Brook replaced her hand on Ravyn's arm. Nat frowned, her lips pursed. John sat back down at the table and sighed. There was a pile of plates stacked on the counter over his shoulder.

"It would be better if we moved as soon as possible, before the Shades find us…but, Ravyn, if you're not up for it…?" John trailed off, his question hanging in the air. Ravyn mentally scanned herself. She felt okay, apart from the little bit of anxiety that was creeping back up on her, and her stomach not feeling too good. But she was sure that, by tonight, she would be fine. She shrugged.

"I'm okay," she told them.

"I still think—"

"We'll do this the old-fashioned way and vote on it, how about that?" Nat suggested. John and Alec nodded. Alec stood behind his chair, forearms crossed and resting on the back of it.

"Perfect. Okay, raise your hand if you want to leave tonight," Nat said and put her hand up, Alec and John following suit. Ravyn, not sure if she was included in this or not, raised her hand anyway. Brook nodded, accepting her defeat.

"Okay. We leave tonight. We can have dinner early, pack the car, and we're out of here no later than six."

*****

Ravyn stared at herself in the bathroom mirror, her hands working to pick out the matted strands on the back of her head. Her fingernails were tinted red from the dried fakes of blood that she kept pulling out and dropping into the sink.

The knock at the door startled her.

"It's Nat. Can I come in?"

Ravyn let out a breath, and took her hands away from her head. She pulled strands of clean hair over the blood, and washed away the dried flakes in the sink.

"Yeah," she said, and the door opened. Ravyn turned around as Nat entered the bathroom and let the door close behind her.

"I just wanted to make sure you're okay," Nat said, glancing Ravyn up and down. Ravyn shrugged.

"Yeah, I'm just trying to… clean up a bit," Ravyn said, her hand going to the back of her head again. She hated how the blood felt in her hair, and how it rubbed against her scalp. She had accidentally pulled a bit of the scab off and it had started bleeding again, creating even more mess for her to clean up.

"Let me help," Nat said and moved towards her. Ravyn turned back around to face the mirror, and Nat stood behind her, looking at the cut on the back of her head.

"You certainly did some damage there," Nat said, and reached around Ravyn to grab one of the crisp white towels hanging up on the wall. She held it under the tap to dampen the edges.

"How did I fall? I don't remember," Ravyn said quietly. She caught Nat's eye in the mirror, and held it for a second before Nat moved behind her again, the dampened towel in one hand. She parted Ravyn's blonde hair, revealing the fresh scab.

"I don't really know either, I wasn't there," Nat told her, but Ravyn sensed a slight edge to her voice. She sighed, and pulled the two sections of hair over her shoulders so Nat could clean down the area.

The towel was cold against her scalp, and the muscles of her back tensed briefly. Nat worked gently, rubbing away all the dried blood, managing to soften it enough to be able to work the matte out of her hair.

"But why don't I remember anything?" Ravyn asked, partly to herself, partly to Nat. Her voice was quiet, and Nat didn't reply straight away, making Ravyn think she hadn't heard her. But Nat stopped what she was doing and stared at Ravyn through the mirror.

"Stress can do that. Also, you hit your head. The two don't make a great combination. I wouldn't worry too much about it," Nat said, and then shot her a brief smile. She draped the towel over the side of the sink, and Ravyn glanced down at it. The once white fabric was tinted a murky red.

Nat's fingers ran lightly over the scab on her scalp, then she pulled Ravyn's hair back into place.

"Done."

Ravyn turned around.

"Thank you," she said, her cheeks burning just a little. Nat flashed her a smile and left the bathroom, leaving her alone once again. Ravyn's fingers went to her scalp, but this time she had to search to find the wound. Eventually she felt it, but it wasn't nearly as noticeable as it had been. It had grown small, barely a cut anymore. Had there really been that much dried blood around it to make it seem so big?

*****

"You good?" Ravyn was jerked from her thoughts and looked up to find John standing over her. Out of the corner of her eye, she saw Nat raise her head too.

Ravyn frowned. "Huh?"

"I asked if you were feeling okay," John said. Ravyn's cheeks heated up, and she nodded to him.

"Oh…yeah. I'm good, thanks," she stammered. John smiled. He held out his fist to her. She looked at it and smirked. She gave him a fist bump, and he patted her shoulder.

Alec walked past them and gave John a punch on the shoulder as he went. John turned and tried to take a swipe at Alec but missed. Alec stuck his tongue out.

Brook scoffed. "Oh, come on, John. You can do better than that." She grinned from her seat beside Ravyn. John turned to Brook with a bemused look on his face, his shadow looming across her. He wrapped her in a bear hug, lifting her from her seat. Brook squealed and gripped the top of his shirt.

"John!" She giggled, trying to squirm from his grip. Ravyn watched with a growing smile on her face. John threw Brook over his shoulder in a fireman's lift, and she screamed. Ravyn laughed, and Alec joined in.

"Put me down!" Brook screamed breathlessly, trying not to laugh.

John just laughed and started spinning in a circle.

"John! I'm going to be *sick*!" Brook burst out laughing, her hair flying out as she was spun around. Ravyn caught brief glimpses of Brook's red face, her mouth open wide as bursts of laughter and harsh breathing escaped her lips.

"You tell her, John! Put her in her place! How dare she say things like that!" Alec encouraged from the sidelines and clapped his hands together as another round of his hearty laughter filled the room.

"You're next, you eejit," John said, setting Brook back on her two feet. Her hair was tangled and messy, falling down in front of her eyes. She brushed it back behind her ears with shaking hands. Her laughter had become almost silent. It was soundless but contagious, and everyone snickered and giggled at the sight of her.

"Shit—" Alec cried out and tried to jump over the back of the sofa as John advanced towards him, but John grabbed him and crushed his arms around Alec's body, lifting him off the ground. Alec shrieked and struggled to break free.

"Settle down, lads," Nat piped up. She had her legs folded under her, and one arm rested on the leather armrest. Her phone was in her lap, and the screen was lit up. A set of grey, tangled headphones hung over her legs, only one earphone in her ear. Ravyn glanced over and found Nat looking at her with a raised eyebrow.

"You always ruin the fun, Nat." John sighed, then chuckled. He squeezed Alec harder, and all the air left his body in a sharp huff. Alec's arms were pinned at his sides, but his hands waved wildly, and he tried knocking his fist against John's hips.

"I'm trying to save us from a noise complaint," Nat said, glancing at John. Then her gaze returned to Ravyn. Her lips tugged upwards. Ravyn's face burned, but she couldn't bring herself to look away. Nat's eyes were so captivating—the colour so harsh and intense, like an endless ocean to swim in before drowning.

Aunt Stephanie's face appeared in her mind, reminding her of what she had left behind and replaced with this. How she had just run away without leaving a note or anything. Would Aunt Stephanie have called the police and reported Ravyn missing? Her scowl remained imprinted behind Ravyn's eyelids, and suddenly she wasn't so sure. She pushed the thoughts from her head. No, this was for the best. She looked back at John and Alec wrestling and play-fighting, putting each other in headlocks and throwing punches at each other's stomach. Her smile dropped, and weights tugged the corners of her lips downwards.

Ravyn closed her eyes and let out a long, shaky sigh.

CHAPTER 7

They were driving on a dark, empty road as the clock ticked over to 5:58 p.m. on the dashboard. Nat was driving, and John was in the front with her, the light from his phone lighting up his face, the occasional comment passing between them. Ravyn was seated in the back behind John, and Brook and Alec chatted away beside her. The radio played softly behind their voices, winding down the day with gentle music. Nat's car was a stunning black Audi, with dark leather seats and tinted windows. It sliced silently through the dusk like a vampire, gliding along the country roads with ease.

Brook and Alec were engaged in their own private conversation that came with the occasional giggle, but Ravyn wasn't interested in what they were saying. She was content leaning her head against the window, lost in her own little world. Outside was dark, and they passed a house occasionally with golden windows, bright flashes in the night. Every so often, her eyes drifted towards the front of the car.

Brook turned to face her. "Ravyn?"

Ravyn snapped out of her daydream. "Hmm?"

"You're not asleep, are you?" she asked, tilting her head. Alec's eyes were on her now, and blood started rising to her face.

"No." She nodded and turned to look back out the window. It was gloomy, but there were stars out, looking down on them and winking. The moon wasn't up yet, and there was no melted silver coating the horizon to announce its arrival, either. Ravyn sighed and let her eyes half close.

"How long till we get there?" Brook asked, leaning forwards between the two front seats.

"Two or three hours, Brook," Nat said, her eyes fixed on the road. Ravyn saw Brook pull a face in the rear-view mirror, and John patted her on the head. She pulled back with a scowl.

"I never remember it being this long. It was *so* much quicker on the way down," she muttered, then rolled her eyes. Ravyn smiled.

"Where are we going again?" she asked.

"Jay has a house for us to stay at for a few days. He'll be meeting us there," Brook explained. Ravyn nodded slowly.

"And…who's Jay?"

"Jay is… Alec, how would you explain what Jay does?" Brook passed the question onto Alec, who frowned.

"He's like the head Ethereal. He's in charge, basically. Helps keep us safe from the Shades, helps train new Ethereal. That kind of thing."

Ravyn nodded.

"Oh, okay."

"He's a cool guy. You'll like him," he said, and Brook smiled in agreement.

"Oh, yeah. Definitely." She nodded.

"Jay is the best," John mumbled from the front. He put his

phone away and turned to face them.

"We should form a Jay appreciation group," Brook said jokingly, and they all laughed. Even Nat chuckled, glancing at them in the mirror.

"I don't think he'd like that very much." John smirked and turned back around in his seat.

Ravyn glanced at Nat again and found her smiling. Her face was glowing in the dim light. She looked into the mirror, and Nat's eyes locked with hers. A blue ocean, full of mysteries and unexplored depths. A deep sapphire blue, with tiny diamonds glinting in the weak light. For that brief moment, they were frozen, gazing at each other.

"Nat!" John shouted, grabbing her arm. Nat tore her eyes away and tried to turn the wheel.

But the world exploded.

A fist of shadow slammed into the front of the car, and Ravyn was launched into the back of John's seat. The seatbelt cut into her shoulder and stomach, and the breath was forced out of her in one sharp exhale. Then she was jerked back, and her head cracked against her headrest. Metal grated against metal, buckling and bending, and the car was flung sideways. They were upside down, and Ravyn tried to grab onto something, but then they crashed back onto the ground, and she was upright again.

She was flung forwards, and her ribs flared with pain. She grunted, barely hearing herself over the roaring of the world around her. They came to a rest as the wheels and crumpled bonnet dug into the soft ground. The car groaned, but it was drowned out by the ringing in her ears. Her vision was blurred, things coming in and out of focus. Black and white spots floated in front of her eyes, eventually popping and blinding her momentarily. She moaned. A thin trickle of warm and sticky blood ran down the side of her face. There was pressure on her legs, but her mind refused to focus on it. She closed her eyes, breathing heavily.

"Everyone okay?" The voice was distant and distorted.

There were other voices, but she couldn't make out any of them, their words barely a mumble. The back of her head was roaring with throbbing pain, pulsing, getting stronger with each thump. The food she ate earlier wanted to come back up.

Then there was a hand on her arm, and her eyes strained to open.

"Ravyn? Hey, are you okay?" It was Brook. Her hair was a mess and hung in clumps around her face, parts of it knotted together. Her dark eyes were wide, her breath laboured, and little puffs of smoke left her mouth with each exhale. The ringing was starting to subside, and her vision was stabilizing.

"Yeah," she mumbled. Her legs were starting to go numb with the pressure, her toes tingling. She tried to shift herself backwards but couldn't move more than a couple of millimetres.

Nat kicked her door open. The metal screamed, and Ravyn cringed at the noise. She was ready to throw up but held it down.

"Everyone out, quick." More doors started opening, more squealing and grinding of metal. A deep chill ran down her spine.

Ravyn opened her door with ease, but when she tried to turn herself, her legs remained stuck. She pulled her legs, but they wouldn't move. Finally, she glanced down at them and found John's seat had been forced backwards and was pinning her legs against her seat.

"Ravyn, can you get out?" Alec asked from the other side of the car. Ravyn tried to pull her legs out again, but it was no use. They wouldn't come free.

Fuck.

She pulled harder, but it just made the crushing sensation worse. The tingling was travelling down her toes and was starting in her feet now. She flexed her toes, but it just made the buzzing sensation worse.

"John! Help Ravyn!" Brook called out. Ravyn tried to push the seat off her, but it wouldn't budge. John appeared at her door and took a look at her situation. Nat glanced in over his shoulder. Ravyn looked up at them with wide eyes, helpless. Nat moved to stand beside him, her eyes on the seat that was crushing Ravyn's legs.

"You pull Ravyn, I'll get the seat," John ordered. Nat managed to squeeze in beside John's bulky frame, and she grabbed Ravyn under her arms. She pulled, and John rammed his shoulder against his seat.

"Guys, hurry. They might come back!" Brook called to them from the front of the car.

John grunted, and Nat pulled harder. As Ravyn's body stretched, her ribs pulled apart and her bones started to separate, but her legs refused to come loose.

"Fuck," John muttered, trying to budge it again. It creaked in protest but didn't move.

He sighed loudly, and Nat stopped pulling.

"Shit," Ravyn muttered. Her throat was starting to tighten. If they came back, and she was stuck like this… Nat put a hand on her shoulder.

"Relax, we'll get you out," she assured her. John pulled the front door open wider, and she stared past the seat towards him. He cracked his knuckles, then spread his fingers wide, loosening them up.

He grabbed the front of the seat.

Rocks climbed into the car, tumbling and rolling over each other as they ascended from the ground. Ravyn looked down and saw that the earth under the door had risen and split open, allowing for the rocky mass to rise out of it. They travelled up along John's body, gripping to his clothes and then rolling down his arms towards his hands.

Ravyn's eyes widened.

The rocks wrapped around his fingers, moulded to his skin, adding a layer of grey, hardened flesh to his hands.

The metal beneath his fingers dented inwards.

More rock moulded to his skin, buckling the metal seat. Then he pulled and the whole thing screeched as it was ripped from the car.

John threw it to the ground, the rocks from his hands flying from his skin and hammering down on it. Blood finally rushed to Ravyn's legs again. It was so warm that it burned her blood vessels. She tapped her foot on the ruined carpet floor, waking it from its slumber.

It took her a second before she could swing her legs out of the car.

John steadied himself against what remained of the car frame.

Magic.

He had used his magic.

Nat grabbed her and pulled her out of the car. She stumbled, her feet still half asleep.

"What do we do now? Where do we go? We can't stay out here!" Brook said hurriedly. She was watching as Nat helped Ravyn out, eyes wide and fingers twitching nervously against her side. Alec was standing beside her, but he was looking around the darkness, his body on full alert.

Ravyn's legs shook, feeling returning to her feet as the

blood rushed back into them. The pins and needles were horrible, stabbing into her whole leg and foot, making it almost impossible to stand on. Nat held her upright, gripping her forearm.

Magic.

It's real.

This is all real.

Fucking hell.

She turned to stare at John with unblinking eyes. His breath was laboured, and he rubbed his forehead with his free hand. She couldn't take her eyes off him, her mind unable to believe what had just happened. It was like a movie, but…it was real. She had seen it happen right in front of her. His eyes caught hers, and he gave her a wink.

A hand of shadow, darker than the night around them, wrapped itself around his throat. John jerked, his hands flying to his neck.

Before Ravyn had any time to react, Nat stepped forwards and flicked her wrist.

Shards of crystal-clear ice formed in the air and stabbed into the Shade's head. It instantly shrivelled up, the shadows melting away to reveal the person beneath. Ravyn caught a glimpse of the young woman's face before she tore her eyes away from the dead body.

So there were real people beneath the shadow.

Oh, god.

Out of the corner of her eye, Ravyn saw shadow ripping at the woman's clothes and hair, pulling pieces off her until she faded into nothing.

"Thanks, Nat," John muttered, massaging his neck.

Ravyn gulped.

Her mind refused to think about what had just happened.

How Nat had just killed someone—

She hadn't known there was a real person beneath that outer shell of swirling shadow. That they weren't just otherworldly monsters with no sense of humanity. No, they were real people hiding behind a façade, people who knew what they were doing when they went in for the kill. People who could feel the life force of their victim drain away, and still seek to spill more blood. She could taste vomit in her mouth, and swallowed quickly before she threw up.

It wasn't a monster that killed her mother, then. It was a human.

The realization brought a stabbing pain to her gut.

"We have to move. There's probably more on the way," she said. Her voice was firm and cold. Her usually sweet tone was laced with darkness. "Let's not stand around, eh? Come on."

Nat started making her way up the grassy bank, which had been destroyed when the car rolled down it.

"To where?" John asked, grabbing Ravyn's arm and breaking her from her trance. He helped her feet remember how to move again, reminding them of what would happen if she just stayed frozen to the spot.

"To the next town. We're not far from it. We'll find somewhere for the night and call Jay."

There was no arguing, no questions, no mention that they had just killed somebody and left their body to rot. No mention of the magic that had just been performed right in front of her eyes, which her brain was still struggling to comprehend.

Everybody helped each other up the muddy bank, and they managed to reach the road without getting too dirty.

They started moving through the darkness, not sure what lay ahead of them. Only a sliver of moonlight showed them the way. They stuck to the edge of the road, following it deeper and deeper into the unknown, further and further away from the safety of the car. Ravyn's mind was alight, adrenaline pumping through her veins at the uncertainty of it all. They were blind, not sure if they were going to be attacked again, not sure if they would run into Shades with their arms open.

But there was nothing else they could do except hope they survived the dark night.

CHAPTER 8

Alec locked the door behind them and tested the handle.

Ravyn's muscles were tight and knotted. The journey from the car to the nearest town had felt like decades, and her legs were aching, shaking, on the verge of collapse. The mixture of adrenaline and lack of exercise over the years crashed over her like a wave, nearly sweeping her off her feet. Her lungs were still burning, and the sensation had travelled up the back of her throat where the cold air set it on fire. And on the brink of exhaustion came exhilaration, a childlike giddiness that she couldn't shake.

The wind, the cold, crisp air filling her lungs and biting at the back of her throat, running through the darkness with a hint of danger in their minds, shadows breathing over their shoulders, hounds nipping at their heels… It was almost refreshing.

It wasn't the freedom she had expected, but this was almost better. This was real, untamed, wild freedom. The adrenaline that still lingered in her blood was excited by it, wanted more of it, trying to hold onto the feeling for as long as it could.

A silence hung over the small hotel room while they all gathered their thoughts and their breath. But Ravyn could feel the static energy that buzzed around them. Or maybe just around her.

She ran her fingers through her hair, pulling out the knots the wind had twisted into the strands. A laugh was trying to push up into her mouth, but she blocked it in her throat.

"John, will you ring Jay?" Nat asked. "Tell him what happened, and that we need someone to come get us."

John nodded. He took out his phone and stepped into the bathroom to make the call in private. The click of the door hung in the air for a moment before slowly drifting to the ground.

"So what do we do now?" Brook said, sitting on the end of one of the beds, which sank low as if it was trying to swallow her whole.

"We wait," Nat said simply.

Brook sighed and fell backwards onto the bed. Alec took the small, dusty, red armchair in the corner and pulled out his phone.

"Fucking screen's cracked," he grumbled under his breath. Nobody responded. Muttered words drifted from the bathroom as John talked to this *Jay* person she had heard so much about. Ravyn went to reach into her pocket, only to find she didn't have one. She patted down her legs, but there was no comforting feeling of a phone against her skin. Her phone was...

In her other clothes.

In the car.

Her shoulders sank. She had grown used to having the

comforting feel of it in her pocket, snuggled against her thigh, that it all felt wrong now. She could have read the news—catch up on what had happened in the world since she'd run away. If there were people looking for her. Maybe she could text Aunt Stephanie and let her know that she was safe…or maybe not. Maybe she wouldn't want her to text. Maybe she had seen Aunt Stephanie for the last time without realising it while she'd trudged to the bus stop under her careful gaze.

Her 'aunt,' she reminded herself and her heart ached.

The thought sat in the pit of her stomach, heavy and invasive, and she didn't quite know how to feel about it.

Her whole childhood had been a lie. She had believed this woman was her relative, her own blood. Someone who would keep her safe and take care of her in the place of her mother. But she was just a stranger she had been made to believe was her aunt. The thoughts all hurt, made punctures in her skin out of which the lies bled as acid and made her flesh sizzle.

She knew she should be angry at her mother, because she had started this lie. But she couldn't find it in herself to be angry at the woman she had loved so much, the woman who's time had been cut so short. Instead, all the flashes of anger were directed at Stephanie herself. The one who had kept up the lie, and never even tried to explain otherwise to Ravyn. Who used this façade of 'aunt' to hammer feelings of guilt into Ravyn.

Her stomach started to become queasy, and she quickly took her mind off the topic. She could think more about it later, but now there were bigger things to worry about.

The room was small, with dull floral wallpaper that was peeling in the corners—a travel lodge for the fresh-faced youths just passing through the town, seeking the big city. The carpet was once a light red but was now stained and dusty.

There were two double beds, two armchairs, and an en suite bathroom that she assumed was just as run-down as the rest of the place. The bed sheets looked like they came straight out of the 1960s and hadn't been changed once. Brook didn't seem to mind, however. She had pulled her legs up onto the bed and curled into a ball, lying on her side and staring quietly at the wall.

Ravyn decided to sit on the other bed, pulling her legs up into a pretzel shape. Even though her legs were weak and she didn't want to risk collapsing, her body itched to just get up and move around. Run again, to the car and back, face the waiting Shades head-on. Bounce on the beds. Just do anything but sit. How could she possibly sit still after what had just happened, and what she had just *seen?* Her blood was practically leaping around inside her, trying to stimulate her muscles to do the same. Then Nat sat beside her, and Ravyn's body became still.

"How are you?" Nat asked quietly. Ravyn shrugged, looking down at her hands which were clasped tightly together on her lap. Her thumbs twitched as they rubbed against each other.

"I'm okay."

"This is not the introduction we wanted to give you," Nat said, sighing.

Ravyn smirked and brought her eyes back up to look into Nat's. "Too late now, I suppose," she said, holding Nat's gaze for a moment before the intensity of her striking blue eyes became too much, and she had to find somewhere else to look.

"Hmm. We'll get everything sorted out when Jay gets here, then hopefully we can start fresh, and you can forget about everything that's happened so far," Nat offered, and Ravyn smiled again. She noticed a bruise starting to form on the side of Nat's chin. Her skin was starting to turn vanilla yellow, with some cinnamon-coloured spots in the very centre.

"Are you okay?" Ravyn asked, reaching out to touch it before thinking better of it and touching her own face instead, showing her where the bruise was.

Nat rubbed her chin and shrugged. "I'll live. I've had worse. Worry about yourself, Ravyn, not me."

Nat smirked and brushed strands of dark hair back behind her ears. Ravyn watched her fingers glide elegantly, gently brushing the side of her face. Even though there were others in the room, they faded from her mind, and she was alone with Nat, just chatting as friends, as if nothing had happened anyway. There was no car crash, no Shades, no magic…

Things were just normal.

And even though she knew the feeling wouldn't last long, she held onto it while it was there, because she didn't know if it would ever return to her again. It wasn't as if she could go back to not knowing all this existed—a whole new world right under her nose. A world she had glimpsed all her life and never even realised it existed.

"The Shade back there… Are they…dead?" Ravyn asked quietly.

Nat stared at her for a moment before she answered. "Yes, they're dead. One thing you should know about our world is that sometimes you will be faced with a situation where there is no other option but to kill them. It's not a nice choice to have to make, but you have to remember that they will not hesitate to kill you if you give them a chance. They're merciless, Ravyn, regardless of what anybody else tells you. And sometimes the only way out of the situation is to kill them. But I'm sure you know that already," Nat said, her eyes never leaving Ravyn's face. Ravyn nodded slowly, willing the lump in her throat to dissolve itself so Nat didn't have to see her gulp it down.

"I mean, yeah, that makes sense," Ravyn replied, still slowly nodding.

She did not sign up for murder when she ran away with Brook.

But it was too late to go back now, too late to change her mind. If she wanted to survive against the Shades, she would have to stay here.

She would have to learn more about magic.

"Does that bother you?" Nat asked slowly, her eyes staring curiously at Ravyn's face. She shrugged, squeezing her shoulders tight to her body as a chill ran through her.

All she could see was blood on the landing.

So much blood…

Stained hands, stained hair, stained knees, stained floor.

"No, not really. I've seen worse."

Nat nodded, her eyes never shifting. She reached over and put her hand on Ravyn's shoulder and gave it a squeeze.

A foreign feeling rose within her, and deep down in the dark pits of her stomach, it scared her. She shouldn't be feeling like this. And yet…for that split second when the feeling first presented itself to her, it didn't matter. Nothing mattered.

"Do the Shades do this a lot, then?" she asked, a pang in her voice. She cleared her throat.

Nat sighed and finally shifted her eyes away. "Eh, not really… We tend to keep to ourselves and stay out of their way. But if our paths happen to cross, then yes, sometimes they do make things *difficult.*" She paused, then shrugged. "I don't want to make it seem like being an Ethereal is a bad thing, 'cause it's not. It's a great community of people from all over the world. The Shades are just a bump in the road of our journey to discovering what it really means to be an Ethereal," Nat said.

Ravyn nodded, digesting the information. "Can I ask something else?"

"Of course."

"Why can't normal people see them?"

"The Shades have two forms. One of them is the shadow form, and the other is a *human* form. Everyone can see them when they use their human form because they just look like normal people, but only we can see them when they are in the other. Make sense?" Nat explained.

"I think so."

Nat offered a smile. "I know it's all a bit confusing. Don't worry, you'll wrap your head around it eventually. We'll try not to overload you with information." Nat gave her a pat on the knee. Ravyn blushed and looked away to smile. Nat's touch was almost electric; tiny bolts of electricity shot through Ravyn's knee and down into her foot, which was still recovering from being crushed.

"I hope so," she sighed. There was so much to digest, so much to know. It was like being back at school, with information being hurled at you and not enough time to learn it before the bell went and the next class began. It was cyphers and glyphs, with only a torn scrap of paper containing a part of the key.

Nat put her hand on Ravyn's knee again and gave it a squeeze. It was uncomfortable and strange, yet pleasant, in a way. The electricity was still there, now a steady current of it flowing into her and along her nerves, igniting her. A chill ran from her knee to her head and brought goosebumps with it. She looked down at her hand, just gently resting there, then dragged her eyes back up to Nat's.

"It's our fault if you're feeling confused. I can't imagine what it must be like learning all this for the first time after not knowing it existed. It's different if you're born into it, because it's almost instinctive." Nat gave her knee another squeeze, then took her hand away.

"Well, I always knew the Shades existed," Ravyn said, and they shared a short chuckle. "I'll get the hang of it. I just might need a few reminders every now and then."

Nat flashed her a grin, and her hand returned to Ravyn's knee, only for a short second, then the space was filled by musty motel-room air.

"I'll make you a handbook to study," she said, laughing.

Ravyn grinned at her. "Do you have one of those handy?"

Nat winked at her. "No, but I'll be your mentor. Ethereal living one-oh-one. Class starts now."

They shared a moment of warm laughter, gentle and comforting. In that moment, the Shades didn't exist. It was just the two of them and the words that drifted between them. Ravyn looked back into those blue, blue eyes, and her smile froze. Nat looked right back at her, their eyes locked in a soft gaze. Heat rose in Ravyn's cheeks, and she blinked, breaking their connection.

The bathroom door opened, and John emerged. The room grew quiet and all eyes turned to him. He put the phone into his pocket and sighed.

"Jay is on his way with Therese. He won't get here until tomorrow, though, so we have to wait here for the night," he announced.

The room sighed and deflated.

"But what if…?" Brook's question hung in the air. She didn't need to finish her sentence. They were all thinking the same thing.

"It'll be fine. We can take turns watching over the place, if that makes everyone feel better?" Nat looked around. Alec nodded from the chair. Brook and John remained silent, but Nat took that silence as a yes.

"I'm hungry," Alec muttered, so suddenly that everybody laughed.

"You're always fucking hungry," John commented, and shook his head. Alec held up his hands in defence.

"Sorry, do you realise how far we've had to walk to get here? I am absolutely starving." Alec's stomach grumbled, adding to his argument. Ravyn smiled, her eyes flicking between the two boys as they bickered. The previous conversation evaporated in the air around them, and instead the room was filled with a light-heartedness that allowed her to finally take a full breath.

"And where do you suppose we're going to find this food? I don't know about you, but I am *not* stepping outside that door again until Jay gets here."

"I'm kind of hungry too," Brook piped up, and John dragged his hands down his face. Ravyn's smile grew. Now that they were talking about food, she noticed the emptiness of her own stomach. She hadn't eaten since that afternoon, well before they had left the apartment.

"I can try to order something to come here," Nat offered, and Ravyn's head turned back to face her. Nat pulled out her phone, and the bright screen lit up her face. The room fell into silence, all eyes on Nat as she searched up somewhere to order food from. Even John watched her, as if he had also suddenly realised how hungry he was.

"Do you just want a chipper?" She said, glancing up. Hungry eyes widened slightly, and they all nodded. Everyone gave their order to Nat, ranging from cheeseburgers and chips to battered cod and a can of beer, and she wrote them down in the notes app of her phone. Nat turned to Ravyn last, a smile on her lips.

"What would you like?" Nat asked her. Ravyn shrugged. She wasn't really in the mood for a burger or anything, and even chips felt too heavy to eat right now. Nothing that anyone else wanted sounded appealing. The high rollercoaster she had been riding early was starting to rapidly descend into exhaustion.

"I think I'll just get a small bag of chips, please."

Nat raised one eyebrow.

"You look like you need more than a bag of chips, Ravyn. I'll get you a milkshake. Get some sugar into you," Nat said, and typed it down. Ravyn smiled her thanks.

Nat called the nearest chip shop, repeating everyone's order and mouthing the estimated delivery time to them. Twenty-five minutes.

Ravyn's stomach growled then, and she wrapped her hands around her midsection.

Nat grinned playfully at her as she hung up the phone.

John and Alec were sitting on either end of a bed, their phones held right up to their faces as they played some game together. Alec randomly kicked out at John every so often, trying to make him lose and John cursed Alec out over it, calling him every name under the sun.

Nat sat back down beside Ravyn.

"You have a tangle in your hair," Nat pointed out, and Ravyn's hand flew to the side of her head. Her fingers pulled through the strands, and got caught in the knot. As she tried to tease it out, Brook told her she had another one on the other side of her head.

"And that's why I don't have long hair," Brook said smugly

from where she was curled up at the head of the bed.

Ravyn muttered curses under her breath as she tried to tease them both out. Single strands pulled painfully on her scalp, nearly ripping the skin off her hair.

"Let me help," Nat said, and reached over. Ravyn took her hands away, and let Nat's fingers replace her own. They moved carefully, plucking strands away from the knots.

"Tell me if I hurt you," Nat mumbled, pulling her fingers through Ravyn's blonde hair as the first tangle came free.

"You're not, don't worry," Ravyn said. Nat shuffled around the back of Ravyn and to the other side of her. She worked her magic again with the second tangle, and Ravyn's hair fell loose again.

"Can I braid your hair?" Nat asked before Ravyn could even say thank you.

"Oh, uh, sure."

"This should stop it getting tangled," Nat said as her fingers worked away, separating her hair into three sections and then braided them together. Ravyn let her eyes close as Nat worked, and her shoulders started to relax. It felt strange, though. To be here, acting like nothing had happened. Like they weren't in a car accident, and almost killed. It was as if everyone had forgotten what had happened just hours ago. But Ravyn's mind refused to let her forget about it that easily.

"There," Nat said as she finished, and let the braid fall over Ravyn's right shoulder. Ravyn glanced over her shoulder at Nat, a smile creeping onto her face.

"Your hair is pretty like that," Nat told her, and Ravyn blushed.

"Thank you."

Before anything else could be said, there was a knock at the door. The smell of hot food wafted into the room, and all heads turned towards the door, smiles growing and mouths ready to feast.

Even though she was hungry, Ravyn didn't feel like eating. She picked at the chips, selecting the smallest ones to eat. The milkshake was good, though. Nat was right—the sugar was doing her good. Her legs no longer felt like they would collapse if she stood on them.

They finished their food and lounged on the beds, allowing the salt-packed meal to digest before they went to sleep. Conversation drifted from one topic to the next, but eventually everyone fell silent.

"I'll take the first watch until midnight," Nat offered, standing up from the bed. "Then there's enough room to share beds, anyway."

Ravyn glanced at Brook, who motioned for her to join her on the other bed. Ravyn moved next to her, and in the short moment where she stood up, her legs almost gave way.

"Sleep here with me tonight," Brook said with a smile. Ravyn nodded, and gave a small smile back. This bed was a lot softer than the other, worn away from all the people who had slept here before her. She continued to slowly sink deeper into the mattress.

"I'll take watch after Nat," Alec offered.

"It's almost midnight. We should all probably get to bed now anyway. It's been a fucking *long-ass* day," John told them, moving towards the other bed.

Brook crawled under the blankets and pulled them tightly around her, and Ravyn followed shortly after. They had nothing to change into—their bags of clothes were buried beneath a car wreck. John was already in bed, facing the other wall. Nat replaced Alec in the chair and switched the light off, whispering goodnight to the room.

Ravyn lay down in the dark, staring at the black ceiling. Part of her longed to stay up with Nat, just chatting to wear off whatever energy was lingering, but her eyes would not stay open any longer. Brook shifted and pulled on the blankets. Ravyn let her take the extra few inches, laying completely still to try to fall asleep quicker.

But her mind was alight and wide awake. It did not want to sleep. Millions of thoughts were spilling over the mental barrier she had tried to set up, starting to gather in a swirling, black pool in her head. She sighed quietly. Her body was exhausted, but her mind wasn't ready to sleep just yet.

This was going to be a long night.

*****

Brook woke her in the morning, gently shaking her shoulder and pulling her from her sleep. Ravyn cracked her eyes open and looked up at the smiling face peering down at her. The bright lights behind the face blinded her, and she scrunched her eyes up, but the impression of Brook's face still floated behind her eyelids. She groaned softly.

"Good morning, sleepy head! Come on, get up!" Brook giggled and sprang off the bed.

"Brook, let her sleep," Alec said from somewhere to her right. Ravyn stretched her arms over her head, and her muscles thanked her for it. She yawned, and her jaw cracked. She opened her eyes slowly, blinking a few times to wake them up. They wanted to shut again and return to the land of empty dreams, but she forced them to stay awake.

She sat up, letting her eyes adjust to the light. Everyone else was already awake. Nat was sitting on the other bed, and she caught her gaze. She smiled her good morning, and Ravyn smiled back. She sat up and pulled the duvet up around her stomach.

"I think we should order breakfast to be delivered," John piped up from the chair where he was lounging, one leg over the arm and hands interlaced behind his head. Ravyn's stomach grumbled at the mention of breakfast. Now she was really starting to feel the hunger, and she regretted not ordering a bigger meal last night.

"That's the only thing we can do, really," Brook said. There was no kitchen, or even a microwave or kettle in the room. The only other option would be to eat out, but after last night, it was safe to assume that nobody really wanted that. Leaving the safety of these four walls was the last thing on their minds.

"I want to take Ravyn out to get some proper clothes first though," Brook continued. That silenced the room. Ravyn raised her eyebrows and slowly turned her head to look at Brook. After the events of yesterday, leaving this place was the last thing on her agenda. There was still no way to be sure that they were safe in here, let alone out there in the open, with other people around them and millions of places where the Shades could hide.

"Brook—" Nat said, but Brook held up her hands.

"She only has one thing to wear. She doesn't even have a jacket, or anything! Before we go, she needs to get a change of clothes," Brook insisted.

Nat pursed her lips and paused for a moment. Everyone looked at her, waiting.

"I don't think it's a good idea. There'll be stuff for her at the house. She can borrow some of my clothes again."

"We won't be long. There should be a shop around here somewhere. We'll be back before breakfast arrives," Brook promised, sitting on the bed next to Ravyn. Ravyn shivered as a wave of cold air took hold of her, just for a second as it wrapped her in an embrace, then faded away.

Nat turned to face Ravyn, her eyes a hard block of ice. "Ravyn, what do you want to do?" she asked. There was a nervous undertone in her voice, lining the edges of her words with concern. Ravyn bit her lip and shrugged. It was not the most logical thing to do, but…she did need a change of clothes. These were Nat's clothes, after all. And…maybe getting out of the room would help her clear her head? Getting out of the clothes, imprinted with Nat's scent and carrying the ghost of her frame, might help too.

"If we're back before breakfast, I suppose we can go," she muttered, glancing at Nat again. Her lips were tight, and her brows drew closer together. Ravyn's chest deflated.

"Alec, will you go with them?" Nat asked, throwing her eyes in his direction for just a split second before returning them to rest on Ravyn.

"Yeah, of course."

"Be quick then. Take some cash." Nat took a crisp fifty-euro note and twenty note from her pocket, handing them to Ravyn. Ravyn looked at the money for a moment, before she reached over to take it. Their fingers grazed each other as Ravyn took the cash from her, and goosebumps rippled up her arms. Ravyn folded the money and tucked it away. Brook stood and took Ravyn's hand, pulling her to her feet.

"Wait…" Ravyn paused. "Nobody else has a change of clothes; we can't just go for me," she said hesitantly. Everyone else's clothes were also in the boot of the crashed car, miles from here.

"We all have our own stuff back at the house. We dropped them off on our way to get you. You need your own clothes, girl," Brook said with a smile, one eyebrow raised. Ravyn nodded slowly, but Brook's words did not calm her nerves. The Shades could be waiting for them to step out before they attacked. They could be hiding right outside the door, ready to pounce as soon as the lock was undone. Waiting for the group to split up, when it was easier to attack—

She folded her arms to stop herself from fidgeting, but her fingers still drummed against her forearms.

It's fine, she told herself. *Get out and clear your head. It will do you good.*

"Okay." She shrugged, and Brook smiled again, showing her teeth this time.

Alec unlocked the door, and they left. Two sets of eyes watched them leave, and the feel of their gaze remained on her back all the way out of the building.

*****

There was a clothes shop just a five-minute walk from the hotel they were staying in. It was small and quaint, so hopefully they would be out of there quickly. Ravyn had been checking over her shoulder the whole way there, but as far as she could tell, they were alone. Well, not completely alone. There were lots of people out already—joggers, early morning shoppers, people on the way to work. She hadn't seen any Shades.

But that still didn't ease her anxiety.

They entered the shop, which looked like it had just opened for the day. There were only two other shoppers in here with them. The whole front wall was windowed, showing mannequins wearing the latest autumnal fashion—fur coats, leather jackets, fluffy boots, tartan patterns. One of them even wore sunglasses and a fedora. An indie band played softly over the speakers mounted to the ceiling.

"Go pick out some things. Make sure it's practical though, if you get what I mean." Brook gave her a wink, and Ravyn nodded. *Practical.* A chill ran through her, sending goosebumps rippling across her skin. Practical... Ravyn stared at the masses of clothes in front of her, not sure where to start. She made a small list in her head—a top, jacket, and trousers or leggings. Boots, maybe, if their funds allowed. Nat's funds, she reminded herself, cringing internally.

She broke off from Alec and Brook and went to look around the shirts and t-shirts. The ripped jeans and off-the-shoulder shirts she liked were not "practical," so she would have to settle for something more "normal." She took a long-sleeved maroon top off the rail and held it out in front of her. It looked nice, and not too restricting either. This would do, she decided, folding it over her arm. Now, a jacket. She looked around and spotted some jackets on the far wall. She walked over to them, Brook and Alec trailing behind her, chatting. Their words floated past her ears, unheard. There were some beautiful denim and leather jackets that she eyed lovingly, but the word "practical" flashed in her mind when she looked at them, so she opted for a light, black fabric jacket that allowed for plenty of unrestricted movement.

You're being overly paranoid, she told herself, but the rational side of her brain beat that thought back with a club. *Better to be safe than sorry!* Her brain beat the thought to a bloody pulp, and then allowed her to continue shopping.

She draped the jacket over her arm too

and went to the trousers section. Again, the word "practical" flashed in front of her when she looked at the ripped jeans, so she tore her eyes away and found a pair of black leggings. Leggings are great for most things, so she took them too and turned back to Brook and Alec.

Brook chuckled.

"You're like Nat when it comes to clothes," she said, taking them from her.

"What do you mean?" Ravyn asked.

Alec smirked. "I'm sure you've noticed," he said, motioning to all of her, "that Nat likes to wear a lot of black too."

Ravyn lifted the corners of her mouth and nodded slowly. "It's a cool colour." She shrugged. There was a little heat in her cheeks, embers burning under her skin, ready to reignite into flames.

"Well—"

"Alec, just because you like to wear neon and walk around like a traffic light does not mean everybody else does," Brook joked, poking him in the ribs. He swatted her hand away.

"I like black too," he protested, smiling. "But sometimes the world is a little dull when everybody wears black and grey." He paused and looked at Ravyn. "No offence." She just grinned and rolled her eyes at him.

"Ravyn looks good in black." Brook ruffled Ravyn's hair.

"I know she does."

"Then stop complaining."

Alec sighed loudly and shook his head at the sky.

"You can't win with her," he muttered, and they all laughed. Brook gave Alec a friendly hug, and he put his arm around her briefly before pushing her off playfully.

"You're forgetting some things." Brook smiled at her. Ravyn frowned. "Shoes? They are filthy." Brook looked down at her feet.

Ravyn blushed and turned around. She made her way over to the shoes. There was a sale on boots, and they were nice ones too. She picked up a black pair that rose halfway up her calves and had a decent inch of platform on them. These were definitely more her style, and she admired them for a moment before turning around to face Brook and Alec.

"At least you'll be able to run in them when the Shades come," Brook said, chuckling.

The muscles in Ravyn's back clenched as a chill ran through them. She chuckled awkwardly, and Alec just smiled, but his eyes narrowed slightly as his eyebrows dipped.

Brook took the money and paid for all the clothes. She left the checkout and skipped towards them, holding a large, brown paper bag.

"Ready?" Brook asked with a smile, handing the bag to Ravyn.

"Are you sure you all don't need something?" Ravyn asked as they were walking out the door.

"I told you, we have things at the house. We should be heading there as soon as Jay comes to get us." Brook gave Ravyn a pat on the shoulder. Alec just nodded.

As they headed back towards the hotel, the streets were buzzing with morning life. The sun was steadily climbing the clouds, making its way towards the top of the sky. But any heat it gave off was eradicated by the cool breeze that whispered silently through the streets, wrapping around the buildings and the people as they walked to wherever they were going. It gave Ravyn a big hug, and she shivered.

A murder of crows squawked overhead, soaring low, looking for scraps.

There was a small corner shop just beside the motel, and

the owner brought the newspaper stand outside as they were walking past. Ravyn glanced over as the aging man walked back into the shop, just wanting to see the headlines. She hadn't heard much of the outside world in…forever, it seemed like. There was only one story on the front page, written all in capital letters, bold and demanding her attention—MURDER INQUIRY AFTER WOMAN FOUND DEAD IN HER HOME. Her stomach lurched.

"Ravyn, come on!" Brook called out to her. They were at the entrance to the hotel, waiting. Alec tilted his head as he looked at her. Ravyn glanced up, her heart racing. Something in that headline demanded her attention. She wanted to pick the paper up, to read more, but she couldn't bring herself to do it. She took a deep breath and went back into the motel with Brook and Alec, her palms sweating.

The mental block that was covering the day she ran away with Brook was starting to erode, but she wasn't sure if she was happy about it. She tried to bring herself back to that night, but her mind wouldn't let her. *In time,* it told her, and she exhaled sharply.

The secrets remained hidden. For now.

Alec knocked on the door, and Nat let them in.

"Breakfast was here before you," she said light-heartedly. Brook scoffed and entered first. Alec followed, and finally Ravyn walked through with her bag, trying not to look at Nat.

"Get anything nice?" Nat asked as Ravyn walked past her.

Ravyn shrugged. "Um, yeah… Thank you for the cash. Brook has your change." She blushed.

"Why don't you get changed before breakfast?" Nat suggested. Ravyn nodded and hurried into the bathroom. She locked the door.

"Fucking hell." She put her head in her hands, elbows

resting on the grimy sink. There was a painful pressure in her skull, wanting to cave it in on her brain. She turned on the tap and splashed cold water on her face. The pressure was travelling down her neck, dead hands around her throat. She took Nat's clothes off and stood there, exposed. There was a dirty mirror above the sink, and she looked into it. Her blonde hair was greasy, her skin was oily, and her eyebrows needed plucking. She stared into her own eyes for a moment. Her reflection looked scared. Those green eyes looked tired, exhausted. Those usually brown flecks in her irises looked like black soot after a fire.

She closed her eyes, gritted her teeth, and pulled on her own clothes. Only then did she look back in the mirror. Yes, she felt a little better now. There was some colour in her lips and her cheeks, making her look less dead. She fixed her hair, parting it at the side and letting stray strands fall around her face. In this light, the top looked more blood red than maroon, but she still liked it. It suited the black jacket well. She half zipped up the jacket, then put Nat's clothes in the bag and left the bathroom, her stomach growling.

The four of them were sitting on the beds, facing each other. They had pulled the one nightstand out in between the beds, and there was a stack of pancakes piled high on a paper plate, and steam was still rising from them. It smelled divine. Her taste buds tingled, lusting for a bite.

Ravyn sat down beside Brook, opposite Nat. She handed the bag over.

"These are yours," she said, and Nat took it with a smile.

"Thanks."

"Thanks for lending them to me," Ravyn said. Nat shrugged. John handed her a paper plate.

"Tuck in." John grinned, his eyes never leaving the food.

He took the top pancake and lifted it close to his face, inhaling deeply and sighing with delight. Ravyn eyed the pancakes but waited for everyone to take one before she did. "Jay said he'll be here around ten," John added.

"That's plenty of time," Brook commented, her mouth half stuffed.

"For what?" John smirked. There was a brief silence.

"To eat."

CHAPTER 9

Jay arrived early. It was a quarter past nine when there was a knock at the door, knuckles rapping gently against the cheap plastic. Everyone had frozen, and heads snapped around to face the door. Muscles had tensed, and wide-eyed glances were thrown at each other. Ravyn's heart had stopped, her blood cold.

John had opened it, and when they saw it was Jay and Therese, there was a sigh of relief, and the tension in the room released. Her heart started pumping again.

Jay was tall, with square shoulders and a strong build. His brown eyes were kind, and he had smile lines developing at the corners of his eyes. His dark brown hair was pulled back into a bun that sat at the base of his neck. His beard was trimmed neatly, falling halfway down his neck. He wore an aging flat cap, like one a farmer would wear, and a baggy, tan sweater. He had an aura of kindness and wisdom around him, a wise father figure who was carrying years of experience on his shoulders.

Therese was a smaller woman, the top of her head barely reaching Jay's shoulder. There was a single streak of grey in her hair, which she kept parted from the rest of her black hair so it fell in front of her shoulder, while the rest was loosely tied back into a ponytail. She had large, round glasses, through which peered hazel eyes.

"So you must be Ravyn," Jay said, holding out his hand. Ravyn shook it and nodded. He had a firm grip.

"I'm Jay, and this is Therese. We hear you've been having some trouble." He smirked and looked around at all the others.

"That's one way to put it," Alec mused. Jay and Therese gave a brief chuckle.

"Well, help has arrived," Therese said. Her voice was smooth as silk, and just as gentle too. They all giggled. Nat stood and let Jay sit down in her place, opposite Ravyn.

"How are you holding up?" he asked, his voice low but pleasant. His eyes took in her face, landing with his gaze locked on hers. She hesitated and shrugged.

"I'm fine," she told him, but really, she wasn't sure how she was. That newspaper had thrown a brick at her, leaving a hole somewhere in her mind, just a small one, but everything behind the wall it had gone through was messy and jumbled, tangled wires that intertwined and twisted into knots, and she wasn't ready to sort through it yet. It was just a peephole into an unknown world, where night ruled and daylight never came.

"Not feeling too overwhelmed with everything?" he asked, tilting his head to the left. She shook her head, and he smiled.

"Good. Once we get you all to the house, you can settle down for a while before we take you home with us. Well, it's not too late to drop out now, and we can set you up with a place somewhere, but…being at Dunfeagh is safer, in my opinion," he told her.

She frowned. "Dunfeagh?" She had never heard of it.

He smiled again. "Where we all live, out of the way of the Shades. We've been there for almost twenty years with no problems, so it must be decent," he replied with another smirk. Ravyn smiled and just nodded. A string twanged in her heart.

A home would be nice, all right.

Somewhere stable, solid and concrete.

She didn't have one with Aunt Stephanie anymore. Not after running away from home with a stranger and a promise of knowledge about a world she did not know of.

Her heart lurched, torn between two sides. There was still rope attached to that home, even though it was frayed and wearing thin. There was still rope attached to *her*, despite the scowls and bruises that came with her. But the other side— the side full of magic and monsters—was so much more appealing. Yet her heart could not let go of all those years of her life.

"But first we need time to gather ourselves, before the Shades come back," Therese said, calmly jumping into the conversation. They all nodded.

"Will they come back?" Ravyn asked slowly.

Jay gave her an understanding smile. "They always come back."

"Why not just…get rid of them?"

The question was met with a moment of silence, and she wanted to shrink down small enough to vanish.

"We are not here to start a war, no matter how desperate they are to start one with us. The Ethereal are not fighters. The Shades… They've been bred to destroy. They don't even know why they hate us anymore, just that they need to kill us."

Jay shrugged.

"Nathan has them all brainwashed," Alec tutted. Ravyn had almost forgotten he was there, sitting quietly beside Jay with his legs crossed and one foot bouncing in the air.

"Nathan?"

Jay sighed and was about to speak, but Alec got there first.

"Their leader, dictator—whatever you want to call him. He's a prick."

"Alec." Jay put his hand on Alec's shoulder. Alec quieted down. "Nathan…just sees the world differently to us. He sees us as competition, even though we don't want his power and control. He wants the rest of the world to know about us, and he won't listen to why that's a bad idea."

Nathan—a new character in this story she was now a part of.

She sighed. Her brain was reaching full capacity now; there wasn't much more information that could be thrown at her without it digesting some of the things it already held first. But her brain seemed to be processing things much more slowly, already overworked and exhausted.

"But enough of that. How is everyone else?" Jay looked around. Nat shrugged, and Ravyn gulped. Nat's hair bounced on her shoulders when she did that. Ravyn tore her eyes away, butterflies in her stomach.

"Good, good," John said. He was leaning against the wall, arms folded. Therese was sitting in the chair beside him, and she smiled when Ravyn's eyes crossed over her.

"Grand," Alec muttered. Ravyn noticed a silence from Brook and glanced at her. She was standing, her spine completely rigid and her shoulders drawn tight. Her narrowed eyes were on Jay, never moving from his figure. Ravyn frowned at her, then looked away.

"What's the plan now, then?" Alec asked.

"We'll be taking you to the safe house. We'll meet up with some others there, make sure there's no Shades lurking about, and then we can all go back home to Dunfeagh. I'm sure by now you all know it is of utmost importance that once we get to the safe house, we go off the grid. There is no contact with the outside world. The Shades cannot follow us home." His tone turned cold and stern. They all nodded, including Ravyn.

"When are we leaving?" Brook asked. It was the first time she had spoken since Jay had gotten here. Her tone was cautious, words playing carefully on her tongue.

A cold chill ran down Ravyn's spine.

"Whenever you are all ready," he replied, shrugging. Out of the corner of her eye, Ravyn noticed Brook draw back from him.

"I'm ready. I would like to get the fuck out of here," Nat piped up. She was standing, facing the beds, arms crossed over her chest and weight shifted onto one leg. Her hair fell in ripples over her shoulders, casting dark shadows across her face.

"Let's go, then." Jay stood. "Therese and I will bring the jeeps around. Grab anything you have with you, and be ready to go. We'll be back shortly."

He gave Ravyn a smile, then left, Therese following behind. The door closed with a click, and the room fell silent—a brewing storm waiting for the first rumble of thunder, a single moment of calm and unease. She had a strange feeling in her stomach.

"We don't have anything to grab," John mumbled, sinking into the chair. He leaned his head back against the wall and closed his eyes.

"I need to piss anyway," Nat said, disappearing into the

bathroom.

Brook started pacing around the room, her nervous fingers pinching at her clothes. Ravyn's eyes followed her for a moment. A shadow crossed Brook's face as she frowned deeply, casting her eyes in darkness.

Ravyn's leg started to tremble, bouncing lightly against the ground.

The feeling in her stomach was spreading.

"All right, antsy pantsy?" Alec asked, moving over to sit beside Ravyn on the bed. Brook just pulled a face at him as she continued to pace. Her narrowed eyes were staring straight down at the ground, watching her feet move across the carpet.

"We're all on edge," Alec muttered to Ravyn. She focused her attention on Alec instead. Brook was making her nervous.

"Yeah. I know."

"You sure you're okay? You were kinda thrown into the deep end," he said. She thought for a moment, then shrugged, even forcing a small smile.

"I don't even know," she replied, giving a half-hearted chuckle. Alec smirked, and slowly nodded.

"I don't blame you. None of this has gone how we planned it. Hopefully now that Jay's here, it will all start to go smoothly," he said, shrugging. "Hopefully."

"Hopefully," she repeated.

Brook's pacing filled the room with a muffled pattering as her feet walked across the dirty carpet. Ravyn watched her feet move anxiously, her hands twitching by her sides. The repetitive noise was starting to drill into her head, making her heart rate increase.

Alec put his arm over her shoulder and gave it a squeeze. The hug startled her, just for a moment, but then she leaned against him and let her head rest against his shoulders. All the anxiety was soothed away as her body relaxed against his.

She had needed that.

The bathroom door opened, and Nat walked out. Alec took his arm away.

"Thanks, Alec," Ravyn whispered to him, and her face started to tingle as tiny fires were lit beneath her skin. He just shrugged and shifted away from her, giving her space.

"Are they here yet?" Nat asked. Alec shook his head, and Ravyn avoided her irritated gaze.

Nat rolled her eyes. "Where the fuck did they park, fucking Belfast?"

"Chill out, Nat, they'll be here soon," Brook mumbled.

"I just want to be out of here as soon as possible. I don't like this…" She trailed off and started pacing. The carpet muffled her footsteps, like they had done with Brook's, but Nat's were heavier, fuller-sounding thuds compared to Brook's light steps. Ravyn watched her as she had done with Brook, but the anxiety and frustration that radiated from Nat was far more intense, bordering on anger.

Ravyn turned her head so she could only see Nat in her peripheral vision, her aura too intense to look directly at. She tried instead to focus on Alec beside her, feeling the warmth radiating from him on the left side of her body.

"It'll be fine. Give them another minute, and if they're not back, we can just go see where they are," Alec said, calmly crossing one leg over his knee.

Ravyn looked down at her hands, flexing her fingers. Her stomach was flipping and tying itself into knots, making her feel sick. The two minutes they had been left on their own felt like an hour. Seconds ticked by painfully slowly, prolonging their torture, enjoying their suffering. Maybe Nat was right, maybe they had been gone too long… *Stop it, Ravyn,* she told herself when her heart surged and lost a beat. She rubbed her hand across her chest. The beat of her heart was far too fast to be a healthy dose of anxiety.

No, it was panicking.

And it was only getting faster.

The door burst off its hinges with a loud boom. Ravyn's head shot up, and her neck cracked. A wave of shadows rolled into the room, falling over itself as tendrils snaked across the floor and along the walls, searching for them, hungry to spill blood.

John shouted and tried to stand, the ground rumbling beneath him as the earth shifted and started rising beneath the floor, making the carpet bulge, but Shades reached out of the wall and grabbed him, pulling him in. He thrashed and struggled to break free before he was swallowed whole by the darkness.

Ravyn was frozen to the spot, watching helplessly as her mind shut down, paralysed by the scene before her. A million images flashed in her mind, images from the past and a projected future of her gravestone, if she was lucky to even get one. Her eyes were wide, staring, her body unmoving.

Nat turned and tried to run towards Ravyn as clumps of water gathered around her fists, but the wall swallowed her. She tried to lash out but was dragged by her hair into the shadows, her screams muffled.

Brook stood still, staring at the approaching sea of death. Shadow creeped over her, and Ravyn could only watch as it consumed her. Brook looked over her shoulder before the shadow slithered across her face, and Ravyn caught the dead look in her eyes before she became part of the growing wave.

Alec grabbed Ravyn and launched them backwards off the bed. Her brain finally rebooted itself, and her body started moving again. Pain exploded in her shoulder as they landed, the crusty carpet hardly breaking their fall.

She grabbed Alec's hoodie, her wide eyes staring helplessly at him.

"Alec—"

A hungry, black snake clamped its jaws around her ankle, and she kicked it off with her other foot. But it was starving, and a simple kick would not stop its search for food.

Alec reached into his pocket and pulled out a box of matches.

Another hungry snake joined the first and looked greedily at them both huddled against the wall. The massive tumbling wave that the snakes had come from was approaching fast, filling the whole room. It hissed and snarled and snapped as it searched for the two remaining survivors.

Alec struck the match, and the flame sparked instantly, its glowing heat bouncing off Ravyn's skin.

He flung it towards the gathering tendrils of shadow, and flames whooshed from the small matchstick. Screams and alarms filled the air, so loud her ears started to ring.

The flames only grew, their orange and red tongues licking the darkness and causing it to shrink away. It screeched, and individual Shades jumped out of the wall, pressing themselves against it and trying to bat away the eager flames.

Alec grabbed Ravyn and pulled her to her feet.

The fire alarm was blaring, screaming at them to leave. The heat was building, singeing the small hairs all over her skin. But Alec started pulling her towards the fire, right into the centre of it. She could only close her eyes and follow him blindly into the heat.

It roared around her, louder than anything she had heard before, and the heat was almost unbearable. But it did not touch her; it was not interested in burning her exposed skin or melting away her new clothes. She risked opening her eyes, and the brightness blinded her. But just as quickly as they had entered the flames, they came to the other side where an open door was waiting for them.

The water sprinklers finally came on and beat back the flames. It rained down on them, saturating them in an instant. Alec pulled her through the door, and she stumbled into the hallway, away from the dying fire and screaming wall of shadow.

A Shade was waiting for them and greeted Alec with a whip of shadow that slashed open his face. Blood splattered onto the floor and wall. Ravyn gasped and tried to pull him back, but he was grabbed by the ankles and flung to the floor. His head cracked as it hit the floor, and she cringed.

He lay unmoving at her feet.

Ravyn stared at the Shade, her eyes unblinking, her heart about to burst through her chest. Her brain was screaming at her to move, but her limbs were heavy and stayed locked into place.

The shadow casing of the Shade melted away, leaving a man in a suit standing there, staring at her with eyes more intense than Nat's. He held out his hand to her, as if he expected her to come willingly.

But her arm did not extend towards him.

All she could think about was Alec's heavy body at her feet, still unmoving, not even a gentle rise and fall of his shoulders. Her lips were trembling, her hands shaking at her sides, the pulse of her heart sending shock waves through her fingers.

The man's fingers beckoned her forwards.

It was so strange how calm he was. Did he know she had no way to escape, no tricks up her sleeve like the others? Did he know she could not fall back on her abilities because she had not been taught how to use them?

She walked towards him, and he smiled.

She had to step over Alec to do so, and it sent a bolt of red-hot fire through her, giving her enough energy to tighten her lips and hold his stare.

All the things she wanted to do to this man came to the front of her mind when he smirked like that. How she wished she could see his body lying in a field while crows pecked at his corpse, and she just watched on with that same stupid smirk that played on his face right now.

The black streak that flew over her head startled her, and she ducked away, her heart jumping multiple beats. Her thoughts turned back to survival.

But the thing wasn't a shadow or a Shade; it was a crow, which launched itself at the man in the suit, screaming and cawing as its wings flapped furiously. The man batted it away, but the bird was vicious, its talons out and mouth wide open.

While she stared in disbelief at the scene in front of her, another Shade grabbed her from behind.

She tried to scream, but there was a hand over her face, crushing her cheeks and jaw. Her arms were grabbed, legs grabbed, hands everywhere, pulling at her, tearing at her. There was a roaring in her ears as the shadows enveloped her, welcoming her to the darkness. It was cold here, extremely cold, and things were ripping at her hair. She tried to pull her own hands to her face, but the Shades' hands holding her were stronger. They had her now, and there was nothing else she could do.

CHAPTER 10

When she woke, she was lying face-up on a cold, uneven floor. Jagged edges of rock poked into her back. There was a fiery pain across her shoulders, and the back of her head thumped like a hammer pounding on metal. She twitched her fingers, scraping her nails along the ground. Dirt and dust collected beneath them, and tiny fragments of stone pressed into her skin. She blinked a few times and squinted her eyes. It was quite dim in here, wherever she was. The light that hung above her was close to dying. It buzzed like a fly and gave the occasional flicker as if it was sucking in its laboured, dying breaths. She closed her eyes again and grimaced as the back of her head started to pound.

"Ravyn?"

It was Nat.

She opened her eyes.

Nat was looking down at her, her face covered in shadow. She had a cut running diagonally across both her lips, and a bruise was blossoming on her cheek. The bruise from the car crash had turned an angry purple. Her hair hung down towards Ravyn like ivy. Ravyn slowly sat up, using her elbows to support her. She grunted. The muscles in her shoulders were knotted tightly and ached when she moved.

"Are you okay?" Ravyn asked, her eyes on the bruise that covered Nat's right cheekbone. It was brown and yellow with some veins of purple starting to show through in the very centre.

Nat gave a small smile and nodded. She put a hand on Ravyn's shoulder and gave it a squeeze. "Are you?"

Ravyn nodded, the nerves in her shoulder tingling. The back of her head was throbbing and pounding her brain, and her shoulders were stiff, but she was sure that was the extent of the damage. Nat took her hand from her shoulder and ran her thumb over Ravyn's jawline. When she took it away, there was blood smeared across it, gathering in the tiny crevices of her fingerprint. Ravyn's fingers went to her jaw and ran over the cut. The edges were hardening as the blood dried and flaked. Her fingers came away red, but it wasn't much. It didn't hurt either, not as much as the throbbing in her head did.

"Where are we?" Ravyn asked, bringing her hand to the back of her skull. It was tender to touch, and she didn't let her fingers linger there longer than they needed to.

"We don't know." There was another voice, but this time a deeper, masculine one.

Ravyn sat up more and saw John leaning against the far wall. It was made of rough, unplastered bricks that were cracking and moulding. There was damp gathering in the corners just below the ceiling, and water trails snaked down the fractures in the bricks. John was resting his head against the wall and looking up at the ceiling. His legs were pulled up to his chest, and he cradled one arm with his other.

"Are you okay?" she asked. He shrugged and flexed his fingers.

"Just sprained, I think," he grunted. Ravyn looked around for the others, but there was nobody else. Her eyes flickered around the room, and she twisted to look behind her, but there was no Brook or Alec hiding in the darkened corners, no Jay or Therese nursing wounds. Her heart skipped a beat, and she swallowed a lump that suddenly formed in her throat.

Alec...

Shit.

No, surely he couldn't be...

"Where are the others?" she asked, panic lacing her voice even though she tried to conceal it. Her stomach tied itself into a tight knot while she waited for an answer.

Nat's face dropped with the question.

And it made Ravyn's heart stop.

"Alec...didn't make it... I don't know about Brook," John mumbled, his words barely reaching her ears. A deafening silence took over, holding them in a moment of sudden stillness. A stabbing pain shot through her heart, and a stake repeatedly stabbed her there, over and over again. She took a sharp breath and let it out slowly. It shook and jittered as it left her lips, the thing she didn't want to believe slowly settling in her mind.

No.

No, that can't be right.

Alec...

NO!

"Alec, he..." she trailed off. Words built in her throat then faded away again before they left her lips. What good would it do to tell them what had happened? He was... He wasn't here anymore.

A sharp pain hit her stomach and she grimaced. It hurt to breathe. Nat put her hand back on Ravyn's shoulder and gave it a squeeze. She didn't say anything. Ravyn looked away from them and instead stared at the wall of metal bars that caged them in like a prison, like animals. Beyond the bars was a room darker than the night. Her jaw clenched, and she tried to focus on the nothingness that lay before them, on that darkness that trapped them here. But his name, his voice, kept filling her head, and soon a single tear pooled in her eye. She tried to blink it away, but it fell before she was able to stop it.

Nat squeezed her shoulder again.

God, no!

Fuck.

"Jay and Therese?" Ravyn asked in a quivering voice.

"We don't know. We don't even know if the Shades got them or not," Nat told her quietly. Ravyn nodded, more tears coming to her eyes.

Alec…

God fucking damn it!

Ravyn gave herself a mental slap.

You will not lose it here.

Not now.

This is not the time.

One leg started to tremble.

Old memories wanted to surface, their meat-hook claws digging deep into her brain, but she screamed at them, and they released themselves from her mind. They fell back into the dark depths of her head that she never dared venture into, choosing to fight back the monsters that came from there instead of slaying them as they slept in their cave, instead of lighting up the depths with flames and exposing all the ugly secrets and whispers and demons that resided there.

Another tear fell quietly.

Her heart was fragile, starting to crack and splinter as it was crushed between cold hands. Her breath shook as she breathed in, her throat starting to swell.

Nat's hand moved to her other shoulder, and she gently pulled Ravyn closer to her chest, holding her in a half hug. Ravyn let her head rest against Nat's collarbone, and her eyelids drooped. But as they did, they pushed more tears to the surface, and they blurred her vision. Her throat continued to tighten as a sob started to rise from her lungs.

So many thoughts were rushing through her mind, a frenzy of desperate, bodiless voices demanding her attention. His name was in all of their voices, His name, and the Shades, and the fire and the crow and—

She wiped the tears from her eyes and pulled herself away from Nat.

"How are we going to get out?" She changed the subject completely, trying to block out his name. Even if everyone else was gone, if they were all... They still had to get out. They couldn't sit around and wait for someone to come rescue them because what if there was no-one? They couldn't just sit and rot in here.

Alec wouldn't want them to sit here and cry. She knew that much. If he was here, he would have cracked a joke and smiled that stupid playful smile of his, urging them to get a move on.

Emotions rushed at her, but she bit her lip hard enough to draw blood and suppressed them. Her eyes burned as more tears tried to push themselves to the surface, but she didn't allow them to.

You can cry when we get out of here, she told herself.
You will not lose it in here.
You will not.

"Ravyn, there is no getting out. We tried everything, and there is no way out," John snapped. Ravyn flinched back from his biting words.

A shadow crossed Nat's face. "John—"

"We tried, Nat! There is no fucking way out!" John smashed the side of his good fist against the wall hard enough to make dust fly and circle around him. Ravyn gritted her teeth.

"What about your—" she tried to ask, but John cut her off.

"We tried! We tried everything!" he shouted. Ravyn bit back her tears and turned her eyes away from his angry face. Nat's jaw was clenched.

John huffed.

A silence hung over them, a poison in the air, only broken by the low buzz of the light above their heads. They sat quietly in their tiny pool of light as the darkness slowly closed in on them, each lost to their own thoughts and jumbled emotions weighted with grief and confusion.

Ravyn swallowed a lump in her throat.

"We can't just sit around and wait," she whispered to Nat, barely breaking the silence. Nat nodded and folded her legs in front of her. She had tears in her eyes that glistened in the low light, softening her eyes to a deep grey. Ravyn wanted to hug her, or just to touch her arm, but she didn't allow herself to. Instead, she closed her eyes, trying to clear her head. Alec's name kept jumping at her, but she did her best to push it back, thinking about anything else but his body, which she had stepped over.

She had stepped over his body instead of helping him.

That realisation stabbed her, multiple times, right in the tender parts of her heart.

Nat was staring at her, and Ravyn lifted her eyes to stare

back. Nat parted her lips, then closed them again with a sigh through her nose, her unspoken words lost forever.

"You all look so sad."

Ravyn jumped, her eyes jerking away from Nat's. They all spun around at the sound of the voice. A man stood outside their cage, staring in at them with a crooked smile on his face. John was on his feet in an instant, and he tried to reach through the bars to grab the man, but a tendril of shadow snagged his wrist, then shoved him back into the cage.

"*Nathan*, you fucker, let us out!" John roared, lunging at the bars again. This time the shadow hit him full force in the chest, knocking him against the back wall. Ravyn was sure she heard John's ribs crack with the force of the impact. John let out a cry and grabbed at his injured arm.

So, this was Nathan.

She recognised him as the same man who'd killed Alec and asked Ravyn to join him in the darkness.

He was tall and slim, wearing a black suit and crisp, white shirt with no tie. He had his hands in his pockets, standing tall and smug. His jet-black hair was slicked back, not a strand out of place. His green eyes caught Ravyn staring.

"Oh, hello again. I'm glad we can meet properly now." He smiled. Ravyn watched him, unblinking. None of the Ethereal spoke.

"There's some bad news, I'm afraid. One of your friends, the boy, he didn't make it." He drew out the last few words, his smile getting bigger as they left his mouth.

"We know," Nat said. Her voice was firm with a hard, sharp edge. John had gone quiet, leaning against the back wall. He didn't look hurt, but his eyes were ablaze, burning through his pupils and into Nathan's head.

"Oh, fantastic—it's not too much of a shock then." He

paced slowly along the full length of the bars, keeping his eye on Ravyn. She matched his stare, trying not to flinch under the intense gaze. Her hands balled into fists, and little tremors ran up her fingers.

Alec's face popped into her mind and lit a fire in her stomach. She pressed her teeth tightly together.

He stopped and peered at her. "You're Carrie's daughter. Olivia, isn't it?" he asked.

At the mention of her mother, a knife went through her heart and blood spurted out her chest. She swallowed a lump in her throat. "Ravyn, actually."

"Ravyn." He pondered the name for a moment. "Very...unique." He seemed to taste the word in his mouth, running his tongue along the back of his teeth and then over his lips. He tilted his head.

"Quiet, just like she was too. The apple doesn't fall far, does it?" He started pacing again. His shoes tapped against the concrete ground. Ravyn remained silent, not letting her eyes leave his body for one second. Her heart was a hammer against her breastbone, beating so hard she thought it might break.

John stood up straighter against the wall. "What the hell do you want?" he growled. Nathan shook his head, tutting.

He opened his mouth, but John charged at him again. And again, the Shadows came between the bars and knocked him backwards. John stumbled and was almost knocked to the ground.

Nathan cleared his throat.

"As I was saying," he continued, glaring at John, "I need a bit of...help. But I'll get to that in a minute. Just sit and be quiet, please." He grinned, showing his teeth. He leaned towards them.

John remained silent.

"Thank you." Nathan ran his tongue between his shark teeth.

There was a brief silence, tension hanging over their heads like a guillotine, ready to kill them if they dared breathe.

"Do you like my new experiment? A little binding in your room, and you're reduced to mere mortals. It was quite simple, actually. I can't believe I didn't think of it sooner. Imagine what it would be like on a bigger scale," he said proudly, grinning. Nobody answered, and his smile faltered.

"I know you're impressed, secretly. Well, if you don't like that experiment, I wonder what you'll think of this one?"

Nathan motioned with his hand for something in the shadows to come forward. Footsteps followed, tapping louder and louder, and soon Brook emerged from the darkness, coming to the edge of the light that spilled from their cage. She stood beside Nathan, eyes half closed and dark circles under them. Black veins popped out around her chin and mouth.

Ravyn's eyes widened, and she struggled to suppress her gasp.

Brook, what have you done?

No, Brook…

John couldn't hold back his anger anymore.

"Brook, I'm going to fucking k—"

A fist of shadows slammed into him, pinning him to the wall this time. Ravyn watched and was in the middle of taking a breath when shadows also slammed into her and Nat, launching them backwards. It wrapped around their wrists and ankles, holding them against the cold brick wall. A strand wrapped around her midsection and pressed her firmly against the brick, preventing air from entering her lungs. Pins and needles were starting to form in her fingertips.

"You've been a great help, haven't you?" Nathan pat Brook's head. Brook simply stared blankly into space. She didn't even flinch. Ravyn stared at her with wide eyes. She wanted to shout at her, to wake her from her trance, but her mouth could not move.

"Yes, you have," Nathan answered for her. "But I'm done with your services. You don't know where Jay is, so I have no use for you anymore." He clicked his fingers and black sparks flew from them.

Brook's body started shaking.

She retched, and the black veins started to spread across her skin. A bulge formed in her throat, starting at the base and working its way up her neck. Brook choked on it, harsh gurgling noises coming from her throat. She was foaming at the mouth, spittle flying into the air and landing on the ground at her feet. Ravyn could only watch, horrified, as Brook tilted her head back, and black shadows started crawling from her open mouth. They formed a hand, which planted itself on her forehead, using it to leverage itself out of her.

Ravyn nearly got sick, catching it in her mouth before it left her body. She swallowed the acidic bile, and it burned as it made its slow way back down to her stomach.

Another hand rose out of Brook's mouth and grabbed onto her shoulder. A slim, shadowy body pushed itself out of Brook as she jerked violently, almost as if she was having a fit.

The thing was finally free and shot into the air, and Brook crumpled to the floor.

They were all stunned into silence.

Nathan smiled again.

"It's something new we're trying out. Good, isn't it?" He held his hand out to the mess of swirling, black shadow which was hovering in the air above Brook. It reached towards him, grabbed his hand, then disappeared up his sleeve. He straightened the fabric it had ruffled, then looked up at them suspended against the wall.

"So, who wants to tell me where Jay is?" His voice was laced with icicles, armed with sharp, pointed tips that would easily pierce skin.

Nobody spoke.

Ravyn couldn't take her eyes off Brook as she lay still on the floor. She was barely even breathing. Her chest rose only a few centimetres before falling again, the movement barely visible. Ravyn's head was spinning, struggling to process what had just happened. There was a hollowness in her chest and stomach, a void that had sucked everything into it. Her body was starting to tremble again.

Brook, oh no, Brook…

"I'll ask one more time, then. Where is Jay?" His sharp voice was getting angrier.

"We don't know," Nat muttered, defeated, her quiet words barely reaching him.

"Sure about that?" Nathan asked smugly, looking directly at Ravyn. Ravyn bit her tongue, keeping herself quiet. His eyes pierced like needles jabbing into her, trying to blind her, trying to pull her retinas out of her, but she stayed quiet. She didn't know where Jay was; none of them did. At least he was still alive, unlike—

Tears stung the back of her eyes, and she quickly forced the thought out of her head.

A Shade came forwards out of the shadows and materialised into a woman. She stepped forwards, put her hand around Nathan's waist, and whispered into his ear. She was also tall, with black hair that was curled perfectly. It looked greasy, like it was held there with a whole bottle of hairspray.

She wore a black dress with a slit up the outside of her leg, which climbed up past her pelvis. She had her septum pierced with a ring that was jewelled at the tip. Her brown skin glowed and shimmered in this light.

"I'll be back. Don't go anywhere," Nathan laughed. He put his arm around the woman's waist, and they walked into the darkness, out of sight.

A snake of shadows opened up the gate into their cell and dragged Brook's limp body through, then closed it with a loud, ringing clang. The shadows which pinned them to the wall released them, and they dropped to the floor. John grunted and clutched his arm.

They were alone again.

CHAPTER 11

Ravyn was the first to go to Brook, though she had stared at Brook's unmoving body for an eternity. They had *all* stared at her, unsure of what to do, what to say about their friend who had just stood on the side of the enemy. But Ravyn couldn't stare at her any longer. She knelt beside her and gently shook her shoulder. Brook didn't respond. She was breathing, but it was shallow and laboured. A thin film of sweat was covering her skin and soaking into her clothes. Her skin looked almost paper white.

"Leave her, Ravyn!" John snapped.

"She—"

"I said fucking leave her!" he shouted, his face turning red. Ravyn stared at him, her eyes wide.

Part of her wanted to. Part of her told her to listen to John and leave her be. She'd betrayed them, after all—

"John, she's hurt." Ravyn struggled to keep the quiver out of her voice, going against every instinct in her body to get the words out of her mouth. Brook had stood beside Nathan while Alec lay dead on the hotel floor.

John stood, towering above them. His jaw was clenched, his brow furrowed. Ravyn's eyes widened as he started towards her. She was about to get up, but Nat jumped between them and pushed him back.

"Don't," she warned.

John shoved her away, pointing at Brook. "She's a fucking traitor! She's the reason Alec is dead! She's the reason we're in here!" he roared, spittle flying through the space between them.

"I know, but you need to calm down—"

"Calm down? Don't tell me to calm down after what she's done!" He started forwards again, but Nat didn't move. They came nose to nose, John standing a good foot above Nat.

"John, sit *down*," Nat growled at him like a wolf, her hand on the centre of his chest. He swatted it away and gave her another shove. She nearly tripped on Brook's limp body.

"Stop!" Ravyn shouted, standing up to meet John. She narrowed her eyes at him. "This is not the time for—"

"Shut up, Ravyn! You don't know anything about what is going on right now. You don't get to decide anything." He turned his attack on her. She balled her fists up and squeezed her shoulders tight to her body.

"She is as much a part of this as you are, Jonathan." Nat drew herself up to full height, her voice a low growl. They were hawks, sharpened claws outstretched as they dived at each other, going for the neck. A flurry of feathers and blood.

"She is not like us, Natalie, and she never fucking will be. I am in charge here. I am going to get us out, and the first thing that I'm going to do is get rid of the *rat*." His eyes jabbed at Brook as he spoke, and he moved to take a step forwards, but Nat slapped him, hard.

His face snapped to one side, the deafening clap of skin on skin bouncing between the walls.

"Sit the fuck down, and stop acting like a dickhead," she snarled.

John stared at her for a few moments while his cheek turned a fierce red, and Ravyn was scared he was going to hit her back. She clenched her fists tighter. Her stomach flipped, and flipped again, making her feel sick. But he shrank away and slid his back down the wall until he sat, staring out at the darkness. Nat backed away from him, and she too sat with her back against the wall, her eyes cast downwards. Ravyn let out a shuddering breath. Nat's claws had torn his throat out, and the lifeless body fell to the earth with its wings reaching towards the heavens, feathers fluttering and falling gracefully alongside the carcass.

Ravyn sat next to Brook, staring down at her peaceful yet pained face.

No words came to her. She sat in absolute silence, trying to bring her mind out of solitary confinement and back into the real world.

We need to get out of here, she thought to herself eventually. *This is exactly what Nathan wants.*

The thoughts screamed at her. They needed to get out, and get out quickly. They couldn't sit around and wait for something to happen. Nat and John didn't seem like they wanted to talk about things like this right now, so it was up to her to haul their sorry arses out of this shithole and back to Jay.

She didn't even know where to start.

There was no magic, and God only knew if there were Shades listening just outside their cage, hiding in the shadows, waiting on that moment when one of them slipped up—

Yes, Shades were listening. They must be; Nathan wouldn't just leave them all unsupervised. Because if one of them started talking, let something slip, thinking he couldn't hear…

Slowly, a plan started to come to mind. The bare bones of one, a weak skeleton with no flesh or muscle to support it, but it was better than nothing. She needed Nathan to willingly let her go, which was going to be hard, but it was worth a shot. It was all she could think of. And if she died, then…

No, she wasn't going to die.

She was going to get them all out, alive.

She looked towards Nat, and their gazes met. She had been watching her with dark, curious eyes.

Ravyn slowly slid herself along the rough floor so she sat beside Nat, her back against the cold wall. It was damp, and she had to lean forwards slightly so it wouldn't seep through her clothes. Nat watched her, lips ever so slightly parted, offering a glimpse of her pearly teeth.

"Do you trust me?" Ravyn leaned over and whispered in Nat's ear. Nat didn't answer for a second, leaning away with a frown to look at Ravyn's full face.

"What?" she asked, her voice a low whisper.

"I need you to trust me," Ravyn whispered back, holding her gaze firmly. Confusion clouded Nat's eyes, but she nodded anyway.

"What are you doing?" Nat put one hand on Ravyn's thigh. The heat from her hand travelled through her leggings and burned her skin. Ravyn closed her eyes while she breathed in deeply, then pushed Nat's hand off her leg. She swallowed a lump filled with *what-ifs*, and it slid its way down to her stomach.

"I'm going to get us out. Just trust me. Take care of Brook," she said before standing up. Nat held her eyes, nodded again, and watched as Ravyn made her way up to the bars. Her heart was starting to pound, telling her this was a bad idea, the kind of bad idea had a coffin waiting for her at the other end.

She slowly inhaled through her nose.

Here goes nothing.

She grabbed the bars and pulled her body into them. The two metal poles pushed painfully against her breasts. They were cold, colder than anything she had ever felt before, and sent a chill all the way down her body. And something was moving beneath them, right at the centre of the metal, sliding up and down the length of the pole. Whatever Nathan had done to this room to prevent them from using their abilities had infected the cage, a hidden darkness moving beneath them. But she didn't let go. She pressed her face between the bars, and the coldness shot up into her brain. She closed her eyes and quietly whispered into the abyss:

"I know where Jay is."

She stood there for a moment, breathing softly, watching out into the deep shadow that covered whatever was in front of them. The single light in their cell was hardly able to penetrate it and only lit the floor just outside the bars. But beyond that, she was hoping that there was a Shade, or Nathan listening in, anyone at all.

Anyone to take the bait.

She waited, counting seconds in her head, asking herself if she should say it again, but the answer came to her quickly. Nathan appeared from the shadows, looking down at her. She took a step back from the metal, her heart lurching at the sight of him. A moment of weakness hit her knees and nearly sent her sprawling on the ground.

I hope you know what you're doing, Ravyn…

"Come with me," he said simply, and a trail of shadow

wrapped around the door and pulled it open. She looked at it, then looked back at John and Nat. John was staring at her, his eyes hard and angry, but the fire behind them had been doused. Nat's eyes flickered between her and Nathan, her emotions hidden.

Neither of them moved.

Nathan tapped his foot. "I don't have all day."

Ravyn had to force her legs to move, and she joined him on the other side of the bars. The gate clanged shut behind her, and she jumped.

Nathan held out his hand to her, and she stared at it for a moment before she took it hesitantly. His skin was warm and soft, a huge difference from the sub-zero ice she had been holding just moments ago. The chill from them remained in her bones, giving a strange sensation of fire and ice on her skin.

He squeezed her hand tight, then led her into the darkness.

She followed him blindly, her heart racing, trying not to trip and fall. She couldn't see anything, but he had no problem navigating their journey. He did not speak to her while they walked. The only sound was the tap of their shoes against the floor. It echoed around them, almost as loud as thunder.

She had no idea how long they walked for, shrouded in a heavy veil of black, but eventually, he stopped, and she knocked into him. She jumped away quickly, pulling her hand out of his. A door opened in front of her. Light spilled out and dazzled her, and she shied away from the glaring beam of light. She covered her eyes, squinting against the brightness. He put his hand between her shoulder blades and gave her a gentle push into the room. She tripped on the way in. Black dots swam around her vision, giving her a headache.

The door clicked shut.

"Have a seat." He gave her another gentle push forwards, towards a wooden table with a chair on either side.

The room was small, but here at least the walls were plastered and painted a pale cream colour. The floor was a marble tile, a few hues darker than the walls. There was a bookcase on one wall that was stuffed with thick, cracked volumes. An ivy plant was placed on top of it, and the leaves trailed down towards the floor. Beside the bookcase was a table that had a tree-like plant on it, one she had seen before but couldn't name. On the opposite side of the room, there were shelves lining the walls that had picture frames and more books. One shelf had a jug of water and some small glasses lined neatly beside it. It seemed too nice of a room for what Nathan planned to do in here.

Her heart was a steady beat of background music now

She pulled a chair out for herself and sat.

He sat opposite her.

Her heart beat a little harder.

Silence hung in the air, thick and stuffy.

"Would you like some water?" he offered. She nodded, and he stood again. He took a jug of water and a small glass cup from the shelf and set it in front of her. She waited for him to sit down before she poured herself a glass. She brought it to her lips with trembling fingers and took a sip. The beating of her heart in her throat made it hard to swallow.

"How are you feeling? That was some argument you all had, I must say." He leaned towards her. She hesitated, then shrugged. Her fingers were drumming against the glass, and her foot wanted to bounce and move, but she kept it rooted firmly to the tile.

She shrugged again. "It's…fine."

A smirk crossed his face. "It doesn't look fine. Having

doubts about your friends, are we?"

She thought carefully for a moment.

You need him to trust you, she reminded herself. *Otherwise, you die.*

"I don't trust John," she told him, surprising herself at how convincing the lie sounded.

"That's understandable. What a temper that boy has," Nathan tutted. "And Natalie too. Both of them can be so hostile sometimes." He leaned back in his seat and folded his arms across his chest. She watched him, consciously keeping her breathing under control.

His jawline was sharp, his cheekbones high and prominent. A crown would suit him, gold and jewelled. A commander of death, smiling at the beheadings, watching as crows picked at the bodies and wishing it was him that tore their flesh open.

"I don't know much about you, Oli—I mean, Ravyn." He smiled when he caught himself. "You seem a little too innocent to be here, facing all of this."

She bit her lip. "I don't know." She didn't know what else to say.

He smiled wider. "What do you even know about this world? Do you know why we're here, or why you've all gotten into this mess?" he asked, and she let his question linger while she thought.

What did she know? Not a whole lot, now that she thought about it. She definitely hadn't known that he could manipulate people—put shadow inside them and control their every move. Images tried to resurface, but she pushed them firmly away.

She gave a shrug. "Not much, really."

That seemed to satisfy him. He leaned towards her again, resting his elbows on the table and leaning on them.

"So they drag you into this world, with no choice, and don't even bother to explain anything to you?" He chuckled, shaking his head. She allowed her lips to lift into a slight smile.

"I know you're a Shade, and we're Ethereal," she told him. She was starting to relax now, her heartbeat starting to calm down, her mind starting to sharpen. On the inside, she was smiling as she reeled in the lure. She couldn't let him see through her, though, so she kept her shoulders hunched and body tight.

Nathan nodded. "That's correct. What else?" He tilted his head expectantly.

"We can do…things. You can manipulate shadows," she said slowly.

He nodded again, tilting his head to the other side. "Anything else? Anything other than the basics?"

She shook her head.

He sighed. "Of course not. I expected more from Jay," he tutted, shaking his head sadly. He looked back up at her. "Did he even tell you who you are?"

She paused. He hadn't, but she knew. The others had told her. Ravyn, the Illusionist, the Ethereal. Daughter of one of the most powerful Illusionists, who had been killed by a Shade while trying to build a new life for herself.

It could have been Nathan that had killed her. It could have been him that stained her floorboards red, that sent her to live with Aunt Stephanie, that ruined everything for her… The thought sent a chill down her body, and goosebumps rose along her skin.

If it was him…

She clenched her fists under the table, and her knuckles wanted to burst through the flesh that coated them. Her jaw clenched, and it took her a second to release it.

"I'm an Illusionist," she spoke softly, casting her eyes down to the table between them. Her eyes traced the lines and knots in the wood, until they led her up his body and back to his face. When she met his eyes once again, he smiled at her.

"An Illusionist." He tasted her words in his mouth, running his tongue along his teeth. "And what is that?"

"I can create illusions. Pretty self-explanatory, I thought." She gave him a smirk.

His smile widened to a grin, and he chuckled. "So she does have a sense of humour, thank the Lords. I thought I'd be bored to death talking to you. But that's not the point. Have you been able to create anything yet? Have you been taught?"

She took a breath before she answered. "No."

"Oh dear. So they drag you into this messy world and don't teach or tell you anything? Do they expect you to fend for yourself?"

Ravyn could tell he was trying to plant seeds of doubt in her mind. But even though she knew, those seeds were starting to bloom. Buds were poking out of the freshly sown soil. She gave herself a mental shake. *No,* she told herself, *you have a job to do. Don't let him stop you. Do it for Brook. Do it for Nat, if anything.*

She changed the subject. "Can I ask you something?"

He nodded. She took a moment, second-guessing herself then doubting her own doubts. But she had to know. What other chance would she get if she didn't seize this one?

"Why was my mother killed?"

Nathan pursed his lips, his eyes searching her blank face. It was taking everything she had to keep any emotion off it—to keep her eyes dry and keep her mouth in a straight line. Then he sighed and leaned back in his chair.

"She was a danger to us all, and she had to be…taken care of."

The words were daggers through Ravyn's heart, rat poison in a cake, a rope around her neck that snapped her vertebrae in two…but she kept her composure and pressed him again.

"She wasn't involved in this world anymore. She just wanted to have a normal life." Tears wanted to come to her eyes and spill down her cheeks, but she kept them pressed down. She just needed to keep him talking for a little longer. She needed more time. She needed his trust.

"I know, Ravyn, but unfortunately my *colleagues* didn't see it that way. They voted to…get rid of her. She was one of the most powerful Ethereal we had ever come across, and even if she was 'retired,' they wanted her gone to make sure she wouldn't do any more damage than she had already done."

She could sense the faked sorrow in his voice, and that just made it all the more painful. Her lip quivered. Her leg trembled. The tears forced their way past her barricades and filled her eyes. She wiped them away quickly while he watched, pitiful.

"What about me?" she asked.

And there it was: the dangerous question. What about her? What did he want? Would he kill her too?

Or let her go?

His shark smile returned.

"You are not a threat to us just yet. You hardly know what you're getting into. You do, however, have some valuable information that we need…" He leaned forwards, arms folded on the table.

She swallowed hard.

Oh God, she thought, panic starting to seep into her blood, infecting her whole body. She only had one plan, and it wasn't a good one by any means. There was a very high chance that it would backfire and she would die—they would all die—but she had to try. It was better than sitting in that damned cell waiting to be rescued.

"Um, yeah…" She bit her lip. "I lied."

His face dropped.

She continued quickly. "I lied because I wanted to talk to you. I hardly know what's going on, I'm scared, I don't know what to do… You're right, they haven't told me anything, and I don't want to be part of this anymore. I just… I need help." She took another deep, shaky breath, examining his face as she did so. He wasn't angry, just…listening carefully. "I don't know where he is, but I can find him. I can get him to come straight here to you, I swear. I just—I just—" She choked on her words, and a single tear slid down her cheek. She made sure he saw it before she wiped it with the back of her sleeve.

"It's okay, Ravyn. I understand," he said softly. She intertwined her fingers on her lap under the table. Tears burned behind her eyes.

"You do?" she whimpered convincingly.

"Of course. It's just what we've been discussing, isn't it? They throw you in the deep end and expect you to learn how to swim on your own. Well, isn't it lucky I'm here to give you a hand?" He smiled, and she gave a brief nod before wiping her eyes again. "And I can tell you're scared. There's no need to be afraid. If you can bring Jay to me, I will have no reason to hurt you, or the others. In fact, I think I can help you in more ways than that, but let's just start with this, eh?"

She knew it was all lies. He wouldn't help her. He would kill them all, starting with Jay and working his way back to her. But those seeds he had planted were growing long stalks and thick roots. This only added to their power in her mind. But her seeds, the ones she had sewn in him, were also blooming.

"Thank you," she whispered, her voice catching on a knot.

Nathan stood up. "Well, there's no time like the present, is there? I'll take you to the town myself, and you can call Jay. Then you'll bring him to me, won't you?" He walked over to her, his fingers dragging along the table.

She looked up at him looming over her, casting a shadow across her body. There was a faint smile on his lips, pushing his cheeks up ever so slightly. Dark shadows covered half his face and neck.

She nodded.

"Can I just ask you one thing first?" Her lip trembled as the words left her. He raised an eyebrow but nodded anyway. "Can I just see Nat? Please?"

She had to let Nat know what was going on. She had to make sure Nat didn't think she was betraying them. Then, she was on her own. She would save them. No matter what.

CHAPTER 12

Two Shades brought Nat into the room, holding her by the arms. They were encased in swirling shadow, a suit of armour, King Nathan's valiant knights. She came in struggling against them, trying to pull herself free, but their shadows had latched onto her arms and curled around her biceps, holding her firmly. It was a punch in the gut to see her like that. When she finally saw Ravyn, she stopped struggling and just stared at her with wide eyes. Ravyn took a deep breath.

Nat's eyes flicked to Nathan, who was standing behind Ravyn.

"What are you doing to her?" she demanded. Fire flashed briefly in her eyes.

Nathan said nothing.

"Nat, it's okay," Ravyn spoke softly, unable to stop her voice from quivering. Nat turned back to her. There was fear crawling behind her eyes, though her face was set hard as stone, trying to mask it.

"Can you let go of her?" Ravyn asked, partly to the Shades, partly to Nathan. Sure enough, after a moment, the Shades dropped her arms.

Nat stood frozen to the spot, just looking at Ravyn with wide, scared eyes, silently begging to know what was going on. Ravyn took a few steps forward so she stood just in front of Nat. She reached her right hand forward slightly and gently took hold of Nat's fingers. Her thumb traced the line that separated her middle and ring finger.

Her heart was pounding, her stomach squeezing so tight that her body wanted to throw up. Her knees were growing weak, shaking as they struggled to support her body weight, but she ignored it all.

Ravyn took another half step forward and hugged Nat.

Nat's arms wrapped around her, returning the tight embrace. Ravyn nestled her face into the space between Nat's shoulder and ear, her face hidden in Nat's silky hair.

"I'm going to get you out of here, I promise," Ravyn whispered, so soft she barely even heard herself. Her lips brushed against the skin of Nat's ear as the words left her mouth, and as she held Nat, she sensed a chill running through her body. Ravyn hugged her tighter.

"I promise," she whispered again, starting to gently rock her.

Nat pulled away and held Ravyn at arm's length, examining her face. Nat's eyes were widened, and a million thoughts were running behind them, masked by her pupils. Nat's lips parted, and her eyebrows raised for a moment before dropping again.

Then she drew forward, and Ravyn's eyes fluttered closed as their lips touched.

Their lips locked together, and Nat wrapped her arms around Ravyn's waist, pulling her closer. Ravyn's hands made their way up to Nat's face and cupped her chin. Their lips brushed gently together like feathers, soft and delicate. She allowed herself to melt into the kiss, to enjoy the moment, a moment she might never relive again if things went wrong.

She pushed the thought out of her mind, and for those few seconds, everything around her faded away and she just focused on the girl in front of her, the one she hadn't allowed herself the freedom to fall for.

And for just those few seconds, everything was okay.

Too soon, though, Ravyn broke off the kiss, dropping her head slightly as she looked down at their bodies pressed against each other, wrapped in the safety of each other's arms. Ravyn's heart beat faster. If only they could stay here. If only it was just them—no Shades, no death, no chaos reigning and destroying the ground under their feet, trying to steal their time from each other. If only…

"Take her away," Nathan spoke, and Ravyn jumped at the sound of his voice.

Slowly, her senses came back to her, and reality set back in. She woke from her daydream as a cold hand dragged her back to the real world. The two Shades grabbed Nat's arms, and Nat struggled against them. She launched herself forwards at Ravyn again and grabbed her face, pulling her into another kiss. Nat wrapped her arms around Ravyn's midsection. The two Shades grabbed Nat's arms again and pulled her fiercely backwards. Ravyn stumbled forwards as Nat was pulled away from her.

They dragged Nat out of the room.

The door slammed shut.

Ravyn stared at it, stared at the place she last saw her. A faint shadow of her lingered in the room, her image just a memory. Ravyn's breath left her quivering. Her throat was tight.

A heavy silence fell over them, and only shifted when Nathan spoke again.

"That was adorable," he chuckled. Ravyn's face heated up. She never turned to him, couldn't look at him. Her eyes were fixed on the door, trying to hold onto the ghost of an image slowly fading away.

"Sometimes I forget how young you all are. Still just teenagers, and Jay is using you as his little soldiers in this…conflict. I would never allow it, personally. You deserve a better life than this. You shouldn't be risking your lives for him…" he trailed off. She shut her eyes tightly, resisting the urge to bring her hands to her ears.

Liar, she hissed at him in her mind.

Murderer.

Monster.

He put his hand heavily on her shoulder. The weight almost made her legs buckle, and she shifted uncomfortably.

"But anyway, we have business to attend to."

*****

"Remember what I told you. You have until midnight to bring him here, or your girlfriend dies." Nathan gave her a cheerful pat on the shoulder. She nodded quickly.

It was early afternoon, the sun peeking through the clouds just over the buildings that stood before her. Ravyn turned her head to Nathan, and he flashed her a smile.

"I'll be waiting," he said, and shadows swirled around him, tearing at his clothes and whipping his hair. He simply melted into them and was gone, just a trail of shadow snaking along the ground, back to his lair.

She turned back around, staring at the town in front of her. The air was crisp and fresh. A cool breeze drifted past her, blowing her hair in front of her face. She pushed it back behind her ears. She was standing on a small gravel path just behind a line of trees. Through the gaps between the trunks, buildings rose and fell, and cars sped along the roads. Birds sang happily overhead in the canopy above her; their sweet song could make the nymphs of the forest dance with joy at the beauty of the sounds. A gentle breeze tugged at her hair again. She was alone in here, but out there were people, lots of people going about their day. None of them saw her hiding in the darkness. None of them looked her way.

She started walking.

She didn't really know where to go, and she didn't know how to get in contact with Jay. That part of her plan she hadn't figured out yet. Maybe she had been too hasty in trying to get out of there, maybe she should have consulted with Nat and John first before she got Nathan's attention. What if she couldn't figure out how to get Jay here, and Nathan killed Nat? And maybe John and Brook too…

Her fingers twitched nervously at her sides. She folded her arms across her chest, tucking her cold hands under her armpits.

"Stop it," she muttered to herself, turning down a path that led her out of the woods and towards the main road.

She would just have to figure something out.

I can do this, she told herself repeatedly as she walked, even though she didn't really believe it.

There were clouds floating around in her head, filled with anxious mutterings, growing slowly as they ate away at her mind.

She walked for a few more minutes with no destination, making a mental map of the town as she went, trying her best to stop herself from jittering and shaking. Her eyes scanned her surroundings, moving too fast to take in any of it. But even still, she started to see places that she recognised—a pub with a blue door and blue window frames, and a house painted pink with hanging baskets of ivy that trailed long enough to nearly reach the ground. For a moment, Ravyn panicked, thinking she had been walking in a circle. But when she stopped and looked around, she realised something.

She was back in the town where they had been staying.

She had walked down here with Brook and Alec to get clothes.

Before…

A flutter of excitement made her heart skip a beat, and she looked around again.

Yes, there was the clothes shop they had been to. She walked towards it, trying to take her mind back to that day. Yesterday? Last week? She didn't know how much time had passed, but that didn't really matter. If she could find her way back to the hotel, she might be able to find a way to contact Jay.

Hopefully.

She stopped outside the store and stared up at it. The glass windows showed her reflection—a scruffy girl with tangled hair and ruffled clothes and wide eyes. She stared at herself for a moment, not really believing what she was seeing, but she eventually dragged her eyes away from herself and looked back up the street. People knocked into her as they passed by, unaware of her life-and-death situation, but she didn't pay much attention to them. She started walking again, retracing old, faded footsteps.

There! The newsagents she had stopped briefly at on the way back. She picked up her pace, hurrying up to the storefront. An old woman with a bright pink scarf wrapped around her stepped shakily down onto the footpath and waddled away. Ravyn stopped at the newspaper stand, just like she had that day, and looked down at the date on the newspapers.

The seventeenth. So it was only the next day. She didn't know if she should be relieved.

"Okay. That's good," she mumbled, briefly reading the bold headline on the newspaper on the top of the stand.

POLICE APPEAL FOR WITNESSES OF TEENAGE GIRL AFTER WOMAN MURDERED.

The headline blared out at her, demanding her utmost attention. *LOOK AT ME!* She gulped, and a part of the wall in her brain crumbled away, and a cloud of dust rose into the air. She reached out and traced her fingers over the words. They stung her, like they were made of nettles. She pulled her hand away, rubbing her fingers with her thumb. She took a shaky breath in and tore her eyes away.

Not a good time, Ravyn, she told herself, starting to walk again, her knees weak and threatening to throw her to the ground.

Somewhere, deep in the back of her mind, she knew.

But she pushed that part of her memory away, for now. She had to focus on what was happening right now. And right now, Nat, John, and Brook were counting on her to get them out. Right now, their lives were on the line, and she didn't have time to think about anything other than that.

The hotel entrance was just up ahead, and she walked inside on shaky legs. There were a few people lingering around the reception, most of them backpackers with bulging rucksacks at their feet. One had a cigarette between his lips, and he blew out a puff of smoke as she stepped inside. The smell made her scrunch up her nose. Another, she saw, eyed her up and down with a stupid smirk on his face. She walked past them, heading down the corridor towards their room.

It was hard to breathe in here.

A curse lay over this place, pungent and bitter.

There was a caretaker dressed in overalls outside the room they had stayed in, hands on his hips and shaking his head. He was a small man with round glasses and grey hair around his temples. She walked up to him.

"What happened?" she asked, staring at the broken door. She knew what had happened; it was burned into her mind. To her surprise, though, the hallway was not scorched or scratched in any way. There was no evidence of the flames that had licked the walls just hours before. She risked a peek inside the room itself and nearly threw up.

The curtains were torn from the window, and there was glass and broken splinters of wood creating some abstract art piece on the floor. The beds were flipped and blankets ripped open, their stuffing adding white clouds to the painting.

There was no blood. And again, no scorch marks or evidence of a fire.

The caretaker looked up at her.

"God only fucking knows. I swear, these backpacking kids that come here are lunatics. Crackheads, fucking crackheads. And they leave me to clean up their junk after 'em. One day, I swear, if I catch them, I will strangle the lot of 'em," he growled in a thick Dublin accent, moving past her and heading back down the corridor. She watched him leave—probably off to get his tools and clean their mess. Once he turned the corner, she stepped quickly inside the room.

As she did, a cold ripple ran through her, almost knocking her to the ground. She put her hand on the wall to steady herself. Death itself was looking down on this room, watching her, ready to take her too. She shivered and tried to ignore the coldness of its stare as she rooted through the debris.

She brushed glass and splinters away, throwing the stuffing of the bedding behind her as she dug through the carnage, trying to find anything at all.

She found a tooth, and her stomach heaved. She quickly kicked it away from her, under one of the mangled beds, and continued her search, trying to rid her mind of the image.

And of his face.

Under one of the torn blankets, there was a phone. She quickly grabbed it and stuffed it in her pocket. She didn't know who it belonged to, but surely it would have Jay's number in it.

It had to.

And if it didn't…

She didn't want to think about that right now.

She took one last look around the room. There was no blood or bits of flesh stuck to the wall. There was just the tooth, buried away until the caretaker found it again. It didn't look like someone had died here, but it sure felt like it.

Her skin crawled, and she shivered.

She hurried out of the room, not wanting to spend another second in there. As she left, Death averted its gaze, and she was safe once again. The cold chill that had invaded her body lifted, and she breathed a sigh of relief. She took a second to compose herself in the corridor, one hand on the wall and leaning heavily against it while her laboured breath returned to normal, before heading back towards the exit. The group of backpackers was still loitering around the reception waiting to be served, and the caretaker was rooting through a closet at the far end of the room.

She stepped out into the frosty air and bit hard on her tongue. There were tears at the backs of her eyes as memories tried to resurface. She shook them away. The phone burned in her pocket, and she fished it out. It had low battery and a cracked screen, but otherwise it worked just fine. The screensaver was a picture of John and another older boy, pulling a stupid pose against a mountainous background. The phone was locked with a password, but on the bottom left corner was an icon of a phone. She swiped up, and a keypad appeared. She ran her tongue over her lips, and started dialling 08—

Names popped up in the contacts, and she scrolled through them until she found Jay. Her heart skipped a beat, and she couldn't stop the smile that rose on her face. She pressed on his name, then held the phone to her ear with trembling hands.

While she waited for him to answer, she started walking down the street, back towards the clothes shop, away from that dreaded place of foul death. She put one hand in her pocket, crossing her fingers so tightly that the blood supply was cut off.

"Hello? John?" Jay's voice brought a wash of relief over her. Her knees wobbled, and she almost crashed to the ground.

"It's Ravyn. Oh my god, Jay—"

He cut her off, his words quick and panicked. "Ravyn! What happened? Where are you?"

Paranoia made her look over her shoulder. What if Nathan was watching? Waiting? What if he had sent Shades out to keep an eye on her, make sure she didn't go against her word. She shook the thoughts from her head. She would just have to risk it.

Her stomach flipped and sent bile racing up her throat. She swallowed it quickly.

"I'm back at the motel. He got us—Nathan got us. He let me go to find you." Words tumbled around in her mind, forming incoherent sentences she had to restrain herself from speaking.

"Okay. Ravyn, I'm coming to get you now. Wait somewhere close by for me, and stay on the phone—"

"Jay, there's not enough battery," she told him.

He paused briefly. "Okay, I'll ring you when I'm passing the motel. I'll be ten minutes, all right? You can explain everything when I'm there. Are you safe right now?" he asked, and she heard shuffling and rustling behind her. She jumped and spun around, but it was just an empty, brown chipper bag rolling towards her. Her heart took a second to restart itself.

She nodded. "Yes."

She hoped so, anyway.

"Okay, good. I'm on the way. Keep the phone with you, and I'll ring you shortly. Find somewhere to wait—a coffee shop or something. It's going to be okay; we'll sort everything out, I promise." His words were coming too quickly, and she was struggling to keep up. She nodded again.

She was starting to feel really sick now.

"Okay."

"Ring me if you need to, okay?"

"Yes."

"I'm on my way now. I'll see you shortly, Ravyn."

"Thank you."

She hung up and slid the phone back into her pocket with shaky hands. Once again, she was on her own.

The sense of loneliness she hadn't felt since before meeting

Brook started to creep back up on her, nipping at her heels and trying to climb up her legs and pull her down to the ground. She walked a little faster, trying to escape its reach. Out of the corner of her eye, she saw a coffee shop with some chairs and tables outside, and she veered towards it. She sat, rubbing her cold hands together. The friction warmed them for a moment, but the cold reappeared the second she stopped.

Her heart was pounding uncontrollably.

Her fingertips were prickling with pins and needles.

A magpie flew down and sat on the back of the chair opposite her. She drew her eyes to it. It hopped along the metal, looking curiously at her, searching for scraps. But when it found none, it gave a squawk, then flew off, and she was alone once again.

CHAPTER 13

When the phone rang again, Ravyn jumped and almost let it fall out of her icy-cold hands. She fumbled with it, answering the call with numb fingers.

"Hello?"

"It's Jay. Where are you?" he asked. She looked over her shoulder into the coffee shop, peering at the name which hung behind the counter, lit up in orange and red.

"Uh, the Westside Coffeehouse. It's only down the road from the hotel," she told him.

"Right, we're almost there. We'll pull up alongside it, and you just hop in, okay?"

She nodded. "Yes."

"See you soon." And he hung up.

Ravyn glanced down at the phone screen, which showed there was only five percent battery left, then put it in her pocket. She would give it back to John later, if—*when* they were freed from Nathan's grasp. She walked to the edge of the path with her arms folded tightly against her chest, trying to retain some warmth. The cold autumn air had penetrated down to her bones, fusing them with ice. She watched cars glide along the road past her. They each sent a gust of biting wind at her as they drove by, and their wheels kicked up dead leaves and sent them swirling onto the path and around her feet. Her foot tapped nervously against the ground. She had been jumping at every shadow and movement out of the corner of her eye since she'd sat down at that cafe, but none of them turned out to be Shades. Still, she wanted to be cautious. She couldn't risk having a Shade follow her, spy on her, and then tell Nathan what was really going on. He would kill them all, and she could not let that happen.

A black jeep flicked its indicators on, slowing as it approached her. It slid to a halt beside her, and her hand froze just as she was about to grab the door handle, a sudden moment of anxiety rushing at her, telling her it was the Shades here to kill her, to drag her back to Nathan and watch as he slaughtered—

She gritted her teeth and opened the back passenger door.

Jay was waiting for her in the back. There were two other people she didn't know sitting in the front. She closed the door, and they started moving again.

"Are you okay? Are you hurt?" Jay asked, helping her put on her seatbelt. She shook her head. He took her chin and tilted her face, pausing to look at the cut on her jaw. Then he nodded to himself and let go. A look of relief washed over his face.

"I'm so glad you're okay. You have no idea how hard we looked for you, and I was starting to think… Anyway, Ryan has an apartment here. We'll head there, then you can tell us everything," he said, motioning to the driver.

He was tall, his bleach-blond hair grazing the roof of the

car. There were thick scars covering the dark skin on his hands, and they disappeared behind his red coat sleeves. He glanced into the mirror, and they made eye contact. He raised his eyebrows in hello, then looked back at the road.

She turned to Jay. "Okay," she said.

He lowered his voice. "You promise me you're all right?"

She nodded again.

It was so warm in the car that her skin was burning, her fingers struggling to move with the sudden temperature change. She flexed them a few times, then squeezed her hands between her thighs.

Jay stared at her for a moment, his eyes soft, then turned back around in his seat. She did the same, staring at the back of the leather headrest in front of her. He put his hand on her shoulder, keeping her within arm's reach in case he lost her again. The gesture was comforting and released some of the anxiety that was gripping the corners of her mind. He squeezed her shoulder then let his hand fall back to the leather seat. She closed her eyes and tried to search for some more sense of relief in her body but found there was none.

Their lives were still at risk.

There was still a gun loaded and pointed at their heads, and it would fire if she didn't figure out a way to save them.

Ravyn was jerked from her half sleep when they went over a speed bump. She rubbed her eyes. They had reached the apartment block, which climbed high into the sky. The building had an underground carpark, and Ravyn stared out the window as they descended into darkness. For a second, they were completely submerged in it, then the yellow glow of artificial lights slowly lit up the car, casting reflections on the windows.

There was a numb chattering in her mind, words mumbled

and lost before she could make sense of them. As much as she tried to block it out, it refused to leave, refused to quiet down.

Nat was still with Nathan.

Brook and John were still with Nathan.

And God only knew what he might be doing to them.

He could have killed them already—

She forced herself to think about something else. But everything else was pain and death anyway, so it didn't help much at all.

They parked near the lift, and everyone got out. Besides Jay and Ryan, there was another woman who she had barely acknowledged on the way over here. She was also tall, thanks to the pair of heels she was wearing, coming up to the tip of Ryan's nose. She had blonde hair with pastel purple and blue highlights running through it that Ravyn adored and had always wanted. She wore dark clothes with silver studs lining the shoulders of her jacket and dark makeup. Her septum and eyebrow piercings glinted in the light. Both of her ears had a number of studs running up them.

She was very pretty.

Ravyn tore her eyes away.

Kissing Nat had been bad-good-*something* enough for today. Her subconscious wouldn't allow her to think of another girl in that way, not now. Maybe when she had worked out the badly creased folds in her mind that was stopping her from accepting it, but not now.

The memory of when Nat had been dragged away, pulled out of Ravyn's arms by the Shades, replayed in her mind and stabbed her in the heart.

I promise.

Her final words to Nat.

They took the lift to the fifth floor, and Ryan fumbled with his keys the whole way up, twisting and turning them in his hands and spinning them on his finger. Ravyn listened to the sound of the metal jingling and scratching against each other, and it only agitated the thoughts floating around her head.

She closed her eyes and took a deep breath. There was a dull pain growing in her chest.

Jay put his hand on her shoulder. "Are you okay?"

Ravyn opened her eyes and nodded at him. There was something in her throat blocking her words, and she didn't want to force it out. Not now. Because when she did, there would be nothing to stop whatever came after them. He stared at her for a moment, searching her face, then took his hand away and clasped them in front of him.

The lift stopped, dropped half a centimetre and sent her heart plummeting, then pinged as the doors slid open. They stepped out and walked a short way to apartment number 9. The hall was narrow, with four apartments on this floor. A row of fluorescent lights lined the centre of the ceiling, emitting a piercingly bright light. The floor was a dark wood that had been worn down, and lighter-coloured scratches and marks decorated it. All the doors were black, and the brass number hanging on them shined in the light. Ryan unlocked the door and let everyone in ahead of him. Once they all filed into the apartment, he closed the door and locked it, then drew three bolts across the door.

Jay flicked on a light, and the room lit up. She blinked, allowing her eyes to adjust before she followed Jay through the short, narrow hallway into the living area. Ryan slid past them and went straight to the kitchen counter and flicked on the kettle. While he did that, Ravyn looked around the room. It was sleek and modern with colour accents and abstract art hanging on the walls, but before she had a chance to take it all in, Jay put one hand on the small of her back and led her to a red leather sofa, facing a TV which was on but muted. There was a cooking show on, and the chef was frying something while flames leapt out of the pan at them. Behind the TV was a window which had an opaque, white curtain drawn across it so she couldn't see out.

She sank down into the leather as her lungs deflated with a sigh, and Jay sat beside her.

"How are you feeling?" he asked quietly. She had lost count of how many times he had asked her the same question, but this was another to add to the list.

She shrugged. "I'm okay." It was an automatic response.

"Do you want to tell us what happened?"

She took a long breath in through her nose.

How the hell was she supposed to explain it all? There were too many layers, too many fresh wounds that would simply bleed out again if she tried to open them.

The chest pain was getting worse, and for a moment, she thought about that time they had learned the symptoms of a heart attack, but quickly pushed the idea out of her head, telling herself to stop being stupid. There were more important things to focus on.

"The Shades attacked us," she started, getting the obvious out of the way. She had never been good with these kinds of serious conversations because these kinds of conversations never happened with Aunt Stephanie. "They…um, they… killed Alec." Her voice grew small as his name found its way back to her, and Jay put his hand on her arm.

Her mind screamed his name at her, so loud she couldn't even ignore it.

It showed her his dead body, his body that she had stepped over and hadn't even tried to help.

Jay nodded slowly, and his eyes started to glisten in the light. He knew. Ravyn continued before her own eyes welled up.

"They took the rest of us to some underground place—"

"Brook, Nat, and John are still in there?"

She nodded. "Yes, but… Brook… She was working with them, the Shades. But it wasn't really her… I don't know how to explain it. There was a Shade inside her…or maybe it was one of Nathan's shadows, I'm not sure." That awful image flashed in her mind, that thing crawling out of Brook's throat. Gnarly hands, sickly thin limbs all composed of shadow … A wave of chills hit her, and she shuddered.

"*Inside* her?" Jay asked with a deep frown, and she nodded.

"Yeah. Nathan was there too. He took it out of her. She's alive…but she's not well. She's really not well, Jay."

Jay stroked his beard, his eyes wandering from her face to the wall behind her. Ravyn's chest felt compressed, like there was a rope around her being pulled tighter and tighter. Her lungs were struggling to expand. She kept her gaze on Jay, very aware of the breath leaving and entering her body. After a moment or two, he looked back to her.

"I've never heard of that happening before… You're absolutely sure?" he asked. Ravyn nodded again.

"Yes, it…came out of her mouth. It looked like a Shade, but I think it might have been just one of Nathan's shadows or something, I really don't know."

She shuddered again, her joints seizing for a brief moment as the shaking took hold of her.

"Hmm…" Jay trailed off, taking hold of a chunk of his beard hair, deep in thought. "Well, that not good. Nathan might be experimenting with new ideas…" Jay let go of his beard and turned his full attention back to her.

"He is. He said he was experimenting, or something like that. He did something to the room we were in, and nobody could use their abilities," she told him. He bit down on his lip, and his eyes narrowed briefly.

"Why did Nathan let you go?" he asked finally.

She hesitated.

Her heart was pounding so loud she was sure he could hear it.

THUD.

THUD.THUD.

"I…"

She didn't know how to tell someone you were going to sacrifice their life for the lives of three others. How do you tell someone that you promised to bring them to meet the devil, and exchange their life for someone else's?

"I told him I would bring you to him. I don't know why I did, I just thought… I thought it would be better if I could find you, then maybe we could get the others out." She looked down at her hands, palms turned towards her face. Her fingers were starting to buzz and tingle like needles piercing her flesh.

Jay gave her arm a squeeze. "You did the right thing. Now we can work on getting the others out of there."

"He said I have to bring you by midnight, or he…he'd kill Nat. And John, and Brook." Her voice got quiet.

Fuck, I shouldn't have left.

What have you done, Ravyn?

What the fuck have you done?

Jay took a moment before he answered. His silence was a vice on her throat, tightening with each passing second.

"We'll figure something out, don't worry. We have loads of time," he said, standing. She watched him as he walked into the kitchen area. Ryan was pouring tea into mugs. The other woman was leaning against the fridge, hands in her pockets. Her eyes caught Ravyn's, and Ravyn looked away. She tilted her face to look down at her hands instead.

The tingling was travelling down her fingers and into her palms now. She knew how this went, it had happened many times before, but she didn't want it to happen here, in front of these people.

Control yourself, for God's sake!

"If you haven't heard, we have a dilemma. We have to get them out by midnight," Jay told the two other Ethereal. Ryan took a mug of tea over to Ravyn, and she looked up as he stood in front of her.

"Thank you," she said as she took it off him. He gave her a quick smile and returned to the counter. Ravyn twisted her body to look towards the three adults trying to find a way to fix her mess.

At least you fucking did something, she told herself, *and didn't rot in that cell.*

The thought didn't help.

"Tammie and Excael are on their way—"

There was a knock at the door.

"Speak of the devil," the woman muttered, walking to the door and out of sight.

Ravyn's body tensed. Her mind immediately imagined Shades bursting through the door and killing them all. Nat lying face down on the floor, blood spreading from her body, her hair matted crimson, and Ravyn would fall to her knees and her tiny fists would ball up as tears streamed down her face and her knees landed in blood and became soaked, her hands covered in blood as she tried to shake Nat awake, but she wouldn't wake up, wouldn't wake up, can't wake up, and she would leave Ravyn forever—

M U M M Y !
W A K E *U P !*
Nathan can't get you here.
You're safe.
There are no Shades.

She tried to tell herself these things, but the words were weak and meaningless against the growing anxiety in her. It had already compromised her chest and stomach, so she wasn't even sure if she could get the tea down. And it was growing, spreading, hungry fingers searching for food. She could feel it, painful and bulging inside her, trying to kill her, trying to consume her.

She gave herself a mental slap.

Three sets of footsteps approached from behind. Her back straightened and all the hair on her body stood completely upright, but they passed her and went into the kitchen. She looked at the woman and the two newcomers—Tammie and Excael, she guessed.

Tammie was short and plump with a kind face. Her dark hair was braided to one side, the end resting on her collarbone. The man was about as tall as Ryan, his light hair tied back in a ponytail. He wore black cargo pants and a dark green jumper. A Celtic tattoo poked out of his collar and travelled up his neck, curling into his hair.

"Thank you for coming," Jay said, greeting Tammie with a kiss on the cheek and Excael with a handshake.

Tammie smiled. "No bother at all."

"I was just explaining that we have until midnight to get the others out."

There was a brief silence, and Ravyn almost choked on it.

"Oh, right." Tammie nodded, but her eyebrows dipped, and a look of worry crossed her face.

"We need to think about how we are going to do this," Jay said, motioning towards the sofas.

Ravyn moved over so she sat at the end, and Jay sat beside her, Tammie beside Jay. The other three sat on the opposite sofa. Amongst all these well-experienced adults, she felt like the odd one out.

"Well, firstly, let me introduce you all to Ravyn, our newest Illusionist." He put a hand on her shoulder. "And Ravyn, let me introduce Tammie, Ryan, Excael, and Clio." He pointed to each one in turn. Ravyn gave them all a quick nod.

"Nice to finally meet you, Ravyn." Tammie looked past Jay to her, smiling. Ravyn smiled back but didn't speak. She felt faint, detached from herself, her body ready to give in.

God, no.

Not now.

Please, not now.

Her fingers were starting to curl into her palms as they became increasingly numb. Her heart was still pounding, pounding, pounding her ribs.

"Let's get straight to it, I suppose, " Ryan said, looking at Jay, who nodded.

"Midnight is not a lot of time to plan, and then *execute* that plan," Excael pointed out. Out of the corner of her eye, Ravyn saw Jay stroke his beard again.

"It's all the time we have," he told them.

"It's not enough—"

"It won't be enough if we don't start doing something productive instead of arguing about how long we have," Clio interrupted. Her voice was sweet with a knife-sharp edge to it. It reminded her so much of Nat. Ravyn's eyes wandered over to her. She was sitting cross-legged and leaning against the arm of the sofa, her chin resting in her palm.

"Clio is right. We don't have time to argue," Jay agreed.

"What do we know about where they are being held?" Ryan asked. Jay looked to Ravyn and gave her an encouraging smile.

"It's beneath an old house. It's big, and dark too. I... I don't know the layout, I just know it's under a house, like a basement, but a lot bigger." Her voice quivered on the last few words, and she cleared her throat. Jay put his hand on her arm and gave it a squeeze, but it didn't help restore her confidence.

The pins and needles were starting in her toes now.

Please, not now, she begged herself.

"It'll be dark so the Shades can hide there," Clio noted. Ravyn nodded at her words.

"Yes, I know," Jay said, but his voice was becoming distant to her. The panic had reached her lungs, and it was filling them with a dark mass, reducing her oxygen. It was getting harder to breathe. Ravyn closed her eyes and focused on her breathing, taking a breath in then a breath out. In and out. But she couldn't keep control over it, no matter how hard she tried. Her body demanded more oxygen, more than she was able to supply it with.

"It won't be easy to get through it, then." She barely recognised Ryan's voice. It was distorted and distant.

"Why don't we just go in and blow the fuckers up?" Excael suggested, which was met with a disapproving mutter.

"The kids, what about the kids?" someone said. Ravyn couldn't place their voice. She opened her eyes, but everything was out of focus. Just a blurry lens she couldn't see through. Her mind was becoming even more distant from her body. Jay's hand became tight around her arm, and she tried to turn her head to him but was met with a wave of dizziness.

The arguing continued, but Jay stood, pulling her with him. His hand moved from her arm to wrap around her middle, and he led her into another room. She followed him blindly, still trying to control her breathing, and her restricted throat was making her breaths audible. Now that the panic had access to her lungs, it was working its way up her throat, caving it in, trying to suffocate her.

"Sit down here. You're all right." Jay sat her down on the edge of a bed and sat beside her. She put her hands over her face, breathing hard and noisily. Jay rubbed her back in slow circles.

"It's okay, Ravyn. Everything's okay," he told her quietly enough that she could barely hear him. She shook her head, choking on air.

No. No, it wasn't all right. They were stuck back there, and she was here, not helping them. Nat was back there. And if she didn't return with Jay, Nathan would kill Nat. And there was her mother on the floor in blood, and Nat was on the floor in blood, and Brook was on the floor and John was on the floor and there was so much blood, all over her hands and her knees and their hair and dripping down the stairs and spilling everywhere and everywhere and so much blood. And he killed them and there was screaming and screaming and screaming in her ears and she didn't know where it was coming from…

Tears were now starting to form in her eyes, but there was no point trying to stop them from spilling. They started rolling down her cheeks seconds after they appeared. Her hands were clenched into fists, and she couldn't unfold them; she couldn't move her fingers at all. Her mind screamed at her that she was dying, that this was the end, that she had failed, and she was going to die! Everyone was going to die because of *her*.

Jay rubbed her back more firmly.

"Ravyn, you're okay. I promise, everything is going to be

fine," he said.

"I shouldn't have left them," she managed to choke out, her own voice foreign to her.

"No, you did the right thing."

"They're going to die because of me," she sobbed.

"No, I promise you they are not. We're going to find a way to get them out, okay? We'll get them out," he assured her, but it didn't work.

They were going to die because of her. She'd killed them by leaving them there. She'd killed Nat by leaving her there. It was a stupid fucking plan she had made, or half made. She hadn't accounted for *this* part, the part where they couldn't get the others out of there and Nathan killed them—

"Listen, we've been in situations like this before, and we always find a way to save them. We will get them out of there, then we are going to stay in a safe house for a few days to get the Shades off our tail. When it's safe again, we'll take you home to Dunfeagh, where you'll be safe. I'll train you how to use your gifts then. How does that sound?"

Good. Unrealistic, perhaps? Delusional? Her head was pounding, but she nodded anyway, just to please him.

"All right, good. I know it's stressful, especially since you've only just been introduced to this world. And I'm stressed too, if I'm honest. I don't want you to get the wrong impression of us, and I especially don't want you to get hurt. The Ethereal are not about fighting or war or anything like that. But it's what we've been thrown into by Nathan and the Shades, so we just have to adapt and get on with it. I don't want you to think that you've been forced into a world full of death and chaos. We have to use our abilities to survive, and since you haven't had the chance to learn yours yet… I mean, it is what it is. Besides, you've been handling yourself pretty well, I think," he finished.

The panic was starting to subside, sinking back down her throat and out of her lungs. She nodded slowly, wiping her eyes. She could finally unfold her fingers, and she flexed them as feeling returned to her flesh.

"Thanks." She forced herself to smile, and he patted her on the back.

"Have you had panic attacks before?" he asked gently.

She nodded, staring at her hands as her fingers moved and the tingling sensation travelled out the tips of her fingers. "A few times."

"I know this must be extremely stressful for you. It's okay to feel scared and anxious, and it's understandable for this kind of thing to happen. If you need to talk to someone, we're all here for you. We're on your side, and we will help you as best we can." His voice soothed her. She nodded slowly.

"One day, this will all be over, and you can see what it really means to be an Ethereal. How beautiful it is to use your gifts for things other than fighting. But for now, we just have to keep surviving how we are," he told her.

"Why don't you want to fight back?" she asked, managing to somewhat keep her voice steady. Jay sighed.

"Because then we give into what they want. We become like them. We only fight when we have to, but we must not forget that we are peacekeepers first and foremost. Besides, it's better to use your brain rather than your fist, hmm?" He smiled.

She nodded, wiping her eyes again. They were sore and puffy. Her lungs were finally free of the acid that had corroded them, and her flesh was starting to knit itself back together.

"I'm sorry for...you know." She pinched the bridge of her nose. He shook his head.

"Ravyn, there's nothing to be sorry for," he assured her,

giving her a squeeze. She shrugged, looking down at her feet resting on the floorboards. Her left leg was trembling slightly, and she pressed it firmly into the wood. "How about a hug?" Jay asked then, and she smiled, nodding.

He wrapped both of his arms protectively around her, and she twisted into him, resting her head on his shoulder. His embrace was warm and comforting, a safety net that saved her from falling. She closed her eyes, reeling in the last of the stray thoughts wandering around her head and tying them down with chains.

"Everything's going to be okay," he told her again, and for the first time, she started to believe him. Maybe everything was going to be okay. The others would be safe, Nat would be safe, and maybe...

No, she told herself. *Don't get your hopes up. That could have been a one-off thing. But maybe...*

It would be nice to kiss her again.

Jay pulled out of the hug and looked into her eyes.

"Now, let's go make some battle plans, shall we?" he said with a smirk.

She couldn't stop the smile making its way onto her lips, and she nodded.

CHAPTER 14

J ay stood next to her, staring at the building in front of
them. It was a single bungalow, and it looked abandoned,
but she knew better than that. The driveway was overgrown,
and weeds were clinging to the side of the house like fingers
reaching up from inside the earth, ready to pull the house back
down with it deep into the darkness of what lay under their
feet. The windows were boarded up, and the door was cracked
down the centre. The roof was ready to cave in. Ravyn
shivered looking at it.

The shadows were strange here. Unnatural, almost. Light
barely seemed to touch this house. It even felt cold here,
colder than the rest of the woods around them, as if it were
encased in a bubble of permanent darkness. The look of it
alone would be enough to drive away any normal person.

It was getting dark now; the sun was starting to set, and the
light had turned rusty orange, but it never touched the house.
Only the surrounding trees had their trunks encased in molten
gold, but the light was cut off in a circular line surrounding the

house.

"Ready?" Jay asked.

She took a moment before she nodded. If this goes arseways...

"You can't let him think that there's something wrong. It will be fine, don't worry," Jay whispered to her. She nodded again and took a deep breath, filling her lungs right to the brim with air.

A robin flew overhead and sat on the top of the house, looking down at them. It was late for him to be out, but he sat and gave one final song, sending off the day and welcoming the night. His sweet tune calmed some of her nerves. She stood up straighter.

They started walking towards the house, lifting their feet high to step over the undergrowth. Nettles stung their legs and brambles snatched their clothes, trying to stop them from entering the house and facing the wickedness it hid beneath its foundations.

Ravyn pushed the rotting door open, and it groaned as the rusty hinges struggled to move. It was dark inside. All the windows had been boarded up, then covered with black plastic. The wind howled through the house like a hungry wolf, ready to feast on them when Nathan tore the life from them. The air was chilly, and goosebumps prickled across her skin.

She took out John's phone, which she had charged at Ryan's apartment, and turned on the torch. Large dust particles floated through the air in front of the light, dancing and swirling as the air was disturbed with their breathing.

They started walking again.

The house had been stripped of furniture, and all the doors had been taken off their hinges. Only the skeleton of the building remained. Water was dripping through holes in the roof and pooling on the wooden floor, causing it to buckle and warp. Ravyn led them to the back of the house, where the wall of shadow stood.

It swirled and moved, covering the entrance to Nathan's little secret home. The gateway to the underworld. They both stared at it, and it stared back.

"We have to go through it," Ravyn whispered, scared to break the silence.

"Hmm." Jay put his hands on his hips, watching as the gate of shadow swirled in an endless cycle. Ravyn took a step towards it, and Jay matched her stride.

She took his hand and pulled them both into the darkness.

It was a storm inside the shadows, whipping at their clothes and pulling at their hair. The shadows roared around them. Not even the light from the phone could shine through it. Ravyn gripped Jay's hand tighter and pushed on through the hurricane. Her foot almost overshot the step down, and she stumbled, catching herself before she fell and broke her neck.

After descending a couple steps, they emerged from the other side of the gateway with their clothes crumpled and their hair a mess.

Ravyn and Jay looked at each other, then Ravyn led the way down.

Jay also turned on his phone torchlight, and they made their way down the narrow steps, further and further into the earth, descending into a dark and cold Hell. Her heart fluttered nervously.

Neither of them spoke as they moved into Nathan's lair. Ravyn was counting the steps—*twenty-five, twenty-six, twenty-seven...*

Finally, after thirty-two steps, they reached flat ground

again. Ravyn stood at the end of the corridor and shone her light down into the darkness. A Shade flitted past her light, whooshing as it went. Ravyn swallowed the lump in her throat. Despite the cold, a sweat was breaking out on her brow. This was it now, no turning back.

This had to work, or they would all die.

She couldn't let them die.

Not when she was the one supposed to be saving them.

She started walking again, and Jay followed behind her. Their footsteps echoed loudly, bouncing off the walls and down the corridor. Surely Nathan would know that they were here. He had to know, didn't he? She didn't want to travel too far and get lost. She had no idea where she was going. She had clung to Nathan while he led her through the darkness, but she'd been unable to memorise the turns and twists he guided her down.

She bit hard on her lip, drawing blood. It was bitter and metallic in her mouth. She pressed her tongue against the wound and grimaced.

Her ears were ringing with the heavy silence that enveloped them.

Another Shade moved past her, a dark shadow leaping across her vision, and she jumped.

They were deep in their territory now, and there was no telling what they would do to them. No telling what Nathan had planned, no telling what tricks he had up his sleeve.

There was a room to their right, the metal door shut, its secrets hidden, and she didn't want to find out what lay behind it. She didn't remember going through any doors on her way out of here, so she walked straight past it.

Up ahead were two more doors, shut tight. She walked slowly past them, glancing over her shoulder as she went to make sure nothing jumped out at her.

It was so dark, their torches mere pinpricks in the black canvas. Anything could be hiding in this gloom.

They came to a fork in the corridor, and she looked down both routes. Down the one to the right, there was a pinprick of light, beckoning them towards it. She crossed her fingers, praying silently that this was it, that they had found the others. The closer they got, the more intense the light became, and she could make out the thick bars across the wall. Her heart skipped a beat, and she sighed with relief.

There were figures in the cell, only dark silhouettes, and one of them stood up.

"Ravyn?" It was Nat who called out. A smile started to push itself onto Ravyn's lips, but she held it back as best as she could. The other figure, John, also stood and looked out between the bars. Brook was still on the floor, unmoving. Ravyn sucked in a sharp breath at the sight of her silhouette.

Ravyn lowered her light, taking it out of their eyes.

"Holy fuck, Ravyn! What—" Nat began, but she was cut off.

"Nice to see you again, Ravyn," a low voice spoke from behind her. Nathan, of course. The two daring knights who willingly entered his lair turned to face him. "And you've brought your friend. How nice of you." He grinned, showing teeth like a shark. They gleamed menacingly in the light.

"Nathan," Jay greeted flatly between clenched teeth.

"Nice of you to join us, Jay. It's been a while, hasn't it?"

"Let them go, Nathan," Jay challenged, moving the phone light up to Nathan's face. Nathan squinted and took a half step backwards. The light on his face cast his eyes in shadow, hidden under his high brow, so he looked almost skeletal.

"Let's not be hasty." Nathan grinned, clasping his hands in

front of his stomach. Behind him, shadows swirled and formed figures, watching, waiting for the blood to spill so they could lap it up like dogs.

"If you let them out, you can take me and do whatever you want with me. Just let them go; they haven't done anything." Jay took a step forward, squaring his shoulders. Ravyn was starting to fidget. Her free hand was clenching and unclenching, fingers tapping her palms and drumming against her thigh.

This had to work.

It *had* to.

There were two sets of eyes staring at the back of her head, burning through her skull. One pair burned through her forehead.

A shaky breath left her mouth.

A whip of shadow lashed out at them both, knocking them off their feet. Ravyn's breath left her mouth in a sharp exhale, and her lungs exploded with pain when she tried to inhale again. She lay on the ground, staring at a dark ceiling.

The phone had been knocked from her hand and lay on the ground to her right, the torch shining up.

"Do you really think I'm that stupid—"

Nathan's words were knocked from his mouth in a gasp.

Ravyn used her elbows to prop herself up, staring at Nathan as he gasped for air. Jay was on his knees, breathing heavily. Shadow gathered around him, swirling angrily.

"A deal is a deal, Nathan. Let them out," Jay spoke slowly, drawing each word out. Nathan gasped and hunched over, his hands on his knees as he finally gulped air.

"Well, that's new," he chuckled, out of breath. He composed himself and straightened his suit.

Ravyn grabbed the phone and pushed herself to her feet.

Jay was up before her, his hands ready at his sides, in case Nathan tried anything again. Ravyn's hand shook as she held the phone, the torch pointed at Nathan's midsection.

"Well, a deal *is* a deal, Ravyn." He raised a hand to the cell. Ravyn flinched out of the way.

Behind her, the cell door creaked and groaned as a wisp of shadow opened it slowly. Ravyn didn't turn, keeping her eyes on Nathan. She gripped the phone tighter and balled up her other hand into a fist. Her fingernails dug into her palm, her knuckles white.

"Did you fucking make a deal with him, Ravyn? What the fuck were—" John's angry voice was cut off by the earth above their head being ripped away.

The ground shook and rumbled, almost knocking her off her feet. It roared and rumbled, soil and rocks falling down on top of them, and suddenly light streamed into the corridor.

Ryan had been waiting up above somewhere with Excael, listening through the phone for the cue of John and Nat being released, the cue to tear the top off this place and get everyone the fuck out.

Ravyn turned on her heel and sprinted to Nat and John. She could barely hear her pounding heart over the roaring of the earth around them. She helped Nat lift Brook's limp body off the floor. She was dead weight in their arms, her limbs hanging down to the ground, her head rolling freely. Nat carried her out of the cell, and then they were running.

Jay had made them an air tunnel to run through, stopping the Shades and Nathan from reaching them. There were Shades flitting everywhere, screeching at their sudden and unexpected exposure, not sure what to do. Nathan was pressed against the wall, flattened by the side of the air tunnel pressing against him. The artery in his neck and the veins in his temples popped under his skin, bulging and pulsing with the beat of his heart. His face was curled into a snarl. Ravyn tore her eyes away from his angry stare.

And they all ran.

Jay led the way, keeping them safe, a bubble of hardened air now surrounding them. It shimmered in the weak light, a soft, transparent white that moved like the wind as it whirled around them. They took the left turn and started running for the stairs. Up above, Ryan and Excael were running alongside them, leaping over the piles of dirt and rock they had created.

They reached the stairs, but a group of Shades formed a wall in front of them, a screaming black mass with arms reaching towards them, fingers outstretched, beckoning them into the cold embrace of death. Before Jay had the chance to do anything, the ground under the wall of Shades exploded, and they were shot into the air before they dispersed, shrieking and screaming.

Ravyn jumped over the hole in the ground, then glanced over her shoulder at Nat. Nat jumped the gap with ease, even with the extra weight in her arms. But as Ravyn was looking behind her, she saw Nathan appear around the corner, clumps of shadow in his fists. His eyes were burning hot, flames leaping out of them and singeing his hair. She looked up to Excael and caught his eye, then pointed at Nathan. He nodded, stopped, and turned back. Ravyn could only catch glimpses over her shoulder as she took the steps two at a time. Nathan was running towards them now, the shadows around his fists growing larger with each step. Then the two walls on either side of the passageway rumbled and closed in, blocking his way.

Nathan roared.

A dark streak of shadow flew upwards, darting faster than

lightning and heading straight for Ryan. It caught the corner of Ravyn's eye, and she stumbled as she turned to watch it fly through the air.

Shit.

Excael was in front of Ryan, and he hadn't seen the Shade flying to kill his friend.

If only the ground would explode again—

But it did, only milliseconds after the thought had appeared in her head. Who made it happen, she didn't know, but the ground erupted around the Shade and made it dart in the other direction, its shrieks adding to the symphony of shrills and screams that had erupted in the forest.

Ravyn turned her full attention back to the steps ahead of her. They were halfway there now. Blood pumped rapidly through her, pounding in her ears. Sweat soaked her clothes and clung to her forehead. Her thighs burned, and her lungs were getting tired, but she didn't slow down.

Ryan and Excael met them at the top of the steps, in the ruins of the house that had collapsed as its foundations were torn away. Both of them were drenched in sweat and breathing heavily. Jay removed the air bubble from around them, and the air popped as the pressure changed, and he stumbled forwards. Ryan caught him before he fell.

Ravyn's ears were ringing. There were no words exchanged; they just shared an inhale and started running again.

The quick change in height was making Ravyn's head spin. Blood was rushing to her head now, and she stumbled over herself. She knocked into Nat and was almost sent sprawling.

Nat lifted Brook and folded her over her shoulder in a fireman's lift, then pushed Ravyn on with her free hand.

The undergrowth snapped at their legs, and Ravyn almost fell again as she kicked a rock hidden in the grass. Pain flared in her toes, and she hissed, staggering as she ran. But Nat was there to push her on, keeping her ahead, keeping her running through the trees and bushes.

Her heart was skipping beats as she ran, her body struggling to keep pace with the others who were much fitter than her.

But they pushed through a bush, and the jeeps came into view. Clio and Tammie were waiting in two separate jeeps parked at the edge of the dirt track, engines running and ready to leave. Tammie met them as they slowed to a stop, helping Nat load Brook into one of the jeeps. Jay grabbed Ravyn by the shoulders and pushed her to the other jeep, where Excael was getting in the front passenger seat. John followed her silently, sitting beside her in the back. The door on the other side of the jeep opened and Nat got in, sitting on Ravyn's other side.

Jay jumped in behind the wheel and pulled the handbrake, the tyres screaming and kicking up muck as they took off, away from that place that reeked of foulness and death.

CHAPTER 15

Nat held her hand tightly as they sat in the back of the car. They didn't talk, but there wasn't much to say anyway. Ravyn just focused on the soft skin of Nat's hand, and how perfectly their fingers fit together, interlocked around each other. She allowed her eyes to close, and she smiled.

The low droning of the car was making her sleepy. The adrenaline had worn off, the excitement of their escape now a distant memory, its sweet taste lingering faintly on the tip of her tongue.

They had all survived.

She had done it.

Condensation was gathering on the windows, fogging them up. Outside was a hazy blur. Only muted colours and shapes could be seen through the veil that coated the glass. Nat wiped the window with her other arm, and a lazy stream of evening sunlight shone through. Above them, dark clouds drifted across the sky, sending down the occasional splashes of raindrops. Lemony sunlight poked through gaps in the clouds, saying its final goodbye to the land before it set and the silver moon took its place.

"Jay, I think there's a car following us," Excael spoke from the front.

Ravyn opened her eyes and saw him peering in the side mirror. Jay adjusted his mirror, and Ravyn shifted her leg slightly to hide their entwined hands from him. Not that he would have been looking, but just in case. Aunt Stephanie was peering through that mirror, a scowl on her face.

If Ravyn could sink backwards and let the black leather swallow her, she would, just to escape that harsh gaze.

Her cheek stung hotly with the ghost of a slap that had nestled itself there before.

"Hmm. Tell the others we'll be taking the scenic route, and we'll meet them there. And tell them to keep an eye out for anyone following them too," he told Excael before changing gears. Excael nodded and took out his phone. The other car had gone a different way, in hopes that they would be harder to track if they split up.

Nat twisted in her seat to look behind them. Ravyn did the same. There was a black Ford pickup behind them, perhaps a little too close to their rear for comfort. There was a glare on the front windscreen, so she couldn't see who was behind the wheel. Just that the jeep was inching closer and closer to their bumper. She turned back around and held Nat's hand tighter.

They were approaching a set of traffic lights, and the light had just flicked to yellow. Jay changed gears again, and they sped through the lights just as it turned red. Ravyn twisted in her seat again and saw that the Ford had done the same.

"Jay—"

"I know, I'm getting rid of them," he said, gunning the engine.

Ravyn was pressed into her seat as Jay picked up the pace, speeding down the slip road and onto the motorway. As they leaned into the curve of the road, Ravyn was pressed into Nat. They cut their way onto the motorway as cars flashed their lights at them, moving into the outside lane and flying past the cars on the inside. Ravyn twisted around again and saw the Ford trying to cut its way into the lane. A truck blasted its horn at the Ford as it rumbled past on the inside lane, and tyres squealed as the pickup was almost run off the road, swerving back into the slip road. She lost sight of it behind the truck, but it reappeared seconds later as it rushed along the hard shoulder, looking for a place to re-join the road before it ran straight into the roadworks just up ahead. It was steadily getting smaller in the distance, and the sound of horns from angry drivers followed them until she could no longer see it.

It was the only time she was glad for roadworks.

Then a bolt of darkness shot towards them, nearly driving them off the road.

Jay weaved his way expertly around cars in both lanes, his eyes flicking between the road ahead and his mirrors, easily doing 150 miles per hour. The streak of shadow tried to keep up, darting around cars and using them as leverage, but it eventually gave up and dispersed into the air.

Jay took the first exit they came to at full speed and had to brake hard as they met traffic at the roundabout. They were all thrown forwards, but Nat moved her arm around Ravyn's waist and caught her before she flew into the front of the car. The seatbelt crushed her ribs, and she stifled a cough.

"Tell the others we'll be twenty minutes, we're coming back around now," Jay told Excael, who nodded and took out his phone again.

Ravyn's heart slowly settled back into a comfortable

rhythm. Nat moved her arm to sit more comfortably around Ravyn's mid-back, her hand on Ravyn's diaphragm. Aunt Stephanie wanted to invade her mind, but Ravyn pulled the curtain and blocked her out.

You will not ruin this for me, she hissed at the memory of that scowling face. *You're not even my aunt, for fuck sake.*

They did not speak, just rested in the comfortable silence of each other's presence.

*****

Ravyn jerked awake at a loud bang and found she was being carried. She turned her head to find the person's face and met Nat's soft blue eyes. Nat gave her a gentle smile.

"That was the door, don't worry," she whispered, and they started climbing the stairs.

Ravyn looked around her. They were in a house with a wide wooden staircase, which they were now ascending. The stairs had glass running from floor to ceiling instead of a banister. The lights on the steps guided them safely to the second floor. There was a dull sound of shuffling feet coming from all directions.

"I can walk, you know," Ravyn whispered to her, and Nat chuckled.

"I know."

But she didn't stop to put her down, so Ravyn rested her head back against Nat's shoulder and let herself be carried upstairs. The gentle rocking of Nat's walk was enough to send her back to sleep, like the rocking of a crib that cradled a new born, the sound of their mother's breath a soft lullaby.

"Are we at that house you've all been talking about?" she asked, her eyes half open.

"Yes," Nat laughed quietly.

"Okay," Ravyn sighed.

Once they were upstairs, Nat carried her down a hall. The walls were painted white, and a polished wooden skirting separated it from the lightly stained wooden floor. There were a few dark scuff marks on the wood, but other than that, the floor looked brand new. Only the light above the stairs was on, and the further they walked down the hall, the darker it became. Nat turned a corner, then kicked one of the doors open. The lights were off, and they were met with darkness as they entered the room. Nat turned and ran her elbow along the wall, finding the light switch and flicking it on.

The lights came to life, blinding Ravyn. She squinted as her eyes adjusted. They were in a small bedroom, with a double bed, a wooden wardrobe, and a large window. The room was fairly plain. The walls were an off-white, as were the bed sheets. The curtains, however, were a dark red, like clotted blood. Her eyes wanted to close again and fall back into a dreamless sleep. Nat kicked the door closed with the back of her heel and walked to the bed.

She put Ravyn down gently on the duvet, then sat beside her, taking her hand again. Ravyn cast her eyes down to their hands, how their fingers interlocked nicely together. Nat's thumb ran up and down Ravyn's. It was a comforting gesture, keeping her mind in this room and not on the last twenty-four hours.

They sat in silence for a few moments, the only noise their quiet breathing. The room was still, undisturbed by their presence, as though it had been expecting them. Ravyn looked around again. The room was plain and simple, but then again, what did she expect? The house probably wasn't lived in for the vast majority of the year. They didn't need luxuries like lamps and paintings, pictures and plants. There would be nobody here to see them. Yet, for a house that was hardly touched, it breathed as though it housed a family of six, full of life and energy.

"I want to kiss you again." Nat's voice broke the quiet, and Ravyn's cheeks flushed red. It was so direct, no skirting around it or testing the waters.

"Oh, um…y-yes?" She didn't know what to say. Her awkward words made her cringe, and she quickly tried to save herself, more words rising in her throat.

But they never got the chance to be spoken, because Nat's hand found its way to Ravyn's face, pulling her attention away from the room and towards Nat's lips, which were now on hers.

Ravyn turned her body towards Nat's, kissing her back. One of Nat's hands stayed on the side of her face, cupping her jaw, while the other traced its way down to her waist and wrapped around it, pulling her in closer.

Nat pulled away first, her lips hovering just out of Ravyn's reach. Ravyn opened her eyes slightly, her breath quivering. Her heart beat hard in her chest, her stomach tying itself in a tight knot. Nat rested her forehead against Ravyn's, her eyes half open.

"I don't think I've said thank you for saving me yet," she said, and Ravyn sensed the smile in her voice.

"I wasn't really the one saving you, that was all Jay." Ravyn closed her eyes again, instead focusing on the comforting feeling of Nat's head against hers. Nat breathed hard out her nose. She interlocked her hands with Ravyn's.

"You were the only one of us who could figure a way out

of there. And, bonus, you didn't just fuck off and abandon us. I would call that saving us," she whispered.

Ravyn shrugged. Her cheeks were too warm. "I'm sorry I left you there in the first place—"

Nat put her finger on Ravyn's lips, hushing her. She tilted her head forwards, and their lips met again. Just like their hands, they fit perfectly together, like they were made to be locked together like this. A lock and key, a perfect fit.

But a knock at the door interrupted them. Ravyn jumped, breaking their bond. Nat pulled away, twisting her body back around into a neutral position, and crossed one leg over the other. The door opened, and Jay stepped in. The burning in Ravyn's cheeks intensified, and she pulled her eyes away from him. For a second, it was Aunt Stephanie who stood there in his place, and Ravyn braced herself for what was to come. But it was just Jay. He closed the door behind him and walked up to them.

"How are you both?" he asked, crouching down in front of them. Ravyn shrugged, glancing over at Nat. She couldn't bring herself to look Jay in the eyes.

"We're fine," Nat spoke for them both. Fine…maybe? Emotions were jumbled, tangled together like a ball of wires, unidentifiable.

Jay nodded slowly, then sighed. "I just wanted to fill you both in on what's happening with Brook. She's…unconscious, but Tammie is working on her. I know you told me what happened to her, Ravyn, but this is something we have never seen before, so if I'm honest, we don't know how to treat her, or if she'll live…" He trailed off, his eyes moving to rest on Ravyn's face. She swallowed his words, but they got stuck in her throat, causing a bulge to form there that tried to press tears from her eyes.

She couldn't lose another friend. Not so soon.

Nathan's face flashed in her mind, and she swiped it away with sizzling red anger.

"How did he do this? I mean, having a shadow inside someone like that should be impossible, shouldn't it?" Nat asked, shifting so she could uncross her legs. A chill ran down Ravyn's back, and the quiver paused in her lower back before releasing at the base of her spine. It should be impossible, but it had happened.

Jay just shrugged, inhaling deeply. "Apparently it's not. We really don't know, Natalie, but whatever Nathan is doing is much more dangerous than we thought. Anyway, I think John is in shock about the whole thing—losing Alec and now all of this. Excael is looking after him, but I think it might help if you went to talk to him soon. You're his friends; he might open up to you." Jay shrugged and scratched his beard before continuing, pain written all over his face. "And...I sent someone back to the hotel yesterday, after the attack. They found Alec's body buried out back, so they've brought it straight to Dunfeagh. His sister said they'll wait for us to get back before they bury him," he finished, his voice soft, his words careful.

Ravyn sucked in a deep breath through her nose, pursing her lips. Alec's name made a pit form in her stomach, and it was starting to greedily suck everything into it. She held back tears.

"When are we going?" Nat asked, her voice low.

Jay paused. "I don't know. I don't know if we should wait and see what happens with Brook, or if we should try to move her home and see if anyone there can do anything. I don't know how long it will be before the Shades stop searching for us, or *if* they will stop searching. We're having a chat about all of this tomorrow morning, so you're welcome to come and talk about it." He nodded to the two of them.

Ravyn glanced at Nat, who had her lips pressed tightly together. A lock of her dark hair had fallen down the side of her face, and it curled under her chin. Ravyn turned back to look at Jay. Her fingers were trembling.

"Okay. Thank you, Jay," Nat said, her words small and weak.

Jay shrugged. "Just get a good rest tonight. I think everyone needs it." He stood, his knees cracking as he did so. "Tomorrow, we figure out our next move. But for now, just rest." He moved towards the door.

Nat stood and followed him over. Ravyn also stood but watched him leave from the bedside. She didn't trust her legs to be able to carry her weight over there. His words had chained her heavy feet to the floor, unable to move.

He put his hand on the handle, then paused. "If you need anything, even if it's just a chat, you can come to me at any time. Okay?"

The two girls nodded.

His eyes met Ravyn's, and she held them for a moment, the eyes of a father she never had, before he looked away, opening the door.

"Goodnight, girls," he said, and Nat gave him a quick hug. He patted her on the back.

"Night. And thank you, again," Ravyn heard Nat whisper to him but didn't hear if he replied. Nat closed the door. This time, she twisted the lock and it clicked into place.

Ravyn persuaded her legs to move, and she walked slowly up behind Nat, each step making her knees wobble, her eyes still burning with hidden tears that she had to bite back. Nat turned around.

"Are you okay?" Ravyn asked quietly, reaching out to touch Nat's arm. Nat just shrugged, taking a slow breath in.

"I don't know."

"Do you want to come sit down again?" Ravyn's hand moved down to take Nat's hand, and she guided her back to the bed. Nat sat and ran her fingers through her hair, tearing out the knots as she did so. Her eyes were glistening with tears. Ravyn pulled their interlocked hands into her lap and gave Nat's hand a squeeze.

"Do you want to…talk about it?" Ravyn asked gently. Nat's eyes moved to match her gaze.

"Ravyn, I really don't want to think about any of this right now."

"Okay. Me neither."

They shared an inhale as they stared into each other's eyes.

A single tear had gathered at the corner of Nat's eye, just waiting for the moment to roll down her cheek. The sight of it made tears appear in Ravyn's eyes, and she blinked them away quickly. She brought her free hand up to Nat's face, and she caught the tear before it fell. Nat leaned her head into Ravyn's hand, her eyes drooping.

Their lips were together again in an instant, a tenderness behind the kiss that hadn't been there before. Nat's hands travelled down the sides of Ravyn's body, then wrapped around her midsection.

Ravyn had to break away to catch her breath, and Nat pressed her forehead against Ravyn's, her breath warm against Ravyn's skin. A smile appeared out of nowhere on Ravyn's face, but she couldn't stop it. She let it spread, and eventually Nat was smiling too.

"Sorry," Ravyn muttered as a short giggle rose in her throat. Nat shook her head, tracing Ravyn's jawline with her thumb.

Her thumb stopped briefly on the scab that was forming over her cut, then continued along to her chin.

"There's nothing to be sorry about," Nat whispered to her.

Ravyn sighed gently and closed her eyes. "I know what you mean about not wanting to think about it all. I don't want to remember any of it. I wish that when I wake up tomorrow, I just forget it all," she admitted.

There was too much spinning and spiralling in her head. She was trying to push it back and keep it at bay, so she could handle things one at a time instead of facing the towering wave that kept building and growing as it sped towards her. It was getting harder to do that though. That wave was still rolling towards her on the shore, ready to consume her and sweep her back out to sea, to drown her in the dark, unexplored depths of the ocean.

"Don't say that," Nat said gently. "It's not about forgetting it; it's about moving forward after it all. I don't want to forget. I just… don't have the energy to think about it right now."

Ravyn smirked. "Well, it's nice to have a bit of a distraction."

"Yeah."

Nobody here was unscathed. Nobody. There were scars that would not heal, wounds that would not close, cuts that would be infected and bruises that would not fade. She could feel every one of them on her skin, a reminder of what had happened.

"When they took me to see you, I didn't know what to think," Nat continued. "I thought you were taking the easy way out and giving yourself over to him." She shook her head. "I wasn't expecting a kiss." She brought her fingers down Ravyn's throat, feeling every crevice and bump on her skin.

Ravyn smiled shyly. "I wasn't either, to be honest."

Nat laughed, her hands running back down her sides again. But this time they didn't wrap around her midsection; they found their way under the fabric and to Ravyn's skin. A bolt of electricity shot through her with the contact.

Ravyn melted into the next kiss, allowing their lips to fit perfectly against each other again. Two jigsaw pieces coming together faultlessly, finally completing the puzzle.

They were two doves with silky white feathers, swirling through the sky as they danced in the midday heat, the sun kissing their backs. The endless blue sky, with wisps of clouds floating across it, was the birds' world to explore. The wind whispered to them, singing sweet music for them to move to, carrying secrets that grazed their ears before they were lost in that ocean sky, in that sapphire blue glowing with the heat.

CHAPTER 16

Ravyn woke desperately needing to pee. She slid slowly out of bed so as not to disturb Nat, who was sleeping on her side, one hand under her head. A few strands of dark hair fell around her face. Ravyn stole a glance at her even though her bladder was about to burst, and her heart melted. She was so *fucking* pretty, but Ravyn had to drag her eyes away. She grabbed the fluffy white robe hanging off the back of the door, slipped it on, and hurried to find the bathroom.

When she got back, she closed the door quietly and slipped the robe off. She folded it over the end of the bed and climbed back under the warm covers, curling up against Nat's even warmer body.

She lay in the semi-darkness for a while, just staring at the dark outline of Nat's face and hair. How her jaw curved, how her hair fell, how her lips were slightly parted, gentle breaths escaping them. There were no sharp corners on her body— everything was a gentle curvature, soft and delicate. Her skin was smooth and silky, like down feathers on a bird. She recalled memories of last night, of their bodies pressed against each other, of the kisses and caresses and gentle innocence's of the late night. It brought a smile to her lips.

The sun eventually poked a light through a gap in the curtains, and it fell across the floor and over the end of the bed, greeting her with a happy good morning. Ravyn turned to face the ceiling and exhaled deeply.

Her mind drifted from thought to thought, and eventually other memories surfaced, memories she just couldn't keep away. Brook, silent and unmoving, barely breathing, lost to the world of sleep. Alec's face appeared in her mind, and his final words to her were whispered in her ears. Alec, who was now dead. She never even got a chance to say goodbye. That was the thought that started the tears. They slowly filled her eyes, then fell silently, running down the sides of her face and curling around her ears.

She closed her eyes.

And behind it all was Nathan. Smiling with his shark teeth, that stupid smirk on his face, delighting in the turmoil he was causing. Nathan, who had tormented her all her life, destroyed everything around her, took everything from her and burnt it in front of her eyes.

Her tears turned angry, and she wiped her cheeks clear.

She thought about knocking those pearly whites in, her fist planted squarely between his teeth as they caved in. She would wipe that stupid fucking grin off his face.

Nat shifted beside her, rolling around to face Ravyn. Then her arm slid across Ravyn's torso, cuddling closer.

"You okay?" Nat whispered, her face buried in the space between Ravyn's head and shoulder. Ravyn nodded, bringing one of her own hands up to hold Nat's. She looked at the intricacy of their hands, how their skin creased, decorated with crisscrossing lines. Their fingers slotted together, an unbreakable bond, delicate yet powerful.

"What's on your mind?" Nat asked.

"Everything," Ravyn admitted quietly, and her chest deflated.

Nat sighed, and nodded. "I know."

"Like, Alec…we were only just talking before it all happened, and he was being so nice, and…" She trailed off, her lungs empty. More tears pricked her eyes, and she wiped them away with her free hand.

"Yeah, I know… It's so strange not having him here anymore. I keep expecting to see him again, that I'll walk around a corner and he'll be there." Nat paused but didn't finish her sentence. A splash of tears hit Ravyn's shoulders.

Ravyn rolled around, breaking their linked fingers, and pressed her forehead against Nat's.

They stayed like that, curled into each other, until their eyes were dry and their breathing was back to its normal rhythm of slow inhales and exhales, breathing life into the air around them. Then Nat unwound herself from Ravyn and sat up, the duvet falling from around her. Ravyn propped herself up on her elbows and turned to face her, watching as she stretched and yawned

"Can I ask something?" Nat asked, her tears now dry. Ravyn nodded.

Nat's fingers traced the long scar that ran from her wrist to her elbow. Her touch was cold. Ravyn pulled her arm away.

There was a moment of quiet.

"What happened?" Nat spoke finally. Ravyn looked away, holding her arm close to her body. The scar was ugly and noticeable, barely healed.

"Shades."

"They did *that* to you? When?"

"A-a while ago. It was before I knew about all of this."

"*Shit…*"

Ravyn shrugged. "It's fine. There's not much I can do about it now."

There was a knock at the door. Both pairs of eyes turned to look towards it.

Jay opened the door slightly and poked his head in. Ravyn's face was instantly on fire, a blazing inferno beneath her skin. She turned her head away from him, and pulled the sheets tighter around her bare body.

"There's breakfast downstairs when you're ready, girls," he said, and Nat gave him a nod. He left, closing the door behind him with a click. Nat sighed, struggling with her hair, parting it to the side and brushing out any knots with her fingers. She looked down at Ravyn while she did.

"There must be a hairbrush somewhere," Ravyn said with a smirk.

"I can't be arsed to find one."

Ravyn 's smile grew, and she rolled her eyes.

Nat tore her fingers through the big knots in her dark hair, untangling it. She winced a few times. Ravyn watched, that smile playing on her lips as her cheeks started to cool. She loved the way Nat's hair fell around her face and cascaded over her shoulders, like gentle waves on the ocean. When Nat was done, she tilted her head back and gave her hair a shake, as though to wake it up. Then she looked down at Ravyn and smiled.

Nat pulled the blankets up from Ravyn's body, swung her leg over, and straddled her. Her spine arched, and her face sank down to meet Ravyn's, and they kissed. Slow and gentle, a cherished memory in the making. And for those precious few moments when their lips were locked, everything in Ravyn's mind melted away, becoming only a distant memory.

Eventually, Nat broke away and slid off the bed. Ravyn sat up and watched as Nat picked up her clothes that had been dumped in a pile on the floor and pulled them on.

"There are clothes in the wardrobe," Ravyn told her, and Nat shrugged.

"Ah, I like these ones though," she said, hitching up her trousers. Ravyn pulled her knees up to her chest and rested her head on the blanket over them.

"Are you coming for breakfast?" Nat asked, walking back over to the side of the bed.

Ravyn lifted her head but shook it. "I'll be down in a minute," she replied.

Nat nodded and kissed the top of her head. "I'll see you down there, then."

Nat left, and Ravyn was alone. Her mind was starting to sharpen again; the fog that had hung over it from last night was lifting, leaving her exposed to the storm that had been brewing inside her.

There was one thing in particular Ravyn couldn't seem to bring her mind away from: the newspapers. Even though the memory of her escape from home was severely out of focus, a dirty camera lens she was trying to see through, there were things starting to piece themselves together.

She didn't want to think too much about it in case things became clearer and she had to face them all.

She shook her head and rubbed her palms over her face.

She propped her elbows on her knees and held her head, staring at the creases and folds in the duvet in front of her, the mountains and ravines it created. The questions spun around her head, making her dizzy. Her stomach did not feel good at all, so she wasn't even sure she could eat breakfast. Maybe she should just stay up here?

She shook her head, more violently this time.

More and more questions popped up, and her head was becoming crowded. And far, far too loud. Now she couldn't even make out what thoughts were coming through; they all just jumbled together in one big, booming mess. She covered her face with her hands.

"Stop it, Ravyn," she muttered to herself, knocking her fist against her temple. But this just dispersed the thoughts even more, so that they became more tangled together, knotting and intertwining.

She picked her clothes up off the floor, trying to just focus on her hands, how her fingers curled around the fabric and lifted them towards her. Once she was dressed, she took a mental inventory and found that most of the thoughts had settled—some lying dormant, others only just starting to get sleepy. But rather than hang around and wake them up again, she left.

Ravyn made her way back along the hall, looking at each door as she passed. They were all closed, their secrets hidden a while longer. Like her room, there were no luxuries in the hall. No paintings, plants, or rugs, no side tables holding wedding photos and pictures of loved ones passed.

She made it to the top of the stairs and started to descend. As she travelled down, voices started to drift towards her, deep in conversation. She followed them down another hallway and through an open door into the kitchen.

It was much brighter in here, and her eyes had to adjust again. There was a glass alcove in the far wall, with the white curtains pulled back, allowing the morning sunlight to stream in. In the alcove was the dining table where Jay, John, Ryan, and Nat currently sat. They glanced up at her as she entered but continued their conversation. Ravyn made her way over to them.

"Morning, Ravyn," Jay greeted her, giving her a smile.

Blood rushed to her cheeks, her mind taking her back to how he found them this morning. "Morning."

"There's food on the counter over there, just grab a plate and load up. Oh, and there's tea in the pot, and you can make coffee if you want," he told her, pointing to the kitchen counter. Ravyn nodded and followed his gesture.

Across the countertop were plates of food, and at the very end were some mugs and a teapot with steam still rising from its spout. This was better than a bed and breakfast. She took a mug and a plate, got herself some tea, then took three slices of toast. She wasn't really sure if she could eat much more than that; her stomach was not feeling like itself this morning, and it grumbled bitterly at the sight of food. After she had gotten her breakfast, she took the plate and steaming mug of tea back to the table and sat opposite Nat.

"Did you sleep okay?" Jay asked her, and she nodded while tiny fires reignited throughout her face. She wrapped her hands around the blue mug. The heat travelled up her arm and down her body, and steam swirled around her face. She brought the mug to her lips and drank.

Nat 's plate was piled high with food, which she was tackling with her knife and fork. She glanced up at Ravyn and flashed her a smile before returning to her food. Ravyn looked down at her toast, and her stomach protested. She picked up a slice anyway and took a small bite.

It tasted like poison in her mouth, and her stomach rejected the prospect of swallowing it.

She looked down to stop people seeing her face scrunch up

as she chewed quickly and swallowed it to get it out of her mouth.

Her stomach didn't like that.

Ryan and Jay returned to their conversation, and Nat occasionally piped in with her mouth half full. Ravyn didn't really pay any attention to their words; her focus was on trying not to throw up. As well as her stomach, there was now a feeling of sickness in her throat. She put down her half-eaten slice of toast and returned to her tea, holding it in both hands close to her face. Its warmth was inviting, and it was welcomed by her taste buds and seemed to please her stomach too.

Her eyes flicked to the left, and she looked at John. Like her, he only had a few slices of toast on his plate, but he hadn't even tried to touch them. He just stared down at it, unmoving except for the slow rise and fall of his shoulders as he breathed. He looked drained, all the life sucked from his eyes, his body a mere vessel of what it used to be.

"Are you okay, John?" Jay asked, and Ravyn quickly looked away from John as he raised his head.

"Yeah."

He looked back down.

"I know you probably don't feel like it, but you need to eat. You need energy," Jay said quietly. Ryan turned to John and gave him a pat on the shoulder.

"If you don't eat, the aeroplane will have to take over." Ryan grinned, picking up a slice of toast. He started flying it through the air, making plane noises. Nat choked on her food and erupted into a coughing fit. Ravyn grinned, and Jay shook his head, but Ravyn saw a smile there too. John's lips tugged upwards, and he hung his head down, his shoulders quivering.

"Open wide." Ryan flew the slice of toast towards John's face and started poking his cheek. John bat his hand away, the smile on his face starting to disappear. His jaw tightened, and his lips pressed together.

"Ryan," Jay admonished gently, and Ryan stopped, putting the slice in John's hand before he turned away. John just put it back on the plate.

A suffocating and awkward lull fell over them, the air heavy with static, like the moments before the first clap of thunder.

"Where are the others?" Ravyn asked quietly, her voice cutting through the stillness.

"Excael and Clio are searching outside to make sure there aren't any stray Shades hanging around. Tammie is with Brook," Jay told her, and she nodded.

"We were just talking about our plan for today," Ryan told her.

"I know the timing is not great, but I think it would be beneficial to teach you how to use your abilities today. How do you feel about that?" Jay asked, one eyebrow raised.

Her eyes widened.

Her heart stopped.

And all the air was sucked out of her lungs.

"Yeah. Yeah, okay," she said after a moment, a smile playing on her lips. She couldn't hold it back. It spread across her face, pushing up her cheeks and lighting up her eyes.

She was finally stepping into this world, for real. She was becoming one of them. One of the Ethereal. Like her mother.

An Illusionist.

Ravyn, the Illusionist.

She had big boots to fill.

But Nathan—

"Perfect, we can start this afternoon. I have some things to sort out first," Jay told her, interrupting her thoughts.

His words got lost amid the excitement that was bubbling

inside her. Her body wanted to jump up and down, to grab Jay by the shoulders and thank him, again and again. But she kept herself rooted to the chair, her feet planted firmly on the floor. Only her smile was out of control, trying to spread even wider than her lips would allow.

"We also think it would be best if we waited here until we can figure out what is wrong with Brook, or at least let Tammie stabilise her enough to make the rest of the journey," Jay continued. Before she had a chance to speak, John cut in.

"What's wrong with her is that she is a traitor. She shouldn't even be here. We should have left that bitch back there with Nathan. It's what she wanted anyway," he growled, his voice rumbling like thunder. Ravyn looked over at him, biting her tongue. Her smile faded quickly, dissolving into nothing. She didn't dare speak.

Ryan patted John's shoulder. "All right, just take a deep breath," he told him gently, but John pushed his hand away.

"Don't tell me to calm down!" His fiery eyes moved to Jay. "Why are you trying to protect her? She betrayed us and nearly got us all killed!" he spat. His hands were clenched into fists on the table. Ravyn sank back in her chair, away from the boiling-red anger that surrounded him.

"Can we not do this so early in the morning?" Nat said, a hint of sarcasm in her voice, but John wasn't in the mood for sarcasm or petty conversations. He stood violently, knocking the table as he did, then stormed off. His booming footsteps marched upstairs.

Some of Ravyn's tea had spilled from her cup and pooled on the glass table.

She let out a shaky exhale.

Every ounce of excitement was nowhere to be seen, like it had never been there in the first place.

"Natalie." From the corner of her eye, Ravyn saw Jay give Nat a scolding look. Nat held up her hands in defence.

"What?" she protested, rolling her eyes. Her cheeks were flushed, her eyes heavy with annoyance.

"Just leave him alone, please. Don't antagonize him," Jay sighed, stroking his beard. Nat just rolled her eyes again.

"You know, you don't have to comment on everything," Ryan mumbled. Nat's head snapped around to look at him, her hair flying and her jaw clenched tight.

"Fuck off, Ryan." She stabbed a sausage on her plate with her fork.

"He's just lost his best friend, Nat," Ryan tried to reason with her. Ravyn sank further into her chair, not ready for another argument. Not yet. The last thing she wanted was to be caught in the middle of a fiery explosion.

"Well, I lost two," Nat growled, ending the conversation.

CHAPTER 17

Ravyn sat in her room on the edge of the bed, hands folded over each other on her lap. She just stared at the wall, not really thinking about anything, but her abdomen was clenched tight, and her throat was threatening to close on her. The house was quiet, still, placid even. There were no raised voices, no banging footsteps, just a dull hush that everyone felt and nobody wanted to disturb.

The silence was better than the arguments. That was one thing she was glad about.

The air was heavy, suffocating her as she sat. She had thought about opening a window when she'd first sat down, but that thought was lost underwater, muffled and drowning silently while her back was turned to it, and she stared at the blankness in front of her.

Nathan occupied most of her thoughts—his smug smile, the crooked crown she wanted to knock off his head.

There was a soft knock at the door, and she snapped out of her daze, looking up.

Nat was standing in the doorway, watching her with one corner of her mouth lifted.

"Sorry to interrupt your thoughts," she said. "Can I come in?"

Ravyn nodded and moved over on the bed to make some space for her. Nat closed the door, and sank down into the mattress beside Ravyn.

"What were you thinking about?" Nat asked, and Ravyn just shrugged. She didn't really want to talk about it right now.

"Just... stuff."

"Stuff," Nat repeated, and gave a short chuckle.

"Yeah. Stuff." Ravyn shrugged again.

"Okay, you don't have to tell me if you don't want to. I came up to ask you something," Nat said slowly, her eyes carefully examining Ravyn's face. Ravyn raised her eyebrows.

"I suppose, I just wanted to ask if this is too much for you?"

Ravyn's eyebrows switched to frowning. She repeated Nat's words in her head, not able to make any sense of them.

"What do you mean?" she asked.

"Like, is *this*," she pointed to herself and then Ravyn, "too much? Us, I mean. Do you need me to give you space, or—"

"No, no!" Ravyn's voice raised higher than she expected, bordering on a shout, and she cleared her throat before continuing. "No, it's not. I...I like being around you."

A smile grew on Nat's face.

"So are you okay to keep sharing this room with me, or do I need to set you up some blankets on the floor somewhere?" Nat joked, and Ravyn chuckled, giving her arm a gentle swat.

"It's okay, I think I can put up with you for a little longer."

"Good, because I like having you in my bed," Nat smirked, and Ravyn hit her arm again.

"Oh, fuck off," Ravyn giggled, and leaned in for a kiss. Nat's lips teased her, kissing her nose instead and then her forehead. Ravyn caught Nat as she was about to stand up, and just about managed to peck her on the lips before Nat pulled away.

Ravyn held her hand, giving her a gentle tug back towards the bed.

"Where are you going?" she asked, pouting. "Stay with me a little longer."

Nat smiled, but shook her head.

"I have big girl business to take care of. Besides, I think Jay is coming up now in a minute to talk to you," Nat told her, and gave Ravyn's hand a squeeze before she dropped it. Ravyn's shoulders sank as she watched Nat cross the room.

"I'll be back later," Nat said, and walked out the door. Ravyn was left alone in the silence of the house again, and the space that Nat had filled in the room was quickly occupied by emptiness. She sighed through her nose, her shoulders sinking further as if there was more and more weights being added to them, waiting to see how much she could take before her bones gave way.

She rubbed her face. The silence and stillness of the house quickly took hold of her again, and all scraps of energy in her body were eaten up by it.

It wasn't long before there was another knock at the door.

Jay stepped into the room. He gave her a smile, and she did her best to return it.

"How are you feeling?" he asked, closing the door behind him.

She shrugged, clasping her hands together on her lap. "I'm okay."

He sat down beside her. "You disappeared this morning,"

he commented.

"I just…needed to step out for a while," she admitted.

He nodded slowly. "I see. I know things were tense this morning, but with everything that's going on, things are…*tough,* for everyone. Natalie and John are just short-tempered, that's all." He paused, then shook his head. "I'll stop myself before I start rambling. Are you sure you're okay? Do you want to talk about anything?" he asked.

She looked down at her hands and shook her head. "Not really. I'm okay."

Jay paused, and Ravyn hoped he wouldn't ask her again. She didn't want to talk. She couldn't put words to what was going on, and even if she could, she didn't want them spoken.

"I came up because I wanted to see if you would like to try to use your abilities?"

The words were barely out of his mouth before she was nodding. The tension in her abdomen released, and she could fill her lungs fully again, brimming with oxygen. A smile spread across her face, pushing up her cheeks and igniting her irises. She had been waiting for this, for her time to become an Illusionist, to follow in her mother's footsteps and use magic—*abilities*, she corrected herself.

"Yes, oh my god!"

He smiled widely at her, his eyes lighting up.

"And what if I were to tell you that you've already used your abilities?"

Her jaw dropped, his words knocking the breath out of her. But his smile made her laugh, and she shook her head.

"No, Jay—" she started, but he cut in ahead of her.

"I'm serious!" He chuckled, and her laughter died down. She stared at him, his words spinning around her head, struggling to sink in. He looked at her for a moment before continuing.

He was joking, he must be.

"I've heard from the others of…strange things happening, which I can only put down to your abilities trying to shine through," he told her. She opened her mouth to talk, but words were not able to rise in her throat. He waited for her to speak, but when she didn't, he continued.

"They told me that when we were running from Nathan, someone made the ground look like it had exploded to protect Ryan, but nobody who has the ability to do that actually did it. And the ground didn't actually explode; it was just an *illusion*…" He trailed off, his words starting to sink into Ravyn's mind. But there were thousands of doubts pushing the idea away. There was no way she could possibly have used her abilities when she didn't even know how they worked. It wasn't possible. Her lips parted again, and she tried to force words up her throat, but everything she wanted to say sounded wrong.

"I… O-okay," she stammered, her brow furrowing deeply. Jay patted her on the shoulder.

"How about I just tell you more about your abilities first? That might make it easier for you to understand," he said gently. She nodded, brushing hair out of her face as she turned her full attention to his words.

"Well, to put it simply, your power is the power to create illusions. They can be whatever you want, wherever you want. For example, you could make a bouquet of flowers appear on the table downstairs while you're still up here, but there wouldn't actually be anything there. It's not real. Make sense?"

She nodded.

"I should warn you, though, using our abilities drains our energy. If you overdo it, it could have serious effects on you, and if you *completely* overdo it, you could…well, die. This is why we only use them when it is absolutely necessary. We don't do it for show or to impress people," he told her, giving her a look. She nodded slowly, digesting all the information being thrown at her. A trickle of excitement was leaving her heart and being pumped throughout her body, invading all the blood vessels and organs inside her. Her smile was growing wider.

The prospect of death passed right over her head, the excitement of finally becoming one of them, one of the Ethereal, would not let her brain dwell on it.

"Okay."

"Your mother described it to me as the power of visualization, like you're forcing yourself to hallucinate. You see something so clearly in your mind that you see it in front of you, in reality. Make sense?"

She thought for a moment, then slowly nodded. "I…think so."

"Because we don't have as much time as I would like, we're going to skip some steps, and I want to see if you can do it now."

Her eyes widened. "Right now?"

He nodded slowly and stroked his chin.

"I have been trying to cut back training time, and some people have been able to access their powers in as little as two days. For the sake of curiosity, and that we might not have two days to learn, I just want to see if you can do it now. Besides, you've already been using them, haven't you? It's okay if you can't do it; I know I'm being hasty, and you might not be able to access your abilities just yet. If you can't, I'll go straight to teaching you how to manage and control your energy."

He tilted his head towards her. She bit her lip, then nodded slowly.

How could he possibly expect her to use them *right now?* It was an idea bred out of madness. But the look he gave her was reassuring, encouraging her to just *try.*

Well, what harm was there in trying?

She had to learn one way or the other, and if being thrown into the deep end was what Jay thought she needed, then she just had to trust him.

Right, okay…

You can do this, she told herself.

But can I?

"What…what do I make?"

"Anything you want. Something simple to start off with though." He put his hand on her shoulder and gave it a squeeze. "Remember, it's like forcing yourself to hallucinate. See it in your mind first."

She turned from him and looked at the space between her and the far wall, the space her gaze had occupied just minutes ago with no intention of using her abilities. Her mind flicked between a few things she could make appear, a nervous excitement building in her stomach.

Eventually she settled on a rainbow. That was easy enough, right? It was just colours in the sky, a beautiful arch stretching over the land, bringing a smile to everyone's face, gracing their day with serenity and a moment of peace, a moment of awe.

She took a long breath in and imagined the empty space of the room in her mind, trying to see the rainbow floating there, arching towards the ceiling before falling again, right there in front of her. She tried to make it so real she could reach out and touch it, but as clear as she saw it in her mind, it did not appear in front of her. She tried again, focusing harder, making the scene as sharp as it would go. She saw every detail, every colour blindingly vivid and saturated, the curve of the rainbow and how it melted away at each end, fading into the air.

But that was only in her mind. In reality, there was nothing, just empty space and a blank wall.

She sighed and shook her head. Her fingers tapped against her lap, drumming frustration into her bones.

"I can't do it," she admitted in defeat, her shoulders sinking. Jay stroked his beard, thinking.

"You saw it clearly?" he asked. She nodded.

"Hmm… Oh, yes, I remember now. To make it appear in this world, you have to shift your mental sight so it merges with your physical sight." As he said this, he held up two fingers, one pointed to his temple, the other in front of his eyes. Slowly, he brought the one at his temple forwards, until it touched his other finger. "You are forcing yourself to hallucinate. You don't just see it in your mind, you see it with your own eyes too."

"But you said I could make things appear downstairs. How do I do that if I have to see it with my own eyes?" she asked, clenching and unclenching her fists. She wanted to knock on her temples with them, to will her brain to just do it, just do this one goddamn thing. But she kept her hands on her lap.

Jay patted her shoulder. "We will worry about that later. Just try this one more time." He gave her a nod, and she sighed.

One last try.

Come on, Ravyn.

She looked back into the empty space and brought her mind back to the rainbow in the room. She focused on it for a few moments, letting her body become still and her thoughts settle. She forgot about Jay, about Nat, about the Shades that might be lurking somewhere nearby. She pushed it all out of her mind, far, far away from her. It was just her and that rainbow, right there in front of her, hovering in the space between her and the far wall. The flaming reds, ocean blues, forest greens, all arching through the air.

When she was solely focused on the rainbow, she tried to bring the image forwards, out of her mind and in front of her. She didn't really know what this meant, but she tried anyway. She tried to push it forwards, keeping the image sharp as she did. She nudged it closer to her skull, teasing it, tempting it, urging it to come forwards. Somewhere in her mind, there was a shift as a blockage was removed, and the image was now in the very front of her mind. Pressure built inside her skull as things shifted and changed. There was a heaviness in her forehead, like her brain was bulging, swelling, trying to expand beyond the capacity of the bone that caged it. Her heart leaped and her hands gripped her thighs, but she did not allow herself to get excited. She couldn't lose focus, not now that she was so close. Her eyes widened, unblinking. She focused on it more, giving the image a push, and it shifted forwards slightly. The pressure in her head intensified, becoming painful. She pushed it again, much harder this time, until it moved from her head, and her eyes blurred as her two sights merged.

And there, in front of her, sat her rainbow in all its colourful glory.

Her heart jumped a mile into the air, and she couldn't stop her grin spreading from ear to ear. Her fingers dug into her thighs, squeezing her muscles, clamping onto them tightly. The pressure in her head was gone, replaced by a sort of emptiness she had never felt before. Her eyes widened even more, her jaw dropping as she stared at this thing in front of her—the thing she had put there, the thing she had *created,* the illusion that she was solely responsible for making appear.

But the excitement caused her vision to stop suddenly, and once again she was looking at empty space.

But she had done it.

For those precious few moments, it had been there.

The world started to tilt as her body leaned forwards, but Jay's arm wrapped around her and held her upright. Her vision blurred, and the excitement in her stomach turned back to feeling like she was going to throw up, worse than it had been this morning. There was fire in her chest, burning her heart and travelling straight down her sternum into her belly. Jay hugged her tight against him.

"You did it," he whispered to her, half chuckling. She managed a smile and closed her eyes. "Wow. Well done, Ravyn. That was incredible!"

She had done it.

She had made an illusion appear right there, right in front of them.

She was an Illusionist.

Even though her body had just run a marathon, her mind was alive and buzzing, high on adrenaline and serotonin. The bird who had just unfurled its wings for the first time and leapt from the nest was now flying, soaring through the skies and clouds for the very first time. Stretched in front was a sky of blue, ripe for exploring. The gates to the world had opened, finally.

After a few minutes, her stomach settled, and she could open her eyes again. Her legs were still weak, her knees quivering, and she wasn't sure if she could support herself if she stood up. But she didn't need to just yet. She sat up straight on her own, without help from Jay, and smiled again, so wide that her mouth ached.

"That was amazing, Ravyn. Well done," Jay praised, joy

ringing in his voice.

Her smile widened, showing her teeth. "Thank you," she whispered.

She was an Illusionist. The fact wouldn't quite sink in; it felt like a fairy tale, a myth, not real at all. But it was, and she had made that rainbow appear.

She thought of her mother, tried to imagine her smiling at her daughter—the one to step up and take her place, the heir to her throne, the next to wear the crown. In that moment, there was a pressure on Ravyn's shoulder as though a hand was there, cold but comforting. Her ears started ringing, and a chill ran through her, but the feeling left within a second of appearing.

She sat up straighter and blinked a few times as her face wanted to frown.

"Using it for the first time drains you a lot," Jay assured her, oblivious to what had just happened, "but it'll get easier the more you practice. Just don't overdo it. I still have to teach you about controlling your energy, but I think you should rest for now."

She nodded, still unsure about what she had just felt, and turned to face Jay.

"What about making things appear in other rooms?" she asked, and he laughed.

"Don't jump ahead of yourself," he chuckled, ruffling her hair. "Yes, you can do that, but it is a lot harder. Your mother told me that it's easier to do it with your eyes closed, so you can use your physical sight to create the room and the object in front of you. You will learn all of this in due course, dear, but for now, I think you need a rest." He gave her a smile.

There was another thought playing in her mind, though, one that would not rest.

One she had been waiting on the answer for.

"But why does Nathan think illusions are a threat? He killed my mother because she was an Illusionist. The illusions aren't real, they can't hurt you. I just—I don't understand," she sighed.

Jay stroked his beard, his lips pursed. His eyes narrowed, deep in thought.

Then he sighed.

"There is a certain level of Illusionism where you can make some illusions become—"

The door flung open with a bang as it hit the wall. Ravyn jumped, her heart stopping dead.

"Jay, Brook is awake."

It was Nat.

Jay jumped off the bed and hurried out the door after Nat. Their feet pounded down the hall, echoing throughout the house. Ravyn stood, but her eyes became unfocused, and she swayed as dizziness hit her. She put her hand on the bedpost to steady herself. Once her vision came back and her head stopped spinning, she followed after them on shaky legs.

Nat's words repeated in her mind, urging her on. Her body grabbed onto whatever energy she had left over and used it to propel her legs forwards.

Her heart was pounding hard in her chest. Her mind was screaming at her legs to move quicker, but her knees were sore and shaking, and she stumbled down the hall.

She didn't know which room was Brook's. One of the doors she passed was half open, and she peered inside.

Brook was indeed awake. She was sitting up in bed, staring blankly at the wall with wide eyes. Ravyn's stomach dropped when she saw her. Ravyn inched forwards, standing just inside the doorway, leaning against it to support her weak muscles.

Jay was sitting on the bed beside Brook, holding her hand tenderly. She didn't pay any attention to him. Her usually slim frame was alarmingly frail and thinner than normal.

"Brook?" Jay said quietly, but Brook didn't register his voice. She continued to stare at the wall, her chest rising and falling in erratic movements.

Nat moved to stand beside Ravyn, her hand gripping Ravyn's arm.

Behind them, there was a patter of footsteps as someone approached them. As they reached the door, Ravyn turned to find John staring at Brook with cold eyes, his lips pressed tightly together. Ravyn's body tensed. John's eyes flicked to her and narrowed as they caught her staring. He turned and walked back up the hall, then slammed his door shut.

The bang made her flinch.

Ravyn swallowed a lump in her throat and turned her attention back to Brook. Tammie was sitting in an armchair at the end of the bed, her face pale and sweaty and her breathing laboured. Jay had told her that morning that Tammie was so advanced in her water manipulation abilities, she could use them to heal others, and it looked like working with Brook had both paid off and taken a toll on her. Brook was alive, at least, but the damage done by Nathan was still unclear. What else had he done to her? Would she still be Brook? Would she remember them, or were they just mere faces with no names?

Ravyn quickly pushed the thoughts away.

"Brook, can you hear me?" Jay tried again, giving Brook's hand a little shake. But Brook was completely spaced out, her head falling slowly to rest on her right shoulder. Her eyelids drooped.

"Girls, perhaps you should go. We'll call you if anything changes," Tammie piped up from her chair, her voice strained and breathless.

Ravyn nodded, despite wanting to just wrap her arms around Brook and hold her, to whisper to her that she would be okay. To tell her that she would make sure Nathan got what he deserved for all this. Her fist clenched.

But she moved outside the room with a heavy heart and a sigh. Nat followed, closing the door gently behind her. It clicked shut, and Brook was taken from them once again.

CHAPTER 18

The walk from Brook's room to their room felt miles long. Ravyn's legs ached every step, and every inch of her being wanted to run back in there and wrap Brook in a bear hug, to whisper in her ear and tell her everything would be okay.

Nat's hand remained on her arm, keeping her steady and keeping her moving. Further away from Brook.

Nathan's face appeared in her mind, and she gritted her teeth. She swatted his image from her mind, but that one glance had brought a thousand emotions rushing at her, trying to break past her barricade, to tear her down and make her bow to him.

The anger firmed up her knees, holding them steady as she walked. Her spine straightened, her steps grew more confident, and Nat seemed to sense it. She loosened her grip on her arm, but never let it go. Her touch was warm, comforting, keeping Ravyn grounded and keeping her mind from taking her to that dark cave where monsters resided.

Back in their bedroom, Ravyn sank onto the bed with a loud sigh. Nat chuckled and sat down beside her, curling her legs under her body. She closed her eyes and leaned her head on Nat's shoulder. The warmth of her body was soothing, calming, a familiar comfort. The rise and fall of Nat's shoulder as she breathed was like waves on the shore, her breath the sound of the sea as it rolled onto the sand.

"What a shit day," Nat said. Ravyn nodded.

"Yeah, what a shit day," Ravyn mumbled, and sighed through her nose. The highs and lows of the past few days were giving her whiplash. One minute you're creating rainbows out of thin air and the next you're staring at your friend suffering silently. She hated it, hated the constant stirring of emotions and memories, hated being tossed upside down and then the right way round again.

She just wanted one day, *one day*, where everything was steady and stable, where there was no rollercoaster to take her to the sky and then plummet her back towards the ground again.

"We just… gotta keep pushing forwards," Nat said. Ravyn nodded again. She let the full weight of her head lean on Nat's shoulder, and her eyes started to close.

"So, were you able to use your abilities?" Nat asked after a moment of quiet and comforting stillness. All other thoughts disappeared, and Ravyn sat up straight, grinning. Her little rainbow popped into her head, shining bright in all its glory, a beautiful array of colours that brought a little life to this otherwise dull room. She nodded. Nat smiled and gave her a kiss.

"Fuck, that was quick!" she said, her smile widening until her teeth poked through her lips. "Well done!"

Ravyn felt herself brighten at the praise. "Thanks."

"It took me two weeks before I could do anything, so you're doing a lot better than me," Nat said, grinning proudly. She gave Ravyn's hair a ruffle, and Ravyn pushed her away, smiling. Then she blushed and gave her a nudge with her elbow. "I don't remember what you said you can do?"

"I can manipulate water."

"That's so cool!"

Nat nudged her back. "Not as cool as being an Illusionist, trust me."

Ravyn shook her head, the corners of her lips tugging upwards. "I'm not that good yet," she told her.

"How does it feel, though, finally being able to use your power after everyone talking about it for so long?" Nat asked with a smile.

Ravyn thought for a moment, taking her mind back to that one second where she'd held the rainbow in the room, right in front of where they were sitting now. That one second had changed everything, and the door she had been peering through for so long was now open, its glorious and terrifying secrets standing before her.

"I just feel like I'm finally good enough to be with all of you." She paused, words silently running across her lips until she found the right ones. "Maybe now I'll be able to fight my own battles," she finished.

Power right at her fingertips, after being hidden deep within her for so long, and unknown to her for years. And now she had unlocked it, grasped it with both hands, and she was never letting it go. Even thinking about it made her body buzz with crackling electricity, igniting fires in her, filled with raw, untamed power waiting to be let out again.

And it felt good.

Nat smiled. "Ravyn, you were *always* good enough to be

with us, for God's sake! I remember when I was getting started… I remember feeling invincible, like I could do anything. It was so amazing." She squeezed Ravyn's hand again, and Ravyn smiled. "But don't overdo it either. I'm sure Jay's told you that already."

"I know. He also said our abilities are not for show, but can you…show me something, maybe? Just something small?" she asked, looking into Nat's eyes, which were the colour of fresh water.

Nat laughed and nodded. "It would be my pleasure," she giggled, and Ravyn grinned.

Nat brought her hand up elegantly, slender fingers poised, and water droplets started to form between them. They were balls of iridescent moisture, clinging to her skin. They curled around her fingers as they merged and grew bigger. The water started swirling upwards out of Nat's palm, first growing a stem, then petals that started to branch off from it. Ravyn watched in awe as a crystal rose formed before her eyes, made entirely of swirling water. She stared at it, at the intricacy of it, and how the water swayed and swirled, shimmering and glowing in the light. Then it dropped, and the water vanished before it even hit Nat's palm.

Ravyn's grin widened. "How did you do that?" she asked, locking the memory away into a box of those she cherished most.

"I take moisture from the air, and then replace it once I'm done." She brought her hand back down to her lap. "Over time, you build up a tolerance to using your abilities, so you can hold it for longer and do more advanced things, like taking moisture from the air. Before, I always had to carry a bottle of water with me, but now…" She trailed off with a smile.

Ravyn nodded, thinking back to what Jay had told her

about her powers.

Her mind spun with possibilities—all the things she could do now, all the doors that had been flung open right in front of her. She was standing at the gates to a new, unexplored world full of secrets and possibilities.

"Do you want to try something for me, now, seeing as we're all showing off? "Nat asked with one eyebrow arched, breaking her thoughts. "Only if you feel able to, though. I remember what it's like starting off."

Ravyn beamed, and she nodded. Excitement burst through her, gathering in the tips of her fingers and making them tingle.

"Sure." She tried to contain her excitement, but her wild, untamable smile gave her away.

She looked out at the empty space again, thinking of something to create for Nat. Something to test herself, something a bit more complicated than a rainbow. She could also make a rose, she thought, but then her idea turned to something Jay had said earlier.

She turned around to face Nat, then looked down at her hands, which were half open and facing towards the ceiling. Ravyn cupped her hands around Nat's, gently framing them. She brought the image of a bouquet of roses to mind, wrapped in brown paper with a pink ribbon tied around the bottom. She forced the image towards the front of her mind, where it became clearer and sharper, high definition. She could see the folds in the paper, the delicate bow that the ribbon formed, and how the V-shaped ends trailed down towards the floor. She could see every petal, so bright and vivid it was almost unnatural. Flaming reds and hot pinks, leaves so green the forests would be jealous. Then, slowly, the image started to come out of her mind as her eyes and her thoughts merged, and the bouquet appeared in Nat's hands, just for a few short moments, then toxic bile started rising in her throat, and she had to close her eyes, cutting off the image. She swallowed it back down, barely managing to stay upright.

Nat wrapped her arm around Ravyn's mid-section, and she squeezed her tightly, so tight it all nearly came back up again. Her head was spinning, her mind smothered by waves, but regardless, she beamed.

"That was amazing!" Nat exclaimed, and she hugged Ravyn tighter.

Ravyn opened her eyes and leaned on Nat's shoulder, allowing her body to rest. Her eyelids were heavy and wanted to close again, to sleep right here, in Nat's arms, where she belonged. She blinked a few times, trying to wake them up.

"Thanks," she muttered, the image of that bouquet in Nat's hands making her smile grow.

Ravyn closed her eyes as she settled into the tight embrace. Yes, it would be nice to just fall asleep here, in her arms… Ravyn gave herself a mental shake. Nat supported her weak body while she regained strength, not speaking a word, but a cozy stillness wrapped around them both. Ravyn rested her head on Nat's shoulder, breathing in the scent of her hair. There was a very faint trace of raspberry shampoo. Her hair was soft and silky against Ravyn's face.

Eventually, Ravyn felt strong enough to hold herself upright, and she did. Nat let her go but kept one hand on her arm, just in case. As Ravyn took a deep breath, her stomach growled.

Nat smirked. "We can get some lunch when you feel strong enough again," she said, and Ravyn smiled, nodding.

"Okay." Her tongue was still heavy.

"That was so cool! I can't believe you only learned how to do that today," Nat remarked.

Ravyn just shrugged, looking down at her hands. Inside, her smile beamed brighter than the sun itself, but her lips were tired and unable to push upwards anymore.

"I'm so excited for you!" Nat continued. "With practice, you will be able to do more and hold them for longer." Nat gave her arm one last squeeze, then took her hand away.

"Hopefully," Ravyn said.

Nat rolled her eyes. "Of course you will. I believe in you." And with that, she leaned over and pecked her on the lips.

A knock at the door interrupted them.

Nat pulled away, rolling her eyes at yet another interruption of their private moments. The door opened, and Jay poked his head in.

"Everything okay, girls?" he asked.

Nat nodded. "Yep."

"I came to tell you that Brook is feeling a little better, and she's been asking for you."

His words stole her breath. That meant she was getting better, that all the work Tammie had done on her was working. She sat up straighter, the lethargy vanishing in an instant.

Maybe things were going to be okay?

If Nathan didn't fuck them up again, a spark of anger told her, lighting up the deep, dark depths of her mind for a split second, and all the demons and monsters hiding back there became visible for that half a second before the darkness submerged them again.

"Oh, okay. We'll be in to see her in a moment, Jay," Nat promised.

Ravyn took a deep breath and nodded.

Resentment growled in those unexplored, out-of-bounds areas deep in her mind, the sound carrying through her head and echoing in her ears.

She gave herself a hard mental slap, knocking away some of the nay-saying thoughts and voices.

Nathan is not important right now—Brook is, she reminded herself.

Jay nodded and left, closing the door behind him.

Nat stood and held out a hand to Ravyn. Ravyn took it, and Nat pulled her to her feet. She swayed, and Nat grabbed her waist to steady her.

"Do you feel well enough to see her?" Nat asked, giving her a once-over. Ravyn nodded, saying nothing. Her knees were weak once again, her feet heavy as lead, but she needed to see Brook.

Nat bit her lip, nodded, and they walked slowly down the hall once again. The journey seemed much longer this time.

Brook was sitting up, her back against the headboard and knees pulled up to her chest under the white duvet. Brook lifted her head and turned to face them. Her face was pale, her eyes sunken and tired. They were bloodshot too. Her usually rosy cheeks were white. She looked like she was hanging on by a thread, clinging by her fingernails to the ledge, but at any moment, those rocks might crumble, and she would be sent tumbling down into the cavern that lay below.

Ravyn walked straight up to the bed and sat down in front of Brook. Her heart sank just looking at her. Tears were forming behind her eyes, but she pushed them away quickly. Nat closed the door and stood just behind Ravyn.

"How are you feeling?" Ravyn asked gently. Brook shrugged, squeezing her shoulders tighter to her body. She looked frail and weak. Her collarbones stuck out. She could pass for a corpse. The sight of her plucked at Ravyn's heartstrings and her tears threatened to overflow.

Ravyn hugged her, careful not to squeeze too tight for fear

that she might shatter and splinter like glass in her arms. Brook hugged her back, her hands resting against Ravyn's back. Brook was ice cold, causing goosebumps to ripple across Ravyn's skin.

"I'm sorry," Brook whispered, and Ravyn hushed her.

"You have nothing to be sorry for, Brook."

"I didn't know what I was doing." Brook's voice cracked, and something panged in Ravyn's chest, sending a shiver down her spine. She wanted to shake those thoughts out of Brook's brain, but she settled for hugging her a little tighter instead. Ravyn couldn't risk breaking her.

Brook reminded Ravyn of the baby raven that had been tossed from the nest all those years ago, back when this all started, back when she'd been unknowingly introduced to this world of madness and chaos. Brook was frail, weak, vulnerable, barely any muscle on her body. She had a near miss with death, and she looked it, too. The tears threatened to come again.

"I know. It's not your fault, Brook," she whispered back, almost choking on her words.

It seemed that Brook's skin had grown thin, and her bones were so prominent. Even the shirt she was wearing was too big for her small body. Ravyn took her mind away from those thoughts, her tears brimming.

"I'm so sorry," Brook said, her words quivering, and there was a splash of a tear on Ravyn's shoulder. Ravyn shook her head, her own stubborn tears ready to fall.

"Don't be," was all she could manage to get out.

Brook started sobbing, gripping at the fabric of Ravyn's shirt with bony fingers. Ravyn closed her eyes, rubbing her hand in circles on her back. As her open palm crossed Brook's back, Ravyn winced at how her spine jutted out. She could feel the bumps of her vertebrae, like knuckles running down her body.

"Alec is dead because of me," Brook sobbed.

The words hit Ravyn hard in the chest, knocking the breath out of her. They robbed her lungs of oxygen, filling them instead with acid that corroded her chest and burned her heart. She shook her head, a tear rolling down her cheek.

"That wasn't you, Brook," she whispered back, shaking her head again. Nat moved forwards and put her hand on Brook's shoulder. Brook released her grip on Ravyn and hugged Nat's waist instead, sobbing.

"I'm so sorry, I'm so sorry," she kept repeating, over and over as her voice got smaller and smaller.

Ravyn's heart crunched as a heavy boot stepped on it. Even after everything that had happened, Brook was still her friend. And this was all Nathan's fault, not Brook's. He did this, not her. The image of his smiling face came to her mind, and she forcefully shoved it back, her blood starting to boil. *Now is not the time to be angry,* she told herself. Brook needed her, needed support from everyone if she was going to get over what he did to her, and what he made her do.

The door creaked open, and Ravyn looked up at Jay with tear-filled eyes.

"I think you should let her rest now," he said quietly.

Ravyn nodded and stood up. She put a hand on Brook's back, then slowly backed away with a piece of her heart missing. Jay helped Nat unhook Brook from her, and he took Ravyn's place on the bed. Brook curled into his arms, still sobbing and mumbling words that Ravyn couldn't hear. Ravyn's teeth were clenched, both angry and sorrowful tears poking her eyes. Nathan's name was flashing in her mind, provoking her, prodding her like a wild animal to see what would happen, wanting her to snap. She tore her eyes away from Brook as more tears spilled down her cheeks.

Nat took her hand. They left quietly.

*****

Ravyn had done nothing for the rest of the day. She didn't have the energy or desire to. She lay in bed, staring at the ceiling, her hands clasped on her stomach.

Nat's muffled footsteps approached her, and Ravyn's eyes watched her as she leaned down over Ravyn's face.

"Come with me," Nat said, taking Ravyn's hand. Ravyn slowly pushed herself up so she sat on the edge of the bed, one leg tucked under her. She raised an eyebrow at Nat.

"Where are you going?" Ravyn asked. Nat only smiled, and tugged her hand. Ravyn sighed and allowed herself to be pulled to her feet. Nat guided her towards the bedroom door.

"Nat, where are we going?" Ravyn asked again. Nat opened the door and threw a glance over her shoulder.

"You'll see. Just follow me and be quiet."

They crept down the hallway, keeping their steps light as they glided over the wooden floors, past the closed bedroom doors and down the stairs. Nat kept Ravyn's hand held tight in her own, guiding her through the house towards an unknown destination.

Nat pulled her into the dark living room. Ravyn reached towards the light switch, but Nat pulled her away.

"Are you going to tell me what we're doing?" Ravyn whispered towards Nat's dark silhouette. Nat glanced back at her again, and Ravyn could sense the cheeky grin on her face.

She finally let go of Ravyn's hand and pushed the curtains aside, revealing one of the large windows that was nearly the height of the wall itself. Outside, it was so dark that the window turned into a mirror, and Ravyn stared at Nat through it.

Nat undid the lock on the window carefully, quietly, and pushed it open. A cold breeze entered the room, and Ravyn shivered.

"Come on," Nat urged her, swinging one of her legs outside. Ravyn stared at her, and shook her head.

"Nat, the Shades—"

"We're only going to the garden. Come on, you can't sit inside all day." Nat waved Ravyn forwards. Ravyn took a hesitant step forward, her mind screaming at her that this was a bad idea. Nat was now on the other side of the window, waiting, her hands on the windowsill.

"I don't know, Nat," Ravyn whispered, taking another step forwards.

"Five minutes?" Nat asked, and Ravyn sighed.

Five minutes couldn't hurt…

She climbed through the window and Nat pushed it closed again, leaving just enough space to slip her fingers through to open again. Ravyn's eyes slowly adjusted to the night, and she slowly spun around, taking in the dark landscape around her.

Nat took her hand once again and led her around the side of the house. Gravel crunched under their feet, but after a few steps the gravel turned to soft grass. Nat let go of Ravyn's hand and lay down on the grass, her body stretched out and her hands behind her head.

Ravyn stared at her for a moment before she did the same, feeling the grass first to make sure it wasn't wet. She lay back and stared at the dark sky, full of twinkling stars. She inhaled a lungful of fresh air, and slowly breathed it back out.

"The Plough," Nat said, pointing towards the constellation. It was upside down, but definitely there. Ravyn drew a line between the stars in her mind, and her lips started to turn upwards. She leaned her head back more, gazing up at the night sky. "It makes up part of Ursa Major. Can you see the legs coming off it?" Nat continued. Ravyn squinted, following Nat's fingers until she could see the shape of the bear in the sky.

It was so calm, so peaceful out here. A gentle breeze hushed them, gliding over their bodies with a cool breath, pulling them away from exhaustion. It caught on some stray strands of hair and let them dance in the air.

"This is nice," Ravyn said in a half-whisper.

"Yeah," Nat replied. She pointed towards the sky again. "Look, you can see Mars."

Ravyn chuckled.

"How do you know all this?" she asked.

"I thought every kid grew up knowing this. My parents used to take me out to star-gaze," Nat told her. Ravyn glanced to her right, where Nat lay, her eyes cast softly on the mystic sky above them. She smiled, then turned to stare back towards the heavens.

They stayed out for as long as their bodies could take it, until the cold chill invaded their bones, and they were forced back into the warmth of the house. They giggled as they crept back up the stairs and to their bedroom to cuddle under the duvet, embracing the warmth of each other's body.

CHAPTER 19

It had been two days, and Brook wasn't any better. The days had been filled by pacing through the various rooms, everyone wondering what was going to happen next. What they were going to do. Jay had spoken to Therese several times, but they both kept agreeing that it was safer to stay put than try move Brook while she was in this state.

Jay also refused to teach Ravyn any more, saying that it was best to conserve her energy; that the first time she casts an illusion was going to take days to recover. She didn't feel drained, or tired. She was itching to learn more, to do more, to explore what other magic her mother had passed down to her. What use was it to keep all this power bottled up inside her right now? At least she had Nat to distract her and keep her company. They had even managed to sneak out a window again and go for a brief walk through the surrounding trees, and the fresh air had felt like a drug.

Now Ravyn lay awake in bed, staring at the dark ceiling above her. Rain tapped at the window, asking her to let it in, telling her it would cleanse her of all this nonsense and chaos that she had been wrapped in, that it would soothe the wounds she was nursing. The wind was howling outside and spraying water droplets at the glass. She had been listening to the noises of the outside world for ages, hoping the sounds of Mother Nature would make her drift off to sleep, but they had no effect on her, and her eyes remained wide open. She inhaled deeply and let it out as a sigh. She didn't know how long she had been lying here, her brain refusing to shut down, even for a few minutes. There was a buzz in her mind, despite the fact that there weren't many conscious thoughts floating around in there. Every time she shut her eyes, no matter how long she held them closed, she could not sleep. The annoyance of the situation was not helping. She pulled the duvet up tighter around herself, getting more comfortable, but it made no difference.

She was still awake.

She knew what would make her tired, but, like both Jay and Nat had warned her, she didn't want to overdo it. *But,* she reasoned, *a little practice couldn't hurt.*

That one second adrenaline rush was too addicting.

It was her drug, her cocaine to ride high on.

She had big boots to fill, after all.

Practice makes perfect.

She sorted through images in her mind, trying to find something a little more challenging than a rainbow or a bouquet. A dog? No… A tree? No…

A storm.

That image lingered in her mind for a few moments, even though she wanted to dismiss it. She wasn't sure if sounds came as part of her Illusionist abilities, and she didn't want to wake Nat, who slept peacefully beside her, one arm over

Ravyn's stomach.

A silent storm then. There didn't have to be thunder—just a single cloud, a swirling deep grey, lit up by lightning streaking through it. A charcoal and ash colour cloud that moved and churned in the air, dancing above her, only broken by the short and sharp flashes as a rod of brilliant, white lightning shot through it. She brought the image to the front of her mind, careful not to add sound effects, just in case. She saw the image as clear as day in her head, then started pushing it outwards.

This one gave resistance, and friction started building up in her head, gathering behind her eyes. But she pushed again, much harder, until it gave way and slid out.

The angry, grey cloud floated above her.

She smiled as she watched it, a few streaks of lightning jolting through it. The cloud swirled, rose, and collapsed on top of itself. The grey held a slight blue tint, dark and ignited by the lightning. She pulled her hand out from under the duvet and raised one finger towards it. Lightning shot down and met it. It pricked her skin like a needle. Once the sharp tip met her fingertip, the stem of the bolt glowed brighter, as if it was gathering energy, building up to a climax. But her hand started to shake then, and her arm was growing weak. She closed her eyes, releasing the illusion with a smile, and her hand fell back to the duvet. She sucked in a deep breath, letting her body rest, but her lack of energy couldn't stop the smile from remaining plastered to her face.

Nat shifted beside her, and Ravyn half opened her tired eyes.

"Don't overdo it," she muttered in Ravyn's ear.

Ravyn nodded, her smile only widening.

That was awesome, she thought. Out loud, however, she

merely responded, "I won't."

Nat cuddled in closer to her, her warm body making Ravyn's skin tingle where their flesh touched.

"That was cool though," Nat said, smiling sleepily.

Ravyn turned her head to look at the dark outline of Nat's face. A few wisps of hair hung over it, and Ravyn pushed them away with shaking fingers. The hairs felt much heavier than they should, and it was hard to move them away. She grinned, her eyes growing tired. It had worked. Of course it had. Ravyn shifted closer to Nat and kissed her.

"Go to sleep, now," Nat said softly, resting her hand on Ravyn's arm and giving it a gentle squeeze. Ravyn nodded.

Nat let out a breath, and it warmed the side of Ravyn's face. She looked back at the ceiling, and her eyes started to close. This was her body finally surrendering to sleep, to rest and regain strength the natural way.

Her eyelids closed, and she pulled her arm back under the duvet. Nat was much warmer than the blanket, and Ravyn welcomed the extra heat. She leaned her head against Nat's, and slowly, gradually, sleep took her to a dark abyss filled with dreams that she would never remember.

*****

Sleep was interrupted by blood-curdling screams. Ravyn jerked awake at the noise, her body tense, muscles clenched so tight they hurt. Her chest was rigid, her lungs barely able to expand, and her heart punched her breastbone.

She quickly recognised the screams as Brook's, and her heart dropped through the floor. She clambered out from under the duvet and pulled on the dressing gown that was still draped over the end of the bed. She hurried out into the hall. Nat hadn't stirred yet, and Ravyn closed the door gently behind her, careful not to wake her again.

Jay ran out of his room just ahead of her, making her jump as he suddenly appeared in front of her. His footsteps pounded the floor, not bothered about who he woke as he sprinted towards Brook. Ravyn followed him to Brook's room, her mind racing so fast she couldn't even make out what thoughts were darting around up there.

The screams grew louder as she approached the open door that led to Brook. Jay hurried inside, leaving the door wide open behind him. Knowing that he was there to help was a relief, but her mind was still spinning out of control. What was happening? What was wrong?

She stopped outside the room, looking in through the open door.

Only a lamp in the corner lit the room, casting a soft, yellow glow on the ceiling. Deep shadows covered their bodies, draping over them like a blanket. Brook was hunched over on her bed, her head on the duvet that covered her knees. Her body was jerking with violent sobs and cries of pain. Jay was sitting next to her, his hand on her back. Ravyn's throat was swelling as she watched. Her fingers twitched against her sides, and she wanted to hug her and comfort her, to hush her and allow her to fall asleep again. Jay glanced up, and his eye caught Ravyn's, just as Tammie pushed her way past Ravyn and into the room.

"Go back to bed, Ravyn," Jay told her.

She nodded slowly, her eyes unable to leave Brook, then slowly backed away, pulling the door closed with her. As it clicked shut, a stake was driven through her chest. Even through the thick wood, she could hear Brook's sobs and the murmured voices that tried to console her and figure out what was wrong. Her heart wrenched, and she put her hand over it. Through her flesh and bone, she could feel the deep thumping of it as it pulsed inside her, scared. She took her hand away and started back down the hallway, her legs heavy. She wanted to go back in there, to hug Brook, to find out what was wrong and tell her that it was going to be okay. Tears stabbed the back of her eyes.

When she looked back, John was standing outside his door, watching her. He was only in his dark red boxer shorts. She noticed scarring along the right side of his torso—three small gashes hugging his ribs. But before she had a chance to examine them further, John disappeared back into his room.

She stood for a moment, allowing her heart rate to come down before she continued walking back to her room.

There was a strange feeling in her stomach, not quite butterflies but something else entirely. A gnawing sensation, toothless gums munching on her stomach lining. It was making her feel sick.

She closed the door quietly, took off the dressing gown, and climbed under the covers once again. Even though they were warm and welcoming, her mind was still begging her legs to return to Brook.

"Is she okay?" Nat asked, her voice sleepy.

Ravyn suppressed a sigh. "I don't know."

Nat leaned her head against Ravyn's shoulder. There was another sobbing cry from Brook, one that clawed at Ravyn's chest and scratched her heart. Tears filled her eyes, and she wiped them away before they could fall. She sat up, hugging her knees to her chest. Her ears picked up another sob, this one much quieter.

The feeling in her stomach was getting more and more uncomfortable.

"Ravyn, lie down," Nat mumbled.

Ravyn ran a hand through her hair, then did just that, though her mind protested loudly. She wanted to go back to Brook, to sit beside her and hold her, tell her it was going to be okay.

But she couldn't.

Nat curled into her, resting one hand on her shoulder. "She's okay, Ravyn. They're looking after her. There's nothing we can do."

Ravyn didn't reply. She just stared up at the ceiling, her hearing far too heightened for her liking. Her body itched to move, to do something to keep her distracted, but she lay completely still, just waiting for there to be some break in the noise so she could fall asleep.

"I don't know, Nat. I feel like something bad is going to happen," she confessed quietly, not even sure if Nat could hear her.

"You're just worried about her. We all are, but Jay and Tammie are doing everything they can for her. Try to get some sleep, Ravyn," Nat mumbled. Her breath was warm against Ravyn's shoulder, her words climbing Ravyn's skin and crawling into her ears, though she didn't really hear them. She was far too focused on the noises outside of their room, on the sobbing and cries of Brook that roamed the hall like a lonely lost soul, trying to find its way home.

Time passed, and eventually Nat's breathing became a slow, steady rhythm, her breath brushing Ravyn's neck. Brook's sobbing gradually faded away, and the house fell silent once again.

She tried to close her eyes, but her mind did not want to

245

sleep. Her eyes were not tired. Her body still itched to move. Her thoughts drifted from one thing to the next, until they eventually landed on the storm cloud she had created just hours ago. Hours, or minutes? She wasn't quite sure, but it didn't really matter to her now.

Perhaps…

No, she told herself. She had done far too much today; there was no way she was going to be able to go even bigger. If she used up all her energy, there was only one thing that would happen.

Death.

You'll regain energy when you sleep, she told herself, almost cheekily, like a challenge to her own mind, to see what she was really capable of. *Just this one time,* her mind whispered to her. *Go a little deeper this time. Go a little bigger.*

Just try it.

It'll help you sleep.

This power was far too addicting.

The more she thought about it, the more she wanted to do it. The thought of it brought a nervous, excited buzz to her fingers and toes. It wasn't the rush of adrenaline she was after this time; it was the sleep. That was what she told herself, anyway. And besides, she could take the day off tomorrow— or today, whichever it was right now—to recover.

Fine, she thought, finally giving in. *Let's do it.*

She brought her mind back to the storm cloud she had created earlier, but this time, the clouds covered the whole ceiling, crashing and swirling angrily, bursting with bolts of lightning. She constructed the image in her mind, building it up layer by layer, cloud by cloud, until she could imagine the storm that would hang over her and Nat, bursting with life, reaching towards the climax of the boom of thunder.

This was dangerously addicting.

Once she was ready, she started pushing it forwards to the front of her mind. As it reached her skull, however, it got stuck and the pressure in her head built quickly, becoming painful. She squinted her eyes and gave it one big shove, and out it came with an agonizing rip in her forehead, and she grimaced. The storm, just as she'd pictured it. Clouds churning over each other, fighting for room. Deep grey with spots of black. Sections of it lit up with lightning striking deep inside the clouds, an epic battle of nature. The lightning struck the walls, the floor, the end of the bed. She could almost smell the crackling ozone that hung in the air around them, crisp and fresh and charged with electricity. The clouds were enraged, hanging menacingly over the room, the storm gods and goddesses battling in the clouds.

But then it started to fade as breathing became hard and her chest grew heavy. As she sucked in a deep breath, it completely disappeared.

Sweat rolled down her skin, soaking into the bed sheets. She closed her eyes and lay still for a moment, her chest tight and constricted. Her heart was skipping beats. It palpitated in her chest. She could barely move her fingers. But as she breathed, and her body absorbed the sweet oxygen, everything began to loosen up, and she could smile to herself.

So that's the limit.

She shook the thoughts from her head. The feeling in her stomach was still there, but her mind was too tired to focus on it right now. She curled into Nat. Their bare bodies fit perfectly together, and Ravyn rested her forehead against Nat's shoulder. Sleep took her quickly.

CHAPTER 20

Ravyn could sense something hanging over her, stirring her from her sleep. Before she opened her eyes, she lay still for a moment, allowing her mind to completely wake up for the second time that night—or morning, she wasn't quite sure yet. At least it wasn't the awful awakening that had happened earlier; this was more of a gentle nudge from her dreams.

She rolled onto her back and slowly opened her eyes.

It took her eyes a moment to adjust to the dark, but once they did, she saw a dark figure standing over her, wisps of smoke trailing out from them and latching onto the air.

She jerked away, knocking into Nat as she did.

"What the—" Nat didn't even finish her sentence before a dark hand reached for them both, their fingers growing longer as they extended towards them, ready to take them and slit their throats. Ravyn's eyes widened.

Nat held up her own hand, and a shard of ice shot from her palm, right into the centre of the Shade's chest. They stumbled backwards, clutching at their chest. They hissed and exploded into fragments of shadow that slowly dissolved into the air.

Fuck.

"Get up and get dressed right now," Nat said, giving her a shove.

Ravyn scrambled out from under the covers, closely followed by Nat. She hurried to pull on her clothes, which were in a pile in the far corner of the room. The hasty beating of her heart travelled to her ears. Alarm bells were ringing in her head, screaming at her to hurry up, hurry up, hurry the fuck up!

"Jay! They're here!" Nat shouted out the door, alarms sounding in her voice. Ravyn looked up at her, standing at the door with only her underwear on, the door opened a crack so she could alert the whole house. If the rest of the house was still alive, that is… Then she banged it shut and continued pulling on her clothes. Ravyn's shaking hands were struggling to dress herself as her mind raced, a million thoughts flying at her and trying to knock her to the ground.

Nat was the first one dressed, and she opened the door just as Ravyn slipped her shirt on over her head, not bothering to put her bra on. She followed Nat out into the hall with her heart pounding in her ears and almost ran into Jay.

"What's going on?" he asked urgently, his eyes flashing between them. His hair was a mess, and he had bags under his eyes from his rude awakening.

"The Shades found us," Nat told him, and his eyes widened.

He took a breath.

Ravyn glanced over her shoulder, fear now starting to kick in. Her hands would not stop shaking. Her mind kept reminding her of what happened the last time the Shades had found them...

It replayed those awful scenes in her mind, holding her eyelids open and forcing her to look at them.

And all that blood that had been spilled. All the blood rolling down the stairs, cascading down like a waterfall. That sticky, red blood all over her hands—

"Shit. Are you okay?" Jay asked, and Ravyn turned back to face him.

Behind him, just a little further up the hall, John came out of his room and looked at them with a frown. Then his face changed, his eyes widening and his mouth dropping. Her body tensed and the hairs on the back of her neck stood bolt upright before words left his mouth.

"Jay!" he shouted, pointing past them. They all spun on the spot as a Shade charged towards them. Jay pushed the two of them away as the Shade jumped, tendrils of shadow snapping out from it and turning to spikes, ready to kill. Jay braced himself, raising his hands, and there was a low boom as the air around them compressed into a wall and hit the Shade. Ravyn's ears popped, then started to ring. She grabbed Nat's arm without even meaning to, holding her tight.

The Shade was forced into the far wall, then a shrieking scream pierced through them as the pressure built and exploded behind the wall of rippling air currents, causing the Shade to fade into the air.

Blood splattered onto the wall and rolled down towards the floor.

For just a second, everything was still and quiet.

The house braced itself for battle.

Jay jumped back into action. He grabbed the two of them and pulled them down the hall towards John, moving quickly.

Ravyn's feet kept tripping over themselves, but Jay held her firmly upright.

Everyone else seemed to appear outside their doors at the same time with sleepy eyes and messy hair, wondering what the hell was going on.

"They're here," Jay said, repeating Nat's words. He grabbed John as they marched past him towards the others. Ravyn's mind screamed at her that they were going to die, that this was the end and there was no getting out of this one. Nathan would not be stupid enough to take prisoners again.

Fuck.

"Ryan, Clio—get Brook and take her to the car. Everyone else, grab what you need and get in the cars. We have to go, now." He spoke calmly, but his words were sharp and pointed.

Everyone nodded in unison.

Nat grabbed Ravyn's arm and pulled her down the stairs, their banging footsteps carrying throughout the whole house. At the bottom of the steps, they took a sharp left and ran down the dark hallway. They hurried past the open kitchen door and took another sharp left that Ravyn hadn't noticed before and went down another short flight of stairs. At the bottom of the steps was a wooden door with three metal bolts drawn across it. Nat pulled them sharply and barged through the door without even allowing herself a breath in between.

The lights came on automatically and revealed two shiny, black Land Rover jeeps parked side by side on a dusty concrete floor. Behind them was a metal shutter door, spanning the length of the whole back wall. There were no windows, no shelves, no spare tyres or cans of petrol. Just the jeeps, ready to be used at a moment's notice.

Then something grabbed her from behind, pulling her backwards, out of Nat's hold. Ravyn gasped and lashed out.

Her elbow connected with soft, spongy shadow and almost went straight through it. One of its hands had a fistful of her hair; the other was around her neck. It squeezed, cutting off her oxygen. She thrashed her arms at it, trying to wiggle out of its grasp. Nat had turned around and was reaching towards Ravyn, but a whip of darkness lashed across her body, and she was thrown to the floor.

Ravyn reached behind her and grabbed the thing's soft head, squeezing as hard as she could. The thing screeched, its shadows loosening for just a moment before its head popped and the shadows slithered away.

Ravyn fell and landed on her back, knocking the breath out of her. She gasped for air, oxygen finally reaching her burning lungs once again. Stars exploded in front of her eyes. Nat grabbed her under the arms and pulled her up, just as John came through the door behind them with a bag.

"Hurry up," he said, moving past them to throw the bag into the back of the first jeep.

Ravyn's head spun, but Nat didn't give her a chance to steady herself. She pulled the back door of the first jeep open, grabbed Ravyn around the waist, and lifted her in roughly. Ravyn fell against the seat. She pushed herself up and clambered over to the far seat, her hands reaching blindly to guide her. Her throat was swollen, and air was struggling to make its way down to her lungs. Nat climbed in after her, and then John hoisted himself up, taking the last seat in the back. As he closed the door, Excael and Tammie came into the garage, each holding a black duffel bag. Excael got into the front passenger seat of their jeep, leaving the duffel at his feet, while Tammie took the second jeep, sitting in the back.

Ryan and Clio came next, carrying Brook between them, who was barely conscious. Ravyn caught John staring at her limp form, his fists clenched.

Ravyn caught his eyes as he shot a warning glance at her. She turned away, watching as they loaded Brook into the back of the other jeep with Tammie. Brook could barely keep her head upright. Ravyn bit her tongue as daggers stabbed her heart. Jay was the last to leave the house, and he locked the door behind him. He took his place in the driver's seat of their car and started the engine. It growled to life.

"They're probably waiting for us outside," Nat commented, voicing their unspoken thoughts. Her words sent a deep chill running down Ravyn's spine, and she bit her lip.

Jay nodded and pressed a button on his fob key. The door behind them started to rattle and slide upwards. Early morning sunlight peeked through the opening, peering in at them, unaware of their danger.

"Probably. I think those ones were to draw us out. But we're safer out there than we are in here," he said, turning to give the thumbs up to Clio, who was driving the other jeep. Ravyn glanced at her as she returned the gesture. Once the shutter door was almost all the way up behind them, Jay stuck the jeep in reverse and put his foot to the floor.

Ravyn was thrown forwards, her seat belt cutting into her chest. Her head nearly hit the back of Jay's seat.

The sun was just starting to creep over the mountains, and the land turned to rust under its glow. Jay jerked the car to the right, and they were thrown sideways. For a moment, it felt like it would tip onto its side, and they would be sitting ducks. Jay spun until he faced forwards, then stuck it in gear and shot off again, down a narrow laneway with tall hedges on either side. Loose stones and dust were kicked up behind them. The road was only made of loose gravel, and they felt every single one under the wheels, but Jay didn't slow down. Ravyn twisted and looked behind them to where Clio was following them, riding a little too close to their rear.

They reached a main road, and Jay took a sharp left. The tyres squealed as they mounted the tarmac.

"Where are we going?" Excael asked him. He was holding onto the handle above the window.

Jay took a moment to reply. "I don't know. We just need to get away from them," he said briskly.

Ravyn took Nat's hand and gave it a squeeze. Her skin was cold. She wanted to say something, but Excael interrupted her thoughts.

"Shit, Jay! Look!" He slapped Jay's arm. Jay looked in his mirror, and Ravyn twisted in her seat again. Behind the other jeep was a wave of shadow, tumbling over itself as it followed them. It swallowed everything it encountered, munching on everything as it raced towards the prize feast.

"Fuck."

The wave of shadow stood as tall as the trees on either side of them, rumbling after them like a tsunami. Ravyn's heart skipped a beat just from looking at it. If that thing plowed into them, it would surely kill them. Jay shifted gears, and the engine responded with a low growl. The other jeep behind them followed suit, racing along the country roads, which were filled with potholes. The thought of a tyre blowing and the Shades catching up to them came into her mind for a split second, but she quickly pushed it away and squeezed Nat's hand tighter. Ravyn looked at her face, how her lips were pressed tightly together and her eyes were staring straight ahead.

I will not let you die, she mentally vowed. *I will* not *let you die.*

Jay let off the accelerator, and the jeep responded instantly, slowing gradually until he took a very sharp left through an open gate. Ravyn was flung against the door and smacked her head off the window. Pain shot through her skull. He straightened out and put his foot down again. The wheels of the car dug into the soft mud, throwing it out behind them. Ravyn glanced around again at the other jeep as they glided to the right, out of the way of the flying clumps of dirt and tufts of grass.

They were out in the open, driving across a long, empty field with some woodland forming a boundary to their right. Everywhere was a mix of different shades of green, blurring past them so fast she couldn't distinguish them from one another.

Jay moved up another gear, and the engine roared.

Out of the corner of her eye, Ravyn caught sight of a shadow as it flitted past them. It moved quickly, just a black streak darting alongside the car. She didn't even have time to register it. Her eyes widened as it moved in front of them, and a Shade formed from it, building itself up to a full figure. Jay touched on the brakes, but didn't stop. He was going to kill it.

The Shade brought its arms up as they hurtled towards it, and a streak of snaking black shadows shot from its fingertips, right towards them. This time, Jay really did hit the brakes hard, and Ravyn was thrown into the back of his seat, her seatbelt forcing all the air out of her lungs.

The shadows hit them, and there was an awful crunching of metal as the nose of the jeep crumpled and buckled, and they flipped.

The seatbelt prevented her from being thrown around like a ragdoll as the jeep flew through the air. It sliced into her stomach as it held her tight against the seat, stopping her from breaking her neck off the roof as they turned upside down. Her hair fanned out in front of her, covering her eyes and getting in her mouth. There was a brief silence, just a fleeting moment where not even the sound of the wind interrupted them as they were hurtled back towards the earth. They crashed back to the ground, and the roof screamed with a crunch of metal as the full weight of the vehicle came down on it. Some parts of it buckled upwards as they landed on rocks, indenting themselves into the aluminum. Momentum flipped it over itself again, and they were upright for a moment as she saw the sky and the trees before being thrown forwards again. Ravyn's neck cracked as her head smacked into her headrest. The car roared as it flipped and tumbled over itself, eventually skidding to a stop on its damaged roof.

She hung there for a moment, black spots exploding in her eyes, her heart racing so fast all its beats just melted into one long thump. The back of her skull ached and throbbed, and she winced. All the blood was rushing to her head, and her vision was coming in and out of focus.

She blinked a few times, slowly releasing her sore fingers from the strap that crossed her chest, and she brought them to her head. She grimaced as she touched her temples but forced herself to feel all around it, checking for blood. It was tender, but there was no blood, thankfully, and she slowly brought her hands to the belt again. The seat belt had cut into her fingers, and small dots of blood swelled where it had broken skin. Over the piercing ringing in her ears, she heard a grunt and looked over.

Excael was tugging at his seatbelt, trying to get it off him.

"Are you okay?" Ravyn asked slowly, her tongue heavy, trying to fall towards the roof of her mouth. He looked around with a frown, then his eyes locked on hers. There was a stream of deep red blood running down the side of his face and onto his scalp. Thin pieces of glass glistened in his hair.

Behind him, the windshield was cracked and broken. There was blood smeared across his tattoo.

"Yeah. Are you?" he asked. She nodded. Her head was pounding, and her ribs were being crushed by the seat belt. She tugged at it, but it didn't loosen.

Then she remembered Nat.

She turned her head quickly, and her neck cracked painfully. Her eyes fell on Nat hanging lifelessly beside her. Her heart stopped, and she frantically brought her hands to Nat's neck to feel for a pulse. Her own heart started beating again when she found one, nice and strong. She put her hand under Nat's nose, and another wave of relief washed over her as Nat's warm breath brushed against her skin. She was alive. For now, at least.

"Nat's okay, but she's been knocked out," Ravyn told Excael.

While she waited for him to check Jay, she tried to look past Nat towards John. Her neck cramped as she tried to lean forwards. He too was unconscious, but she could see the faint rise and fall of his shoulders as he breathed. Sudden pain struck her head and she grimaced, holding the back of her skull.

"John too," she winced.

"Jay's fine. I don't think he's broken anything, thank God." Excael twisted around to her again. His face was starting to go red as it filled with blood.

"What do we do now?" Ravyn asked.

"I don't know."

Ravyn looked out her own shattered window and saw the other jeep laying on its side, the body crumpled and the paint all scratched away. She couldn't see inside it. If everyone here had all survived, then they must have too, right? They would be okay. They had to be. She thought about telling Excael they needed to get out and check the others, but something caught her eye and stopped her words from forming.

Just past the other jeep, the wall of shadows that had been following them was tumbling into the field. It was shrinking as it moved, eventually fading away and leaving only the shadowy figures of the Shades behind. There were a lot of them, all standing there, observing the scene that lay in front of them—the scene they had created—as though they were looking at an art piece painted by a great master.

"Um, they're here," she whispered hoarsely, not letting her eyes leave the huge group of Shades that stood in the grass, admiring their handiwork. One of them started walking towards the cars, and the others followed. Their black casing melted away, and they became people again.

Nathan led the group.

Fuck.

She sucked in a shaky breath through clenched teeth.

"Oh, shit," Excael muttered, starting to tug at his seatbelt again. Ravyn did the same, feeling around for the buckle to release her. The belt was tight against her, holding her firmly against the seat and refusing to let her go. She tried to pull it away from her, to give her room to breathe, but it would not loosen.

"You stay here, okay? I'll take care of this," Excael said before releasing himself from the grasp of the polyester seat belt. His body thumped as it landed on the roof of the car. Glass crunched under him.

Ravyn frantically shook her head at him, making herself dizzy. "You—"

"Don't worry about me. I got this." He flashed her a smile then kicked his door open. Her mouth dropped as she tried to protest, but he quickly pulled himself out of the wreckage and stood outside, dusting himself off. She watched as he rounded their overturned car, a limp in his step. Some of the glass shards he had landed on were poking out of his clothes, blood gathering beneath them.

She wanted to scream at him to stop, but the sounds didn't make it out of her mouth. She knew Nathan would not take prisoners this time. He was going to kill them all, and there would be no mercy.

The Shades grew still. Even from this distance, she could see a smirk on Nathan's face.

There was a rumble in the ground under them, a mighty beast waking from a deep slumber, crawling towards the surface. She bit hard on her lip, staring out at Excael. He stood with his weight on one leg, his trousers torn and blood caking his dirty body. All the muscles in his neck were strained, hands outstretched painfully wide, fingers pointed towards the ground. Every tendon and muscle in him appeared to be straining as he summed up his powers deep within the earth. The ground around him started cracking, chunks of grass and muck shooting into the air.

Before he had a chance to unleash the power of Mother Nature on the Shades, Nathan raised one hand towards him.

"Excael!" Ravyn screamed, but it was too late. A spear of dark matter shot from Nathan's outstretched palm and drove deep into Excael's chest. It went straight through him, then splintered into thousands of shadow fragments that raced back into Nathan's palm.

Excael stumbled backwards, his hands over the gaping hole in the centre of his chest. Blood fell like a waterfall from the wound, pattering as it hit the ground. She could hear it from inside the car, that sickening sound that made her skin crawl and her stomach retch. He sank to his knees and fell forwards, his face buried into the dirt.

For a second, his body resembled her mother's, lying face-down in her own blood on the landing. There was a screaming in Ravyn's ears, a high-pitched shriek of a child from long ago. Her vision blurred, and he became Excael again.

And he was dead.

"No, no, no! Oh my god!" Ravyn whispered to herself, her body seizing up. Her eyes were locked on his corpse.

Shit.

Oh, shit.

No, no, no, no, no!

Pain stabbed her heart as it beat uncontrollably in her chest. She clutched at her rib cage and cried out. Tears filled her eyes.

Nathan started advancing towards the cars again, his hands in his pockets like nothing had happened. Like he hadn't just killed a man, or like he didn't care that he had. There was that smirk again, that stupid smug smile. Her hands clenched into fists, balled up against her breasts. She snapped her out of her trance, and her heart kicked back into gear, pounding as it pumped blood and adrenaline rapidly around her body. One single tear slid from her eye and rolled into her hairline. Her top lip was curling back in a snarl, her fists clenching tighter.

Something clicked in her mind, heightening her senses. Everything sharpened—her sight, her smell, her thoughts. Every crack in the glass beside her glowed. The scent of mud and blood drifted up her nostrils, and she scrunched up her nose. She could almost taste Excael's metallic blood on her tongue. She had to survive. And if she was going to survive, pacifism was not going to work anymore. Not against Nathan. She had to get out of here, and make sure everybody else did too. She couldn't see any movement in the other car, so she could only guess that she was alone in this fight. But she didn't know if she could do anything to protect everyone. Sure, she was an Illusionist, but what would illusions do right now? What good were they? She couldn't make anything real happen, like Excael did, like Nat did.

No, she told herself. *You can do something. You have to.*

She quickly scanned through her mind, trying to find something she could use to send them scurrying in the opposite direction. She could make it look like Jay got out of the car and used his abilities, but she quickly shut that idea down. She didn't know the extent of Jay's abilities, not like Nathan probably did. He would pick out the lie in a second, and it would all be over. She would die; they would all die.

She could make one of the Shades betray Nathan. That would surely draw his attention. She quickly formed an illusion in her mind—a small wave of shadow swallowing both cars and making a run for it, into the trees. There she could release the illusion, and they wouldn't know. They would keep hunting, searching for something that even didn't exist. She just needed it to last long enough to lead them away. If she could hold that storm above the room last night, she could hold this too. Right?

Please let this work, she begged her own mind. *Please.*

She took a few deep breaths, forcing her body to calm down. She ignored the erratic thumping in her chest, ignored her tight throat, ignored the burning in her eyes as tears threatened to fall. The headache was getting worse, but she pushed it away and replaced it with the film reel of what would happen. As she pulled it towards the front of her mind, it started to get painful, like a bullet ricocheting inside her skull. It pulled on all her energy, sucked it in and grew bigger and bigger.

The pain was almost unbearable, a blunt knife sawing into her skull, tearing chunks of bone and flesh from her head as the illusion tried to escape. She couldn't even scream as it forced its way to the front of her mind.

She scrunched her eyes closed and gritted her teeth, pulling harder until it finally snapped out and into reality.

She kept her eyes closed, seeing it all play out as if from above, watching down on them. Her mind was no longer connected to her body. It floated above them, watching on as a goddess in the sky would. A small wave of shadow tumbling over itself scuttled past Nathan and the other Shades, then rose and spread as it submerged both cars in its darkness, taking hold of them. Nathan stopped in surprise, a deep frown on his face. The wave moved again, picking up speed as it pulled the wreckages further down the field.

"What? Hey!" Nathan shouted, his voice distorted. The wave turned into the trees and raced through the undergrowth.

The real cars were invisible, still upturned on the grass, protected from his view.

"What the fuck! Don't just fucking stand there; get him! Go catch that fucking *moron!*" he screamed at his followers, who stood dumbfounded behind him. One by one, their black shadow casing enveloped them, and they raced after the illusion. Sweat started to form on Ravyn's forehead. She had released the wave of darkness, but she had to hold the invisibility over the two cars for just a little longer, just until Nathan left.

He stood for a second, fists clenched at his sides and a vein popping out in his temple. His own wave washed over him then, carrying him after the others.

She released everything with a sigh, her limbs falling weak

and dangling towards the roof of the car. She retched as bile rose in her throat, the acidic taste burning her mouth. She swallowed it back down again, trying to work against gravity. A laugh was building, but she didn't have the energy to push it out, so it hung in her chest for a few moments while she slowly regained her energy. Her eyes were heavy, her vision darkening around the edges.

Energy rushed to her weakened muscles, and gradually, breathing became easier. Eventually she was able to raise her hand and fumble around for the buckle. She found it and pressed it slowly, but that didn't stop her from falling out of the seat and landing on her side. She grunted, sharp pain shooting through her ribs. She lay there for a moment, curled up in a ball, and finally, the laugh came. She covered her mouth and giggled into her numb fingers.

The laugh stopped, and she hugged her knees tighter against her chest, breathing heavily. Minutes ticked past painfully slowly as she could barely even raise her arm, but eventually, she had gathered enough energy to pull herself out of the wreckage.

The door was jammed, but the window was cracked. She threw her weight against it, eventually pushing through it. Glass rained down on her, and she shook it off. Some of it stuck into the skin around her neck and hands, and she carefully brushed them away. Blood smeared across her skin, but she didn't care. She dragged herself out through the broken window, scraping her sides as she did so and tearing through the fabric of her jacket. She grunted, her arms weak and shaking frantically. Once she was out of the car, she lay on the glass-covered ground, staring up at the brightening sky.

The clouds were sparse yet dark, a promise of rain. A murder of crows flew overhead, shouting down to her, their words masked behind the squawking of their voices. She blinked a few times, slowing her breathing, then pushed herself up and crawled over to the other wreckage. Her arms shook and her muscles strained as she dragged her body over, but adrenaline kept her going, urging her on, begging her to move. She didn't know how long she would have until the Shades figured it out. There was no time for lying around and waiting to feel better.

And if she died, if her energy reserves became used up and her heart gave in, then at least she had kept the others safe until they woke up and could hopefully get away themselves.

She ignored the thought.

You are not dying today, Ravyn, she told herself firmly.

Once she had reached the other overturned jeep, she used it to pull herself to her feet. The jagged metal sliced her fingertips open. A rush of dizziness swept over her, nearly knocking her back down again. She held onto the crumpled metal frame to steady herself, her eyes closed and her lungs labouring.

Eventually, she opened her eyes again and let go of the frame. Bright red blood stained the place where she'd held, and drops of it fell from her hands. She wiped her hands against her thighs, and her fingers stung.

There was a nagging feeling in the pit of her empty stomach that they were all dead. Nobody had tried to escape from the wreckage yet. She had passed Excael's body on the way here but refused to look at it. She couldn't, not if she wanted to get out of here alive. There was no time for mourning. They could do that later, when they were safe. But not now. She knew Nat, John, and Jay were okay, just unconscious. She could deal with that. But if Brook, Tammie, Clio, and Ryan were dead, she wasn't so sure how she could cope. They had already lost enough people to this fucking stupid war; they didn't need to lose any more.

The windscreen was heavily damaged and parts of it were stained red. Her heart dropped straight through Hell itself. She crouched to look inside.

Ryan, she knew instantly, was dead. His head had smashed into the windscreen and split open. Blood gushed from a large open wound the size of her hand. She could see his red-stained skull beneath the torn flesh on his forehead. His unseeing eyes stared straight ahead, glossed over like marbles.

He wasn't breathing.

She jerked away from the car and threw up. Vomit landed in front of her and splashed onto her shoes. Water streamed from her eyes as she retched.

Fuck, no.

Oh no.

No, no, no!

Ravyn closed her eyes and forced herself to calm down once again. She took control of her breathing, taking long inhales and long exhales. The sour taste of sick lingered in her mouth, and she spit on the ground. She stayed still for a minute or two, hands on her knees, bringing her shaking body back under control. Now was not the time to be freaking out.

You have to check on the others, she told herself. *Don't look at him, just check the others.*

She slowly straightened up, giving her head a shake. Her mind was screaming at her, telling her to hurry up, that there wasn't enough time to be taking the piss and standing around waiting for something to happen. She took another long breath in, brushed her dirty hair out of her face, and was about to start back towards the car when there was a chuckle behind her.

CHAPTER 21

S he froze, her limbs locking into place.

She knew that laugh. She knew the voice that carried the laugh. She knew the smile that would undoubtedly be on his face, a smile she despised more than anything in this world.

Shit.

"My God, you are sneaky, aren't you," he said, and she could almost hear the smirk on his lips. Ravyn bit hard on her tongue, forcing her body to wake up again and break out of this trance.

She turned slowly to face Nathan.

He stood with his hands in his pockets, a dark expression on his face. His eyebrows were set in a straight line, eyes hard and focused. One side of his mouth was lifted slightly. His suit was a little ruffled, and his black shoes had mud caked around the soles. She stared at him, carefully picking her words, but he saved her breath.

"Clever, though, I'll give you that," he said, taking his hands out of his pockets to adjust the sleeves of his suit.

As Ravyn stared at him, anger started to build in her stomach. It was hot, red hot and made her cheeks flush. Ryan and Excael were dead because of him. Alec was dead because of him. Brook was hurt, Nat was hurt, John and Jay were hurt... Her jaw clenched, and her teeth ground against each other as everyone's faces appeared in her mind.

"So I've heard," she said sarcastically.

A grin slowly spread over his face, and he licked his lips. "Oh, Ravyn. I know you're scared, and you can try to cover it with sarcasm all you want, but I can hear it in your voice. You can't fool me again."

She pursed her lips and clasped her hands in front of her. There was no way she could use her powers again, not yet. She was too weak, and he knew her tricks now. He would see right through anything she could try. If she had a bit more time, if she could save up some more energy, she could pull off something big again. But for now, she couldn't rely on her illusions to get her out of this.

"You tricked me with Jay. That was very annoying, Ravyn. *Very* annoying, and it cost me a lot. I will admit, I should have seen it coming, but you just seemed so...genuine and naïve. Little Ravyn, scared and alone, in need of guidance. Silly me. And now, you try to use those little illusion powers of yours to trick me again, make me think one of my own betrayed me," he tutted, shaking his head. "I didn't think you would be able to learn so quickly. I thought we'd have more time to get to know each other and play this little game. Once again, silly me."

Ravyn shifted her weight to her other leg. His grin grew wider. Shark teeth flashed at her, and her anger grew hotter, starting to simmer in her stomach.

"I won't underestimate you again, trust me. I have learned

my lesson."

"I'm good, though, aren't I? With my abilities. I only learned how to use them a few days ago, you know," she told him, allowing her own little smirk to appear on her lips, masking the flames that were rising up her throat. His brow furrowed, just for a second, before it relaxed again.

Keep him talking.

"But do you know what that means, darling?" he asked.

She shook her head.

He took a step forward, and she took one back.

"You are now my biggest threat, and that means you have to die."

She gulped, thinking quickly.

"A teenager is your biggest threat?" she said.

That smug smile faded, and his lips set in a hard line. "Don't get cocky, now," he warned.

"Is that a threat?" she teased.

His jaw clenched. "I could turn every single one of your friends against you, just like I did with Brook. I could do it to you too. Only…sometimes the process can be quit…*damaging.* Fatal, even. What if I were to try it on Natalie first, hmm? Would you like to watch me rip your girlfriend apart from the inside out?"

Her heart skipped a beat. The smirk on her face dropped, and her body wanted to throw up. Her imagination showed her horrific images of a meaty body missing chunks of flesh, oozing with blood. Bones poking through what remained of the mangled flesh, skin hanging in drapes over the gaping wounds—

She cleared her throat, her stomach on the verge of retching again.

"Brook was only the second successful test I've had. I've

been experimenting for years, trying to see if I could do it. I lost count of how many bodies were splattered over the walls. Sometimes I still find bits of rotting flesh on the floors. Do you really want that for your friends?" he continued, hammering the gruesome images into her mind with thick, rusty nails.

"You don't have the balls to do that," Ravyn spat through clenched teeth. He laughed loudly, and the sound carried on the wind into the forest behind her. "I would kill you before you even had the chance."

"No, sweetheart, you wouldn't. Stop playing games, now. You might be a quick learner and have a smart-arse mouth, but you still have absolutely no idea what you are doing or what you are getting yourself into—"

"You don't know anything about me or what I can do," she snarled.

There were too many ghosts surrounding her, too many bodies lying behind her to stop the words from leaving her mouth.

Easy now, Ravyn, she told herself. But the fire in her stomach was only burning brighter.

He took a step towards her, gracefully gliding over the grass. She moved with him, taking a step backwards. This was their dance, slow and simple, easy movements that followed the beat carried in the wind.

"Enough—"

"Why don't you just leave? We're not doing anything, we just want to get home," she said, cutting him off.

"And let you run around unsupervised? I don't think so. You know nothing about this world, Ravyn. Stop pretending like you do."

"You sound like a lunatic."

He sighed, rolling his eyes. "What you don't understand, Ravyn, is that our world is not separate from the normal world. You can say you want to live in peace all you like, but it's never going to happen. You all have this idea of a perfect, utopian lifestyle that you are never going to achieve. Because eventually, the other world will find out about us, whether you like it or not. We can't exist in secret for much longer. And what happens when they find out? They're going to turn on us, because humans can't accept that there are things higher than them in the food chain. They will hunt us down and kill us. Are you going to just run and hide then, like you always do?" He snorted with laughter. "What Jay and the rest of you scumbags don't understand is that there has to be *one* overarching power, so that when the time comes that the world finds out about us, we take control instantly and squash any sort of rebellion before it even happens. We become the government, and they will learn to live under us. I just need to get rid of any competition and make it crystal clear who is in charge here, so that when the time comes, the Shades are ready," he said, cocking his head to the right. "You're just a child playing dress-up as an adult. You wouldn't understand."

She pursed her lips. "You're not making any sense; you're still just a fucking lunatic."

He laughed and took another step forward. She matched him, taking a step back, keeping the same distance between them. She would need it for when she ran.

"At least I'm not the one who murdered an innocent victim and started the world's awakening to our existence."

His words brought a thousand memories flooding back to her all at once. They almost swept her off her feet as they came like a wave, crashing into her mind and nearly throwing her to the ground.

She tried to shake the memories from her head, but they refused to go. They flashed in front of her eyes, making her stumble backwards. Mummy on the floor, blood everywhere, sitting in a doctor's office screaming about the Shadow Person, a baby bird all alone... They flashed in front of her eyes like a picture album. One snapped up her attention quickly—leaving Aunt Stephanie's house. She was going to stop them. Going to take her freedom. There was a knife.

A knife.

And Ravyn had taken it.

She had stabbed her.

She had killed Aunt Stephanie.

Even though she had suspected it for a while now, remembering the whole event in clear detail was a punch to the gut, a ton of metal crushing down on her, trying to bury her beneath this battlefield. Before, everything had been blurry and out of focus; now, she could watch it over again in high definition and surround sound. She closed her eyes, but Aunt Stephanie's face was there, looking down at her with saddened eyes and a pitiful smile. Her cheek stung again, and again, and again, then metallic blood filled her mouth as her lip burst and bruises reappeared on her back. Words screamed in her ears, shrieking at her, swearing at her, bursting her ear drums.

Stop.

Stop it, she told herself repeatedly, fanning away the memories like smoke. That was all they were, after all—mists of the past that she couldn't dwell on right now if she wanted to see her next birthday.

"Hit a nerve, did I?" Nathan's chuckle was the final rope she needed to pull herself back into reality. She blinked a few times, readjusting to her surroundings and situation. Her head was still spinning. Nathan was tilting from side to side with that same fucking smile she hated more than anything. She sucked in a deep breath through clenched teeth.

"*You're* the one who started it all," she growled, closing her fists.

She had killed someone.

Stop it, Ravyn.

He chuckled.

"We were only having a bit of fun with you."

"I didn't find it very funny."

"Well, I did. You were as much of a threat to me then as a fly, but I still had to keep tabs on you, didn't I? I couldn't just let the daughter of one of the most powerful Illusionists in the world run around unchecked, could I?"

"Seems like I'm taking after her," Ravyn muttered, then instantly regretted it. That was like sticking a target on her forehead, the red bullseye centre glowing, waiting to be struck for the prize to be won. He smirked and clasped his hands over his belly. Her vision was slowly returning to normal.

"It does seem like that, yes. Which is why I must…dispose of you, as quickly as possible."

He took two steps forwards, and she took one back.

"Just tell me one thing first," she asked, now starting to execute her one and only plan, praying that her memories wouldn't get in the way. The one and only thing she could do right now to hopefully save herself and the others. She just had to keep his focus on her and her alone. He raised his eyebrows. "Am I your biggest threat right now?" she asked.

"I think I've made it pretty clear that you are."

"Do you care about getting Jay anymore?"

"I will once you're dead." A smile grew slowly on his lips. She dug into her energy reserves, gathering as much stamina as she could.

"Good to know," she said, flashing him a smile before she twisted on one foot and started running towards the trees. Behind her, Nathan started laughing.

Old instincts kicked back in. Sprinting over short distances was never really her strength; she was more of an endurance runner. But regardless, she would have to sprint today like the hounds of Hell were behind her. Her thighs burned as she ran, reminding her how unfit she had gotten since she'd had to leave school. She couldn't even remember how long ago that was. But that didn't matter right now; she just had to run.

The hairs on the back of her neck stood bolt upright, and she ducked her head. A spear of shadow shot right over her, catching some strands of stray hair and severing them. She wanted to look back at him, to just take one glance over her shoulder, but she didn't allow herself. She had to run.

"Oh, Ravyn, you are a tricky little *bitch*," Nathan called out from behind her, his own heavy footsteps starting to run towards her.

She jumped a ditch, landing on the opposite bank with a thud. Gorse scraped her legs as she ran through it and into the trees. They welcomed her with open arms, embracing her with the cold mist that lingered between the trunks.

Her heartbeat was steadily getting louder in her chest, and a sweat was breaking out on her forehead and under her arms. Everywhere was aching. Her mind was whispering to her that she couldn't do it, that she was too weak. But she just kept her breathing steady as she ran, focusing on picking a path through the trees rather than her body's struggle.

Another spear planted into the tree beside her, leaving a deep scar. It vapourised, and the wisps of shadow trailed back to Nathan, who she could hear was just coming through the gorse. He grunted as he pushed his way through the spikes, probably ruining his expensive suit as he did so.

"Fuck this," he panted, and something started whizzing through the air towards her. She jumped sideways, tucked her head to her chest and bringing her hands up to cover it. A ball of shadow shot right past her, tentacles of darkness trailing behind it. It hit a tree, and the tree groaned and swayed, shaking violently as it bounced the ball back towards Nathan.

Ravyn took a sharp left, her eyes scanning her surroundings quickly to pick out a good route through the trees and away from Nathan. Roots stuck out of the ground and threatened to trip her up, to grab her ankles and hold her until Nathan caught up.

Another spear shot past her, barely missing her ear.

He was swearing and stumbling behind her, but she ignored his angry noises and focused on keeping one foot in front of the other. The muscles in her legs were starting to cramp and tighten. There was another ditch just up ahead. It looked a lot bigger than the last one, and she wasn't sure if she could jump it, but she was sure as hell going to try. She couldn't turn around, couldn't turn back towards the jeeps. The ditch might slow him down a bit and allow her more time to get away. She picked up speed, pushing past the pain and tightness in her legs, dead twigs and leaves snapping under her heavy feet.

The closer she got to the ditch, the more she started to doubt herself. It was too big. Far too big to jump. It looked like an old, dried-up riverbed, weaving its way around the trees. *No,* she told herself, *you're not going to make it.* But the closer it drew, she could see there were footholds on the opposite bank. Rocks and tree roots, small animal burrows… If she could even get her feet into one of those, she could haul herself up and keep running.

She jumped.

It was too big.

She put her hands out to try and grab onto something, but her ribs slammed into the hard muck and rocks on the bank, her arms barely making it over the top of the wall. All the air in her lungs was knocked out of her and left her lips in a sharp huff. She bounced off it and landed on her back in the ditch, on rocky ground. Her head spun, white sparks exploding in front of her eyes. Sharp pain shot through her back and travelled around her ribs.

She winced as she tried to take a breath in, her lungs tight and heavy. She lay still for a few moments, the world above her spinning, fireworks exploding in the canopy. She blinked a few times, then closed her eyes, the pain starting to travel down to her stomach. She groaned, clutching her stomach, sudden tears jabbing her eyes.

Get up, she told herself. *He's coming, get the fuck up.*

Even with her eyes closed, the world still spun around her, and she started falling, twisting and turning and spinning around and around as she fell deep into the earth—

Get up.

She opened her eyes and stared at the trees overhead, looking down on her with worry. Some branches extended down towards her, a helping hand there to pull her to her feet.

Get the fuck up!

She planted her arms on either side of her torso and grunted as she pushed herself to sit. The pain in her back and ribs became hotter, the tips of white-hot needles sinking deeper into her bones, and she moaned. As she sat up, her stomach retched, and she doubled over. Her vision blurred as tears filled her eyes.

She ground her teeth against each other and pushed herself

to her knees. She started crawling. Rocks cut into her hands and knees, but she kept moving, down the riverbank. Her stomach retched again, and her arms buckled under her. Her face hit the ground, and she scrambled desperately to push herself back up.

"Well, well, well. The great warrior has fallen."

Nathan's voice was a cannonball to the back of the head. He was out of breath and annoyed.

Ravyn turned herself around so she sat, facing him up there on the ridge. She was gasping, her lungs struggling to expand, barely able to hold onto oxygen. The pain in her ribs jabbed them with every breath.

"You really are so fucking annoying, you know. But I think you've emptied your bag of tricks now, haven't you?" He grinned at her. She wasn't really listening. Instead, she was scanning thousands of thoughts on how to survive this situation.

She couldn't run anywhere; she couldn't hide either. There was only one thing left that she could do, and she quickly worked to manufacture an illusion that would hopefully stun him long enough for her to gain some ground away from him.

Hopefully.

But the odds weren't looking good, and a single thought told her she should prepare to die.

Nathan walked closer, shadows swirling around his fists. Her heart skipped a beat when she saw them, but she looked away and brought herself inside her mind.

"It's been fun. But you're in my way, fucking up my plans with and without your silly little illusions. Just like your mother did, all those years ago, and you know what happened to her…" He cocked his head, raising his hands.

She forced the illusion out of her mind with a scream. It

was agonizing as it tore out of her, ripping her forehead open as it blasted into reality. The ground under Nathan exploded, shooting upwards in a furious rumble. Tree roots and rocks blasted into the air, carrying Nathan with them.

Only, he was flung off his feet with the illusion.

A gaping hole gawked at her.

She stared at the carnage with wide eyes, breathing hard, sweat rolling down her strained face. Yes, the ground really had exploded, and she wasn't just imagining it. It wasn't just her illusion.

It had actually happened.

She couldn't see Nathan anymore. He had been thrown out of sight with the eruption. Bits of dirt and stone started raining down on her, and she covered her head with her arms. The rocks pattered down onto her forearms, and dirt fell into her eyelashes. She blinked it out of her eyes.

A sudden wave of dizziness hit her, and her heart struggled to beat, missing every fifth or sixth pulse.

She threw up what was left in her stomach.

Ravyn sat for a few moments, her head spinning once again, staring at the uplifted earth in front of her. Tree roots poked out of the freshly exposed soil, as if checking to make sure it was safe. Rocks caked in dirt that had been launched into the air lay loose on the ground around her.

No… That wasn't possible.

The whole thing was an illusion; there was no way that it had actually exploded.

But it had, and the evidence was clear in front of her.

She closed her eyes, but everything around her still spun. She never felt herself falling backwards, just the blunt pain to the back of her head as she hit the ground. She moaned and rolled onto her side, curled into the fetal position. Everywhere hurt. Her bones ached. Her muscles throbbed. Ligaments and tendons twinged painfully.

You have to get up, she told herself, but the thought was distant.

Go back to the others.

Get up!

She opened her eyes, breathing hard. Her mouth was dry. She didn't feel like she could get back to them. No, she was too tired. She just wanted to sleep, right here. Sleep for a thousand years, maybe only woken at true love's kiss. No, she just wanted to lay here for a while. She tried to flex her hands, but they barely moved.

Get up, Ravyn!

GET UP NOW!

The scream in her head startled her, and she blinked rapidly, her vision slowly coming back into focus, though it was darkened around the edges. Everything around her still quivered, but she pushed herself up to kneel. Her body tried to resist, tried to keep her on the ground, but she gritted her teeth and pushed past the urge.

She winced, then slowly started to rise to her feet, using the freshly exposed dirt wall beside her to help her up. Blood rushed from her head, and she swayed, her vision going black for a moment. Her knees threatened to buckle under her any second now. The ground looked so inviting, even with all the dirt and rocks… Just for a few moments, just until—

She put one foot forward, then the other.

One foot, another foot.

She was walking.

Her lungs were struggling to absorb the oxygen she sucked in through her mouth.

She knew where she needed to go. The only question was

would this riverbed take her back out to the field? Back to Jay, and Nat? Back to the battlefield littered with bodies and drenched in blood? She didn't know, but she followed it anyway.

*****

Eventually, she saw sunlight beaming through the trees in front of her. This was the edge of the forest, but the riverbed didn't cut through it. It swerved around, following the tree line further down to the right. She looked at the wall of steep mud and rock in front of her with tired, drooping eyes and sighed.

She still wanted to sleep, just a few moments, then she could get out over the ditch. She just needed to sleep.

She examined the wall in front of her and saw one single tree root poking out of the soil about halfway up. She could reach it easily—it was only at shoulder height for her—but she just didn't know if she would have the strength to pull herself up it.

Her vision darkened around the edges, and she stumbled forwards. She rested her head against the dirt wall and groaned. Her legs were shaking violently. They wanted to rest, just to sit down for a second, maybe lie down…

She shook her head clear.

She brushed away some dirt from the top of the root and rested her elbows on it.

Oh yes, here would be a nice place to rest.

Stop it.

She put some weight on the root, testing it. It held steady. She brought one leg up slowly, searching for a hole or stone in the dirt to help her up. She caught one and pushed her body upwards, bringing her other knee onto the root. Her stomach lurched, but she had already thrown up everything inside her. Here, she could see over the top of the ridge and out into the field. The grass was glistening with gold light, swaying gently in the breeze. Her eyes were getting heavier though, ready to close, and the inviting lull of sleep was near.

She brought her arms over the top of the wall of dirt and boosted herself over it with a grunt, then lay on the ground, facing the sky.

She lay still.

The wind rustled the leaves above her, praising her for her perseverance. They clapped gently overhead, a standing ovation. Birds chirped and whistled somewhere nearby, adding to nature's song of applause.

Despite her body telling her to stay here for a few moments and appreciate the kind gesture of the forest, she got up and started walking again. Everything was starting to sway again, and she stumbled a few times, but she made it past the trees and into the field.

She squinted at the brightness of the sun beating down on her, trying to blind her. One knee buckled, and she was almost sent sprawling. She saved herself at the last moment, determined to stay on her feet. It took a few seconds for her eyes to adjust, then she looked around for any sign of the wreckages.

To her left, the two jeeps were still overturned. And it looked like there were people standing outside the jeeps too. Relief washed over her and nearly sent her to the ground. She tried to smile, but the muscles in her face had no energy left. She couldn't make out who the people were; for all she knew they might be Shades—they were just black blobs slowly getting more and more out of focus, but regardless, she started stumbling towards them.

About halfway there, one of the figures noticed her, and they all stopped to turn and look.

Then one started running towards her, but she couldn't keep herself upright any longer. Her vision was growing dark, her eyelids heavy and her breathing laboured, and it crossed her mind that she might be dying. This could be it. Her heart was giving up, her body ready to give over to the gentle pull of death.

Even with her blurred vision, the raven hair that billowed out behind the running figure made her heart skip a beat. It was Nat.

As soon as Nat reached her, she wrapped her in a hug, but Ravyn slipped into darkness and became dead weight in Nat's arms.

CHAPTER 22

The first thing Ravyn noticed was that she was moving, swaying slightly from side to side, and there was a heavy thump that vibrated through her every time the person carrying her took a step. She allowed herself to be carried— her body was still tired and wanted to go back to sleep, but her mind wouldn't let her. It was wide awake, ready to go, ready to fight. Her head was resting on someone's chest, and she brought her attention to their heartbeat. The slow, steady, rhythmic thump was soothing, like a lullaby, wishing her to rest again and let this person take care of her.

The air was cool around her, cradling her body. There was rustling all around as people walked alongside them. Twigs snapped and leaves crunched underfoot as the group made their sombre way to wherever they were going.

She stayed still for a few more moments, eyes closed and hands limp on her stomach. But curiosity got the better of her—who was carrying her, where were they going, was Nat okay?

Ravyn slowly opened her eyes.

Trees passed her slowly, the same trees that she had seen earlier today. Or was it yesterday? The day before that, even? She didn't know how long she had been out for. They were walking through the forest where she had fought Nathan. Where she made an actual explosion, made him fly off his feet. Was he alive? Perhaps she hadn't made that explosion happen, and there really was a hidden mine or bomb there that he had triggered somehow. A stash of explosives someone was trying to keep hidden from prying eyes. That was way more likely than her making it happen.

Illusions couldn't do that.

No, how could they? Illusions weren't real, they were just an illusion. It was in the name. Just her own hallucination that she could make others see too.

Ravyn closed her eyes again, a headache starting to form behind them. The back of her head was still tender. Maybe the whole thing had been a dream—she'd hit her head pretty hard, after all. Maybe it was a figment of her bruised and confused imagination? Maybe she had been knocked out when the car flipped, and everything after that had been a dream.

Ryan and Excael could still be alive if that was the case.

She allowed herself to be carried for a bit longer while her body slowly regained some strength. She opened her eyes again and brought her hands up to rub them.

"Ravyn's awake." It was John carrying her. His familiar voice was a relief to hear.

Ravyn turned her head to look over her right shoulder and saw Jay in front of her. She blinked a few times. He had a cut on his forehead, which had scabbed over, but dried blood still caked his skin under it. There were dried flakes of blood in his beard. John stopped, and Jay walked up to her. He gave her a smile.

"How are you feeling?" he asked.

She shrugged and yawned. "I'm okay. I think I can walk myself," she told him, despite being terribly comfortable where she was in John's arms.

John set her down gently, and Ravyn held onto his shoulder as she regained her balance. Now that she was standing, her body strained as her muscles were suddenly woken up and forced to stretch. Nat appeared in the corner of her eye, watching with those pretty eyes of hers. Ravyn brought her attention to her legs and tried to get one to move in front of the other, but she stumbled instead, and Jay caught her as she fell. He lifted her back to her feet.

"I think you need to rest a little longer. Why don't we stop here for a bit, let Ravyn get some energy back?" he said, holding Ravyn upright. Her legs were sore, with pins and needles stabbing her toes. She gripped Jay's shirt with trembling hands, trying to stay upright, but her body was heavy, almost too heavy for her to hold up by herself.

Jay helped her sit down with her back against a tree trunk, then sat beside her. She looked up at Nat, who gave her a smile before sitting down against a trunk a bit away from her. There were cuts on her hands and arms. Her hair was a mess, full of tangles and knots. Brook was there too and sat beside Nat with her legs curled under her. She didn't look up once. She had a yellowish bruise forming on her cheek but otherwise looked unharmed. There were some bloodstains on the cuffs of her top but no wounds on her skin.

Tammie stayed standing. There were blood stains and rips all over her clothes but no cuts. None that Ravyn could see anyway, and then she remembered Tammie could heal wounds. Of course. John crouched in front of a tree to her left. He also had some blood stains and rips on his clothes, but no visible wounds.

Clio wasn't with them.

So it hadn't been a dream then.

Another dead.

The thought hurt.

Ravyn watched them all for a moment or two, her eyes flicking between them. She watched Nat in particular and wanted her to be closer, wanted to feel the warmth of her skin and kiss all her wounds until they healed. She wanted to tell her that everything was going to be okay, that she would make sure nothing like this ever happened again. Everyone looked defeated, ready to raise the white flag above their heads.

"Are you okay?" Jay asked, breaking her out of her daze, and she turned around to face him. He looked at her gently, his head tilted slightly to the right.

"Yeah," she replied, nodding.

"What happened earlier?"

"Ehm…Nathan was there. He…" She stopped herself. He had killed Excael. Killed him. She had watched him die, watched his body crumple to the ground in front of her. Nathan had killed the others too, the ones who weren't here. Ryan, and she guessed Clio too—both dead. Dead.

Fucking *dead*.

She sighed as she held back tears.

Don't cry, she ordered herself.

A lump was starting to form in her throat.

"I knew Nathan would be there. But where did the rest of the Shades go? Where did *you* go?" Jay prompted her. She turned away from him, staring at a daisy in the grass. Some of the petals were baby pink, the others an off-white. Its yellow face stared at her, questioning, waiting for secrets to be spilled and absorbed into the soil.

"I…created an illusion, and it made the Shades leave. I thought Nathan went with them too, but he came back on his own… I just ran into the woods, and he followed me. It was weird, Jay, I don't know what happened, but…" Ravyn paused, trying to figure out how she could explain what had happened.

An explosion, under his feet. Like what she had made back in their escape from his underground lair, or whatever that place was. But that hadn't been real, and this was. She couldn't do that; she couldn't just make that happen.

"What happened?" Jay asked, gently taking her out of her thoughts. He put a hand over hers, warm and comforting.

"I made an illusion to try and daze him so I could get away… I tried to make it look like the ground under him exploded, but…it actually did. He was thrown off his feet. I don't know what happened." She sighed loudly and gave a half-hearted shrug. The whole scene replayed in her mind through a hazy filter, like a broken TV with bad signal. The boom, the ground shooting upwards, and Nathan… Nathan being thrown backwards. Her headache pulsed, forcing her to stop thinking about it. Jay did not speak for a few moments, until Ravyn looked up at him. He was stroking his beard.

"Hmm." He pursed his lips and narrowed his eyes. "That is…strange. Normally it would take years, even decades, before someone could do what you just did. But you've only just learned how to use your powers…" He trailed off. Ravyn frowned at him.

He took his hand away from hers.

"Wait, what?"

She mentally shook her head. No, there was no way. There was no way she could do anything like that.

Jay pressed his lips tighter together and took his hand away from his face. "Some Illusionists have the power to make their illusions a reality, like what you just did. I think I mentioned it to you before. Your mother was able to do it, but it took her years of training and hard work to be able to access that part of her abilities. But you've done it already, Ravyn. I don't really understand how that's possible." Jay shook his head. "I can make wild guesses. Perhaps the stress you were under activated it as a survival tactic. Did you try anything different this time, feel anything different?" he asked.

She shook her head, her mind reeling with his words.

His hand went back to his beard. "That's…unusual. I can't give you much more of an answer now, Ravyn, but maybe I will be able to when we return to Dunfeagh and we talk more about it and really dissect what happened." Jay gave her a smile. She returned it quickly, but there were questions on her lips, waiting for their turn to speak.

"I still don't understand what you mean about the illusions becoming real," she told him.

He nodded slowly and shifted where he sat to a more comfortable spot. "Illusionists don't just have the ability to create illusions, they can also solidify them and make them happen in the real world, like what happened with Nathan and the ground exploding. I'm sure you already know from Nathan that Illusionists are deemed too dangerous to have running around. But why would they be if all they can do is make illusions? That's not all they can do, and that's why Nathan and the Shades think they are so dangerous. It is not like me, or Therese, or John, where we have a specific set of abilities. I manipulate air, and I can only do that. John can manipulate the ground and the earth, and that is all he can do. You, however, and all other Illusionists, have the ability to make your illusions a reality. You can make the ground explode, like you did. You can make a building collapse, make the sea rise, make a gunman appear and shoot actual bullets. Do you see what I mean?" He tilted his head.

She nodded slowly, still trying to wrap her head around it. The headache was preventing her from processing it quickly. Words spun around and around in her mind before they finally made sense.

"But how do I make it happen? I...I don't remember what I did differently with Nathan." She leaned her head back against the trunk of the tree, sighing. Her mind was working overtime. Her eyes were getting heavy again, but she couldn't sleep. Not now. There was so much going on, and she needed to be awake and alert. There was so much still to learn, so much unknown information she needed to uncover.

"First, you need to understand how to control the energy you use when casting illusions. It's something we all have to learn once we understand the basics of our abilities. Once you learn that, it's just about pouring enough energy into the illusion that it manifests itself as a real thing. It's hard to put that much energy into something; your body generally will not allow you to do it, and that is why it takes so long to learn how." He gave her a smile. "Maybe not though. You continue to surprise me, Ravyn."

She pressed her lips tightly together. She brought her eyes to Nat for a moment, who was crafting a daisy chain crown.

She would look beautiful wearing it. A princess of the forest, one of the woodland fae that wandered through the trees. A friend of the deer and foxes, the birds and the bunnies. Wherever she walked, flowers would grow and bloom.

But her thoughts turned dark and clouded, and reality set back in.

She turned back to Jay.

"I already used my abilities before I made that happen, so is that why I'm so tired now? Have I used too much energy?" she asked.

"If I'm honest, Ravyn, you should be dead right now," Jay said. Ravyn looked up in alarm. "Making illusions real takes a huge amount of energy, and most people spend days recovering after they do it. It is only used if absolutely necessary. You had already used a lot of energy with your other illusions, so I'm surprised your heart had enough energy left to beat after that, let alone walk back to us. It could just be the stress or the adrenaline, but as I said, you continue to amaze me." He gave her another smile, and she tried to return it, though her lips barely lifted.

Fucking hell…

She closed her eyes for a few moments, her body wanting to drift back to sleep. Thinking was tiring. Sitting was tiring. Digesting all of this was tiring.

She just wanted to sleep.

But there were more questions to ask, answers to seek, and secrets to uncover.

"Is that why my mother didn't do that…on the night it happened? She didn't create a real illusion because it would have taken too much out of her?" she asked quietly, hoping John, Nat, and the others wouldn't hear.

"I wasn't there that night, so I can only guess. She probably didn't want to do it in case she passed out, leaving you on your own with the Shade," he replied. His words stung her deeply, bringing old, dusty memories to the surface.

She batted her eyelids open. Her throat was starting to close in, a sign of tears coming, but she couldn't allow them to fall yet. Not now.

The forest floor turned to blood, and her mother's body appeared right there, right in front of her, face down, drowning in the sea of red.

Ravyn lifted her eyes, and the scene melted away.

"Was it Nathan that killed her that night?"

There was a moment of silence, and her body braced itself for the answer.

"I think so, yes."

Jay put his hand on her shoulder, rubbing circles with his thumb. Her throat was closing, tightening, constricting her airways. Tears jabbed the back of her eyes, but she never let them fall. Her mind kept taking her back to that night, the night her mother died. When she was stolen from her, ripped from her hands and taken to another world without a goodbye. They didn't speak for a few moments, and Ravyn closed her eyes again, ready to give into sleep, but she kept seeing his smiling face in front of her, grinning with those stupid teeth, teeth she would gladly knock out of his head. He had done too much damage, destroyed too many lives. Thoughts of Nathan brought a sudden realisation to her.

She opened her eyes.

"Nathan might still be here," she said, her voice cracking. She cleared her throat. Her heart started becoming noticeable in her chest. If he was still here, he would be pissed.

Pissed at her, more specifically, and ready to kill her.

"I know. I'm hoping he went back to wherever he's hiding out now though. If he's injured, I doubt he'll be hanging around, but I'm not taking any chances. Once you feel better, we'll keep moving."

"To where?"

"Well, we've no car and no phones. We can't call anyone for help. We're on our own here, so the best thing we can do is try to stay out of sight, try to avoid any lurking Shades, and make our way back to the house and hope it isn't crawling with them. If it is, it's a long way to the nearest village."

"Won't somebody know we're in trouble if we don't contact them? What about Therese?"

"They will realise that we haven't made contact in a while and hopefully send somebody out. But that might not be until tomorrow, or the day after. They know our situation, so they might think we're keeping low and staying hidden." Jay sighed. He looked worried. There was a hint of fear in his eyes, afraid of the possibilities that lay before them, most of which ended in death.

Ravyn nodded slowly, and once again, her eyes closed, and her body started to drift into a sleep, even though she didn't really want to sleep. She wanted to stay up, to talk to Jay, to see Nat in that beautiful daisy crown. But a powerful wave came over her, knocking away all her consciousness and finally getting her to rest.

*****

She woke to the sound of voices and gently opened her eyes. She was lying on her side, on somebody's coat. It was dark, but there was a light source coming from somewhere in front of her. A fire, she guessed, as the sounds of crackling and hissing drifted towards her ears. Its warmth just about reached her, heating her upper body. The sweet smell of burning wood floated towards her and lovingly greeted her nostrils.

She closed her eyes and mentally scanned herself. She was

still tired, but not as tired as she had been when she'd fallen asleep. There was a dull throbbing in her back and head, but other than that, she was okay. She opened her eyes again, rubbed them, then sat up.

They had built a fire and pulled two logs up beside it. Or maybe they had already been there, she didn't know. She *did* know this was not the same place where she had fallen asleep though. The trees were much older, and moss clung to the bark. The thick branches formed a high roof above them, keeping them sheltered. They had wanted to keep moving, which was fair enough given their circumstances. They needed to get back to the house, and they needed to get away from Nathan.

Jay was chatting to Tammie and John. The fire cast a warm glow on their faces. John wasn't really saying much, but he listened in and gave the occasional smile, something she hadn't seen him do in a long time. It was nice to see.

Nat, who had been standing at the fire warming her hands, walked over to her and crouched down.

Ravyn gave her a sleepy smile. "Hey."

Nat smiled back. "Welcome back to the land of the living," she said, taking Ravyn's hand and giving it a squeeze. "You're cold. Come sit beside the fire."

Nat stood, pulling Ravyn with her. Ravyn wobbled as she stood, but Nat held her arm and waited patiently for her to regain her balance. Her legs were weak under her as they walked the few steps around one of the logs, and she grasped Nat's hand tightly, afraid of falling.

They sat. Brook was on the other end of the log, staring into the fire. It danced in her eyes, flickering and swaying with the wind. Ravyn stared at her for a few moments but turned back to Nat when Brook didn't look over to her. Here, the warmth of the fire was much more powerful, almost too hot against her tender skin.

Jay gave her a smile and a nod, then went back to his conversation with Tammie. John just glanced at her. Their words were carried up into the canopy with the smoke, lost to her ears.

"You good?" Nat asked her in a low voice. Ravyn shrugged. The warmth from the fire was pleasant, heating the whole front part of her body, and her skin was growing accustomed to the heat. The fire crackled and sparks shot up into the air, dancing like fireflies in front of her eyes.

"Yeah, I'm okay."

"You sound a lot better."

Ravyn gave her a smile, then changed subject. "What are we doing now?" she asked.

"We're making our way back to the house. It's taking a while 'cause we're taking a longer route to make sure we don't run into any Shades, but everyone needs to take it slow today. We'll be there tomorrow, but for now, it's better we all rest here. We'll take turns keeping watch, just in case."

Ravyn nodded before admitting quietly, "You scared me. I thought you were dead in the jeep."

Nat squeezed her hand. "You scared me too when you disappeared like that, then came back and fainted on me, so I guess that makes us even." She smiled. Ravyn returned it, then leaned her head on her shoulder. She wanted to kiss her, even just peck her on the cheek, but having multiple eyes all around her was very off-putting. Aunt Stephanie's gaze was in there among them, watching her out of the corner of her eye. She decided to just keep her head on Nat's shoulder.

"I think you need to go back to sleep," Nat said.

"I'm okay."

"Hmm…" Nat exhaled sharply in a huff.

"I've rested too much today already."

"Well, you need more. I heard what you did. It's fucking impressive, it really is, but I also heard it knocks the living daylights out of you. You need to sleep."

"I want to stay up for a while."

Nat smirked. "On your head be it."

"How are *you*, though?" Ravyn asked, raising her head from Nat's shoulder. She examined Nat's face. Her eyes did not sparkle like they usually did. They were not filled with diamonds and emeralds, crystals shining in the sunlight. Her eyes were dull, tired, beaten.

"I'm fine. Tammie worked her magic on me. You shouldn't be worrying about me, anyways." Nat rolled her eyes.

"You can't stop me," Ravyn said. Nat shook her head, but Ravyn saw the smile on her lips.

Nat's company was enchanting, her presence something Ravyn cherished. She couldn't stop thinking about her, about the feeling she got when they were together. It was something magical, something Ravyn couldn't put words to, but she relished every moment.

Brook gasped suddenly, the noise jarring Ravyn from her thoughts. Everyone turned to Brook. Ravyn had to peer around Nat to see her. Jay was on his feet instantly, crouching down in front of her.

Brook was trembling, her eyes wide and staring blankly into the fire. Beads of sweat rolled down her face and disappeared under her shirt. Jay took her clenched hands and spoke softly to her, but her unseeing eyes stared straight through him.

"What's wrong?" Ravyn whispered to Nat. Her heart skipped a beat as she looked at Brook, at the muscles in her neck bulging as she gasped for air.

"We don't know. She had one of these episodes earlier, and Jay said she had one back at the safehouse. It's because of what that dickhead Nathan did to her," Nat growled angrily under her breath. Ravyn swallowed a lump in her throat and watched as Brook slowly came out of her partially unconscious state.

Ravyn looked away, tears pricking her eyes. She wiped them quickly with the back of her sleeve.

Brook hung her head, her messy hair concealing her face. Jay stayed with her for a few more moments, whispering gentle words, his arm around her shoulders. The fire crackled and hissed at them, flames popping. It was the only noise. Nobody spoke. Everyone stared into the fire, feeding it their emotions and thoughts, stoking it with unheard shouts and sobs.

Sparks shot into the air and danced above them.

Ravyn was getting tired again. The fire, the warmth, was making her drowsy. She didn't want to go to sleep though, not again. She had just woken up, after all, and she wanted to spend time with Nat. She wanted to make sure Brook was okay.

"You look exhausted, Ravyn," Nat said, as if reading her mind.

Ravyn shook her head. "I'm fine."

Nat gave her a nudge. "Just lie down for a few minutes. Get some strength back."

Ravyn finally gave in, and Jay got her a blanket to lie down on beside the fire. He had pulled the bags from the wreckages, and thankfully, they weren't too damaged. She lay on her side, her back to the flames and an arm under her head. Thoughts were starting to float around her mind as she lay there. Not the Ethereal, not illusions, just…her old life. Before all this. Before she had been cast into this chaotic world, before the bodies had started to pile.

HELENA BRADY

Brook joined her on the ground, spreading a blanket out alongside hers. She lay down on her back, looking up at the dark branches above them. Neither of them said anything for a few moments.

"You okay?" Ravyn asked quietly. Brook turned her head to face her. She was looking better. Colour had returned to her face, and her skin had started to plump out again.

"I don't know."

"I know the feeling."

"All this is my fault, isn't it?"

"No, of course not."

"It is, Ravyn."

"It's Nathan's fault, not yours."

Brook sighed and didn't respond.

"How did it happen though? How did he do that to you?"

"I…" Brook paused, turning her head back to face the sky. The light from the fire caught on the tears in her eyes. "I don't really remember. I just know it was a few days before we were sent to get you. I feel like I'm missing a day's memory, like there's something there, but I can't find it. I know I felt…*off*, but I couldn't figure out why. I didn't know he had done anything, or that something was wrong. I should have known when Jay made me feel really uncomfortable at the motel, but I didn't pay any attention to it."

"Maybe it will come back to you, one day."

Brook huffed. "I don't know if I want it to."

Ravyn nodded. That was understandable. It was probably best that she didn't remember. They spent a few minutes in silence, listening to the chatter and the fire's crackle and pop.

"Do you remember when we first met?" Ravyn asked her.

Brook looked over once again. "Yeah, why?"

"Did I kill somebody?"

Brook went silent. She bit her lip, then narrowed her eyes. Ravyn knew what was coming, her intuition was screaming at her, but she wanted that confirmation to solidify the fact in her brain.

"Yes," Brook admitted.

"My aunt Stephanie?"

"Yes."

Brook turned her face away again, and Ravyn did the same, rolling over so she faced the heavens. She couldn't see the sky through the canopy of trees above them, but she could imagine it—the millions of stars and the moon casting a silver light down on them. They would whisper sweet melodies into their ears as they slept tonight. Maybe there were shooting stars, comets filled with stardust, a tail of blue and purple streaking across the cosmos.

It would be beautiful but unseen.

She closed her eyes.

She had killed someone, and the universe knew. The heavenly moon knew.

If you can kill Aunt Stephanie, you can kill Nathan.

The thought came out of nowhere but stuck in her mind, glowing neon and holding her attention. *You killed someone already, why not kill Nathan? You're already a murderer, what difference would it make?*

No, she told herself. *I am not killing anybody else.*

But you can end this, just kill him.

Kill Nathan.

Get it over with, just fucking kill him. He killed Alec, he hurt Brook, then he killed Excael, Ryan, and Clio. He's a monster, Ravyn, and you have to stop him. Because if you don't, he will kill everyone just to get to you.

No, she told herself firmly, but the thoughts kept coming, taking over her mind. She fell asleep thinking of murder.

CHAPTER 23

Smoke climbed the sky in the distance, rising from where the safehouse was supposed to be. Thick and black, polluting the air. The closer they got, the more worried Ravyn became. Her stomach had tied itself into a knot. She was sure the house was no longer standing, absolutely sure of it, and she knew everybody else was thinking the same thing.

But they kept walking anyway. Nobody spoke. Silence hung over their heads, heavy on their shoulders, trying to drag them to the ground, to get them to give up all hope.

The smell of burning confirmed it before they had even seen the wreckage.

When they finally did reach the house, it was just a shell—smouldering, smoking embers glowing in the soot and ashes. Everything had burnt; only the brick structure remained standing, but it was blackened and weakened by the fierce flames that had consumed it. The doors, the furniture, everything else was now charcoal and dust gathered in piles on the ground. The second floor had collapsed, and the roof had caved in. A few tile slates were shattered in front of the house, covered in ash. Everything was destroyed.

Ravyn closed her eyes and sighed. Her fists hung by her side, clenched so tight her knuckles were white.

"What do we do now?" Nat asked.

Nobody answered. They all just continued staring at the destruction in front of them. Some of the bushes had been burnt back, unable to escape the hungry flames. Holes had been eaten out of the hedges, and the surrounding leaves were blackened and burnt. The smoke was clinging to the back of Ravyn's throat, coating it with a thick, greasy film.

Jay finally spoke. "Looks like we're on our own now. We'll have to get to a village or town and try to get somebody out to us."

Ravyn looked at the back of his head, at his slumped shoulders. He was exhausted, she could tell. The air around him was sombre.

Why not fight back? she asked in her mind but brushed away the thought.

"The nearest town is miles away. We're in the middle of nowhere, Jay." Tammie's voice was small and weak. Ravyn looked at how Tammie's hands were fidgeting nervously in front of her stomach. Her eyes were wide and scared.

"I know, but what else can we do?" he said, turning to face them. Ravyn examined his face. Tired. Drained. His eyes were sunken, dark circles cast beneath them. His wrinkles were more noticeable, and he looked much older. A pang of sorrow snapped in her stomach.

Kill Nathan, the thoughts whispered to her. *Kill him and end this fucking war that he insists on waging. This has to end. The killing, the destruction, it has to end, and Nathan is not backing down.*

So you have to rise and meet him instead.

"We better start walking then," Jay said, pushing through them. The air around them was cold, wrapping around their bones and souls, gripping their bodies with icy fingers. They followed him back down the stony track to the road, then took a right and kept going.

The clouds in the sky were dark grey with some patches that were completely black. She glanced angrily up at them, warning them against raining, sending her words of caution straight to the storm gods themselves.

You can kill Nathan, kill him, kill him.

Get rid of him.

She pushed the thoughts away, keeping her attention on her feet, walking on cracked tarmac with grass poking through it. Her feet were tired and sore, but she ignored it as best she could. There was nothing else they could do except walk this lonely road and hope they made it to a town.

Or kill Nathan.

Stop it, Ravyn.

Don't you think it would make things better if he was dead?

Yes, but—

Do it, then. He has murdered so many of your kind; he took your mother from you, he took Alec from you. He tried to kill Nat. He hurt Brook. He needs to be taken care of, or more people will die. You *will* die.

The thoughts kept coming, tainting and blackening her mind, turning her mood grim.

I'm not a murderer, she tried to tell herself, but she knew she already was. She had killed once, but as much as she searched for some remorse, she felt none. Had Aunt Stephanie deserved it? Ravyn didn't know, she couldn't really remember, but it was done now, and she couldn't go back and change it. She didn't know if she would want to, anyway. If Aunt

Stephanie was still alive, would Ravyn be here? Would she have escaped with Brook, or been locked away in her room while Shades continued to haunt and torture her?

If she just got rid of Nathan…

Her thoughts turned to imagining her and Nat living peacefully in their own house, maybe getting married one day, but that was a while away. Ravyn didn't want kids, never had, and she didn't know how Nat felt about the situation, but she was sure they could figure it out. She had never felt this way about someone before, she had never been able to see herself with someone for the rest of her life until she met Nat. They hadn't known each other that long, after all, but…she knew it was something special. A smile came to her face just thinking about it. She tried not to get ahead of herself, she wasn't even sure if they were officially a *thing*, but…it would be nice. She glanced over at Nat, who walked beside her. Nat caught her eye, giving Ravyn a smile before turning back around.

Yes, it would be nice.

But you have to get rid of Nathan first.

That thought was not so nice.

I'm not going to kill anybody else, she told herself.

Well then, have fun spending the rest of your life running from him, always looking over your shoulder, losing people close to you as he kills them all and tries to find you.

He wants you, *Ravyn.*

He will kill you, and anybody who gets in his way.

You have to kill him first.

Kill him before he kills you and everyone you love.

Yes. The thought came from nowhere but solidified in her brain the instant it appeared there.

Ravyn would kill him. She would kill him and take everything from him, just like he'd taken everything from her—her mother, her friends, her old life. He was the catalyst of all this annihilation.

I am going to kill you, Nathan, she told him mentally, reaching out to him, wherever he was. Her face hardened, eyes narrowed and thoughts sharpened.

No more running.

She was going to do what the rest of them were afraid to do. Then she was going to go home, to be with Nat and live the rest of her life knowing she did not have to worry about Nathan sneaking into her house at night to murder the person she loved the most, just because she was more powerful and more dangerous than he would ever be. Because she had something he craved, something he wanted so desperately he was prepared to blow up the world for it.

A smile slowly pushed its way onto her lips again. Nat grabbed her hand and gave it a squeeze. She leaned over and whispered, "What's the smile for?"

Ravyn moved closer to her.

"I was thinking about you," she whispered back. Nat grinned at her and leaned her head on Ravyn's shoulder as they walked. If killing Nathan meant saving Nat and the others from an unholy fate, then she would do it in a heartbeat.

Yes, she was going to find Nathan and kill him.

Maybe he would come for her, but either way, he was going to die.

Then, she could be at peace.

*****

The sun was starting to set when they reached the village,

half hidden by the buildings that rose from the earth. It burned deep orange in the sky. The horizon was a blend of pink and purple, with dark cotton-wool clouds floating gently in front of the sun. Flocks of birds danced overhead, flying back to their nests for the night. Ravyn took her time to appreciate it while Jay and Tammie—the ones who didn't look like they'd just crawled out of a thorn bush—went to check them in to a bed and breakfast.

Nat was still holding her hand, their fingers intertwined. Brook stood to one side of them, John to the other. Brook's head hung down, her hair in front of her face. Ravyn glanced at her, and her heart ached.

With her other hand, she took Brook's. Brook's fingers closed gently around Ravyn's, and she finally lifted her head.

"They have two rooms. We got the last ones, luckily," Jay said, approaching them from the right, dangling a set of keys in his hands. He handed them to Nat, then gave her his bag, the one that had survived the crash. "Me, Tammie, and Brook will take one room. You three take the other. Tammie is already there." He motioned with his head for them to follow him. He looked better, more alert and energetic. He walked with his head up, back straight and an air of confidence. The corner of her mouth lifted slightly.

"Do they have a phone?" Nat asked.

"Uh-huh. We're going to get settled first, make sure we don't have any surprise visitors, then we will call Therese. She'll arrange for us to be collected."

"And after that?"

Jay looked over his shoulder at them. "I don't know yet. But we have time to figure it out."

The bed and breakfast was above a pub. The building was painted yellow, with dark wooden window frames and a dark roof. Flower boxes hung from the upstairs windows, filled with bright pink and lemon-coloured plants. There were some benches outside with large, multi-coloured umbrellas sticking out of the middle of them and little heaters attached to the pose. Some people sat outside—mostly older people with greying hair and weathered skin—talking and laughing. The pints on the tables were almost empty, with white froth clinging to the side of the glasses.

They used the separate entrance to the rooms at the side of the pub. The steps leading up were steep and creaked as they ascended. There was barely enough room for her to squeeze between the walls.

The hallway was also incredibly narrow, barely enough room for two people to walk side by side. There were six rooms in total—three on the left, three on the right. Jay pointed Nat to one on the end.

"You're there. We're here." He stopped outside a door in the middle of the hallway. "If there's any problems, just knock. We'll let you settle in, then we'll meet up with you and work out what to do next." He opened the door and let Brook in ahead of himself.

Nat led the way down to their room and unlocked it. The door had once been painted white, but most of the colour had been chipped off, revealing the dark brown door beneath. Nat went in first and switched on the lights.

The room smelled musty, with some lavender air freshener trying its best to cover it but not doing a very good job. There were three single beds fitted into the small space, with hardly enough room to walk between them. It was very cramped. There was one window on the back wall, with stained cream curtains pulled over it.

"Home sweet home," Nat muttered, taking one of the beds

against the wall, sitting on the end of it. Ravyn took the one beside her, and John the next one over. The room had a low ceiling and felt very confined, like they were trapped in a room that just continued to shrink, trying to squash them. But it was only for one night, Ravyn told herself. It was better than the forest floor. Her aching shoulders would appreciate a mattress to sleep on tonight.

"Do me a favour, you two," John said as he lay down on the bed, propping the pillow up behind him. "Keep your hands off each other tonight, please. I would like to have a good sleep."

Nat laughed heartily, and Ravyn blushed. Heat rose in her cheeks and up to the top of her head. She looked down at her hands.

"Don't be daft," Nat scoffed.

"We all know what you're like, Nat."

Nat threw her pillow at John's head, but he caught it and launched it back at her. Ravyn had to duck out of the way to avoid being caught in the crossfire. They laughed, and even Ravyn managed a small chuckle, though bonfires still burned in her cheeks.

"Fuck off," Nat laughed, flinging the pillow back over before giving him the finger. John responded by holding up both his middle fingers to her. Ravyn's smile widened as her blush eased.

"You're feeling better obviously," Nat commented then, settling back down onto the bed. She pulled the other pillow behind her back and leaned against the wall. Ravyn's eyes flicked to John, and he sighed. A brief pained expression flashed on his face.

"I suppose."

"Good. I'm glad," Nat said, her voice becoming soft. John

smirked and shrugged.

"I just… can't wait to get back to Dunfeagh, and see everyone again," John said. Ravyn nodded, watching his face. She still had no idea where this Dunfeagh was, or *what* it was, but she couldn't wait to get there either. But she knew Nathan would not let them reach their destination so easily. She pressed her lips together.

"We've had some hell of a detour," Nat chuckled.

There was a knock at the door. John got up and opened it, letting Jay, Brook, and Tammie into the room. The small space became even smaller as more bodies crammed into it, stealing more air and making the room stuffy.

Brook took a seat beside Nat, wearily eyeing John, who sat back on his bed on the other side of the room. Tammie and Jay chose to remain standing. The ceiling was nearly touching the top of Jay's head.

Jay pursed his lips, and his hand went to stroke his beard, but he stopped himself and folded it back across his chest instead.

"Firstly, I suppose I wanted to…apologize." He paused. Ravyn raised her eyebrows. "None of this should have happened. I shouldn't have sent you to get Ravyn on your own, I should have been more cautious. Maybe if I had been, we wouldn't be stuck here, and maybe some people would still be alive. I thought by sending you lot it would be easier, because you're all teenagers, and it would make Ravyn feel more comfortable. I should have gone, I shouldn't have let you go on your own."

Out of the corner of her eye, she saw John stiffen. Her heart was starting to beat faster, thudding against her ribs. She looked at Nat and held her eyes for a moment before turning back to Jay.

"You don't have anything to apologize for, Jay," Nat said.

Jay shook his head. "No, I do, and I am sorry for everything that has happened."

"Nobody knew this was going to happen. We couldn't have. *You* couldn't have. We had no reason to be more cautious or do things differently. The plan was perfect, and there was no indication that things could have gone the way they did," Nat countered, her voice stern. Ravyn looked down at her hands and nodded in agreement, but part of herself told her that she was the one that had caused all this. Nathan wanted her, after all. They were just trying to save her from misery and take her back to her *real* home; everything they had done had been for her.

She had to fix it.

She had to make things right.

That was her responsibility.

"Nat's right, Jay," John spoke quietly, and Ravyn raised her head again. She looked at him as he sighed. "It's nobody's fault, except that fucker Nathan... It's not your fault either, Brook." He turned to look across the room at her, and Brook's spine straightened, her slim body becoming rigid under his gaze. "I'm...sorry."

Brook just nodded, her dark eyes glossy with tears. Nat put a hand on her back.

A sudden stillness fell as the air softened and a hush took over them.

"What a good therapy session," Nat said with a smirk, and they all chuckled.

"So we all agree that nobody here is to blame for anything that has happened? Anybody else want to get something off their chest?" Tammie spoke for the first time in ages. She looked a bit better, not as pale or as weak. She was starting to emanate that warm presence she had back when Ravyn first met her. It set Ravyn at ease, relaxing her muscles and slowing her heartbeat.

"I think we should just kill Nathan," John mused quietly. Ravyn was about to nod when Jay spoke.

"I would have to disagree."

"Jay, he is going to keep coming back, again and again. If we just kill him—"

"If he dies, Isabella will take over, and she is much worse than Nathan, trust me. She is…insane—"

"Kill her too then."

"It would take a lot to kill the two of them, and I am not comfortable putting that many lives on the line."

"Um," Ravyn interrupted. "Who is Isabella?"

"She's Nathan's girlfriend. She was there in the cell, the one with that black dress," Nat told her. Ravyn nodded. She remembered her all right.

"Oh."

"She likes to… torture people. Nathan would use her to get people to talk. We've…had a run-in before. It wasn't pretty." Jay stroked his beard, and his body shuddered as a chill ran through it.

Ravyn bit her lip.

"Hence my argument—kill them both," John continued. "Then we have a chance to get home, while the Shades re-group and fight over who their next dictator will be."

"I have to agree with John on that one," Nat said. "Getting rid of the two of them would make it a hell of a lot easier to get home without being attacked. And when we're home, Ravyn will be able to train, and then we will all be safer with her around. It's just common sense."

Ravyn blushed. Nat was carrying a lot of high expectations

for her, ones she wasn't even sure she would be able to meet.

"What happened to being peaceful people? Ethereal are peaceful beings; we don't kill unnecessarily," Tammie challenged, almost pleadingly. Her hands were clasped in prayer at her chest. Ravyn looked back up at her and her worried face.

"It is necessary, Tammie. It's the best thing for us right now," John said.

"It really isn't. We just need to get home, that's the best thing for us."

"We can't do that. Nathan will find us. He's probably on his way here now, for all we know. We can't risk him following us home. There would be a massacre."

Everyone fell silent, reflecting on the thought. No, they absolutely could not lead Nathan home to Dunfeagh, wherever that was. John was right. They would have to get rid of Nathan, one way or another.

She would have to get rid of him.

This was her fight, after all.

He wanted her.

"Nathan will come here, no doubt about it," Jay spoke up after a moment of quiet. "But we just don't know when. It could be within the hour, or tomorrow morning. I think the best thing for us right now is to accept that fact and act accordingly. We will sleep here tonight, and we can take turns keeping an eye outside, just in case. I will phone Therese now, and I'll have her send somebody out to us in the morning. I will have a word with her about all this, and we can decide what to do in the morning."

Everyone nodded, though Ravyn caught the eye-roll from both John and Nat.

Jay clapped his hands together, putting on a fake smile.

"Great. I'll go ring Therese, and I'll be back up in a few minutes."

He left, and a silence fell over the room that nobody wanted to break. Ravyn lay down and folded her hands across her stomach. She stared up at the rough, low ceiling. The paint was wearing away, and she spotted mould growing in one of the corners. There was a creak to her left as John stood up from the bed, walking around to Nat and Brook's bed. Ravyn turned her head to watch him slowly make his way around her bed. Brook stiffened but didn't pull away as John sat next to her. He hugged her gently, cradling her small frame in his arms, and eventually, Brook put her arms around him and started sobbing.

Ravyn turned away and went back to staring at the ceiling, tears jabbing her eyes. She let them have their moment of reconciliation in private—old friends finally reuniting after making it through troubled waters. Waters that Nathan had caused and pushed them into, hoping they would drown.

She closed her eyes.

I have to kill him.

CHAPTER 24

Jay came back about half an hour later and told them Therese was sending people tonight, and they would be here early tomorrow morning to pick them all up.

He didn't mention killing Nathan or Isabella.

Ravyn wanted to talk to him, so she followed him out as he was bringing Tammie and Brook back to their room.

"Jay," she called, and he stopped. Tammie just glanced back at her, then continued with Brook into their room.

Ravyn waited for the door to shut.

"Yes, Ravyn?" Jay asked, smiling at her.

"I want to know how to do it. The things you said—controlling energy and all that."

Jay scrunched up his face, the light in his eyes dimming. "I don't think that's a good idea right now—"

"What if he comes back though? Illusions won't be enough to stop him," she pushed. They most certainly wouldn't. She needed to know how to create reality. That was the only way she was going to be able to kill him.

Jay thought for a moment, stroking his beard.

"I still don't think now is a good time. We can handle him, and besides, your illusions are effective. They worked last time, didn't they?" he said, shrugging.

"Not really. Nathan knew, and he came back."

"But it worked for the others."

"Jay, please. Just tell me—"

"Ravyn." He stepped closer to her and put a hand on her shoulder. It was heavy resting there, weighing her down. It kept her grounded, kept her from reaching these powers that were hidden somewhere inside her. It was the anchor chaining her to the bottom of the ocean. "Don't worry, okay? I know you want to get involved, but you are doing enough already. You are amazing, you really are. You are developing powers at an exceptional rate, but I still worry you might burn yourself out. Remember what I told you? You can die if you use too much energy, and I don't want that to happen to you. We should train you more, absolutely, but not now. When we get home, I promise I will train you. I promise, okay? Just not now." He took his hand away, but her shoulders remained slumped.

Ravyn nodded slowly, looking down. Her fingers twitched at her sides. "Okay."

"Get some rest. You need it." He patted her shoulder, then went to his room.

Ravyn stood alone in the narrow hallway for a moment, her stomach curling and twisting. Every cell in her body was screaming at her.

"Fuck," she muttered. She brought her hands to her temples and squeezed, letting out a long sigh.

No, I have to learn, she told herself.

Her mother jumped to her mind, her face blurry and out of

focus. Ravyn could barely remember what she looked like. She could remember blue eyes, like Nat's. But did she have long or short hair? Was it blonde, like Ravyn's, or maybe it was brown? Red? She reached into her memory and tried to grasp at a ghost, tried to pull the image of her mother closer but her face never became any clearer. The thought made tears appear in her eyes, ready to fall. She blinked them away. She leaned her head back and sighed at the ceiling.

I need to learn.

She went back into her mind, this time searching for something simple to do, the blurred memory of her mother egging her on. Maybe this would connect the two of them again, mother and daughter connected by an unbelievable force, a power so great that people would kill to have it. She was her mother's blood; this power ran in her veins and she was not going to let Jay or anyone else hold her back from it. She had to learn how to do it. There was no alternative. It was learn, or die.

Nathan would not wait for her to practice.

He would kill them before Jay even got the chance to explain it to her.

Something simple—turning the lights off. That was manageable, right? Yes, she could make that happen. It was easy enough, nothing too challenging. Not as challenging as the thing she had done already.

She brought herself deep inside her mind, coming out of the real world so only her body remained on this earth, until she wasn't aware of the room anymore, just the world in her mind. Everything around her faded, until it was only her and those lights. Just her and the lights, tucked away into her own little world. A world where anything she wanted could happen. She was the God, and she made the rules.

And in that world, the lights that ran down the hall flicked off, one by one.

She half-opened one eye, to find a world where the lights were still very much on and working. Her shoulders slumped, and she closed her eye again.

Her minds vision took over, and she created the scene before her yet again. She stood still, minutes ticking by slowly as she created the room, the lights, until she could even sense the air that was trapped in the space. And she pushed it out of her mind, but still, nothing.

The lights remained on.

Frustration grew, and she balled up her fists at her side. She ran her fingers through her hair, and shook her head. She pressed her lips together, and closed her eyes one more time.

One last try, for her mother.

She created the room again, created an alternate world that would soon be conjoining with her own. She just needed to really *see* it.

She slowed her breathing, allowing this world to consume her until she couldn't even sense her own body.

She focused on it, saw it so vividly that she could even see the tiny dust particles floating in the air that were invisible to her eyes, then started to push it forwards, to the front of her skull. She pushed it harder, launching it forwards, and it accelerated quicker and quicker. The further she pushed it, the more power she put behind it, until the momentum pushed it out of her head, and she was suddenly brought back to her body with a jolt, watching as the lights flicked off, one by one.

She sucked in a deep breath, her knees wobbling. Sweat clung to her skin, fat beads rolling down her face and neck. She tasted sweet metal in her mouth.

She was surrounded by darkness.

The lights were off.

She put her hand on the wall, steadying herself. Her legs shook, and her hands trembled, but still she smiled. Then she laughed with what little energy remained in her body.

"I did it," she whispered to herself, laughing again.

She closed her eyes and took a few deep breaths before returning to her room, careful how she placed her feet so she didn't fall, hoping the others didn't catch a whiff of what she was doing. Her head was spinning, the world tilting from left to right in front of her eyes, her knees ready to break. She lay down on her bed, smiling to herself.

She'd done it.

Nat climbed into the bed beside her, lying on her side with one arm draped lazily over Ravyn's stomach. Ravyn's eyes were getting tired, but she kept herself awake, replaying the moment it had happened over and over again in her head. Each time it played in her mind, pride swelled inside her.

She had figured it out.

It had been the momentum.

Yes, that was it.

The power behind it.

The force of the push, propelling it forwards so fast the friction didn't even have time to develop. All her energy reserves had been drawn upon, a hungry wolf pulling everything it laid eyes on into its munching mouth. It wanted everything, leaving no scraps or discarded bones. Nothing was wasted.

It was energy so fierce, so feisty, that it would not let anything stop it.

Back in the woods, she recalled, it had taken all the energy she could muster to project her illusion into the world, to solidify it so much that it had become real. And even though it still took energy to make the non-real illusions, this was another beast that had woken in her mind, one that had crawled out of the dark depths she never dared to explore, but one she was glad to feed.

She smiled again, her lips barely able to push themselves towards her tired eyes.

"What's so funny?" Nat whispered to her.

Ravyn shook her head. "Nothing."

"Tell me," Nat said, nudging her.

Ravyn turned her head to look at Nat's curious face. "I figured it out."

"Figured what out?"

"How to make them real. The illusions. I know how to do it."

Nat propped herself up on her elbow and looked down at Ravyn. Her eyes were narrowed slightly, and her lips were set in a straight line. Ravyn sighed, her moment of pride faltering. She knew what was coming.

"I don't think that's a good idea. Jay said that was only for extreme circumstances because it drains so much energy. You have wasted so much energy already. It's dangerous to be doing this, Ravyn."

"Well, I have to learn, don't I? I can't learn when I'm about to be killed." Ravyn closed her eyes.

"Ravyn. Listen to me. You are using too much energy. You have done too much since you first learned how to make illusions. You're really pushing the boundaries. I don't want something bad to happen to you. I don't want to lose you," Nat whispered sternly. Ravyn opened her eyes again and stared at her.

She knew Nat was only looking out for her. It was one of the many things she loved about Nat. But she couldn't allow her words of warning to sink in, because Nat's life was on the line, and Ravyn was not prepared to have her taken away, just like her mother had been. She would not allow that fateful night to repeat itself.

She would not let Nathan take the person she loved most again.

"I know, I just… Never mind. I'm done now, I just wanted to see if I could do it again," she muttered, closing her eyes again.

Nat lay back down beside her, and she snuggled in close. Their fingers locked together, and Nat took their hands and rested them on Ravyn's stomach. There were nerves tingling in Ravyn's stomach, telling her that this was a bad idea. That she shouldn't be doing this alone.

But what other option did she have?

Would she just give up on life so easily, die without a fight? Would she just let Nat suffer all the terrible things Nathan would do when he found them?

She breathed deeply, allowing her breaths to eat away the nerves. John shifted in the bed beside her, then she faded into sleep.

She needed to conserve her energy for what she was going to do.

*****

She opened her eyes, and the room was dark. She blinked a few times, allowing her sight to adjust to the dim light. She turned her head and saw that Nat was sleeping in her own bed, her back to Ravyn. She looked the other way and saw John

318

sleeping on his stomach, one leg out of the duvet and hanging down off the bed. She turned back to face the ceiling.

Her heart was pounding.

Time to go, part of her brain told her.

No, you're not ready, the other part said.

She sat up and looked over to where Nat was sleeping soundlessly. She thought about giving her a kiss goodbye, to gently lay her lips on the top of her head, just in case…

She shook her head.

She will die if you don't go.

Ravyn put her hand on her chest, and her heart thumped rapidly against it, wanting to be free of her body, afraid to go ahead with her stupid plan. Ravyn took her hand away and swallowed a lump in her throat.

They will all die if you don't go.

She peeled the duvet off herself and put her feet on the carpeted floor. It was hard and crusty. She looked down and noticed she wasn't wearing shoes. Had she been wearing them when she fell asleep? She was sure she had, so Nat probably took them off her. She bent over and reached under the bed, feeling around for them.

Her fingers knocked against her boots. She grabbed her boots and slowly slid them onto her feet, careful not to make too much noise. Then she stood and looked over to Nat for a moment, taking in her figure in case this was the last time she saw her. A single tear skimmed down her cheek, and she wiped it away.

All their memories together surfaced. It was short and sweet but beyond precious. Memories she would take to her waiting grave. It had been nice while it lasted. It had been enough to make her final days happy.

She hoped that they would know to lay her beside her

mother. Two untimely deaths, two Illusionists that had done their best to protect the ones they love most.

She quietly left the room, closing the door behind her with a soft click.

The hall lights were still out. Her walk towards doom would be a dark one, leading her to the gates of Hell. She stuck close to the wall as she crept towards the exit so the floors didn't creak. She passed by Jay's room even slower, testing the floor before she completely put her foot down, just to be safe. She didn't know if he was sleeping or keeping an eye out the window, waiting for Death to arrive and claim them all. She would have to be careful that they didn't see her sneak out. They would try to stop her if they did.

And if that happened, only misery and eternal sleep could follow.

And none of them deserved that.

A chill ran down her spine, making her legs shake, nearly throwing her to the ground.

She reached the top of the narrow stairs and looked down them. Her stomach was starting to flip and knot itself, but she took a deep breath and slowly descended the stairs, once again testing the steps and sticking close to the wall.

Bad idea, Ravyn, part of her mind screamed at her. *Go back to bed! Go back to bed! You will die!*

I will not die, she told it. *I can do this.*

Once she reached the bottom, she closed her eyes and inhaled deeply. Her heart was pounding harder, and her stomach was full of butterflies, bouncing around inside her and making her sick.

She put her hands on her head and took another deep breath. She looked back up the stairs and was nearly about to abandon everything, but she reminded herself why she was doing this. He needed to be stopped, and it was her duty to make sure he was. He had caused too much damage, infected too many wounds.

He was after her now. And she would not be responsible for another needless death in this stupid war he was needlessly fighting.

"Come on, Ravyn. You got this," she whispered to herself before undoing the bolt across the door and stepping outside.

The cold air hit her like a ton of bricks, nearly knocking her off her feet. She shivered and closed the door behind her.

The village was quiet, eerily quiet. The wind whistled as it blew between the buildings, calling her forwards, enticing her with promises of mysteries unknown to the human race. It lured her out of the building like a stranger with candies, leading her into the unknown. There were no lights on in any of the windows. Everybody was asleep, in bed.

Except her.

On her way to die.

She shook the thought quickly from her head.

No, I am not going to die.

I am going to kill Nathan.

And Isabella.

They will pay for what they did to us.

To me.

Her thoughts returned to her mother, to that night that had been carved into her flesh and left a scar so deep her skin was barely holding itself together. The night Ravyn saw Death for the first time, standing over her mother's body like an angel ready to take her to another world of everlasting sleep.

If Nathan could kill, then so could she.

If Nathan could walk around pretending to be the angel of death, she could do Death's bidding and strip him of that false crown. He did not deserve to wear it.

She had killed before, after all. Her hands already knew the aching hunger of murder. Death was her friend.

She started walking, careful to stay out of sight of the B&B's windows.

She didn't really know where to go; she just knew she had to get out of the village. She couldn't risk anyone else getting caught up in her war. She didn't want anyone else to die. There had been enough death already, and all because Nathan wanted to get to her, because he wanted her dead. Because she had what he craved, and he wanted her out of his way to reach his unattainable goal.

They had all sacrificed themselves for her.

She clenched her fists.

I am going to fucking kill you, Nathan, she told him mentally, grinding her teeth together. Her heartbeat started to slow, beating hard and steady. She picked up the pace, marching against the wind. It pushed against her, trying to turn her around and tell her to go back, back to safety. It had realised she was serious about this, that it wasn't a silly, childish game. *Let the others do the fighting. You don't even know what you're getting yourself into,* it whispered to her, but she just shook her head and kept walking.

You're going to lose, you're going to die, get this stupid idea out of your head and turn around, the wind howled at her with another forceful blow.

She squared her shoulders, straightened her back, and walked right through it.

I can destroy everything, if I want to, she told it, *and I am going to tear him apart.*

The wind died down, watching solemnly as she walked along the side of the road through the darkness, her jacket blowing out behind her like a cape and her hair tangling around itself.

A smile started to form on her face, and she unclenched her fists.

Her fingertips tingled with power, a storm brewing, waiting to be let loose and raise Hell out of the ground, ready to consume Nathan and all the other Shades who stood in her way. A thunderstorm was gathering, clouds clashing and rumbling, lightning waiting to strike down anything that dared get too close.

This isn't you, Ravyn, a thought told her. *Just forget about all this. Go home, just turn around and go home! Forget about this, forget about Nat, leave it all behind you.*

She pushed it forcefully out of her mind.

The smile on her face grew, and the power started to buzz within her. It was a loaded gun, waiting to fire, waiting for her to set her eyes on her target and blow his brains out.

CHAPTER 25

A Shade was following her.

She could hear it flitting and darting around behind her, keeping tabs on where she was going, making sure she was alone. That was good. That meant Nathan was coming.

And she would make him bow to her. He did not deserve to wear that crown he liked to pretend he owned.

She was still wandering the streets of the village, away from the B&B where the others slept peacefully, unaware of what she was doing. Unaware of the murder she was going to commit.

But if it meant saving them, she would do anything.

She stopped walking.

She stood in a small square, surrounded by old stone buildings and parked cars. To her right was a small playground, abandoned at night. The swings creaked with the wind, playing her an eerie tune. She looked up at the sky, drinking in the starlight, allowing it to calm her nerves.

The waning moon shone down on her, illuminating the

land with liquid silver, giving her just enough light to see the world around her. The Lady of the Moon wished her luck in her battle. Stars shone brightly, the sky full of constellations. She found the ones that Nat had shown her a few days ago as they stretched out on the grass, blissfully unaware of all that was about to happen. She looked around her, noting her escape routes, just in case this went tits up.

The Shade flitted about behind her, watching as she stood there.

If Nathan wanted her, he could come and get her.

She was not going anywhere.

After a few moments, she heard it whoosh up behind her. She slowly turned and found herself staring directly at Nathan.

The moonlight cast him in silver, making the shadows of his face darker than the night sky itself. His eyes were shrouded in shadow, only glints of silver floating in them.

"Hello, Ravyn," he crooned, smiling.

She didn't reply.

He raised an eyebrow at her, but when he realised he would get no answer, he sighed.

"That's just rude," he commented, shaking his head. He took a step backwards and observed her whole body. "You've seen better days."

"So have you," she shot back. Behind her, she could sense more Shades gathering. The pressure of the air shifting as they arrived was getting uncomfortable.

Nathan smirked. He was wearing a new suit—fresh, crisp, and probably quite expensive. His metal cufflinks twinkled at her like diamonds, and he adjusted them when he noticed her staring.

She had a few illusions ready in the back of her mind, just in case he tried to pull something unexpected in an attempt to catch her off guard.

A seed of fire had planted itself in her stomach, and the burning flowers were just starting to bloom, dancing with flames and shooting sparks into her bloodstream.

God, I hope you can do this again, Ravyn, she thought to herself, then regretted it. She pushed it away and turned her attention back to Nathan, the man she was going to kill tonight.

The man she would kill with no regrets.

"They don't know you're here, do they?" he tutted, looking over his shoulder. She followed his gaze and saw the woman, Isabella, standing patiently with her hands behind her back. She was wearing a black dress again, but this one had a sweetheart neckline with lace sleeves and a lace front covering her cleavage and the base of her neck.

Isabella grinned at her.

She had a shark smile too.

Ravyn smiled back, showing her own teeth.

Nathan turned around.

"You're all on your own, Ravyn. You're going to die alone. How sad." He drew his lips down to frown at her and clasped his hands in front of his stomach.

She shrugged again. "I kicked your arse on my own last time, didn't I?" She smirked.

His eyes narrowed, and his lips drew back up into a straight line. He tutted again and shook his head.

"Don't be cocky. It doesn't suit you."

"You said that last time too," she reminded him.

Her heart was starting to pound now, knocking against her ribs and reminding her that she could die tonight, but she took a few breaths and calmed it. Her fingertips were still tingling, power pooling there, waiting to be unleashed. That flower was growing taller, its petals ablaze. The very centre of it was white-hot molten lava.

Nathan growled. "Isabella wants to have a little fun with you before I take your head from your shoulders. I hope you don't mind," he said, ignoring Ravyn's comment. Isabella started walking forwards, her hips swaying.

Shadow swirled around her, picking up her hair and pulling at her dress.

Before Ravyn could call forth one of her illusions, a shadow struck her across the cheek, knocking her to the ground. She grunted as she landed, scraping her palms.

Another shadow took hold of her wrists, clamping them to the ground. She tried to pull away, but they held her tight and cut off her blood supply.

Oh, shit.

"Hello, dear. We haven't met yet," Isabella said, and Ravyn looked up.

Isabella towered over her, smiling down at her through red lips.

Ravyn pulled one of her illusions forward, but her thoughts were interrupted as a shadow latched onto her jaw and forced her to look Isabella straight in the eye.

"Oh, the things I could do to a pretty girl like you," Isabella mused.

A single thread of shadow traced Ravyn's lips. It was sharp, and nearly cut straight through the soft skin. She clamped her mouth shut, her eyes widening as memories of Brook came flooding back to her, taking over her mind and occupying the space she needed to form an illusion.

Come on, Ravyn, she told herself. *Calm down!*

She pushed the memories aside and replaced them with a crystal-clear image. She started gathering the energy, drawing it up her arms and into her mind. The flower shot right up through her middle, past her chest, and up the back of her neck, unleashing its fury into her mind. She narrowed her eyes at Isabella.

Isabella raised one hand elegantly, using shadow to form a knife. It had a long, sharp tip that winked at her, eyeing her flesh like a starved bear.

She put the burning power behind the illusion, and it built up speed, travelling faster and faster towards the front of her mind. She pushed it towards her skull and out into the world.

A spear shot through the middle of Isabella's chest, the bloody tip poking out between her breasts, ruining her lovely dress and taking that smile off her face.

The shadows holding Ravyn disintegrated into the air.

Ravyn's vision blurred, and she sucked in air, filling her lungs and sending oxygen to every part of her body. Her sight came back just in time to see Isabella splutter blood from her mouth, some of which landed on Ravyn's legs and soaked into her already ruined trousers, before collapsing.

There was a moment of deafening silence. It rang loud in Ravyn's ears, almost bursting her eardrums. The world held its breath, then Nathan roared and fell to the ground beside Isabella's body, which had landed just beside Ravyn. She shoved herself away from him and his dead mistress. Nathan screamed Isabella's again, shaking her shoulders, trying to wake her. The end of the spear poked out of her back, and deep crimson blood started to soak the ground around her body. Her eyes had rolled back in her head, and her jaw hung loose, blood oozing from her lips. Her dress became saturated with it, dyeing it a burnt maroon colour.

Ravyn stood up slowly, breathing hard. Her hands were starting to shake and tremble.

Power gathered in her fingertips again, and she slowly

started to regain her strength. It pumped through her body with each thump of her heart, powering all her muscles and organs, keeping them alive and strong.

Some Shades started advancing towards her, and she quickly prepared another illusion, but Nathan gave a roar like a wild animal, and she flinched away. His hands were soaked in his beloved's blood. His new suit was stained with dirt and red clots.

"She's mine! She's mine to kill!" he screamed at the Shades. They backed off, resuming their previous positions, watching the events unfold, placing their bets on the victor.

He rose slowly, turning to glare at her. His brow furrowed to cast dark shadows over his eyes. In his irises, she could see his bloodlust, wild and untamed. He bared his teeth at her. They were fangs, ready to tear her flesh from her bone.

She gulped.

"You fucking bitch!" he cried, marching towards her. She took a step backwards, eyes wide, quickly trying to form something in her mind.

He threw his arm out, and shadow slammed into her from the side, throwing her off her feet and launching her across the cobbled ground. The breath was knocked out of her, her lungs completely deflated as she crashed into the ground. She cried out as white spots exploded in front of her eyes, blinding her.

He roared, and shadows shot from his whole body. They shattered windows, pierced through cars, streamed like missiles towards the night sky. Car alarms wailed, house alarms shrieked and tore through her eardrums. She covered her head with her arms, missing a black shard by inches.

There was a boom, then, and the earth shook. More shadow streamed out from him, moving like a wave along the ground. It spread towards her, and she stumbled away, but it was too fast. It latched onto her feet and dragged her to the ground.

Fuck.

The pressure in the air changed, and her ears popped. She looked up and saw Jay running towards her. A ripple of air currents moved in front of him, shimmering in the moonlight and flashing orange from the hazard lights of ruined cars. He sent them forwards, and they threw Nathan off his feet.

The shadows let go of Ravyn.

"Get up."

Nat was beside her then, her hands under her arms. She dragged Ravyn to her feet, and Ravyn gripped her bicep. They stared at each other and shared an inhale.

"What are you doing? Don't run off on your own like that, you could have been killed!" Nat snapped. Ravyn released her arm.

"I was trying to—"

"The whole family has decided to join in! Saves me looking for you all, at least," Nathan laughed, brushing himself off.

"Nathan, you need to leave," Jay growled. Nathan just laughed again, and the Shades descended on them.

It was a towering wave, climbing the air as it reached over Nathan and crashed down on top of them all. Ravyn was thrown to the ground again, and Nat was pulled away from her. The roaring of the shadows around them drowned out all the other noises, so loud her eardrums felt like they might burst.

The ground under her rumbled, the pavement shaking and cracking as the earth below them opened up and started to swallow the Shades. They screamed and shrieked and shot themselves back into the air, back into the safety of the night sky.

Ravyn coughed, dust flying all around her. As the darkness lifted, she looked towards John and Brook. Their hands were planted to the ground, drawing on the energy of the earth. Sweat rolled off their skin, shining in the silver light.

Ravyn heaved in a breath and finally stood once again.

Nathan was in front of Jay, his face twisted into a snarl.

He planted a punch right into Jay's nose. Then a shard of shadow slashed at his face.

Ravyn gasped.

Jay stumbled backwards, clutching his face. Even at this distance, she could see the blood splatter onto the ground. She pulled an illusion into her mind, striking a match and lighting it on fire.

It was time for Nathan to die.

But before she could unleash it all, Tammie came running from the shadows. She grabbed Jay and started pulling him away, back to safety where she could heal him. But Nathan extended his hand towards them both.

"No!" Ravyn screamed, the illusion jolted from its place and no longer ready to fire.

His shadow dagger shot straight through Tammie's head.

Her body collapsed, and Jay fell on top of her. He tried to scramble away, but another shadow pinned him to the ground.

Ravyn's heart dropped, all the burning fire in her fading instantly.

Ravyn took a step to run, but Nat pushed her out of the way. She stepped in front, her muscles straining. In her hands, there was water, swirling around her fingers, starting to freeze. The particles of ice were almost glowing as they shot towards Nathan.

He stepped out of the way, but one struck his leg. He

roared in pain, stumbling backwards. More shards of ice, with sharpened tips made to pierce flesh, rained down on him.

"Enough!" he roared, swiping his hand through the air.

Shadows closed around Nat's ice and crushed them. More shadow rose from the ground and grabbed her arms, her hair, pulling her towards the cobbles. Ravyn grabbed at the dark matter, trying to rip it off her. But another strand took hold of her and pulled her down with Nat.

She heard screams from Brook and John.

Shit.

No, no, no.

This wasn't supposed to happen.

Ravyn, you can't let him win.

"I have had enough of you fucking Ethereal! How *dare* you kill my Isabella, Ravyn! I will fucking *kill you!*" Nathan screamed, his footsteps stomping towards her. Fury twisted on his face, his teeth bared.

Ravyn turned her head to try and look at him, but instead, her eyes found people, ordinary people, staring out their windows at the scene before them. Some had phones to their ears, others stared with their mouths wide open. They were getting caught up in a war that wasn't theirs.

She should never have come here.

She should have gone outside the village, where there would be no unnecessary casualties. It was just like Nathan himself had said—the world was going to find out eventually. And this was it.

There was no more hiding from the real world.

Nathan came into view, his darkened face glaring down at her with a hatred so hot it burned her skin. Her eyes widened, and his foot stomped down on her chest.

She cried out, all the air in her lungs vanishing.

She gasped for breath, her ribs on fire.

"Nathan, don't you dare—" Nat shouted above all the harsh noise in the air, and a blast of water hit him square in the chest. He stumbled away, nearly tripping on his own shadows.

Ravyn rolled over, struggling to get her breathing under control. Everywhere hurt, but her lungs were on another level of pain. Nathan stomped back towards her, shadow swirling angrily around his hands. She pushed herself onto her knees, but then tendrils of shadow wrapped around her waist and threw her down again. She slammed into the ground, then rolled. Pain flared in her ribs and back, radiating throughout her whole body. She winced, trying to scramble to her feet. Her arms buckled, and her face hit the tarmac.

The ground rumbled once again as Brook tried to throw Nathan off, but he spun and landed a kick to her ribs.

Nat was on her feet now, but Nathan spun on the spot. Shadows flew from his fingers and wrapped around her throat. She choked, the harsh noise pricking Ravyn's ears.

Anger bubbled within her once again. That fire sparked, reigniting itself in the pit of her stomach.

"Don't touch her!" Ravyn screamed, pushing herself to her feet. Nathan's face whipped around to her, his eyes holding the look of a wild animal. He outstretched his hands, and a blanket of shadow covered all that was behind him—cars, bikes, plants, Nat, and the others. It pinned them to the ground, starving them of oxygen.

Ravyn's heart stopped beating for just a second, and her whole body froze.

Then shadows gathered around her, and she was pulled from her trance as her body braced itself. They wrapped around her pelvis and dragged her, face-down, across the ground and back towards Nathan. Rocks cut into her and tore her flesh open as they pulled her, and she cried out, thrashing and trying to free herself. The shadows had a firm grip on her legs that only tightened as she struggled, cutting off her blood supply. She tried to grab at the ground of grass as she was yanked towards him, but it only tore the skin from her fingers. Her fingernails filled with dirt, and her palms opened and bled. Her mind was going a million miles an hour, too fast to form an illusion, too fast to do anything about this except fall at his feet and beg for mercy.

She stopped at Nathan's feet as the shadows released her and returned to Nathan's hand. She looked up at him, breathing hard and fast, tears gathering in her widened eyes. Blood ran from the slashes on her face, warm and sticky against her skin.

Calm down, she told herself. *You can't win if you're panicking.*

She tried to slow down her breathing, but her lungs demanded more oxygen than she was capable of inhaling, and she struggled to keep herself in control of it. Her body needed more, more, more. Her hands were shaking uncontrollably. They were cut and bloody, coated with a thick layer of dirt. The moonlight turned her blood to dark, liquid gold, Nathan's prize money.

Nathan shook his head at her. His lips curled in a snarl. His eyes were manic, wild and furious.

"I've had enough of you. You and your *fucking* illusions! You're just like your mother; the two of you are so *fucking annoying*, always pissing on my plans, getting in my way. I've had enough! I have had *enough*! You killed Isabella, you son of a bitch!" He spat at her, and she turned her head out of the way just in time. Her lungs were finally starting to obey her, and her mind was starting to calm.

But a fist of shadow slammed into her ribs and she heard a crack. She tried to scream as burning pain consumed her chest, but all the air had been knocked out of her and she forgot how to inhale.

She gasped in air once her brain realised she was dying, and violent coughs shook her torso, springing more tears to her eyes. They blurred her vision. Nathan grinned at her, then brought his foot up and stamped back down on her chest.

She howled in agony.

"You think you can just saunter in here and try to take me down, hmm? You think that because you won last time you can beat me again? You are still just a stupid child, Ravyn, acting like you're bigger than you are. When I'm done with you, I will drag the rest of your fucking friends out here to see your corpse, then I will rip their fucking hearts right from their chests. I'll leave Natalie till last, and stuff her fat gob with your remains so she can suffocate and pay for your stupid brain-dead decisions!" He roared at her, leaning down to scream it in her face. Her eyes widened.

"Don't you fucking dare," she spluttered at him, and he punched her jaw.

Blood started gathering in her mouth, coppery and acidic. Her face scrunched up in pain, and her throat was barely able to contain her cry.

Shadows lifted her to her feet, then suspended her in the air by her arms. She didn't fight. She didn't struggle. Her lungs ached but she didn't lose control over them. She didn't scream or cry, despite the almost unbearable pain taking hold of her body. She just kept herself calm. Every breath made a bullet of pain shoot through her, but she ignored it.

She started forming an illusion in her mind, searching for the power to put behind it.

The seedling bloomed once again, spitting fire and smoke through her body. It curled around her spine like a snake, using it as a support to grow taller, towards her mind. The bud opened and unfurled its petals, revealing a blazing inferno that set her whole body alight.

Nathan snarled at her.

A shadow knife formed in his hand, the blade sharp and curved. It grew into a machete with a razor sharp edge. It looked menacingly at her throat, wanting to spill blood, wanting to hear that sickly patter of blood falling to the ground.

Calm down, Ravyn, she told herself.

He raised the knife. It swirled in his palm, sharpening its blade to a paper-thin point that could slice through bone.

"I have had enough of you and your fucking stupid Ethereal friends!" He snapped, his eyes manically wide.

She took the power and energy from the raging flower and started gathering it behind her illusion. Then she started to push forwards, push faster. The fire drove it onwards at an impossible pace, racing through her mind with sparks flying behind it. Friction started to develop under it, trying to slow it down, but she put more power and more energy behind it, pushing it further and further, faster until—

It exploded out of her, like a bullet through her head, and she screamed. The air popped, and a low boom rattled the surrounding area. The wind was pushed backwards, and some of the remaining Shades were knocked off their feet.

Nathan's chest exploded and shadow poured out of him, swirling up towards the sky, twisting and writhing as it shot upwards, heading for the watching Heavens. The trails of smoky shadow started to solidify and became blacker than the darkest night. It pulsated, growing and twisting into shapes as the beast inside unfurled its wings and stretched outwards. It formed a raven, wings spread wide, beak open towards the cosmos as it screamed a battle cry, crowing loudly, making the air pop and world quiver once again.

Nathan's pained face dragged itself around to look at her, hatred in his eyes. He bared his teeth and screamed, slashing his hand through the air towards her.

A shard of shadow plunged into her chest.

The shadows holding Ravyn faded away, and she dropped to the ground.

All the shadow disappeared, and the village fell deathly silent, no longer trapped by the darkness.

Nathan's limp body thumped as it fell beside her.

"*Ravyn!*" Nat screamed.

Her body forgot how to work, forgot how to breathe, how to move. She lay there, completely still, her life fading away. It wasn't even painful. It was just... death. Her friend. Her lungs struggled to expand, her chest barely rising. She stared up at the stars, at her mighty raven which was still in the sky above them, looking down at her. It crowed, beating its wings and flapping air down at her. Loose stones were thrown around and cars roofs were dented, their alarms screaming. She sucked it in, taking in all the oxygen and lifeforce it beat down on her, trying to grab a few more moments of life.

"Ravyn!" Nat screamed again, her feet pounding towards her.

The raven gave one final mighty squawk, and flew away, up into the stars to join the awe-struck Gods and Goddesses that resided there.

Stillness followed.

Quiet.

The world held its breath.

"Oh my God, Ravyn!" Nat was beside her now, staring down at her. Her tears splashed onto Ravyn's face. Nat pulled her up, holding her in a hug, screaming her name over and over again, her grip getting tighter and tighter.

Ravyn closed her heavy eyes, letting herself relax into her lover's body. She could feel the warm blood that pumped from her chest, soaking into Nat's clothes and staining them red.

"Ravyn, please. Oh my god, Jay! Help me! Jay!" Nat was screaming, choking on her words. Sobs took her over, sending little jolts through Ravyn. But she didn't mind, she just wanted to be here, in Nat's arms.

It was the best she could have asked for, given the circumstances.

"Thank you, for everything," Ravyn managed to whisper, the words finally spoken. They had been locked in her chest for too long, and they needed to be released. She would not get another chance. Her throat tightened, and a single tear welled in her eye.

Nat never heard her words.

"*Jay!* John! Help me!" Nat was still crying, her hands now pressing on Ravyn's wound. More pounding footsteps added to the symphony of noise around them.

Death appeared then, extending its hand down towards her.

And with her final breath, she took that hand, allowing herself to be carried away.

CHAPTER 26

B irds woke her, pulling her from her deep slumber. They sang all around her, gently taking her back to reality. Ravyn lay for a moment, just listening to them sing their sweet tunes, and she even managed to smile.

A single raven soared overhead, peering down at her before flying to find its breakfast.

"Please, please, please!" she heard then, a sweet but strained voice speaking over the birds. She knew that voice, she had heard it many times before...

Oh God.

Before her fight with Nathan.

Before she'd killed him, and he killed her.

Ravyn opened her eyes.

The sky stared back at her. It was starting to brighten, the sun rising somewhere behind her. The heavens were orange, fading into purple and blue. The ground under her was cold, the tarmac offering no softness or comfort.

"She's awake."

"Ravyn! Oh my god!"

Nat's pale face appeared then, tear tracks marked on her cheeks, her eyes bloodshot and glistening. Her hand flew to her mouth, and she started sobbing.

Ravyn managed to drag one hand over the ground to touch Nat's leg. Nat's hand took hers, and she squeezed it tight, bringing it to her chest.

Jay's face came into view then. His nose was definitely broken, and dried blood stained his face. He smiled at her, relief washing over his features.

"Welcome back," he said, unable to stop his smile from spreading.

Ravyn didn't have the energy to keep her eyes open any longer. She let them flutter closed and took a deep breath. As she did, a dagger of pain shot through her chest, and she winced. There was a tight knot under her sternum, and she slowly raised her other hand to feel it.

Her clothes had been torn and were crusted with dried blood. And right in the centre of where they had been ripped, her skin had been knotted back together. She frowned as her fingers traced over it, feeling all the bumps and ridges of her new scar. It was rough and tender to touch.

Nat took her hand away.

Ravyn opened her eyes and stared into Nat's glossy, blue orbs.

"You...you did that?" Ravyn croaked out, her throat like sandpaper. Nat gave a pained smile and pulled one of Ravyn's hands to her face to kiss her numb fingers.

"She spent all night working on you," John said. Ravyn glanced in the direction of his voice, but she could only see the top half of his face.

"Seems you weren't the only one who unlocked more

advanced abilities without training, Ravyn," Jay said with a chuckle. Ravyn managed a smile, and her gaze returned to Nat. Tears still flowed from her eyes and fell around Ravyn's face.

"Thank you," Ravyn muttered, her voice still raw. Nat kissed her fingers again and again.

"I know you're not feeling well, Ravyn, but we need to go," Jay continued, soft but firm. "People have seen what happened here, and we can't stay. The place is already crawling with Police and even the Army. Brook is keeping them away from here."

Ravyn nodded, still breathing in that sweet fresh air that was pouring life into her veins. She wiggled her toes, coaxing away the pins and needles that still had hold of them.

Nat helped her sit up before wrapping her in a hug.

It was like being wrapped in a blanket of silk, so soft and tender. So sweet and loving. Ravyn just about managed to hug Nat back, burying her face into the crook of Nat's neck and breathing in her sweet scent.

She didn't want to let go.

But Nat did, and instead gave her a kiss.

Ravyn decided that this moment had been worth dying for.

*****

She slept most of the journey to Dunfeagh, leaning on Nat's shoulder with Nat's arm protectively around her. Ravyn dreamed of birds pecking at decaying bodies in an empty street, tearing at the flesh and discarding bones for the foxes to enjoy when they crept out as the sun fell. She woke as they went over a bump in the road, and she blinked a few times.

She sat up straighter, and Nat kissed her cheek but kept her arm around her.

Ravyn never wanted to leave her arms again.

The sun was already going down in the sky once more. The horizon burned dark orange. It didn't feel like that long since the sun had risen, and it was already falling out of the sky. She sighed and leaned her head back on Nat's shoulder.

They were driving through a rocky landscape, one which Ravyn didn't recognise at all. She stared out the window as the jagged landscape rose and fell in unnatural landforms. The peaks were sharp and pointed, ready to impale anything that got too close. It started closing in around them, encasing them.

"Where are we?" she whispered to Nat.

"We're almost home."

"But where are we?"

"The Ethereal made this place. It's hidden from wandering eyes, so it's not on a map."

"You made this?" She sat up straighter, looking out the front window. Her neck cricked, and she grimaced. Everywhere still hurt, her whole body throbbing and her chest aching.

It was Jay who spoke this time, from the front passenger seat. "It's our sanctuary. Somewhere safe for us. We designed it and made it that way. We even made the land." He pointed out the window, and Ravyn followed his gesture. They were surrounded by rocky mountains, with jagged edges and steep cliff faces, a palette of every shade of grey. The sun was setting to their left, right behind a pointing peak.

"Wow."

Everyone chuckled.

"Welcome home, Ravyn. I'm so glad you're here," Nat whispered in her ear, kissing her cheek.

*****

They passed by a town—an actual town in a valley between the mountains—and headed towards a large house sitting on the outskirts of the urban area. It was a beautiful building with high windows and arched double doors. The two jeeps pulled up in front of it.

The front doors opened, and Therese came out, followed by a few other people Ravyn didn't know. The car doors opened then, and cool, fresh air filled the interior, pulling her from the lingering hold of sleep. Goosebumps rippled across her skin.

Nat climbed out of the jeep, then turned to help Ravyn out. Ravyn took her hand, and slowly set her feet on the ground. Her legs ached as her muscles were forced to straighten. She used the side of the jeep and Nat's firm grip to support her as she started walking slowly towards the front of the house. Everybody else was heading in that direction, finally meeting up with loved ones they hadn't seen in so long. People were being embraced, and tears were being shed. Jay kissed Therese, then hugged her.

Nobody was there to meet Ravyn or Nat.

Nat helped Ravyn towards the house, past the embraces and tears and bear hugs. Every step was painfully slow, each one shooting fire up her legs and towards her heart, but she gritted her teeth and walked, one arm around Nat.

"Nat, take Ravyn to the sitting room and let her rest," Jay said as they passed him.

The hallway they entered was huge, with a wide staircase

leading to the second floor. Nat took Ravyn past it, past the modern paintings that hung on the cream walls, past the large potted plants that could use some water.

She pushed open the door to the sitting room and led Ravyn over to one of the sofas.

They sat in silence, their hands clasped together. Neither of them wanted to let go.

"Do your parents not know you're back yet?" Ravyn asked quietly, careful not to disturb the calmness that enveloped this room.

Nat bit her lip and shrugged. "They don't live here anymore. They've moved on."

Ravyn raised her eyebrows. "Oh."

"Yeah, they…got a new place in the south of France. It's nice, I think."

Ravyn paused, staring at Nat's face, trying to see past her words. Her eyes gave it away as they glossed over with more tears.

"You didn't go?" Ravyn asked carefully, squeezing her hand tighter.

Nat took a breath and shrugged. "No, I… There wasn't enough money for me to move too. I don't really care. If I had gone, I never would have met you." Nat forced a smile, and Ravyn's heart panged. She pressed her lips tight together, giving a small smile in return. She leaned her head on Nat's shoulder and let her eyes half close.

"Thank you for saving me," Ravyn said, changing the subject. She pulled Nat's hand to her chest, right over the new scar that Nat had made there.

Nat let her head rest against the top of Ravyn's. "I couldn't lose you, Ravyn. I—" Nat choked on her words. Tears formed in Ravyn's eyes then, and she blinked them away rapidly. The pain of her scar travelled deeper beneath her flesh and struck her heart.

They stayed in each other's arms, breathing slow, until the tears dried. It was just the two of them, nobody else. Just the two of them in each other's company. It was these moments Ravyn loved the most—the quiet love, the unspoken words, the heat of each other's bodies against each other, basking in the moment.

It was times like these that made her realise how much she loved this girl.

Even though she had spoken the words already, she didn't think Nat had heard them. They'd been her final words, the ones she wanted to make sure Nat knew. Ravyn needed her to know.

"Nat?" Ravyn whispered. Nat turned her face to nestle against Ravyn's hair, her breath tickling Ravyn's ear. "Thank you, for everything. I can't say thank you enough. Being with you has been more than amazing, and—"

Nat pressed her finger to Ravyn's lips, hushing her. This insignificant moment that would have otherwise been forgotten was now implanted into both of their minds, a memory that would never fade.

She had never known how it felt to have someone care so much about you, to be ready to die for that person, to give your life in exchange for theirs. She briefly wondered if that's how her mother had felt about her. But why wouldn't she have? Why would she have died that night if she hadn't?

The memory made her heart ache because she couldn't remember her mother's face clearly. Only the blood, only her hair, only the coldness of her skin. And those blue eyes.

Nat whispered something back, drawing her back to the moment. Ravyn barely heard her words, but still she smiled.

Her heart lit up, warmth spreading through her body. It was infectious, it was pure and innocent, and it was something words couldn't explain. "But don't you dare do anything like that again!" Nat warned.

They both laughed before sharing a tender kiss.

CHAPTER 27

Alec was cremated that night, along with Ryan, Clio, Excael, and Tammie. Their bodies had been retrieved and brought home shortly after Ravyn and the others had arrived. Alec's body had been here for a few days, waiting for their return. His sister had insisted that they wait. Ravyn had met her earlier, and they'd exchanged a teary hug. Ravyn had apologised, but her words fell on deaf ears.

It's not your fault, his sister had said. *You killed the person who is responsible, and I am so grateful for that.*

But Ravyn still felt guilty. A cremation was not something anybody had planned for when they'd first set out to find her.

Although the bodies that burned tonight were not the only souls that had been taken by Death since Brook had first approached her.

Nat let Ravyn borrow one of her dresses—a deep, sea blue that fell just past her knees—and a pair of shoes to wear with it. The dress had a ribbon around the waist that Nat had tied into a bow for her. She had also given Ravyn a bit of makeup, and Ravyn had put on some mascara. Nat wore a simple black, sleeveless dress and a pair of heels. The tears in her eyes had not gone away all evening.

The bodies were burned outside, on the edge of the town. Hundreds of Ethereal gathered, watching silently, saying their goodbyes and their prayers, and passing condolences to the loved ones of those who had died trying to bring Ravyn home. Some of them hugged Ravyn, some of them merely nodded to her, and others would not look in her direction. The weight of all the bodies had piled on her, making her shoulders sink. Her heart was a pincushion, and thousands of pinpricks struck her. Their ghosts would linger here, probably forever.

Ravyn closed her eyes and took Nat's hand. The heat of the fire warmed her face, even at this distance. The rest of her body was cold, covered in goosebumps.

I killed him, don't worry, she told their ghosts in her mind. *He's gone. He's gone for good. Nobody else will die because of him, I promise.*

And if you see him, wherever you are, kick him in the balls for me.

Brook was standing beside them, and Ravyn took her hand too. Nat took John's hand.

They watched silently. The smoke trailed up towards the sky, carrying their souls with it to wherever they went after death. She hoped that wherever they went, they would find peace.

"This won't be the end of it," Brook said quietly. They all looked at her. "The Shades will find someone new to be in charge. Maybe someone more powerful. Maybe the Shades in other countries will come here and try to take over because Nathan's dead."

Nathan. He had gotten what he wanted, in the end. The world knew. It had started as hushed whispers, but like a virus it spread rapidly through the population and still it was growing.

Jay had told her that the Giant Bird, people thought, signified the end of days. A bad omen, an angry spirit that has been awoken by the gods who despised the destruction and hate of humanity. Many called it fake, many believed.

At least it was kind of funny.

"It will take them a while though," John replied. "They've been brainwashed; they can't think for themselves. We have time to figure out what to do about it."

"I suppose."

"We'll be fine," Nat said, nudging Ravyn. "We have the most powerful person alive now right beside us."

Ravyn nudged her back, shaking her head with a smile. There was still a lot to learn, and Jay had promised he would teach her everything he knew. He'd promised to tell her everything her mother had told him.

"That's true." Brook gave her a wink.

Ravyn rolled her eyes. "No—"

"Shh, don't lie. Just accept it." Nat gave her hand a squeeze. A smile played on Ravyn's lips, and she pushed it away. Maybe she was the most powerful, maybe she wasn't, but she didn't mind either way. She was just happy to be here, beside her friends, beside Nat. Finally at home.

There would be peace, just for a while, but it was enough.

That peace was what she had been chasing after for so long, and now she finally had a grasp of it.

The smile came back, and she closed her eyes.

Maybe she could find out more about her mother here, and find out the real extent of her powers. Maybe she could meet other Illusionists, and learn from them, train with them. And yes, maybe one day she would follow in her mother's footsteps and become as powerful as her.

Ravyn reeled her thoughts back in.

Yes, maybe she could do those things later, but for now, she just gave Nat's hand a squeeze and watched the fire burn.

ACKNOWLEDGEMENTS

This book has been in the works for almost five years now and been through so many different drafts and rewrites to get it to this stage. I've had help from so many different people along the way, without whom this book would not be in your hands today.

Firstly, a huge thank you to my Critique Partner, Carolina! Caro, without you this book would still be sitting in a computer file collecting digital dust. You've helped me make it go from absolute shite to a story worthy of publishing. Thank you so much for all the times you've read ILLUSION, all the feedback you've given me, and all the encouragement and excitement along the way. I am so grateful to call you my friend and CP! I am so excited to follow you on your own author journey, and I'll be there to support you all the way!

Thank you to everyone who read the very first version of ILLUSION, and gave me helpful feedback on the story. All that feedback helped me to completely rewrite the story and make it into the best version of itself. So, a huge thank you to Ms. Dilley, my English teacher; thank you to Pauline, thank you to my parents and my grandparents.

Thank you to Patrick, my go-to for all design-related issues and questions, as well as help with my website.

Thank you to my friends Emma and Sabra for all the support and encouragement.

Thank you to my editor, Nicki, from Richards Corrections.

You really worked your magic on this book and polished it to perfection. Thank you so much for all your kindness and support, and all your helpful feedback.

Thank you to my writer friend Liz Sheehan. Chatting to you about our books really brightened the day, and I can't wait to see where your author career takes you!

Thank you to the author community on Instagram and Twitter. You guys are amazing, and really hype me up on days I'm just not feeling it. It's been amazing getting to know you all!

Finally, a huge thank you to YOU, the reader. Thank you for picking up this book and giving it a chance. It means the world to me to know that you decided to read this little book of mine, and I hope you enjoyed it!

ABOUT THE AUTHOR

Helena is the Irish author of two novels. Her debut novel, THE SECRETS OF THE FOREST, was published when she was just 17 years old. ILLUSION is her second novel. When she is not writing, Helena spends her time cuddling with her dogs, practicing yoga, and doing all sorts of witchy things.

You can find her on social media here:
Facebook — Author Helena Brady
Instagram — @authorhelenabrady
Twitter — @HelenaB_author
Website — www.authorhelenabrady.com

Support the author and leave a review on Goodreads and Amazon!

Printed in Great Britain
by Amazon